THE COMPLETE TALES OF HENRY JAMES
VOLUME EIGHT: 1891–1892

THE COMPLETE TALES OF

HENRY JAMES

EDITED WITH AN

INTRODUCTION BY

LEON EDEL

8

1891–1892

J. B. LIPPINCOTT COMPANY
PHILADELPHIA AND NEW YORK

CONTENTS

INTRODUCTION: 1891–1892

THE thirteen tales included in this volume were published by Henry James during 1891 and 1892 in conformity with his decision to confine himself to short fiction while he was writing plays. He seems to have been able to produce on the average a story a month while his play *The American* was running in London and the provinces and three of his comedies were being circulated among the managers. And while some of these tales (like "Nona Vincent") reflect James's willingness to concern himself with trifles and potboilers, others like "The Marriages," "The Real Thing," "The Private Life" or "The Chaperon" take their places among his short masterpieces. Unlike his tales of the 1870's and the 1880's, which were long and leisurely, James sought in these stories a concentrated narrative, and kept before himself constantly the example of Maupassant who was nearing the end of his short career in story-telling across the Channel. To be sure, James himself, in such a tale as "Four Meetings," had anticipated Maupassant—or more exactly had learned the lesson of writers such as Merimée, Turgenev, Flaubert, from whom Maupassant also derived. But what he envied his French confrère was the ability to sketch in detail with great rapidity, to plunge the reader at one stroke into the midst of the situation: the foreshortening of painting applied to prose. James studied closely Maupassant's "mastery of statement." And this explains his reiterated allusion in his working notebooks to the example of the French writer—"the sketch, picture, vision—à la Maupassant," or "as admirably compact and *selected* as Maupassant," or "on the rigid Maupassant system." At moments Maupassant becomes the muse—"Oh spirit of Maupassant, come to my aid!"

It must be said that Maupassant came to his aid only in the most limited way. For try as he would, Henry James was too reflective and too intellectual to achieve that simplifying of passion and emotion which characterised Maupassant's work. He did not live on as easy terms with his senses and his appetites. There is not a tale in this volume—unless it be the little story of "The Visits"—that is "Maupassantesque." James's art as a story-teller is more relaxed, more urbane, more profound—and also more compulsive: he must get his picture; he must insert every relevant detail; he is less in a hurry to push to the heart of his anecdote; he cannot resist looking at what is to be seen by the way. James's "Maupassant phase" may be judged therefore as an attempt to imitate his fellow-writer's concision rather than his image of life. And as for Maupassant's philosophy James had little sympathy with it—there was too much in the French writer's stories of the monkeys in the monkey-cage. Maupassant was, in a word, too carnal; he looked too closely at sex, and as James remarked, there was much else that he accordingly missed.

James invoked Maupassant but he remained Henry James, and the tales in this volume can be grouped in accordance with characteristic Jamesian themes. Among these are the four tales which study with consummate art what we might call today "social conditioning"—Brooksmith, the butler, who in perception and feeling has moved outside his backstair status and can't move back; the upper-middle-class couple in "The Real Thing," who try very hard, but are unable to change their status by being artist's models; the artist, in "The Private Life" (inspired by Robert Browning), who is a bore in public and a genius in private, or the individual who is brilliant in public and has no existence in private (Lord Leighton); and the youth, in "Greville Fane," brought up on the theory that writers are made, not born. People are what they are, James seems to be saying; only art transfigures. The butler is really an artist; the son of Greville Fane can never be one. There is no turning of a silk purse into a sow's ear. And the stodgy Major and Mrs Monarch, in their polished leather and excellent tweeds, can never be anything but "the real thing"—and are useless to the artist who imagines reality better than life itself.

"The Marriages" and "The Chaperon" belong to a different side of James's social observation and they are among his finest tales. On the surface they remind us of "Pandora," the self-made girl, who has firm control of her family and obtains a position for her fiancé from no less a personage than the President of the United States. Rose Tramore, in "The Chaperon," is a kind of Pandora; she sets herself the unenviable task of restoring her *déclassée* mother to London society. This she achieves by a tenacity of purpose and a kind of filial stubbornness that "society" ultimately rewards. It is the same society which Mrs Headway conquered in "The Siege of London," and which Laura Wing feared in "A London Life," a society that will accept its erring daughters not from any sense of decorum or morality but simply because it is amused. The daughter of "The Marriages," Adela Chart, is a different sort of "managerial" person: on the grounds of decorum and invoking her love for her dead mother, she prevents her father from remarrying: meddles, in other words, in her father's life, and in a malign way. James's achievement in this tale is to have seen clearly all its psychological values: for what he makes equally apparent—and wholly without benefit of Freud—is the girl's driving need to take possession of her father, and her fear of having this possession violated. James thus shows us how a young girl, under the guise of filial piety and filial self-righteousness, can turn passionate jealousy into an exercise of power. Robert Louis Stevenson was among James's readers who relished this tale:

> I pore on you, dote on you, clasp you to heart,
> I laud, love, and laugh at you, Adela Chart,

And thank my dear maker the while I admire
That I can be neither your husband nor sire.

In another stanza Stevenson suggests that, "You're a by-way to suicide, Adela Chart.

But to read of, depicted by exquisite James,
O, sure you're the flower and quintessence of dames."

"Lord Beaupré" (Beauprey in the serial version) and the tale "Collaboration" belong to a different thematic range in James's story-telling. At first glance, the story of the English peer, pursued by women who want to marry him, and the story of the German and French artists who seek to overcome national feelings in the realm of their art, may seem to have little in common. Yet both express what we have observed in many of James's tales, the difficulty of men with womenfolk. They imply that life would be greatly simplified if women could be removed from the lives of certain men. Lord Beaupré is happy enough so long as he need not commit himself, and egotistical enough to accept an "arrangement" by which his friend shields him from his female pursuers—even though she finds the arrangement intolerable and suffers from a distressing confusion of feeling. In similar fashion, the broken engagement in "Collaboration" leaves the French and German artists free to pursue their careers together: it is the masculine-feminine collaboration that is dispensed with—and the men without women, dedicated to art, find happiness together. The implication may be homosexual: but the ground in James is not that of sex—as it might be in Gide or other modern writers. What is stated in these tales, rather, is a fundamental emotional incompatibility between the sexes—an incompatibility, James implies, far greater than French and German antagonism after the Franco-Prussian war. These tales are corollary to stories such as "Sir Edmund Orme" and "The Wheel of Time" which portray men who cannot fathom women or who misunderstand and lose them. In "The Wheel of Time" James toys with the ironic predicament of a woman rejected for her plainness in youth, who becomes beautiful in middle-age; and tells of her double revenge, for her son rejects the daughter of the man who rejected her, and for the same reason. The children thus relive the drama of their elders. This reliving of an old experience is also a part of "Sir Edmund Orme" (as in an earlier tale it was the theme of "The Diary of a Man of Fifty"). The ghost of Sir Edmund Orme returns to make certain that there will be no duplication of an old mistake—that the young lover will not be jilted by the young woman whose mother had jilted Sir Edmund.

Sir Edmund is the first of James's highly individualised ghosts—ghosts as unlike the traditional phantoms of English fiction as his American girls are unlike its traditional heroines. A ghost was most ghostlike, James held, when it walked in broad daylight, shorn of all Gothic trappings. It was too obvious to have clanking chains, bloodstains, secret stairways and dead of night for one's phantoms. The "gruesome, gross and obvious" needed refinement. James refined it by invoking "the strange and sinister embroidered on the very type of the normal and easy." Sir Edmund Orme calmly takes his place in church beside those whom he haunts; he behaves as if he belongs there and not in the least like some spirit damned. It is afterwards that we discover that he is visible only to the woman he is punishing and the man he is safe-guarding. He is a ghost with constabulary functions: he is beneficent and protective, but also threatening. Thus began the series of ghostly tales which James wrote during the 1890's and even after the turn of the century, one of them, "The Turn of the Screw," destined to become a classic. The genre, as James enlarged and refined it, became a study of forms of anxiety and of "psychological" ghosts of a distinctly modern kind. "Sir Dominick Ferrand" (originally titled "Jersey Villas," when it appeared in a magazine) and

"Nona Vincent" are not ghost stories, but they contain elements of what we today would call "extra-sensory perception," and the first of the two stories reverts to the theme of "The Aspern Papers"—an old desk and its secret drawer yielding documents which must be burned, one by one, in the interest of privacy. But the tale is a mere echo of the earlier masterpiece, testifying only to the fact that the theme of "the private life" continued to haunt James—as it would beyond 1900.

We see thus, in these tales written rapidly during this period, congruity of theme even when James attempts different genres—his ghost story for instance is but another way of retelling such stories as "Louisa Pallant" or "The Diary of a Man of Fifty"—stories of men who have been jilted or have misunderstood women, or of women who have on their side been wronged and whom time avenges; daughters who aid their mothers, or seek to meddle destructively in the lives of their fathers. In all the tales James is returning constantly to the principal preoccupation of his fiction, the study of personal relations and, in particular, familial relations; and with this the observation of the many forms that reality can take.

There remains the little tale of "The Visits" (originally titled "The Visit"), which like the others has its predecessors. It is related to "The Aspern Papers" and "A London Life," in its use of the woman who "proposes" or makes some overture to the man; but it has in it still another element—the panic-state of the girl, who indeed in this instance dies of her terror. Passion released and avowed can kill. This would seem to be the inner statement of certain of James's tales, as it would be that of his melodramatic novel, *The Other House,* where it becomes the motive for a murder.

LEON EDEL

New York University

BROOKSMITH

WE are scattered now, the friends of the late Mr Oliver Offord; but whenever we chance to meet I think we are conscious of a certain esoteric respect for each other. "Yes, you too have been in Arcadia," we seem not too grumpily to allow. When I pass the house in Mansfield Street I remember that Arcadia was there. I don't know who has it now, and I don't want to know; it's enough to be so sure that if I should ring the bell there would be no such luck for me as that Brooksmith should open the door. Mr Offord, the most agreeable, the most lovable of bachelors, was a retired diplomatist, living on his pension, confined by his infirmities to his fireside and delighted to be found there any afternoon in the year by such visitors as Brooksmith allowed to come up. Brooksmith was his butler and his most intimate friend, to whom we all stood, or I should say sat, in the same relation in which the subject of the sovereign finds himself to the prime minister. By having been for years, in foreign lands, the most delightful Englishman any one had ever known, Mr Offord had, in my opinion, rendered signal service to his country. But I suppose he had been too much liked—liked even by those who didn't like *it*—so that as people of that sort never get titles or dotations for the horrid things they have *not* done, his principal reward was simply that we went to see him.

Oh, we went perpetually, and it was not our fault if he was not overwhelmed with this particular honour. Any visitor who came once came again—to come merely once was a slight which nobody, I am sure, had ever put upon him. His circle, therefore, was essentially composed of *habitués*, who were *habitués* for each other as well as for him, as those of a happy *salon* should be. I remember vividly every element of the place, down to the intensely Londonish look of the grey opposite houses, in the gap of the white curtains of the high windows, and the exact spot where, on a particular afternoon, I put down my tea-cup for Brooksmith, lingering an instant, to gather it up as if he were plucking a flower. Mr Offord's drawing-room was indeed Brooksmith's garden, his pruned and tended human *parterre*, and if we all flourished there and grew well in our places it was largely owing to his supervision.

Many persons have heard much, though most have doubt-less seen little, of the famous institution of the *salon*, and many are born to the depression of knowing that this finest flower of social life refuses to bloom where the English tongue is spoken. The explanation is usually that our women have not the skill to cultivate it—the art to direct, between suggestive shores, the course of the stream of talk. My affectionate, my pious memory of Mr Offord contradicts this induction only, I fear, more insidiously to confirm it. The very sallow and slightly smoked drawing-room in which he spent so large a portion of the last years of his life certainly deserved the dis-tinguished name; but on the other hand it could not be said at all to owe its stamp to the soft pressure of the indispensable sex. The dear man had indeed been capable of one of those sacrifices to which women are deemed peculiarly apt; he had recognised (under the influence, in some degree, it is true, of physical infirmity), that if you wished people to find you at home you must manage not to be out. He had in short accepted the fact which many dabblers in the social art are slow to learn, that you must really, as they say, take a line and that the only way to be at home is to stay at home. Finally his own fireside had become a summary of his habits. Why should he ever have left it?—since this would have been leaving what was notoriously pleasantest in London, the compact charmed cluster (thinning away indeed into casual couples), round the fine old last century chimney-piece which, with the exception of the remarkable collection of miniatures, was the best thing the place contained. Mr Offord was not rich; he had nothing but his pension and the use for life of the somewhat superannuated house.

When I am reminded by some uncomfortable contrast of to-day how perfectly we were all handled there I ask myself once more what had been the secret of such perfection. One had taken it for granted at the time, for anything that is supremely good produces more acceptance than surprise. I felt we were all happy, but I didn't consider how our happiness was managed. And yet there were questions to be asked, questions that strike me as singularly obvious now that there is nobody to answer them. Mr Offord had solved the insoluble; he had, without feminine help (save in the sense that ladies were dying to come to him and he saved the lives of several), established a *salon;* but I might have guessed that there was a method in his madness—a law in his success. He had not hit it off by a mere fluke. There was an art in it all, and how was the art so hidden? Who, indeed, if it came to that, was the occult artist? Launching this inquiry the other day, I had already got hold of the tail of my reply. I was helped by the very wonder of some of the conditions that came back to me—those that used to seem as natural as sunshine in a fine climate.

How was it, for instance, that we never were a crowd, never either too many or too few, always the right people *with* the right people (there must really have been no wrong people at all), always coming and going, never sticking fast nor overstaying, yet never popping in or out with an indecorous familiarity? How was it that we all sat where we wanted and moved when we wanted and met whom we wanted and escaped whom we wanted; joining, according to the accident of inclination, the general circle or falling in with a single talker on a convenient sofa? Why were all the sofas so convenient, the accidents so happy, the talkers so ready, the listeners so willing, the subjects presented to you in a rotation as quickly fore-ordained as the courses at dinner? A dearth of topics would have been as unheard of as a lapse in the service. These speculations couldn't fail to lead me to the fundamental truth that Brooksmith had been somehow at the bottom of the mystery. If he had not established the *salon* at least he had carried it on. Brooksmith, in short, was the artist!

We felt this, covertly, at the time, without formulating it, and were conscious, as an ordered and prosperous community, of his evenhanded justice, untainted with flunkeyism. He had none of that vulgarity—his touch was infinitely fine. The delicacy of it was clear to me on the first occasion my eyes rested, as they were so often to rest again, on the domestic revealed, in the turbid light of the street, by the opening of the house-door. I saw on the spot that though he had plenty of school he carried it without arrogance—he had remained articulate and human. *L'Ecole Anglaise*, Mr Offord used to call him, laughing, when, later, it happened more than once that we had some conversation about him. But I remember accusing Mr Offord of not doing him quite ideal justice. That he was not one of the giants of the school, however, my old friend, who really understood him perfectly and was devoted to him, as I shall show, quite admitted; which doubtless poor Brooksmith had himself felt, to his cost, when his value in the market was originally determined. The utility of his class in general is estimated by the foot and the inch, and poor Brooksmith had only about five feet two to put into circulation. He acknowledged the inadequacy of this provision, and I am sure was penetrated with the everlasting fitness of the relation between service and stature. If *he* had been Mr Offord he certainly would have found Brooksmith wanting, and indeed the laxity of his employer on this score was one of many things which he had had to condone and to which he had at last indulgently adapted himself.

I remember the old man's saying to me: "Oh, my servants, if they can live with me a fortnight they can live with me for ever. But it's the first fortnight that tries 'em." It was in the first fortnight, for instance, that Brooksmith had had to learn that he was exposed to being addressed as "my dear fellow" and "my poor child." Strange and deep must such a probation have been to him, and he doubtless emerged from it tempered and purified. This was written to a certain extent in his appearance; in his spare, brisk little person, in his cloistered white face and extraordinarily polished hair, which told of responsibility, looked as if it were kept up to the same high standard as the plate; in his small, clear, anxious eyes, even in the permitted, though not exactly encouraged tuft on his chin. "He thinks me rather mad, but I've broken him in, and now he likes the place, he likes the company," said the old man. I embraced this fully after I had become aware that Brooksmith's main characteristic was a deep and shy refinement, though I remember I was rather puzzled when, on another occasion, Mr Offord remarked: "What he likes is the talk—mingling in the conversation." I was conscious that I had never seen Brooksmith permit himself this freedom, but I guessed in a moment that what Mr Offord alluded to was a participation more intense than any speech could have represented—that of being perpetually present on a hundred legitimate pretexts, errands, necessities, and breathing the very atmosphere of criticism, the famous criticism of life. "Quite an education, sir, isn't it, sir?" he said to me one day at the foot of the stairs, when he was letting me out; and I have always remembered the words and the tone as the first sign of the quickening drama of poor Brooksmith's fate. It was indeed an education, but to what was this sensitive young man of thirty-five, of the servile class, being educated?

Practically and inevitably, for the time, to companionship, to the perpetual, the even exaggerated reference and appeal of a person brought to dependence by his time of life and his

infirmities and always addicted moreover (this was the exaggeration) to the art of giving you pleasure by letting you do
things for him. There were certain things Mr Offord was
capable of pretending he liked you to do, even when he didn't,
if he thought *you* liked them. If it happened that you didn't
either (this was rare, but it might be), of course there were
cross-purposes; but Brooksmith was there to prevent their
going very far. This was precisely the way he acted as moderator: he averted misunderstandings or cleared them up. He had
been capable, strange as it may appear, of acquiring for this
purpose an insight into the French tongue, which was often
used at Mr Offord's; for besides being habitual to most of the
foreigners, and they were many, who haunted the place or
arrived with letters (letters often requiring a little worried
consideration, of which Brooksmith always had cognisance),
it had really become the primary language of the master of the
house. I don't know if all the *malentendus* were in French, but
almost all the explanations were, and this didn't a bit prevent
Brooksmith from following them. I know Mr Offord used to
read passages to him from Montaigne and Saint-Simon, for he
read perpetually when he was alone—when they were alone,
I should say—and Brooksmith was always about. Perhaps
you'll say no wonder Mr Offord's butler regarded him as
"rather mad." However, if I'm not sure what he thought
about Montaigne I'm convinced he admired Saint-Simon. A
certain feeling for letters must have rubbed off on him from
the mere handling of his master's books, which he was always
carrying to and fro and putting back in their places.

I often noticed that if an anecdote or a quotation, much
more a lively discussion, was going forward, he would, if busy
with the fire or the curtains, the lamp or the tea, find a pretext
for remaining in the room till the point should be reached. If
his purpose was to catch it you were not discreet to call him
off, and I shall never forget a look, a hard, stony stare (I caught
it in its passage), which, one day when there were a good

many people in the room, he fastened upon the footman who
was helping him in the service and who, in an undertone, had
asked him some irrelevant question. It was the only manifestation of harshness that I ever observed on Brooksmith's part,
and at first I wondered what was the matter. Then I became
conscious that Mr Offord was relating a very curious anecdote, never before perhaps made so public, and imparted to
the narrator by an eye-witness of the fact, bearing upon Lord
Byron's life in Italy. Nothing would induce me to reproduce
it here; but Brooksmith had been in danger of losing it. If I
ever should venture to reproduce it I shall feel how much I
lose in not having my fellow-auditor to refer to.

The first day Mr Offord's door was closed was therefore a
dark date in contemporary history. It was raining hard and
my umbrella was wet, but Brooksmith took it from me exactly
as if this were a preliminary for going upstairs. I observed
however that instead of putting it away he held it poised and
trickling over the rug, and then I became aware that he was
looking at me with deep, acknowledging eyes—his air of
universal responsibility. I immediately understood; there was
scarcely need of the question and the answer that passed
between us. When I did understand that the old man had
given up, for the first time, though only for the occasion, I
exclaimed dolefully: "What a difference it will make—and to
how many people!"

"I shall be one of them, sir!" said Brooksmith; and that
was the beginning of the end.

Mr Offord came down again, but the spell was broken, and
the great sign of it was that the conversation was, for the first
time, not directed. It wandered and stumbled, a little frightened, like a lost child—it had let go the nurse's hand. "The
worst of it is that now we shall talk about my health—*c'est la
fin de tout*," Mr Offord said, when he reappeared; and then I
recognised what a sign of change that would be—for he had
never tolerated anything so provincial. The talk became

ours, in a word—not his; and as ours, even when *he* talked, it could only be inferior. In this form it was a distress to Brooksmith, whose attention now wandered from it altogether: he had so much closer a vision of his master's intimate conditions than our superficialities represented. There were better hours, and he was more in and out of the room, but I could see that he was conscious that the great institution was falling to pieces. He seemed to wish to take counsel with me about it, to feel responsible for its going on in some form or other. When for the second period—the first had lasted several days—he had to tell me that our old friend didn't receive, I half expected to hear him say after a moment: "Do you think I ought to, sir, in his place?"—as he might have asked me, with the return of autumn, if I thought he had better light the drawing-room fire.

He had a resigned philosophic sense of what his guests— our guests, as I came to regard them in our colloquies—would expect. His feeling was that he wouldn't absolutely have approved of himself as a substitute for the host; but he was so saturated with the religion of habit that he would have made, for our friends, the necessary sacrifice to the divinity. He would take them on a little further, till they could look about them. I think I saw him also mentally confronted with the opportunity to deal—for once in his life—with some of his own dumb preferences, his limitations of sympathy, *weeding* a little, in prospect, and returning to a purer tradition. It was not unknown to me that he considered that toward the end of Mr Offord's career a certain laxity of selection had crept in.

At last it came to be the case that we all found the closed door more often than the open one; but even when it was closed Brooksmith managed a crack for me to squeeze through; so that practically I never turned away without having paid a visit. The difference simply came to be that the visit was to Brooksmith. It took place in the hall, at the familiar

foot of the stairs, and we didn't sit down—at least Brooksmith didn't; moreover it was devoted wholly to one topic
and always had the air of being already over—beginning, as
it were, at the end. But it was always interesting—it always
gave me something to think about. It is true that the subject
of my meditation was ever the same—ever "It's all very well,
but what *will* become of Brooksmith?" Even my private
answer to this question left me still unsatisfied. No doubt Mr
Offord would provide for him, but *what* would he provide?
that was the great point. He couldn't provide society; and
society had become a necessity of Brooksmith's nature. I must
add that he never showed a symptom of what I may call sordid solicitude—anxiety on his own account. He was rather
livid and intensely grave, as befitted a man before whose eyes
the "shade of that which once was great" was passing away.
He had the solemnity of a person winding up, under depressing circumstances, a long established and celebrated business;
he was a kind of social executor or liquidator. But his manner
seemed to testify exclusively to the uncertainty of *our* future.
I couldn't in those days have afforded it—I lived in two rooms
in Jermyn Street and didn't "keep a man;" but even if my
income had permitted I shouldn't have ventured to say to
Brooksmith (emulating Mr Offord), "My dear fellow, I'll
take you on." The whole tone of our intercourse was so
much more an implication that it was *I* who should now want
a lift. Indeed there was a tacit assurance in Brooksmith's whole
attitude that he would have me on his mind.

One of the most assiduous members of our circle had been
Lady Kenyon, and I remember his telling me one day that her
ladyship had, in spite of her own infirmities, lately much
aggravated, been in person to inquire. In answer to this I
remarked that she would feel it more than any one. Brooksmith was silent a moment; at the end of which he said, in a
certain tone (there is no reproducing some of his tones), "I'll
go and see her." I went to see her myself, and I learned that

he had waited upon her; but when I said to her, in the form of a joke but with a core of earnest, that when all was over some of us ought to combine, to club together to set Brooksmith up on his own account, she replied a trifle disappointingly: "Do you mean in a public-house?" I looked at her in a way that I think Brooksmith himself would have approved, and then I answered: "Yes, the Offord Arms." What I had meant, of course, was that, for the love of art itself, we ought to look to it that such a peculiar faculty and so much acquired experience should not be wasted. I really think that if we had caused a few black-edged cards to be struck off and circulated —"Mr Brooksmith will continue to receive on the old premises from four to seven; business carried on as usual during the alterations"—the majority of us would have rallied.

Several times he took me upstairs—always by his own proposal—and our dear old friend, in bed, in a curious flowered and brocaded *casaque* which made him, especially as his head was tied up in a handkerchief to match, look, to my imagination, like the dying Voltaire, held for ten minutes a sadly shrunken little *salon*. I felt indeed each time, as if I were attending the last *coucher* of some social sovereign. He was royally whimsical about his sufferings and not at all concerned—quite as if the Constitution provided for the case—about his successor. He glided over *our* sufferings charmingly, and none of his jokes—it was a gallant abstention, some of them would have been so easy—were at our expense. Now and again, I confess, there was one at Brooksmith's, but so pathetically sociable as to make the excellent man look at me in a way that seemed to say: "Do exchange a glance with me, or I sha'n't be able to stand it." What he was not able to stand was not what Mr Offord said about him, but what he wasn't able to say in return. His notion of conversation, for himself, was giving you the convenience of speaking to him; and when he went to "see" Lady Kenyon, for instance, it was to carry her the tribute of his receptive silence. Where would the speech of his betters have been if proper service had been a manifestation of sound? In that case the fundamental difference would have had to be shown by *their* dumbness, and many of them, poor things, were dumb enough without that provision. Brooksmith took an unfailing interest in the preservation of the fundamental difference; it was the thing he had most on his conscience.

What had become of it, however, when Mr Offord passed away like any inferior person—was relegated to eternal stillness like a butler upstairs? His aspect for several days after the expected event may be imagined, and the multiplication by funereal observance of the things he didn't say. When everything was over—it was late the same day—I knocked at the door of the house of mourning as I so often had done before. I could never call on Mr Offord again, but I had come, literally, to call on Brooksmith. I wanted to ask him if there was anything I could do for him, tainted with vagueness as this inquiry could only be. My wild dream of taking him into my own service had died away: my service was not worth his being taken into. My offer to him could only be to help him to find another place, and yet there was an indelicacy, as it were, in taking for granted that his thoughts would immediately be fixed on another. I had a hope that he would be able to give his life a different form—though certainly not the form, the frequent result of such bereavements, of his setting up a little shop. That would have been dreadful; for I should have wished to further any enterprise that he might embark in, yet how could I have brought myself to go and pay him shillings and take back coppers over a counter? My visit then was simply an intended compliment. He took it as such, gratefully and with all the tact in the world. He knew I really couldn't help him and that I knew he knew I couldn't; but we discussed the situation—with a good deal of elegant generality—at the foot of the stairs, in the hall already dismantled,

where I had so often discussed other situations with him.
The executors were in possession, as was still more apparent
when he made me pass for a few minutes into the dining-
room, where various objects were muffled up for removal.

Two definite facts, however, he had to communicate; one
being that he was to leave the house for ever that night
(servants, for some mysterious reason, seem always to depart
by night), and the other—he mentioned it only at the last,
with hesitation—that he had already been informed his late
master had left him a legacy of eighty pounds. "I'm very
glad," I said, and Brooksmith rejoined: "It was so like him
to think of me." This was all that passed between us on the
subject, and I know nothing of his judgment of Mr Offord's
memento. Eighty pounds are always eighty pounds, and no
one has ever left *me* an equal sum; but, all the same, for Brooksmith, I was disappointed. I don't know what I had expected—
in short I was disappointed. Eighty pounds might stock a
little shop—a *very* little shop; but, I repeat, I couldn't bear
to think of that. I asked my friend if he had been able to save
a little, and he replied: "No, sir; I have had to do things." I
didn't inquire what things he had had to do; they were his
own affair, and I took his word for them as assentingly as if
he had had the greatness of an ancient house to keep up;
especially as there was something in his manner that seemed
to convey a prospect of further sacrifice.

"I shall have to turn round a bit, sir—I shall have to look
about me," he said; and then he added, indulgently, magnanimously: "If you should happen to hear of anything for
me——"

I couldn't let him finish; this was, in its essence, too much
in the really grand manner. It would be a help to my getting
him off my mind to be able to pretend I *could* find the right
place, and that help he wished to give me, for it was doubtless painful to him to see me in so false a position. I interposed
with a few words to the effect that I was well aware that wher-

ever he should go, whatever he should do, he would miss our old friend terribly—miss him even more than I should, having been with him so much more. This led him to make the speech that I have always remembered as the very text of the whole episode.

"Oh, sir, it's sad for *you*, very sad, indeed, and for a great many gentlemen and ladies; that it is, sir. But for me, sir, it is, if I may say so, still graver even than that: it's just the loss of something that was everything. For me, sir," he went on, with rising tears, "he was just *all*, if you know what I mean, sir. You have others, sir, I daresay—not that I would have you understand me to speak of them as in any way tanta- mount. But you have the pleasures of society, sir; if it's only in talking about him, sir, as I daresay you do freely—for all his blessed memory has to fear from it—with gentlemen and ladies who have had the same honour. That's not for me, sir, and I have to keep my associations to myself. Mr Offord was *my* society, and now I have no more. You go back to conver- sation, sir, after all, and I go back to my place," Brooksmith stammered, without exaggerated irony or dramatic bitterness, but with a flat, unstudied veracity and his hand on the knob of the street-door. He turned it to let me out and then he added: "I just go downstairs, sir, again, and I stay there."

"My poor child," I replied, in my emotion, quite as Mr Offord used to speak, "my dear fellow, leave it to me; we'll look after you, we'll all do something for you."

"Ah, if you could give me some one *like* him! But there ain't two in the world," said Brooksmith as we parted.

He had given me his address—the place where he would be to be heard of. For a long time I had no occasion to make use of the information; for he proved indeed, on trial, a very difficult case. In a word the people who knew him and had known Mr Offord, didn't want to take him, and yet I couldn't bear to try to thrust him among people who didn't know him. I spoke to many of our old friends about him, and I found them all governed by the odd mixture of feelings of which I myself was conscious, and disposed, further, to entertain a suspicion that he was "spoiled," with which I then would have nothing to do. In plain terms a certain embarrassment, a sensible awkwardness, when they thought of it, attached to the idea of using him as a menial: they had met him so often in society. Many of them would have asked him, and did ask him, or rather did ask me to ask him, to come and see them; but a mere visiting-list was not what I wanted for him. He was too short for people who were very particular; nevertheless I heard of an opening in a diplomatic household which led me to write him a note, though I was looking much less for something grand than for something human. Five days later I heard from him. The secretary's wife had decided, after keeping him waiting till then, that she couldn't take a servant out of a house in which there had not been a lady. The note had a P.S.: "It's a good job there wasn't, sir, such a lady as some."

A week later he came to see me and told me he was "suited"—committed to some highly respectable people (they were something very large in the City), who lived on the Bayswater side of the Park. "I daresay it will be rather poor, sir," he admitted; "but I've seen the fireworks, haven't I, sir?—it can't be fireworks *every* night. After Mansfield Street there ain't much choice." There was a certain amount, however, it seemed; for the following year, going one day to call on a country cousin, a lady of a certain age who was spending a fortnight in town with some friends of her own, a family unknown to me and resident in Chester Square, the door of the house was opened, to my surprise and gratification, by Brooksmith in person. When I came out I had some conversation with him, from which I gathered that he had found the large City people too dull for endurance, and I guessed, though he didn't say it, that he had found them vulgar as well. I don't know what judgment he would have passed on his actual patrons if my relative had not been their friend; but under the circumstances he abstained from comment.

None was necessary, however, for before the lady in question brought her visit to a close they honoured me with an invitation to dinner, which I accepted. There was a largeish party on the occasion, but I confess I thought of Brooksmith rather more than of the seated company. They required no depth of attention—they were all referable to usual, irredeemable, inevitable types. It was the world of cheerful commonplace and conscious gentility and prosperous density, a full-fed, material, insular world, a world of hideous florid plate and ponderous order and thin conversation. There was not a word said about Byron. Nothing would have induced me to look at Brooksmith in the course of the repast, and I felt sure that not even my overturning the wine would have induced him to meet my eye. We were in intellectual sympathy—we felt, as regards each other, a kind of social responsibility. In short we had been in Arcadia together, and we had both come to *this!* No wonder we were ashamed to be confronted. When he helped on my overcoat, as I was going away, we parted, for the first time since the earliest days in Mansfield Street, in silence. I thought he looked lean and wasted, and I guessed that his new place was not more "human" than his previous one. There was plenty of beef and beer, but there was no reciprocity. The question for him to have asked before accepting the position would have been not "How many footmen are kept?" but "How much imagination?"

The next time I went to the house—I confess it was not very soon—I encountered his successor, a personage who evidently enjoyed the good fortune of never having quitted his natural level. Could any be higher? he seemed to ask—over the heads of three footmen and even of some visitors. He made me feel as if Brooksmith were dead; but I didn't dare to inquire—I couldn't have borne his "I haven't the least idea, sir." I despatched a note to the address Brooksmith had given me after Mr Offord's death, but I received no answer. Six months later, however, I was favoured with a visit from an elderly, dreary, dingy person, who introduced herself to me as Mr Brooksmith's aunt and from whom I learned that he was out of place and out of health and had allowed her to come and say to me that if I could spare half-an-hour to look in at him he would take it as a rare honour.

I went the next day—his messenger had given me a new address—and found my friend lodged in a short sordid street in Marylebone, one of those corners of London that wear the last expression of sickly meanness. The room into which I was shown was above the small establishment of a dyer and cleaner who had inflated kid gloves and discoloured shawls in his shop-front. There was a great deal of grimy infant life up and down the place, and there was a hot, moist smell within, as of the "boiling" of dirty linen. Brooksmith sat with a blanket over his legs at a clean little window, where, from behind stiff bluish-white curtains, he could look across at a huckster's and a tinsmith's and a small greasy public-house. He had passed through an illness and was convalescent, and his mother, as well as his aunt, was in attendance on him. I liked the mother, who was bland and intensely humble, but I didn't much fancy the aunt, whom I connected, perhaps unjustly, with the opposite public-house (she seemed somehow to be greasy with the same grease), and whose furtive eye followed every movement of my hand, as if to see if it were not going into my pocket. It didn't take this direction—I couldn't, unsolicited, put myself at that sort of ease with Brooksmith. Several times the door of the room opened, and mysterious old women peeped in and shuffled back again. I don't know who they were; poor Brooksmith seemed encompassed with vague, prying, beery females.

He was vague himself, and evidently weak, and much embarrassed, and not an allusion was made between us to Mansfield Street. The vision of the *salon* of which he had been an ornament hovered before me, however, by contrast, sufficiently. He assured me that he was really getting better, and his mother remarked that he would come round if he could only get his spirits up. The aunt echoed this opinion, and I became more sure that in her own case she knew where to go for such a purpose. I'm afraid I was rather weak with my old friend, for I neglected the opportunity, so exceptionally good, to rebuke the levity which had led him to throw up honourable positions—fine, stiff, steady berths, with morning prayers, as I knew, attached to one of them—in Bayswater and Belgravia. Very likely his reasons had been profane and sentimental; he didn't want morning prayers, he wanted to be somebody's dear fellow; but I couldn't be the person to rebuke him. He shuffled these episodes out of sight—I saw that he had no wish to discuss them. I perceived further, strangely enough, that it would probably be a questionable pleasure for him to see me again: he doubted now even of my power to condone his aberrations. He didn't wish to have to explain; and his behaviour, in future, was likely to need explanation. When I bade him farewell he looked at me a moment with eyes that said everything: "How can I talk about those exquisite years in this place, before these people, with the old women poking their heads in? It was very good of you to come to see me—it wasn't my idea; *she* brought you. We've said everything; it's over; you'll lose all patience with me, and I'd rather you shouldn't see the rest." I sent him some money, in a letter, the next day, but I saw the rest only in the light of a barren sequel.

A whole year after my visit to him I became aware once, in dining out, that Brooksmith was one of the several servants who hovered behind our chairs. He had not opened the door of the house to me, and I had not recognised him in the cluster of retainers in the hall. This time I tried to catch his

eye, but he never gave me a chance, and when he handed me
a dish I could only be careful to thank him audibly. Indeed I
partook of two *entrées* of which I had my doubts, subsequently converted into certainties, in order not to snub him.
He looked well enough in health, but much older, and wore,
in an exceptionally marked degree, the glazed and expressionless mask of the British domestic *de race*. I saw with dismay
that if I had not known him I should have taken him, on the
showing of his countenance, for an extravagant illustration of
irresponsive servile gloom. I said to myself that he had
become a reactionary, gone over to the Philistines, thrown
himself into religion, the religion of his "place," like a foreign
lady *sur le retour*. I divined moreover that he was only
engaged for the evening—he had become a mere waiter, had
joined the band of the white-waistcoated who "go out."
There was something pathetic in this fact, and it was a terrible
vulgarisation of Brooksmith. It was the mercenary prose of
butlerhood; he had given up the struggle for the poetry.
If reciprocity was what he had missed, where was the reciprocity now? Only in the bottoms of the wine-glasses and
the five shillings (or whatever they get), clapped into his
hand by the permanent man. However, I supposed he had
taken up a precarious branch of his profession because after
all it sent him less downstairs. His relations with London
society were more superficial, but they were of course more
various. As I went away, on this occasion, I looked out for
him eagerly among the four or five attendants whose perpendicular persons, fluting the walls of London passages, are
supposed to lubricate the process of departure; but he was
not on duty. I asked one of the others if he were not in the
house, and received the prompt answer: "Just left, sir. Anything I can do for you, sir?" I wanted to say "Please give him
my kind regards;" but I abstained; I didn't want to compromise him, and I never came across him again.

   Often and often, in dining out, I looked for him, sometimes accepting invitations on purpose to multiply the chances of my meeting him. But always in vain; so that as I met many other members of the casual class over and over again, I at last adopted the theory that he always procured a list of expected guests beforehand and kept away from the banquets which he thus learned I was to grace. At last I gave up hope, and one day, at the end of three years, I received another visit from his aunt. She was drearier and dingier, almost squalid, and she was in great tribulation and want. Her sister, Mrs Brooksmith, had been dead a year, and three months later her nephew had disappeared. He had always looked after her a bit—since her troubles; I never knew what her troubles had been—and now she hadn't so much as a petticoat to pawn. She had also a niece, to whom she had been everything, before her troubles, but the niece had treated her most shameful. These were details; the great and romantic fact was Brooksmith's final evasion of his fate. He had gone out to wait one evening, as usual, in a white waistcoat she had done up for him with her own hands, being due at a large party up Kensington way. But he had never come home again, and had never arrived at the large party, or at any party that any one could make out. No trace of him had come to light—no gleam of the white waistcoat had pierced the obscurity of his doom. This news was a sharp shock to me, for I had my ideas about his real destination. His aged relative had promptly, as she said, guessed the worst. Somehow and somewhere he had got out of the way altogether, and now I trust that, with characteristic deliberation, he is changing the plates of the immortal gods. As my depressing visitant also said, he never *had* got his spirits up. I was fortunately able to dismiss her with her own somewhat improved. But the dim ghost of poor Brooksmith is one of those that I see. He had indeed been spoiled.

pretending to look at a picture. She was so far from agreeing with Mrs Churchley that it was an hour she particularly disliked. She was conscious of the queerness, the shyness, in London, of the gregarious flight of guests, after a dinner, the general *sauve qui peut* and panic fear of being left with the host and hostess. But personally she always felt the contagion, always conformed to the flurry. Besides, she felt herself turning red now, flushed with a conviction that had come over her and that she wished not to show.

Her father sat down on one of the big sofas with Mrs Churchley; fortunately he was also a person with a presence that could hold its own. Adela didn't care to sit and watch them while they made love, as she crudely formulated it, and she cared still less to join in their conversation. She wandered further away, went into another of the bright, "handsome," rather nude rooms—they were like women dressed for a ball —where the displaced chairs, at awkward angles to each other, seemed to retain the attitudes of bored talkers. Her heart beat strangely, but she continued to make a pretense of looking at the pictures on the walls and the ornaments on the tables, while she hoped that, as she preferred it, it would be also the course that her father would like best. She hoped "awfully," as she would have said, that he wouldn't think her rude. She was a person of courage, and he was a kind, an intensely good-natured man; nevertheless, she was a good deal afraid of him. At home it had always been a religion with them to be nice to the people he liked. How, in the old days, her mother, her incomparable mother, so clever, so unerring, so perfect—how in the precious days her mother had practiced that art! Oh, her mother, her irrecoverable mother! One of the pictures that she was looking at swam before her eyes. Mrs Churchley, in the natural course, would have begun immediately to climb staircases. Adela could see the high bony shoulders and the long crimson tail and the universal coruscating nod wriggle their business-like way through the rest of

the night. Therefore she *must* have had her reasons for detain-
ing them. There were mothers who thought every one wanted
to marry their eldest son, and the girl asked herself if *she*
belonged to the class of daughters who thought every one
wanted to marry their father. Her companions left her alone;
and though she didn't want to be near them, it angered her
that Mrs Churchley didn't call her. That proved that she was
conscious of the situation. She would have called her, only
Colonel Chart had probably murmured, "Don't." That
proved that he also was conscious. The time was really not
long—ten minutes at the most elapsed—when he cried out,
gayly, pleasantly, as if with a little jocular reproach, "I say,
Adela, we must release this dear lady!" He spoke, of course,
as if it had been Adela's fault that they lingered. When they
took leave she gave Mrs Churchley, without intention and
without defiance, but from the simple sincerity of her anxiety,
a longer look into the eyes than she had ever given her before.
Mrs Churchley's onyx pupils reflected the question; they
seemed to say: "Yes, I *am*, if that's what you want to know!"
    What made the case worse, what made the girl more sure,
was the silence preserved by her companion in the brougham,
on their way home. They rolled along in the June darkness
from Prince's Gate to Seymour Street, each looking out of a
window in conscious dumbness; watching without seeing the
hurry of the London night, the flash of lamps, the quick roll
on the wood of hansoms and other broughams. Adela had
expected that her father would say something about Mrs
Churchley; but when he said nothing, it was, strangely, still
more as if he had spoken. In Seymour Street he asked the
footman if Mr Godfrey had come in, to which the servant
replied that he had come in early and gone straight to his
room. Adela had perceived as much, without saying so, by a
lighted window in the third story; but she contributed no
remark to the question. At the foot of the stairs her father
halted a moment, hesitating, as if he had something on his

mind; but what it amounted to, apparently, was only the dry "Good-night" with which he presently ascended. It was the first time since her mother's death that he had bidden her good-night without kissing her. They were a kissing family, and after her mother's death the habit had taken a fresh spring. She had left behind her such a general passion of regret that in kissing each other they seemed to themselves a little to be kissing her. Now, as, standing in the hall, with the stiff watching footman (she could have said to him angrily, "Go away!") planted near her, she looked with unspeakable pain at her father's back while he mounted, the effect was of his having withheld from other and still more sensitive lips the touch of his own.

He was going to his room, and after a moment she heard his door close. Then she said to the servant, "Shut up the house" (she tried to do everything her mother had done, to be a little of what she had been, conscious only of mediocrity), and took her own way upstairs. After she had reached her room she waited, listening, shaken by the apprehension that she should hear her father come out again and go up to Godfrey. He would go up to tell him, to have it over without delay, precisely because it would be so difficult. She asked herself, indeed, why he should tell Godfrey when he had not taken the occasion—their drive home was an occasion—to tell herself. However, she wanted no announcing, no telling; there was such a horrible clearness in her mind that what she now waited for was only to be sure her father wouldn't leave his room. At the end of ten minutes she saw that this particular danger was over, upon which she came out and made her way to Godfrey. Exactly what she wanted to say to him first, if her father counted on the boy's greater indulgence, and before he could say anything, was, "Don't forgive him; don't, don't!"

He was to go up for an examination, poor fellow, and during these weeks his lamp burned till the small hours. It was for the diplomatic service, and there was to be some frightful number of competitors; but Adela had great hopes of him— she believed so in his talents, and she saw, with pity, how hard he worked. This would have made her spare him, not trouble his night, his scanty rest, if anything less dreadful had been at stake. It was a blessing, however, that one could count upon his coolness, young as he was—his bright, good-looking discretion. Moreover he was the one who would care most. If Leonard was the eldest son—he had, as a matter of course, gone into the army and was in India, on the staff, by good luck, of a governor-general—it was exactly this that would make him comparatively indifferent. His life was elsewhere, and his father and he had been in a measure military comrades, so that he would be deterred by a certain delicacy from protesting; he wouldn't have liked his father to protest in an affair of *his*. Beatrice and Muriel would care, but they were too young to speak, and this was just why her own responsibility was so great.

Godfrey was in working-gear—shirt and trousers and slippers and a beautiful silk jacket. His room felt hot, though a window was open to the summer night; the lamp on the table shed its studious light over a formidable heap of text books and papers, and the bed showed that he had flung himself down to think out a problem. As soon as she got in she said to him: "Father's going to marry Mrs Churchley!"

She saw the poor boy's pink face turn pale. "How do you know?"

"I've seen with my eyes. We've been dining there—we've just come home. He's in love with her—she's in love with him; they'll arrange it."

"Oh, I say!" Godfrey exclaimed, incredulous.

"He will, he will, he will!" cried the girl; and with this she burst into tears.

Godfrey, who had a cigarette in his hand, lighted it at one of the candles on the mantelpiece as if he were embarrassed.

As Adela, who had dropped into his armchair, continued to sob, he said, after a moment: "He oughtn't to—he oughtn't to."

"Oh, think of mamma—think of mamma!" the girl went on.

"Yes, he ought to think of mamma;" and Godfrey looked at the tip of his cigarette.

"To such a woman as that, after *her!*"

"Dear old mamma!" said Godfrey, smoking.

Adela rose again, drying her eyes. "It's like an insult to her; it's as if he denied her." Now that she spoke of it, she felt herself tremendously exalted. "It's as if he rubbed out at a stroke all the years of their happiness."

"They were awfully happy," said Godfrey.

"Think what she was—think how no one else will ever again be like her!" the girl cried.

"I suppose he's not very happy now," Godfrey continued vaguely.

"Of course he isn't, any more than you and I are; and it's dreadful of him to want to be."

"Well, don't make yourself miserable till you're sure," the young man said.

But his sister showed him confidently that she *was* sure, from the way the pair had behaved together and from her father's attitude on the drive home. If Godfrey had been there he would have seen everything; it couldn't be explained, but he would have felt. When he asked at what moment the girl had first had her suspicion, she replied that it had all come at once, that evening; or that at least she had had no conscious fear till then. There had been signs for two or three weeks, but she hadn't understood them—ever since the day Mrs Churchley had dined in Seymour Street. Adela had thought it odd then that her father had wished to invite her, in the quiet way they were living; she was a person they knew so little. He had said something about her having been very civil

to him, and that evening, already, she had guessed that he had
been to Mrs Churchley's oftener than she had supposed. To-
night it had come to her clearly that he had been to see her
every day since the day she dined with them; every afternoon,
about the hour she thought he was at his club. Mrs Churchley
was his club,—she was just like a club. At this Godfrey
laughed; he wanted to know what his sister knew about clubs.
She was slightly disappointed in his laugh, slightly wounded
by it, but she knew perfectly what she meant: she meant that
Mrs Churchley was public and florid, promiscuous and man-
nish.

"Oh, I dare say she's all right," said Godfrey, as if he
wanted to get on with his work. He looked at the clock on the
mantelshelf; he would have to put in another hour.

"All right to come and take darling mamma's place—to sit
where *she* used to sit, to lay her horrible hands on *her* things?"
Adela was appalled—all the more that she had not expected
it—at her brother's apparent acceptance of such a prospect.

He coloured; there was something in her passionate piety
that scorched him. She glared at him with her tragic eyes as if
he had profaned an altar. "Oh, I mean nothing will come of
it."

"Not if we do our duty," said Adela.

"Our duty?"

"You must speak to him—tell him how we feel; that we
shall never forgive him, that we can't endure it."

"He'll think I'm cheeky," returned Godfrey, looking
down at his papers, with his back to her and his hands in his
pockets.

"Cheeky, to plead for *her* memory?"

"He'll say it's none of my business."

"Then you believe he'll do it?" cried the girl.

"Not a bit. Go to bed!"

"*I'll* speak to him," said Adela, as pale as a young priestess.

"Don't cry out till you're hurt; wait till he speaks to *you*."

"He won't, he won't!" the girl declared. "He'll do it without telling us."

Her brother had faced round to her again; he started a little at this, and again, at one of the candles, lighted his cigarette, which had gone out. She looked at him a moment; then he said something that surprised her.

"Is Mrs Churchley very rich?"

"I haven't the least idea. What has that to do with it?"

Godfrey puffed his cigarette. "Does she live as if she were?"

"She has got a lot of showy things."

"Well, we must keep our eyes open," said Godfrey. "And now you *must* let me get on." He kissed his sister, as if to make up for dismissing her, or for his failure to take fire; and she held him a moment, burying her head on his shoulder. A wave of emotion surged through her; she broke out with a wail:

"Ah, why did she leave us? Why did she leave us?"

"Yes, why indeed?" the young man sighed, disengaging himself with a movement of oppression.

II

A D E L A was so far right as that by the end of the week, though she remained certain, her father had not made the announcement she dreaded. What made her certain was the sense of her changed relations with him—of there being between them something unexpressed, something of which she was as conscious as she would have been of an unhealed wound. When she spoke of this to Godfrey, he said the change was of her own making, that she was cruelly unjust to the governor. She suffered even more from her brother's unexpected perversity; she had had so different a theory about him that her disappointment was almost an humiliation and she needed all her fortitude to pitch her faith lower. She wondered what had happened to him and why he had changed. She would have trusted him to feel right about anything, above all about such a matter as this. Their worship of their mother's memory, their recognition of her sacred place in their past, her exquisite influence in their father's life, his fortunes, his career, in the whole history of the family and welfare of the house— accomplished, clever, gentle, good, beautiful and capable as she had been, a woman whose soft distinction was universally proclaimed, so that on her death one of the Princesses, the most august of her friends, had written Adela such a note about her as princesses were understood very seldom to write: their hushed tenderness over all this was a kind of religion, and also a sort of honour, in falling away from which there was a semblance of treachery. This was not the way people usually felt in London, she knew; but, strenuous, ardent, observant girl as she was, with secrecies of sentiment and dim originalities of attitude, she had already made up her mind that London was no place to look for delicacies. Remembrance there was hammered thin, and to be faithful was to be a bore. The patient dead were sacrificed; they had no shrines, for people were literally ashamed of mourning. When they had hustled all sensibility out of their lives, they invented the fiction that they felt too much to utter. Adela said nothing to her sisters; this reticence was part of the virtue it was her system to exercise for them. *She* was to be their mother, a direct deputy and representative. Before the vision of that other woman parading in such a character, she felt capable of ingenuities and subtleties. The foremost of these was tremulously to watch her father. Five days after they had dined together at Mrs Churchley's he asked her if she had been to see that lady.

"No indeed, why should I?" Adela knew that he knew she had not been, since Mrs Churchley would have told him.

"Don't you call on people after you dine with them?" said Colonel Chart.

"Yes, in the course of time. I don't rush off within the week."

Her father looked at her, and his eyes were colder than she had ever seen them, which was probably, she reflected, just the way her own appeared to him. "Then you'll please rush off to-morrow. She's to dine with us on the 12th, and I shall expect your sisters to come down."

Adela stared. "To a dinner party?"

"It's not to be a dinner party. I want them to know Mrs Churchley."

"Is there to be nobody else?"

"Godfrey, of course. A family party."

The girl asked her brother that evening if *that* was not tantamount to an announcement. He looked at her queerly, and then he said, "*I*'ve been to see her."

"What on earth did you do that for?"

"Father told me he wished it."

"Then he *has* told you?"

"Told me what?" Godfrey asked, while her heart sank with the sense that he was making difficulties for her.

"That they're engaged, of course. What else can all this mean?"

"He didn't tell me that, but I like her."

"*Like* her!" the girl shrieked.

"She's very kind, very good."

"To thrust herself upon us when we hate her? Is that what you call kind? Is that what you call decent?"

"Oh, *I* don't hate her," Godfrey rejoined, turning away as if his sister bored him.

She went the next day to see Mrs Churchley, with a vague plan of breaking out to her, appealing to her, saying, "Oh, spare us! have mercy on us! let him alone! go away!" But that was not easy when they were face to face. Mrs Churchley had every intention of getting, as she would have said—she was perpetually using the expression—into touch; but her good intentions were as depressing as a tailor's misfits. She could never understand that they had no place for her vulgar charity; that their life was filled with a fragrance of perfection for which she had no sense fine enough. She was as undomestic as a shop-front and as out of tune as a parrot. She would make them live in the streets, or bring the streets into their lives—it was the same thing. She had evidently never read a book, and she used intonations that Adela had never heard, as if she had been an Australian or an American. She understood everything in a vulgar sense; speaking of Godfrey's visit to her and praising him according to her idea, saying horrid things about him—that he was awfully good-looking, a perfect gentleman, the kind she liked. How could her father, who was after all, in everything else, such a dear, listen to a woman, or endure her, who thought she was pleasing when she called the son of his dead wife a perfect gentleman? What would he have been, pray? Much she knew about what any of them were! When she told Adela she wanted her to like her, the girl thought for an instant her opportunity had come—the chance to plead with her and beg her off. But she presented such an impenetrable surface that it would have been like giving a message to a varnished door. She wasn't a woman, said Adela; she was an address.

When she dined in Seymour Street, the "children," as the girl called the others, including Godfrey, liked her. Beatrice and Muriel stared shyly and silently at the wonders of her apparel (she was brutally overdressed!) without, of course, guessing the danger that tainted the air. They supposed her, in their innocence, to be amusing, and they didn't know, any more than she did herself, that she patronised them. When she was upstairs with them, after dinner, Adela could see her looking round the room at the things she meant to alter; their mother's things, not a bit like her own and not good enough for her. After a quarter of an hour of this, our young lady felt sure she was deciding that Seymour Street wouldn't do at all, the dear old home that had done for their mother for twenty years. Was she plotting to transport them all to her horrible Prince's Gate? Of one thing, at any rate, Adela was certain: her father, at that moment, alone in the dining-room with Godfrey, pretending to drink another glass of wine to make time, was coming to the point, was telling the news. When they came upstairs, they both, to her eyes, looked strange: the news had been told.

She had it from Godfrey before Mrs Churchley left the house, when, after a brief interval, he followed her out of the drawing-room on her taking her sisters to bed. She was waiting for him at the door of her room. Her father was then alone with his *fiancée* (the word was grotesque to Adela); it was already as if it were her home.

"What did you say to him?" the girl asked, when her brother had told her.

"I said nothing." Then he added, colouring (the expression of her face was such), "There was nothing to say."

"Is that how it strikes you?" said Adela, staring at the lamp.

"He asked me to speak to her," Godfrey went on.

"To speak to her?"

"To tell her I was glad."

"And did you?" Adela panted.

"I don't know. I said something. She kissed me."

"Oh, how *could* you?" shuddered the girl, covering her face with her hands.

"He says she's very rich," said Godfrey simply.

"Is that why you kissed her?"

"I didn't kiss her. Good-night," and the young man, turning his back upon her, went out.

When her brother was gone Adela locked herself in, as if with the fear that she should be overtaken or invaded, and

during a sleepless, feverish, memorable night she took counsel of her uncompromising spirit. She saw things as they were,
in all the indignity of life. The levity, the mockery, the in-
fidelity, the ugliness, lay as plain as a map before her; it was
a world *pour rire*, but she cried about it, all the same. The
morning dawned early, or rather it seemed to her that there
had been no night, nothing but a sickly, creeping day. But
by the time she heard the house stirring again she had determined what to do. When she came down to the breakfast-
room her father was already in his place, with newspapers and
letters; and she expected the first words he would utter to be
a rebuke to her for having disappeared, the night before, without taking leave of Mrs Churchley. Then she saw that he
wished to be intensely kind, to make every allowance, to con-
ciliate and console her. He knew that she knew from Godfrey,
and he got up and kissed her. He told her as quickly as
possible, to have it over, stammering a little, with an "I've a
piece of news for you that will probably shock you," yet
looking even exaggeratedly grave and rather pompous, to inspire the respect he didn't deserve. When he kissed her she
melted, she burst into tears. He held her against him, kissing
her again and again, saying tenderly, "Yes, yes, I know, I
know." But he didn't know, or he could never have done it.
Beatrice and Muriel came in, frightened when they saw her
crying, and still more scared when she turned to them with
words and an air that were terrible in their comfortable little
lives: "Papa's going to be married; he's going to marry Mrs
Churchley!" After staring a moment and seeing their father
look as strange, on his side, as Adela, though in a different
way, the children also began to cry, so that when the servants
arrived, with tea and boiled eggs, these functionaries were
greatly embarrassed with their burden, not knowing whether
to come in or hang back. They all scraped together a decorum,
and as soon as the things had been put on the table the Colonel
banished the men with a glance. Then he made a little affec-

tionate speech to Beatrice and Muriel, in which he assured them that Mrs Churchley was the kindest, the most delightful, of women, only wanting to make them happy, only wanting to make him happy, and convinced that he would be if they were and that they would be if he was.

"What do such words mean?" Adela asked herself. She declared privately that they meant nothing, but she was silent, and every one was silent, on account of the advent of Miss Flynn, the governess, before whom Colonel Chart preferred not to discuss the situation. Adela recognized on the spot that, if things were to go as he wished, his children would practically never again be alone with him. He would spend all his time with Mrs Churchley till they were married, and then Mrs Churchley would spend all her time with him. Adela was ashamed of him, and that was horrible—all the more that every one else would be, all his other friends, every one who had known her mother. But the public dishonour to that high memory should not be enacted; he should not do as he wished.

After breakfast her father told her that it would give him pleasure if, in a day or two, she would take her sisters to see Mrs Churchley, and she replied that he should be obeyed. He held her hand a moment, looking at her with an appeal in his eyes which presently hardened into sternness. He wanted to know that she forgave him, but he also wanted to say to her that he expected her to mind what she did, to go straight. She turned away her eyes; she was indeed ashamed of him.

She waited three days, and then she took her sisters to see Mrs Churchley. That lady was surrounded with callers, as Adela knew she would be; it was her "day" and the occasion the girl preferred. Before this she had spent all her time with her sisters, talking to them about their mother, playing upon their memory of her, making them cry and making them laugh, reminding them of certain hours of their early childhood, telling them anecdotes of her own. None the less she assured them that she believed there was no harm at all in Mrs Churchley, and that when the time should come she would probably take them out immensely. She saw with smothered irritation that they enjoyed their visit in Prince's Gate; they had never been at anything so "grown up," nor seen so many smart bonnets and brilliant complexions. Moreover, they were considered with interest, as if, as features of Mrs Churchley's new life, they had been described in advance and were the heroines of the occasion. There were so many ladies present that Mrs Churchley didn't talk to them much; but she called them her "chicks" and asked them to hand about tea-cups and bread and butter. All this was highly agreeable and indeed intensely exciting to Beatrice and Muriel, who had little round red spots in *their* cheeks when they came away. Adela quivered with the sense that her mother's children were now Mrs Churchley's "chicks" and features of Mrs Churchley's life.

It was one thing to have made up her mind, however; it was another thing to make her attempt. It was when she learned from Godfrey that the day was fixed, the 20th of July, only six weeks removed, that she felt the importance of prompt action. She learned everything from Godfrey now, having determined that it would be hypocrisy to question her father. Even her silence was hypocritical, but she couldn't weep and wail. Her father showed extreme tact; taking no notice of her detachment, treating her as if it were a moment of *bouderie* which he was bound to allow her and which would pout itself away. She debated much as to whether she should take Godfrey into her confidence; she would have done so without hesitation if he had not disappointed her. He was so strange and so perversely preoccupied that she could explain it only by the high pressure at which he was living, his anxiety about his "exam." He was in a fidget, in a fever, putting on a spurt to come in first; sceptical moreover about his success and cynical about everything else. He appeared to agree to the general axiom that they didn't want a strange woman thrust into their home, but he found Mrs Churchley "very jolly as a person to know." He had been to see her by himself; he had been to see her three times. He said to his sister that he would make the most of her now; he should probably be so little in Seymour Street after these days. What Adela at last determined to say to him was that the marriage would never take place. When he asked her what she meant and who was to prevent it, she replied that the interesting couple would give it up themselves, or that Mrs Churchley at least would after a week or two back out of it.

"That will be really horrid then," Godfrey rejoined. "The only respectable thing, at the point they've come to, is to put it through. Charming for poor father to have the air of being 'chucked.'"

This made her hesitate two days more, but she found answers more valid than any objections. The many-voiced answer to everything—it was like the autumn wind around the house—was the backward affront to her mother. Her mother was dead, but it killed her again. So one morning, at eleven o'clock, when Adela knew her father was writing letters, she went out quietly and, stopping the first hansom she met, drove to Prince's Gate. Mrs Churchley was at home, and she was shown into the drawing-room with the request that she would wait five minutes. She waited, without the sense of breaking down at the last, the impulse to run away, which was what she had expected to have. In the cab and at the door her heart had beat terribly, but now, suddenly, with the game really to play, she found herself lucid and calm. It was a joy to her to feel later that this was the way Mrs Churchley found her; not confused, not stammering nor prevaricating, only a little amazed at her own courage, conscious of the immense responsibility of her step and wonderfully older than her years. Her hostess fixed her at first with the waiting eyes of a cashier, but after a little, to Adela's surprise, she burst into tears. At this the girl cried herself, but with the secret happiness of believing they were saved. Mrs Churchley said she would think over what she had been told, and she promised Adela, freely enough and very firmly, not to betray the secret of her visit to the Colonel. They were saved—they were saved: the words sung themselves in the girl's soul as she came downstairs. When the door was opened for her she saw her brother on the step, and they looked at each other in surprise, each finding it on the part of the other an odd hour for Prince's Gate. Godfrey remarked that Mrs Churchley would have enough of the family, and Adela answered that she would perhaps have too much. None the less the young man went in, while his sister took her way home.

III

ADELA CHART saw nothing of her brother for nearly a week; he had more and more his own time and hours, adjusted to his tremendous responsibilities, and he spent whole days at his crammer's. When she knocked at his door, late in the evening, he was not in his room. It was known in the house that he was greatly worried; he was horribly nervous about his ordeal. It was to begin on the 23d of June, and his father was as worried as himself. The wedding had been arranged in relation to this; they wished poor Godfrey's fate settled first, though it was felt that the nuptials would be darkened if it should not be settled right.

Ten days after her morning visit to Mrs Churchley Adela began to perceive that there was a difference in the air; but as yet she was afraid to exult. It was not a difference for the better, so that there might be still many hours of pain. Her father, since the announcement of his intended marriage, had been visibly pleased with himself, but that pleasure appeared to have undergone a check. Adela had the impression which the passengers on a great steamer receive when, in the middle of the night, they hear the engines stop. As this impression resolves itself into the general sense that something serious has happened, so the girl asked herself what had happened now. She had expected something serious; but it was as if she couldn't keep still in her cabin—she wanted to go up and see. On the 20th, just before breakfast, her maid brought her a message from her brother. Mr Godfrey would be obliged if she would speak to him in his room. She went straight up to him, dreading to find him ill, broken down on the eve of his formidable week. This was not the case, however, inasmuch as he appeared to be already at work, to have been at work since dawn. But he was very white, and his eyes had a strange and new expression. Her beautiful young brother looked older; he looked haggard and hard. He met her there as if he had been waiting for her, and he said immediately: "Please to tell me this, Adela: what was the purpose of your visit, the other morning, to Mrs Churchley—the day I met you at her door?"

She stared—she hesitated. "The purpose? What's the matter? Why do you ask?"

"They've put it off—they've put it off a month."

"Ah, thank God!" said Adela.

"Why do you thank God?" Godfrey exclaimed roughly.

His sister gave a strained, intense smile. "You know I think it's all wrong."

He stood looking at her up and down. "What did you do there? How did you interfere?"

"Who told you I interfered?" she asked, flushing.

"You said something—you did something. I knew you had done it when I saw you come out."

"What I did was my own business."

"Damn your own business!" cried the young man.

She had never in her life been so spoken to, and in advance, if she had been given the choice, she would have said that she would rather die than be so spoken to by Godfrey. But her spirit was high, and for a moment she was as angry as if some one had cut at her with a whip. She escaped the blow, but she felt the insult. "And *your* business, then?" she asked. "I wondered what that was when I saw *you*."

He stood a moment longer frowning at her; then, with the exclamation "You've made a pretty mess!" he turned away from her and sat down to his books.

They had put it off, as he said; her father was dry and stiff and official about it. "I suppose I had better let you know that we have thought it best to postpone our marriage till the end of the summer—Mrs Churchley has so many arrangements to make:" he was not more expansive than that. She neither knew nor greatly cared whether it was her fancy or a reality that he watched her obliquely, to see how she would take these words. She flattered herself that, thanks to Godfrey's preparation, cruel as the form of it had been, she took them very cleverly. She had a perfectly good conscience, for she was now able to judge what odious elements Mrs Churchley, whom she had not seen since the morning in Prince's Gate, had already introduced into their relations with each other. She was able to infer that her father had not concurred in the postponement, for he was more restless than before, more absent, and distinctly irritable. There was of course still the question of how much of this condition was to be attributed to his solicitude about Godfrey. That young man took occasion to say a horrible thing to his sister: "If I don't pass it will be your fault." These were dreadful days for the girl, and she asked herself how she could have borne them if the hovering spirit of her mother had not been at her side. Fortunately, she always felt it there, sustaining, commending, sanctifying. Suddenly her father announced to her that he wished her to go immediately, with her sisters, down to Overland, where there was always part of a household and where for a few weeks they would be sufficiently comfortable. The only explanation he gave of this desire was that he wanted them out of the way. "Out of the way of what?" she queried, since, for the time, there were to be no preparations in Seymour Street. She was willing to believe that it was out of the way of his nerves.

She never needed urging, however, to go to Overland, the dearest old house in the world, where the happiest days of her young life had been spent and the silent nearness of her mother always seemed greatest. She was happy again, with Beatrice and Muriel and Miss Flynn, and the air of summer, and the haunted rooms, and her mother's garden, and the talking oaks and the nightingales. She wrote briefly to her father, to give him, as he had requested, an account of things; and he wrote back that, since she was so contented (she didn't remember telling him that), she had better not return to town at all. The rest of the season was not important for her, and he was getting on very well. He mentioned that Godfrey had finished his exam; but, as she knew, there would be a tiresome wait before they could learn the result. Godfrey was going abroad for a month with young Sherard—he had earned a little rest and a little fun. He went abroad without a word to Adela, but in his beautiful little hand he took a chaffing leave of Beatrice. The child showed her sister the letter, of which she was very proud and which contained no message for Adela. This was the worst bitterness of the whole crisis for that young lady—that it exhibited so strangely the creature in the world whom, after her mother, she had loved best.

Colonel Chart had said he would "run down" while his children were at Overland, but they heard no more about it. He only wrote two or three times to Miss Flynn, upon matters in regard to which Adela was surprised that he should not have communicated with herself. Muriel accomplished an upright little letter to Mrs Churchley—her eldest sister neither fostered nor discouraged the performance—to which Mrs

Churchley replied, after a fortnight, in a meagre and, as Adela thought, illiterate fashion, making no allusion to the approach of any closer tie. Evidently the situation had changed; the question of the marriage was dropped, at any rate for the time. This idea gave the girl a singular and almost intoxicating sense of power; she felt as if she were riding a great wave of responsibility. She had chosen and acted, and the greatest could do no more than that. The grand thing was to see one's results, and what else was she doing? These results were in important and opulent lives; the stage was large on which she moved her figures. Such a vision was exciting, and as they had the use of a couple of ponies at Overland she worked off her excitement by a long gallop. A day or two after this, however, came news of which the effect was to rekindle it. Godfrey had come back, the list had been published, he had passed first. These happy tidings proceeded from the young man himself; he announced them by a telegram to Beatrice, who had never in her life before received such a missive and was proportionately inflated. Adela reflected that she herself ought to have felt snubbed, but she was too happy. They were free again, they were themselves, the nightmare of the previous weeks was blown away, the unity and dignity of her father's life were restored, and, to round off her sense of success, Godfrey had achieved his first step toward high distinction. She wrote to him the next day, as frankly and affectionately as if there had been no estrangement between them; and besides telling him that she rejoiced in his triumph, she begged him in charity to let them know exactly how the case stood with regard to Mrs Churchley.

Late in the summer afternoon she walked through the park to the village with her letter, posted it and came back. Suddenly, at one of the turns of the avenue, half-way to the house, she saw a young man looking toward her and waiting for her—a young man who proved to be Godfrey, on his march, on foot, across from the station. He had seen her, as he took his short cut, and if he had come down to Overland it was not, apparently, to avoid her. There was none of the joy of his triumph in his face, however, as he came a very few steps to meet her; and although, stiffly enough, he let her kiss him and say, "I'm so glad—I'm so glad!" she felt that this tolerance was not quite the calmness of the rising diplomatist. He turned toward the house with her and walked on a short distance, while she uttered the hope that he had come to stay some days.

"Only till to-morrow morning. They are sending me straight to Madrid. I came down to say good-by; there's a fellow bringing my portmanteau."

"To Madrid? How awfully nice! And it's awfully nice of you to have come," Adela said, passing her hand into his arm.

The movement made him stop, and, stopping, he turned on her, in a flash, a face of something more than suspicion—of passionate reprobation. "What I really came for—you might as well know without more delay—is to ask you a question."

"A question?" Adela repeated with a beating heart.

They stood there, under the old trees, in the lingering light, and, young and fine and fair as they both were, they were in complete superficial accord with the peaceful English scene. A near view, however, would have shown that Godfrey Chart had not come down to Overland to be superficial. He looked deep into his sister's eyes and demanded: "What was it you said that morning to Mrs Churchley?"

Adela gazed at the ground a moment; then, raising her eyes: "If she has told you, why do you ask?"

"She has told me nothing. I've seen for myself."

"What have you seen?"

"She has broken it off—everything's over—father's in the depths."

"In the depths?" the girl quavered.

"Did you think it would make him jolly?" asked her brother.

"He'll get over it; he'll be glad."

"That remains to be seen. You interfered, you invented something, you got round her. I insist on knowing what you did."

Adela felt that she could be obstinate if she wished, and that if it should be a question of organizing a defense she should find treasures of perversity under her hand. She stood looking down again a moment, and saying to herself, "I could be dumb and dogged if I chose, but I scorn to be." She was not ashamed of what she had done, but she wanted to be clear. "Are you absolutely certain it's broken off?"

"He is, and she is; so that's as good."

"What reason has she given?"

"None at all—or half a dozen; it's the same thing. She has changed her mind—she mistook her feelings—she can't part with her independence; moreover, he has too many children."

"Did he tell you this?" said Adela.

"Mrs Churchley told me. She has gone abroad for a year."

"And she didn't tell you what I said to her?"

"Why should I take this trouble if she had?"

"You might have taken it to make me suffer," said Adela. "That appears to be what you want to do."

"No, I leave that to *you;* it's the good turn you've done me!" cried the young man, with hot tears in his eyes.

She stared, aghast with the perception that there was some dreadful thing she didn't know; but he walked on, dropping the question angrily and turning his back to her as if he couldn't trust himself. She read his disgust in his averted face, in the way he squared his shoulders and smote the ground with his stick, and she hurried after him and presently overtook him. She accompanied him for a moment in silence; then she pleaded: "What do you mean? What in the world have I done to you?"

"She would have helped me; she was all ready to do it," said Godfrey.

"Helped you in what?" She wondered what he meant;

if he had made debts that he was afraid to confess to his father and—of all horrible things—had been looking to Mrs Churchley to pay. She turned red with the mere apprehension of this and, on the heels of her guess, exulted again at having perhaps averted such a shame.

"Can't you see that I'm in trouble? Where are your eyes, your senses, your sympathy, that you talk so much about? Haven't you seen these six months that I've a cursed worry in my life?"

She seized his arm, she made him stop, she stood looking up at him like a frightened little girl. "What's the matter, Godfrey—what *is* the matter?"

"You've vexed me so—I could strangle you!" he growled. This idea added nothing to her dread; her dread was that he had done some wrong, was stained with some guilt. She uttered it to him with clasped hands, begging him to tell her the worst; but, still more passionately, he cut her short with his own cry: "In God's name, satisfy me! What infernal thing did you do?"

"It was not infernal; it was right. I told her mamma had been wretched," said Adela.

"Wretched? You told her such a lie?"

"It was the only way, and she believed me."

"Wretched how—wretched when—wretched where?" the young man stammered.

"I told her papa had made her so, and that *she* ought to know it. I told her the question troubled me unspeakably, but that I had made up my mind it was my duty to initiate her." Adela paused, with the light of bravado in her face, as if, though struck while she phrased it, with the monstrosity of what she had done, she was incapable of abating a jot of it. "I notified her that he had faults and peculiarities that made mamma's life a long worry—a martyrdom that she hid wonderfully from the world, but that we saw and that I had often pitied. I told her what they were, these faults and peculiarities;

I put the dots on the *i*'s. I said it wasn't fair to let another person marry him without a warning. I warned her; I satisfied my conscience. She could do as she liked. My responsibility was over."

Godfrey gazed at her; he listened, with parted lips, incredulous and appalled. "You invented such a tissue of falsities and calumnies, and you talk about your conscience? You stand there in your senses and proclaim your crime?"

"I would have committed any crime that would have rescued us."

"You insult and defame your own father?" Godfrey continued.

"He'll never know it; she took a vow she wouldn't tell him."

"I'll be damned if *I* won't tell him!" Godfrey cried.

Adela felt sick at this, but she flamed up to resent the treachery, as it struck her, of such a menace. "I did right—I did right!" she vehemently declared. "I went down on my knees to pray for guidance, and I saved mamma's memory from outrage. But if I hadn't, if I hadn't"—she faltered for an instant—"I'm not worse than you, and I'm not so bad, for you've done something that you're ashamed to tell me."

Godfrey had taken out his watch; he looked at it with quick intensity, as if he were not hearing nor heeding her. Then, glancing up with his calculating eye, he fixed her long enough to exclaim, with unsurpassable horror and contempt: "You raving maniac!" He turned away from her; he bounded down the avenue in the direction from which they had come, and, while she watched him, strode away across the grass, toward the short cut to the station.

IV

GODFREY'S portmanteau, by the time Adela got home, had
been brought to the house, but Beatrice and Muriel, who had
been informed of this, waited for their brother in vain. Their
sister said nothing to them about having seen him, and she
accepted, after a little, with a calmness that surprised herself,
the idea that he had returned to town to denounce her. She
believed that would make no difference now—she had done
what she had done. She had somehow a faith in Mrs Churchley. If Mrs Churchley had broken off she wouldn't renew. She
was a heavy-footed person, incapable of further agility. Adela
recognised too that it might well have come over her that
there were too many children. Lastly the girl fortified herself
with the reflection, grotesque under the circumstances and
tending to prove that her sense of humor was not high, that
her father, after all, was not a man to be played with. It
seemed to her, at any rate, that if she *had* prevented his marriage
she could bear anything—bear imprisonment and bread and
water, bear lashes and torture, bear even his lifelong reproach.
What she could bear least was the wonder of the inconvenience she had inflicted on Godfrey. She had time to turn
this over, very vainly, for a succession of days—days more
numerous than she had expected, which passed without bringing her from London any summons to come up and take her
punishment. She sounded the possible, she compared the
degrees of the probable; feeling however that, as a cloistered
girl she was poorly equipped for speculation. She tried to
imagine the calamitous things young men might do, and could
only feel that such things would naturally be connected either
with money or with women. She became conscious that after
all she knew almost nothing about either subject. Meanwhile

there was no reverberation from Seymour Street—only a sultry silence.

At Overland she spent hours in her mother's garden, where she had grown up, where she considered that she was training for old age, for she meant not to depend upon whist. She loved the place as, had she been a good Catholic, she would have loved the smell of her parish church; and indeed there was in her passion for flowers something of the respect of a religion. They seemed to her the only things in the world that really respected themselves, unless one made an exception for Nutkins, who had been in command all through her mother's time, with whom she had had a real friendship, and who had been affected by their pure example. He was the person left in the world with whom, on the whole, she could talk most intimately about her mother. They never had to name her together—they only said "she;" and Nutkins freely conceded that she had taught him everything he knew. When Beatrice and Muriel said "she" they referred to Mrs Churchley. Adela had reason to believe that she should never marry, and that some day she should have about a thousand a year. This made her see in the far future a little garden of her own, under a hill, full of rare and exquisite things, where she would spend most of her old age on her knees, with an apron and stout gloves, a pair of shears and a trowel, steeped in the comfort of being thought mad.

One morning, ten days after her scene with Godfrey, upon coming back into the house shortly before lunch, she was met by Miss Flynn with the notification that a lady in the drawing-room had been waiting for her for some minutes. "A lady" suggested immediately Mrs Churchley. It came over Adela that the form in which her penalty was to descend would be a personal explanation with that misdirected woman. The lady had not given her name, and Miss Flynn had not seen Mrs Churchley; nevertheless the governess was certain that Adela's surmise was wrong.

"Is she big and dreadful?" the girl asked.

Miss Flynn, who was circumspection itself, hesitated a moment. "She's dreadful, but she's not big." She added that she was not sure she ought to let Adela go in alone; but this young lady felt throughout like a heroine, and it was not for a heroine to shrink from any encounter. Was she not, every instant, in transcendent contact with her mother? The visitor might have no connection whatever with the drama of her father's frustrated marriage; but everything, to-day, to Adela, was a part of that.

Miss Flynn's description had prepared her for a considerable shock, but she was not agitated by her first glimpse of the person who awaited her. A youngish, well-dressed woman stood there, and silence was between them while they looked at each other. Before either of them had spoken, however, Adela began to see what Miss Flynn had intended. In the light of the drawing-room window the lady was five-and-thirty years of age and had vivid yellow hair. She also had a blue cloth suit with brass buttons, a stick-up collar like a gentleman's, a necktie arranged in a sailor's knot, with a golden pin in the shape of a little lawn-tennis racket, and pearl-grey gloves with big black stitchings. Adela's second impression was that she was an actress; her third was that no such person had ever before crossed that threshold.

"I'll tell you what I've come for," said the apparition. "I've come to ask you to intercede." She was not an actress; an actress would have had a nicer voice.

"To intercede?" Adela was too bewildered to ask her to sit down.

"With your father, you know. He doesn't know, but he'll have to." Her "have" sounded like "'ave." She explained, with many more such sounds, that she was Mrs Godfrey, that they had been married seven mortal months. If Godfrey was going abroad she must go with him, and the only way she could go with him would be for his father to do something.

He was afraid of his father—that was clear; he was afraid even to tell him. What she had come down for was to see some other member of the family face to face ("fice to fice" Mrs Godfrey called it), and try if he couldn't be approached by another side. If no one else would act, then she would just have to act herself. The Colonel would have to do something —that was the only way out of it.

What really happened Adela never quite understood; what seemed to be happening was that the room went round and round. Through the blur of perception accompanying this effect the sharp stabs of her visitor's revelation came to her like the words heard by a patient "going off" under ether. She denied passionately, afterwards, even to herself, that she had done anything so abject as to faint; but there was a lapse in her consciousness in relation to Miss Flynn's intervention. This intervention had evidently been active, for when they talked the matter over, later in the day, with bated breath and infinite dissimulation for the schoolroom quarter, the governess had more information, and still stranger, to impart than to receive. She was at any rate under the impression that she had athletically contended, in the drawing-room, with the yellow hair, after removing Adela from the scene and before inducing Mrs Godfrey to withdraw. Miss Flynn had never known a more thrilling day, for all the rest of it too was pervaded with agitations and conversations, precautions and alarms. It was given out to Beatrice and Muriel that their sister had been taken suddenly ill, and the governess ministered to her in her room. Indeed Adela had never found herself less at ease; for this time she had received a blow that she couldn't return. There was nothing to do but to take it, to endure the humiliation of her wound.

At first she declined to take it; it was much easier to consider that her visitor was a monstrous masquerader. On the face of the matter, moreover, it was not fair to believe till one heard; and to hear in such a case was to hear Godfrey himself.

Whatever his sister had tried to imagine about him she had not arrived at anything so belittling as an idiotic secret marriage with a dyed and painted hag. Adela repeated this last word as if it gave her some comfort; and indeed where everything was so bad fifteen years of seniority made the case little worse. Miss Flynn was portentous, for Miss Flynn had had it out with the wretch. She had cross-questioned her and had not broken her down. This was the most important hour of Miss Flynn's life; for whereas she usually had to content herself with being humbly and gloomily in the right, she could now be magnanimously and showily so. Her only perplexity was as to what she ought to do—write to Colonel Chart or go up to town to see him. She bloomed with alternatives, never having known the like before. Toward evening Adela was obliged to recognise that Godfrey's worry, of which he had spoken to her, had appeared bad enough to consist even of a low wife, and to remember that, so far from its being inconceivable that a young man in his position should clandestinely take one, she had been present, years before, during her mother's lifetime, when Lady Molesley declared gayly, over a cup of tea, that this was precisely what she expected of her eldest son. The next morning it was the worst possibilities that seemed the clearest; the only thing left with a tatter of dusky comfort being the ambiguity of Godfrey's charge that his sister's action had "done" for him. That was a matter by itself, and she racked her brains for a connecting link between Mrs Churchley and Mrs Godfrey. At last she made up her mind that they were related by blood; very likely, though differing in fortune, they were cousins or even sisters. But even then what did her brother mean?

Arrested by the unnatural fascination of opportunity, Miss Flynn received before lunch a telegram from Colonel Chart—an order for dinner and a vehicle; he and Godfrey were to arrive at six o'clock. Adela had plenty of occupation for the interval, for she was pitying her father when she was not rejoicing that her mother had gone too soon to know. She flattered herself she discerned the providential reason of that cruelty now. She found time however still to wonder for what purpose, under the circumstances, Godfrey was to be brought down. She was not unconscious, it is true, that she had little general knowledge of what usually was done with young men in that predicament. One talked about the circumstances, but the circumstances were an abyss. She felt this still more when she found, on her father's arrival, that nothing, apparently, was to happen as she had taken for granted it would. There was a kind of inviolable hush over the whole affair, but no tragedy, no publicity, nothing ugly. The tragedy had been in town, and the faces of the two men spoke of it, in spite of themselves; so that at present there was only a family dinner, with Beatrice and Muriel and the governess, and almost a company tone, the result of the desire to avoid publicity. Adela admired her father; she knew what he was feeling, if Mrs Godfrey had been at him, and yet she saw him positively gallant. He was very gentle, he never looked at his son, and there were moments when he seemed almost sick with sadness. Godfrey was equally inscrutable and therefore wholly different from what he had been as he stood before her in the park. If he was to start on his career (with such a wife!—wouldn't she utterly blight it?) he was already professional enough to know how to wear a mask.

Before they rose from table the girl was wholly bewildered, so little could she perceive the effects of such large causes. She had nerved herself for a great ordeal, but the air was as sweet as an anodyne. It was constantly plain to her that her father was deadly sad—as pathetic as a creature jilted. He was broken, but he showed no resentment; there was a weight on his heart, but he had lightened it by dressing as immaculately as usual for dinner. She asked herself what immensity of a row there could have been in town to have left his anger so spent. He went through everything, even to sitting with his son after dinner. When they came out together he invited Beatrice and Muriel to the billiard-room; and as Miss Flynn discreetly withdrew Adela was left alone with Godfrey, who was completely changed and not in a rage any more. He was broken, too, but he was not so pathetic as his father. He was only very correct and apologetic; he said to his sister, "I'm awfully sorry *you* were annoyed; it was something I never dreamed of."

She couldn't think immediately what he meant; then she grasped the reference to the yellow hair. She was uncertain, however, what tone to take; perhaps his father had arranged with him that they were to make the best of it. But she spoke her own despair in the way she murmured: "O Godfrey, Godfrey, is it true?"

"I've been the most unutterable donkey—you can say what you like to me. You can't say anything worse than I've said to myself."

"My brother, my brother!" his words made her moan. He hushed her with a movement, and she asked, "What has father said?"

Godfrey looked over her head. "He'll give her six hundred a year."

"Ah, the angel!"

"On condition she never comes near me. She has solemnly promised; and she'll probably leave me alone, to get the money. If she doesn't—in diplomacy—I'm lost." The young man had been turning his eyes vaguely about, this way and that, to avoid meeting hers; but after another instant he gave up the effort, and she had the miserable confession of his glance. "I've been living in hell," he said.

"My brother, my brother!" she repeated.

"I'm not an idiot; yet for her I've behaved like one. Don't ask me—you mustn't know. It was all done in a day, and since then, fancy my condition—fancy my work!"

"Thank God you passed!" cried Adela.

"I would have shot myself if I hadn't. I had an awful day yesterday with father; it was late at night before it was over. I leave England next week. He brought me down here for it to look well—so that the children sha'n't know."

"He's wonderful!" she murmured.

"He's wonderful!" said Godfrey.

"Did *she* tell him?" the girl asked.

"She came straight to Seymour Street from here. She saw him alone first; then he called me in. *That* luxury lasted about an hour."

Adela said, "Poor, poor father!" to this; on which her brother remained silent. Then, after he had remarked that it had been the scene he had lived in terror of all through his cramming, and she had stammered her pity and admiration at such a mixture of anxieties and such a triumph of talent, she demanded: "Have you told him?"

"Told him what?"

"What you said you would—what *I* did."

Godfrey turned away as if at present he had very little interest in that inferior tribulation. "I was angry with you, but I cooled off. I held my tongue."

Adela clasped her hands. "You thought of mamma!"

"Oh, don't speak of mamma," said the young man tenderly.

It was indeed not a happy moment; and she murmured: "No; if you *had* thought of her"—

This made Godfrey turn back at her, with a little flare in his eyes. "Oh, *then* it didn't prevent. I thought that woman was good. I believed in her."

"Is she *very* bad?" his sister inquired.

"I shall never mention her to you again," Godfrey answered, with dignity.

"You may believe that *I* won't speak of her. So father doesn't know?" she added.

"Doesn't know what?"

"That I said that to Mrs Churchley."

"I don't think so, but you must find out for yourself."

"I shall find out," said Adela. "But what had Mrs Churchley to do with it?"

"With *my* misery? I told her. I had to tell some one."

"Why didn't you tell me?"

Godfrey hesitated. "Oh, you take things so beastly hard— you make such rows." Adela covered her face with her hands, and he went on: "What I wanted was comfort—not to be lashed up. I thought I should go mad. I wanted Mrs Churchley to break it to father, to intercede for me and help him to meet it. She was awfully kind to me; she listened and she understood; she could fancy how it had happened. Without her I shouldn't have pulled through. She liked me, you know," Godfrey dropped. "She said she would do what she could for me; she was full of sympathy and resource; I really leaned on her. But when you cut in, of course it spoiled everything. That's why I was so angry with you. She couldn't do anything then."

Adela dropped her hands, staring; she felt that she had walked in darkness. "So that he had to meet it alone?"

"*Dame!*" said Godfrey, who had got up his French tremendously.

Muriel came to the door to say papa wished the two others to join them, and the next day Godfrey returned to town. His father remained at Overland, without an intermission, the rest of the summer and the whole of the autumn, and Adela had a chance to find out, as she had said, whether he knew that she had interfered. But in spite of her chance she never found out. He knew that Mrs Churchley had thrown him over and he knew that his daughter rejoiced in it, but he appeared not to have divined the relation between the two facts. It was strange that one of the matters he was clearest about—Adela's secret triumph—should have been just the thing which, from this time on, justified less and less such a confidence. She was too sorry for him to be consistently glad. She watched his attempts to wind himself up on the subject of shorthorns and drainage, and she favoured to the utmost of her ability his intermittent disposition to make a figure in orchids. She wondered whether they mightn't have a few people at Overland; but when she mentioned the idea her father asked what in the world there would be to attract them. It was a confoundedly stupid house, he remarked, with all respect to *her* cleverness. Beatrice and Muriel were mystified; the prospect of going out immensely had faded so utterly away. They were apparently not to go out at all. Colonel Chart was aimless and bored; he paced up and down and went back to smoking, which was bad for him, and looked drearily out of windows, as if on the bare chance that something might arrive. Did he expect Mrs Churchley to arrive, to relent? It was Adela's belief that she gave no sign. But the girl thought it really remarkable of her not to have betrayed her ingenious young visitor. Adela's judgment of human nature was perhaps harsh, but she believed that many women, under the circumstances, would not have been so forbearing. This lady's conception of the point of honour presented her as rather a higher type than one might have supposed.

Adela knew her father found the burden of Godfrey's folly very heavy to bear and was incommoded at having to pay the horrible woman six hundred a year. Doubtless he was having dreadful letters from her; doubtless she threatened them all with a hideous exposure. If the matter should be bruited Godfrey's prospects would collapse on the spot. He thought Madrid very charming and curious, but Mrs Godfrey was in England, so that his father had to face the music. Adela took a dolorous comfort in thinking that her mother was out of *that*—it would have killed her; but this didn't blind her to the fact that the comfort for her father would perhaps have been greater if he had had some one to talk to about his trouble. He never dreamed of doing so to her, and she felt that she couldn't ask him. In the family life he wanted utter silence about it. Early in the winter he went abroad for ten weeks, leaving her with her sisters in the country, where it was not to be denied that at this time existence had very little savour. She half expected that her sister-in-law would descend upon her again; but the fear was not justified, and the quietude of such a personage savoured terribly of expense. There were sure to be extras. Colonel Chart went to Paris and to Monte Carlo and then to Madrid to see his boy. Adela wondered whether he would meet Mrs Churchley somewhere, since, if she had gone for a year, she would still be on the Continent. If he should meet her perhaps the affair would come on again: she caught herself musing over this. Her father brought back no news of her, and seeing him after an interval, she was struck afresh with his jilted and wasted air. She didn't like it; she resented it. A little more and she would have said that that was no way to treat such a man.

They all went up to town in March, and on one of the first days of April she saw Mrs Churchley in the park. She herself remained apparently invisible to that lady—she herself and Beatrice and Muriel, who sat with her in their mother's old bottle-green landau. Mrs Churchley, perched higher than ever, rode by without a recognition; but this didn't prevent Adela from going to her before the month was over. As on her great previous occasion she went in the morning, and she again had the good fortune to be admitted. But this time her visit was shorter, and a week after making it—the week was a desolation—she addressed to her brother at Madrid a letter which contained these words:

"I could endure it no longer—I confessed and retracted; I explained to her as well as I could the falsity of what I said to her ten months ago and the benighted purity of my motives for saying it. I besought her to regard it as unsaid, to forgive me, not to despise me too much, to take pity on poor *perfect* papa and come back to him. She was more good-natured than

you might have expected; indeed, she laughed extravagantly.
She had never believed me—it was too absurd; she had only,
at the time, disliked me. She found me utterly false (she was
very frank with me about this), and she told papa that she
thought I was horrid. She said she could never live with such
a girl, and as I would certainly never marry I must be sent
away; in short she quite loathed me. Papa defended me, he
refused to sacrifice me, and this led practically to their rupture. Papa gave her up, as it were, for me. Fancy the angel, and
fancy what I must try to be to him for the rest of his life!
Mrs Churchley can never come back—she's going to marry
Lord Dovedale."

THE CHAPERON

I

An old lady, in a high drawing-room, had had her chair moved close to the fire, where she sat knitting and warming her knees. She was dressed in deep mourning; her face had a faded nobleness, tempered, however, by the somewhat illiberal compression assumed by her lips in obedience to something that was passing in her mind. She was far from the lamp, but though her eyes were fixed upon her active needles she was not looking at them. What she really saw was quite another train of affairs. The room was spacious and dim; the thick London fog had oozed into it even through its superior defences. It was full of dusky, massive, valuable things. The old lady sat motionless save for the regularity of her clicking needles, which seemed as personal to her and as expressive as prolonged fingers. If she was thinking something out, she was thinking it thoroughly.

When she looked up, on the entrance of a girl of twenty, it might have been guessed that the appearance of this young lady was not an interruption of her meditation, but rather a contribution to it. The young lady, who was charming to behold, was also in deep mourning, which had a freshness, if mourning can be fresh, an air of having been lately put on. She went straight to the bell beside the chimney-piece and pulled it, while in her other hand she held a sealed and directed letter. Her companion glanced in silence at the letter; then she looked still harder at her work. The girl hovered near the fire-place, without speaking, and after a due, a dignified interval the butler appeared in response to the bell. The time had been sufficient to make the silence between the ladies seem long.

The younger one asked the butler to see that her letter should be posted; and after he had gone out she moved vaguely about the room, as if to give her grandmother—for such was the elder personage—a chance to begin a colloquy of which she herself preferred not to strike the first note. As equally with herself her companion was on the face of it capable of holding out, the tension, though it was already late in the evening, might have lasted long. But the old lady after a little appeared to recognise, a trifle ungraciously, the girl's superior resources.

"Have you written to your mother?"

"Yes, but only a few lines, to tell her I shall come and see her in the morning."

"Is that all you've got to say?" asked the grandmother.

"I don't quite know what you want me to say."

"I want you to say that you've made up your mind."

"Yes, I've done that, granny."

"You intend to respect your father's wishes?"

"It depends upon what you mean by respecting them. I do justice to the feelings by which they were dictated."

"What do you mean by justice?" the old lady retorted.

The girl was silent a moment; then she said: "You'll see my idea of it."

"I see it already! You'll go and live with her."

"I shall talk the situation over with her to-morrow and tell her that I think that will be best."

"Best for her, no doubt!"

"What's best for her is best for me."

"And for your brother and sister?" As the girl made no reply to this her grandmother went on: "What's best for them is that you should acknowledge some responsibility in regard to them and, considering how young they are, try and do something for them."

"They must do as I've done—they must act for themselves. They have their means now, and they're free."

"Free? They're mere children."

"Let me remind you that Eric is older than I."

"He doesn't like his mother," said the old lady, as if that were an answer.

"I never said he did. And she adores him."

"Oh, your mother's adorations!"

"Don't abuse her now," the girl rejoined, after a pause.

The old lady forbore to abuse her, but she made up for it the next moment by saying: "It will be dreadful for Edith."

"What will be dreadful?"

"Your desertion of her."

"The desertion's on her side."

"Her consideration for her father does her honour."

"Of course I'm a brute, *n'en parlons plus*," said the girl. "We must go our respective ways," she added, in a tone of extreme wisdom and philosophy.

Her grandmother straightened out her knitting and began to roll it up. "Be so good as to ring for my maid," she said, after a minute. The young lady rang, and there was another wait and another conscious hush. Before the maid came her mistress remarked: "Of course then you'll not come to *me*, you know."

"What do you mean by 'coming' to you?"

"I can't receive you on that footing."

"She'll not come *with* me, if you mean that."

"I don't mean that," said the old lady, getting up as her maid came in. This attendant took her work from her, gave her an arm and helped her out of the room, while Rose Tramore, standing before the fire and looking into it, faced the idea that her grandmother's door would now under all circumstances be closed to her. She lost no time however in brooding over this anomaly: it only added energy to her determination to act. All she could do to-night was to go to bed, for she felt utterly weary. She had been living, in imagination, in a prospective struggle, and it had left her as exhausted as a real fight. Moreover this was the culmination of a crisis, of weeks of suspense, of a long, hard strain. Her father had been laid in his grave five days before, and that morning his will had been read. In the afternoon she had got Edith off to St Leonard's with their aunt Julia, and then she had had a wretched talk with Eric. Lastly, she had made up her mind to act in opposition to the formidable will, to a clause which embodied if not exactly a provision, a recommendation singularly emphatic. She went to bed and slept the sleep of the just.

"Oh, my dear, how charming! I must take another house!" It was in these words that her mother responded to the announcement Rose had just formally made and with which she had vaguely expected to produce a certain dignity of effect. In the way of emotion there was apparently no effect at all, and the girl was wise enough to know that this was not simply on account of the general line of non-allusion taken by the extremely pretty woman before her, who looked like her elder sister. Mrs Tramore had never manifested, to her daughter, the slightest consciousness that her position was peculiar; but the recollection of something more than that fine policy was required to explain such a failure to appreciate Rose's sacrifice. It was simply a fresh reminder that she had never appreciated anything, that she was nothing but a tinted and stippled surface. Her situation was peculiar indeed. She had been the heroine of a scandal which had grown dim only because, in the eyes of the London world, it paled in the lurid light of the contemporaneous. That attention had been fixed on it for several days, fifteen years before; there had been a high relish of the vivid evidence as to his wife's misconduct with which, in the divorce-court, Charles Tramore had judged well to regale a cynical public. The case was pronounced awfully bad, and he obtained his decree. The folly of the wife had been inconceivable, in spite of other examples: she had quitted her children, she had followed the "other fellow" abroad. The other fellow hadn't married her, not having had time: he had lost his life in the Mediterranean by the capsizing of a boat, before the prohibitory term had expired.

Mrs Tramore had striven to extract from this accident something of the austerity of widowhood; but her mourning only made her deviation more public, she was a widow whose husband was awkwardly alive. She had not prowled about the Continent on the classic lines; she had come back to London to take her chance. But London would give her no chance, would have nothing to say to her; as many persons had remarked, you could never tell how London would behave. It would not receive Mrs Tramore again on any terms, and when she was spoken of, which now was not often, it was inveterately said of her that she went nowhere. Apparently she had not the qualities for which London compounds; though in the cases in which it does compound you may often wonder what these qualities are. She had not at any rate been successful: her lover was dead, her husband was liked and her children were pitied, for in payment for a topic London will parenthetically pity. It was thought interesting and magnanimous that Charles Tramore had not married again. The disadvantage to his children of the miserable story was thus left uncorrected, and this, rather oddly, was counted as *his* sacrifice. His mother, whose arrangements were elaborate, looked after them a great deal, and they enjoyed a mixture of laxity and discipline under the roof of their aunt, Miss Tramore, who was independent, having, for reasons that the two ladies had exhaustively discussed, determined to lead her own life. She had set up a home at St Leonard's, and that contracted shore had played a considerable part in the upbringing of the little Tramores. They knew about their mother, as the phrase was, but they didn't know her; which was naturally deemed more pathetic for them than for her. She had a house in Chester Square and an income and a victoria—it served all purposes, as she never went out in the evening—and flowers on her window-sills, and a remarkable appearance of youth. The

income was supposed to be in part the result of a bequest from
the man for whose sake she had committed the error of her
life, and in the appearance of youth there was a slightly impertinent implication that it was a sort of afterglow of the
same connection.

Her children, as they grew older, fortunately showed signs
of some individuality of disposition. Edith, the second girl,
clung to her aunt Julia; Eric, the son, clung frantically to
polo; while Rose, the elder daughter, appeared to cling mainly
to herself. Collectively, of course, they clung to their father,
whose attitude in the family group, however, was casual and
intermittent. He was charming and vague; he was like a clever
actor who often didn't come to rehearsal. Fortune, which but
for that one stroke had been generous to him, had provided
him with deputies and trouble-takers, as well as with whimsical opinions, and a reputation for excellent taste, and whist
at his club, and perpetual cigars on morocco sofas, and a
beautiful absence of purpose. Nature had thrown in a remarkably fine hand, which he sometimes passed over his children's
heads when they were glossy from the nursery brush. On
Rose's eighteenth birthday he said to her that she might go to
see her mother, on condition that her visits should be limited
to an hour each time and to four in the year. She was to go
alone; the other children were not included in the arrangement. This was the result of a visit that he himself had paid
his repudiated wife at her urgent request, their only encounter
during the fifteen years. The girl knew as much as this from
her aunt Julia, who was full of tell-tale secrecies. She availed
herself eagerly of the license, and in course of the period that
elapsed before her father's death she spent with Mrs Tramore
exactly eight hours by the watch. Her father, who was as inconsistent and disappointing as he was amiable, spoke to her
of her mother only once afterwards. This occasion had been
the sequel of her first visit, and he had made no use of it to ask
what she thought of the personality in Chester Square or how

she liked it. He had only said "Did she take you out?" and when Rose answered "Yes, she put me straight into a carriage and drove me up and down Bond Street," had rejoined sharply "See that that never occurs again." It never did, but once was enough, every one they knew having happened to be in Bond Street at that particular hour.

After this the periodical interview took place in private, in Mrs Tramore's beautiful little wasted drawing-room. Rose knew that, rare as these occasions were, her mother would not have kept her "all to herself" had there been anybody she could have shown her to. But in the poor lady's social void there was no one; she had after all her own correctness and she consistently preferred isolation to inferior contacts. So her daughter was subjected only to the maternal; it was not necessary to be definite in qualifying that. The girl had by this time a collection of ideas, gathered by impenetrable processes; she had tasted, in the ostracism of her ambiguous parent, of the acrid fruit of the tree of knowledge. She not only had an approximate vision of what every one had done, but she had a private judgment for each case. She had a particular vision of her father, which did not interfere with his being dear to her, but which was directly concerned in her resolution, after his death, to do the special thing he had expressed the wish she should not do. In the general estimate her grandmother and her grandmother's money had their place, and the strong probability that any enjoyment of the latter commodity would now be withheld from her. It included Edith's marked inclination to receive the law, and doubtless eventually a more substantial memento, from Miss Tramore, and opened the question whether her own course might not contribute to make her sister's appear heartless. The answer to this question however would depend on the success that might attend her own, which would very possibly be small. Eric's attitude was eminently simple; he didn't care to know people who didn't know *his* people. If his mother should ever get back into society perhaps he would take her up. Rose Tramore had decided to do what she could to bring this consummation about; and strangely enough—so mixed were her superstitions and her heresies—a large part of her motive lay in the value she attached to such a consecration.

Of her mother intrinsically she thought very little now, and if her eyes were fixed on a special achievement it was much more for the sake of that achievement and to satisfy a latent energy that was in her than because her heart was wrung by this sufferer. Her heart had not been wrung at all, though she had quite held it out for the experience. Her purpose was a pious game, but it was still essentially a game. Among the ideas I have mentioned she had her idea of triumph. She had caught the inevitable note, the pitch, on her very first visit to Chester Square. She had arrived there in intense excitement, and her excitement was left on her hands in a manner that reminded her of a difficult air she had once heard sung at the opera when no one applauded the performer. That flatness had made her sick, and so did this, in another way. A part of her agitation proceeded from the fact that her aunt Julia had told her, in the manner of a burst of confidence, something she was not to repeat, that she was in appearance the very image of the lady in Chester Square. The motive that prompted this declaration was between aunt Julia and her conscience; but it was a great emotion to the girl to find her entertainer so beautiful. She was tall and exquisitely slim; she had hair more exactly to Rose Tramore's taste than any other she had ever seen, even to every detail in the way it was dressed, and a complexion and a figure of the kind that are always spoken of as "lovely." Her eyes were irresistible, and so were her clothes, though the clothes were perhaps a little more precisely the right thing than the eyes. Her appearance was marked to her daughter's sense by the highest distinction; though it may be mentioned that this had never been the opinion of all the world. It was a revelation to Rose that she herself might look a little like that.

She knew however that aunt Julia had not seen her deposed sister-in-law for a long time, and she had a general impression that Mrs Tramore was to-day a more complete production—for instance as regarded her air of youth—than she had ever been. There was no excitement on her side—that was all her visitor's; there was no emotion—that was excluded by the plan, to say nothing of conditions more primal. Rose had from the first a glimpse of her mother's plan. It was to mention nothing and imply nothing, neither to acknowledge, to explain nor to extenuate. She would leave everything to her child; with her child she was secure. She only wanted to get back into society; she would leave even that to her child, whom she treated not as a high-strung and heroic daughter, a creature of exaltation, of devotion, but as a new, charming, clever, useful friend, a little younger than herself. Already on that first day she had talked about dressmakers. Of course, poor thing, it was to be remembered that in her circumstances there were not many things she *could* talk about. "She wants to go out again; that's the only thing in the wide world she wants," Rose had promptly, compendiously said to herself. There had been a sequel to this observation, uttered, in intense engrossment, in her own room half an hour before she had, on the important evening, made known her decision to her grandmother: "Then I'll *take* her out!"

"She'll drag you down, she'll drag you down!" Julia Tramore permitted herself to remark to her niece, the next day, in a tone of feverish prophecy.

As the girl's own theory was that all the dragging there might be would be upward, and moreover administered by herself, she could look at her aunt with a cold and inscrutable eye.

"Very well, then, I shall be out of your sight, from the pinnacle you occupy, and I sha'n't trouble you."

"Do you reproach me for my disinterested exertions, for the way I've toiled over you, the way I've lived for you?" Miss Tramore demanded.

"Don't reproach *me* for being kind to my mother and I won't reproach you for anything."

"She'll keep you out of everything—she'll make you miss everything," Miss Tramore continued.

"Then she'll make me miss a great deal that's odious," said the girl.

"You're too young for such extravagances," her aunt declared.

"And yet Edith, who is younger than I, seems to be too old for them: how do you arrange that? My mother's society will make me older," Rose replied.

"Don't speak to me of your mother; you *have* no mother."

"Then if I'm an orphan I must settle things for myself."

"Do you justify her, do you approve of her?" cried Miss Tramore, who was inferior to her niece in capacity for retort and whose limitations made the girl appear pert.

Rose looked at her a moment in silence; then she said, turning away: "I think she's charming."

"And do you propose to become charming in the same manner?"

"Her manner is perfect; it would be an excellent model. But I can't discuss my mother with you."

"You'll have to discuss her with some other people!" Miss Tramore proclaimed, going out of the room.

Rose wondered whether this were a general or a particular vaticination. There was something her aunt might have meant by it, but her aunt rarely meant the best thing she might have meant. Miss Tramore had come up from St Leonard's in response to a telegram from her own parent, for an occasion like the present brought with it, for a few hours, a certain relaxation of their dissent. "Do what you can to stop her," the old lady had said; but her daughter found that the most she could do was not much. They both had a baffled sense that Rose had thought the question out a good deal further than they; and this was particularly irritating to Mrs Tramore, as consciously the cleverer of the two. A question thought out as far as *she* could think it had always appeared to her to have performed its human uses; she had never encountered a ghost emerging from that extinction. Their great contention was that Rose would cut herself off; and certainly if she wasn't afraid of that she wasn't afraid of anything. Julia Tramore could only tell her mother how little the girl was afraid. She was already prepared to leave the house, taking with her the possessions, or her share of them, that had accumulated there during her father's illness. There had been a going and coming of her maid, a thumping about of boxes, an ordering of four-wheelers; it appeared to old Mrs Tramore that something of the objectionableness, the indecency, of her granddaughter's prospective connection had already gathered about the place. It was a violation of the decorum of bereavement which was still fresh there, and from the indignant gloom of the mistress of the house you might have inferred not so much that the daughter was about to depart as that the mother was about to arrive. There had been no conversation on the dreadful subject at luncheon; for at luncheon at Mrs Tramore's (her son never came to it) there were always, even after funerals and other miseries, stray guests of both sexes whose policy it was to be cheerful and superficial. Rose had sat down as if nothing had happened—nothing worse, that is, than her father's death; but no one had spoken of anything that any one else was thinking of.

Before she left the house a servant brought her a message from her grandmother—the old lady desired to see her in the drawing-room. She had on her bonnet, and she went down as if she were about to step into her cab. Mrs Tramore sat there with her eternal knitting, from which she forebore even to raise her eyes as, after a silence that seemed to express the fulness of her reprobation, while Rose stood motionless, she began: "I wonder if you really understand what you're doing."

"I think so. I'm not so stupid."

"I never thought you were; but I don't know what to make of you now. You're giving up everything."

The girl was tempted to inquire whether her grandmother called herself "everything"; but she checked this question, answering instead that she knew she was giving up much.

"You're taking a step of which you will feel the effect to the end of your days," Mrs Tramore went on.

"In a good conscience, I heartily hope," said Rose.

"Your father's conscience was good enough for his mother; it ought to be good enough for his daughter."

Rose sat down—she could afford to—as if she wished to be very attentive and were still accessible to argument. But this demonstration only ushered in, after a moment, the surprising words "I don't think papa had any conscience."

"What in the name of all that's unnatural do you mean?" Mrs Tramore cried, over her glasses. "The dearest and best creature that ever lived!"

"He was kind, he had charming impulses, he was delightful. But he never reflected."

Mrs Tramore stared, as if at a language she had never heard, a farrago, a *galimatias*. Her life was made up of items, but she had never had to deal, intellectually, with a fine shade. Then while her needles, which had paused an instant, began to fly again, she rejoined: "Do you know what you are, my dear? You're a dreadful little prig. Where do you pick up such talk?"

"Of course I don't mean to judge between them," Rose pursued. "I can only judge between my mother and myself. Papa couldn't judge for me." And with this she got up.

"One would think you were horrid. I never thought so before."

"Thank you for that."

"You're embarking on a struggle with society," continued Mrs Tramore, indulging in an unusual flight of oratory. "Society will put you in your place."

"Hasn't it too many other things to do?" asked the girl.

This question had an ingenuity which led her grandmother to meet it with a merely provisional and somewhat sketchy answer. "Your ignorance would be melancholy if your behaviour were not so insane."

"Oh, no; I know perfectly what she'll do!" Rose replied, almost gaily. "She'll drag me down."

"She won't even do that," the old lady declared contradictiously. "She'll keep you forever in the same dull hole."

"I shall come and see *you*, granny, when I want something more lively."

"You may come if you like, but you'll come no further than the door. If you leave this house now you don't enter it again."

Rose hesitated a moment. "Do you really mean that?"

"You may judge whether I choose such a time to joke."

"Good-bye, then," said the girl.

"Good-bye."

Rose quitted the room successfully enough; but on the other side of the door, on the landing, she sank into a chair and buried her face in her hands. She had burst into tears, and she sobbed there for a moment, trying hard to recover herself, so as to go downstairs without showing any traces of emotion, passing before the servants and again perhaps before aunt Julia. Mrs Tramore was too old to cry; she could only drop her knitting and, for a long time, sit with her head bowed and her eyes closed.

Rose had reckoned justly with her aunt Julia; there were no footmen, but this vigilant virgin was posted at the foot of the stairs. She offered no challenge however; she only said: "There's some one in the parlour who wants to see you." The girl demanded a name, but Miss Tramore only mouthed inaudibly and winked and waved. Rose instantly reflected that there was only one man in the world her aunt would look such deep things about. "Captain Jay?" her own eyes asked, while

Miss Tramore's were those of a conspirator: they were, for a moment, the only embarrassed eyes Rose had encountered that day. They contributed to make aunt Julia's further response evasive, after her niece inquired if she had communicated in advance with this visitor. Miss Tramore merely said that he had been upstairs with her mother—hadn't she mentioned it?—and had been waiting for her. She thought herself acute in not putting the question of the girl's seeing him before her as a favour to him or to herself; she presented it as a duty, and wound up with the proposition: "It's not fair to him, it's not kind, not to let him speak to you before you go."

"What does he want to say?" Rose demanded.

"Go in and find out."

She really knew, for she had found out before; but after standing uncertain an instant she went in. "The parlour" was the name that had always been borne by a spacious sitting-room downstairs, an apartment occupied by her father during his frequent phases of residence in Hill Street—episodes increasingly frequent after his house in the country had, in consequence, as Rose perfectly knew, of his spending too much money, been disposed of at a sacrifice which he always characterised as horrid. He had been left with the place in Hertfordshire and his mother with the London house, on the general understanding that they would change about; but during the last years the community had grown more rigid, mainly at his mother's expense. The parlour was full of his memory and his habits and his things—his books and pictures and *bibelots*, objects that belonged now to Eric. Rose had sat in it for hours since his death; it was the place in which she could still be nearest to him. But she felt far from him as Captain Jay rose erect on her opening the door. This was a very different presence. He had not liked Captain Jay. She herself had, but not enough to make a great complication of her father's coldness. This afternoon however she foresaw complications. At the very outset for instance she was not pleased with his having arranged such a surprise for her with her grandmother and her aunt. It was probably aunt Julia who had sent for him; her grandmother wouldn't have done it. It placed him immediately on their side, and Rose was almost as disappointed at this as if she had not known it was quite where he would naturally be. He had never paid her a special visit, but if that was what he wished to do why shouldn't he have waited till she should be under her mother's roof? She knew the reason, but she had an angry prospect of enjoyment in making him express it. She liked him enough, after all, if it were measured by the idea of what she could make him do.

In Bertram Jay the elements were surprisingly mingled; you would have gone astray, in reading him, if you had counted on finding the complements of some of his qualities. He would not however have struck you in the least as incomplete, for in every case in which you didn't find the complement you would have found the contradiction. He was in the Royal Engineers, and was tall, lean and high-shouldered. He looked every inch a soldier, yet there were people who considered that he had missed his vocation in not becoming a parson. He took a public interest in the spiritual life of the army. Other persons still, on closer observation, would have felt that his most appropriate field was neither the army nor the church, but simply the world—the social, successful, worldly world. If he had a sword in one hand and a Bible in the other he had a Court Guide concealed somewhere about his person. His profile was hard and handsome, his eyes were both cold and kind, his dark straight hair was imperturbably smooth and prematurely streaked with grey. There was nothing in exis-tence that he didn't take seriously. He had a first-rate power of work and an ambition as minutely organised as a German plan of invasion. His only real recreation was to go to church, but he went to parties when he had time. If he was in love with Rose Tramore this was distracting to him only in the same sense as his religion, and it was included in that department of his extremely sub-divided life. His religion indeed was of an encroaching, annexing sort. Seen from in front he looked diffident and blank, but he was capable of exposing himself in a way (to speak only of the paths of peace) wholly inconsistent with shyness. He had a passion for instance for open-air speaking, but was not thought on the whole to excel in it unless he could help himself out with a hymn. In conversation he kept his eyes on you with a kind of colourless candour, as if he had not understood what you were saying and, in a fashion that made many people turn red, waited before answering. This was only because he was considering their remarks in more relations than they had intended. He had in his face no expression whatever save the one just mentioned, and was, in his profession, already very distinguished.

He had seen Rose Tramore for the first time on a Sunday of the previous March, at a house in the country at which she was staying with her father, and five weeks later he had made her, by letter, an offer of marriage. She showed her father the letter of course, and he told her that it would give him great pleasure that she should send Captain Jay about his business. "My dear child," he said, "we must really have some one who will be better fun than that." Rose had declined the honour, very considerately and kindly, but not simply because her father wished it. She didn't herself wish to detach this flower from the stem, though when the young man wrote again, to express the hope that he *might* hope—so long was he willing to wait—and ask if he might not still sometimes see her, she answered even more indulgently than at first. She had shown her father her former letter, but she didn't show him this one; she only told him what it contained, submitting to him also that of her correspondent. Captain Jay moreover wrote to Mr Tramore, who replied sociably, but so vaguely that he almost neglected the subject under discussion—a communication that made poor Bertram ponder long. He could never get to the bottom of the superficial, and all the proprieties and conventions of life were profound to him. Fortunately for him old Mrs Tramore liked him, he was satisfactory to her longsightedness; so that a relation was established under cover of which he still occasionally presented himself in Hill Street—presented himself nominally to the mistress of the house. He had had scruples about the veracity of his visits, but he had disposed of them; he had scruples about so many things that he had had to invent a general way, to dig a central drain. Julia Tramore happened to meet him when she came up to town, and she took a view of him more benevolent than her usual estimate of people encouraged by her mother. The fear of agreeing with that lady was a motive, but there was a stronger one, in this particular case, in the fear of agreeing with her niece, who had rejected him. His situation might be held to have improved when Mr Tramore was taken so gravely ill that with regard to his recovery those about him left their eyes to speak for their lips; and in the light of the poor gentleman's recent death it was doubtless better than it had ever been.

He was only a quarter of an hour with the girl, but this gave him time to take the measure of it. After he had spoken to her about her bereavement, very much as an especially mild missionary might have spoken to a beautiful Polynesian, he let her know that he had learned from her companions the very strong step she was about to take. This led to their spending together ten minutes which, to her mind, threw more light on his character than anything that had ever passed between them. She had always felt with him as if she were standing on an edge, looking down into something decidedly deep. Today the impression of the perpendicular shaft was there, but it was rather an abyss of confusion and disorder than the large bright space in which she had figured everything as ranged and pigeon-holed, presenting the appearance of the labelled shelves and drawers at a chemist's. He discussed without an invitation to discuss, he appealed without a right to appeal. He was nothing but a suitor tolerated after dismissal, but he took strangely for granted a participation in her affairs. He assumed all sorts of things that made her draw back. He implied that there was everything now to assist them in arriving at an agreement, since she had never informed him that he was positively objectionable; but that this symmetry would be spoiled if she should not be willing to take a little longer to think of certain consequences. She was greatly disconcerted when she saw what consequences he meant and at his reminding her of them. What on earth was the use of a lover if he was to speak only like one's grandmother and one's aunt? He struck her as much in love with her and as particularly careful at the same time as to what he might say. He never mentioned her mother; he only alluded, indirectly but earnestly, to the "step." He disapproved of it altogether, took an unexpectedly prudent, politic view of it. He evidently also believed that she would be dragged down; in other words that she would not be asked out. It was his idea that her mother would contaminate her, so that he should find himself interested in a young person discredited and virtually unmarriageable. All this was more obvious to him than the consideration that a daughter should be merciful. Where was his religion if he understood mercy so little, and where were his talent and his courage if he were so miserably afraid of trumpery social penalties? Rose's heart sank when she reflected that a man supposed to be first-rate hadn't guessed that rather than not do what she could for her mother she would give up all the Engineers in the world. She became aware that she probably would have been moved to place her hand in his on the spot if he had come to her saying "Your idea is the right one; put it through at every cost." She couldn't discuss this with him, though he impressed her as having too much at stake for her to treat him with mere disdain. She sickened at the revelation that a gentleman could see so much in mere vulgarities of opinion, and though she uttered as few words as possible, conversing only in sad smiles and headshakes and in intercepted movements toward the door, she happened, in some unguarded lapse from her reticence, to use the expression that she was disappointed in him. He caught at it and, seeming to drop his field-glass, pressed upon her with nearer, tenderer eyes.

"Can I be so happy as to believe, then, that you had thought of me with some confidence, with some faith?"

"If you didn't suppose so, what is the sense of this visit?" Rose asked.

"One can be faithful without reciprocity," said the young man. "I regard you in a light which makes me want to protect you even if I have nothing to gain by it."

"Yet you speak as if you thought you might keep me for yourself."

"For *yourself.* I don't want you to suffer."

"Nor to suffer yourself by my doing so," said Rose, looking down.

"Ah, if you would only marry me next month!" he broke out inconsequently.

"And give up going to mamma?" Rose waited to see if he would say "What need that matter? Can't your mother come to us?" But he said nothing of the sort; he only answered—

"She surely would be sorry to interfere with the exercise of any other affection which I might have the bliss of believing that you are now free, in however small a degree, to entertain."

Rose knew that her mother wouldn't be sorry at all; but she contented herself with rejoining, her hand on the door: "Good-bye. I sha'n't suffer. I'm not afraid."

"You don't know how terrible, how cruel, the world can be."

"Yes, I do know. I know everything!"

The declaration sprang from her lips in a tone which made

him look at her as he had never looked before, as if he saw
something new in her face, as if he had never yet known her.
He hadn't displeased her so much but that she would like to
give him that impression, and since she felt that she was doing
so she lingered an instant for the purpose. It enabled her to see,
further, that he turned red; then to become aware that a carriage had stopped at the door. Captain Jay's eyes, from where he
stood, fell upon this arrival, and the nature of their glance made
Rose step forward to look. Her mother sat there, brilliant, conspicuous, in the eternal victoria, and the footman was already
sounding the knocker. It had been no part of the arrangement
that she should come to fetch her; it had been out of the question—a stroke in such bad taste as would have put Rose in
the wrong. The girl had never dreamed of it, but somehow,
suddenly, perversely, she was glad of it now; she even hoped
that her grandmother and her aunt were looking out upstairs.

"My mother has come for me. Good-bye," she repeated;
but this time her visitor had got between her and the door.

"Listen to me before you go. I will give you a life's devotion," the young man pleaded. He really barred the way.

She wondered whether her grandmother had told him that
if her flight were not prevented she would forfeit money.
Then, vividly, it came over her that this would be what he
was occupied with. "I shall never think of you—let me go!"
she cried, with passion.

Captain Jay opened the door, but Rose didn't see his face,
and in a moment she was out of the house. Aunt Julia, who
was sure to have been hovering, had taken flight before the
profanity of the knock.

"Heavens, dear, where did you get your mourning?" the
lady in the victoria asked of her daughter as they drove away.

II

LADY MARESFIELD had given her boy a push in his plump back and had said to him, "Go and speak to her now; it's your chance." She had for a long time wanted this scion to make himself audible to Rose Tramore, but the opportunity was not easy to come by. The case was complicated. Lady Maresfield had four daughters, of whom only one was married. It so happened moreover that this one, Mrs Vaughan-Vesey, the only person in the world her mother was afraid of, was the most to be reckoned with. The Honourable Guy was in appearance all his mother's child, though he was really a simpler soul. He was large and pink; large, that is, as to everything but the eyes, which were diminishing points, and pink as to everything but the hair, which was comparable, faintly, to the hue of the richer rose. He had also, it must be conceded, very small neat teeth, which made his smile look like a young lady's. He had no wish to resemble any such person, but he was perpetually smiling, and he smiled more than ever as he approached Rose Tramore, who, looking altogether, to his mind, as a pretty girl should, and wearing a soft white opera-cloak over a softer black dress, leaned alone against the wall of the vestibule at Covent Garden while, a few paces off, an old gentleman engaged her mother in conversation. Madame Patti had been singing, and they were all waiting for their carriages. To their ears at present came a vociferation of names and a rattle of wheels. The air, through banging doors, entered in damp, warm gusts, heavy with the stale, slightly sweet taste of the London season when the London season is overripe and spoiling.

Guy Mangler had only three minutes to reëstablish an interrupted acquaintance with our young lady. He reminded her that he had danced with her the year before, and he mentioned that he knew her brother. His mother had lately been to see old Mrs Tramore, but this he did not mention, not being aware of it. That visit had produced, on Lady Maresfield's part, a private crisis, engendered ideas. One of them was that the grandmother in Hill Street had really forgiven the wilful girl much more than she admitted. Another was that there would still be some money for Rose when the others should come into theirs. Still another was that the others would come into theirs at no distant date; the old lady was so visibly going to pieces. There were several more besides, as for instance that Rose had already fifteen hundred a year from her father. The figure had been betrayed in Hill Street; it was part of the proof of Mrs Tramore's decrepitude. Then there was an equal amount that her mother had to dispose of and on which the girl could absolutely count, though of course it might involve much waiting, as the mother, a person of gross insensibility, evidently wouldn't die of cold-shouldering. Equally definite, to do it justice, was the conception that Rose was in truth remarkably good looking, and that what she had undertaken to do showed, and would show even should it fail, cleverness of the right sort. Cleverness of the right sort was exactly the quality that Lady Maresfield prefigured as indispensable in a young lady to whom she should marry her second son, over whose own deficiencies she flung the veil of a maternal theory that *his* cleverness was of a sort that was wrong. Those who knew him less well were content to wish that he might not conceal it for such a scruple. This enumeration of his mother's views does not exhaust the list, and it was in obedience to one too profound to be uttered even by the historian that, after a very brief delay, she decided to move across the crowded lobby. Her daughter Bessie was the only one with her; Maggie was dining with the Vaughan-Veseys, and Fanny was not of an age. Mrs Tramore the younger showed only an admirable back—her face was to her old gentleman—and Bessie had drifted to some other people; so that it was comparatively easy for Lady Maresfield to say to Rose, in a moment: "My dear child, are you never coming to see us?"

"We shall be delighted to come if you'll ask us," Rose smiled.

Lady Maresfield had been prepared for the plural number, and she was a woman whom it took many plurals to disconcert. "I'm sure Guy is longing for another dance with you," she rejoined, with the most unblinking irrelevance.

"I'm afraid we're not dancing again quite yet," said Rose, glancing at her mother's exposed shoulders, but speaking as if they were muffled in crape.

Lady Maresfield leaned her head on one side and seemed almost wistful. "Not even at my sister's ball? She's to have something next week. She'll write to you."

Rose Tramore, on the spot, looking bright but vague, turned three or four things over in her mind. She remembered that the sister of her interlocutress was the proverbially rich Mrs Bray, a bankeress or a breweress or a builderess, who had so big a house that she couldn't fill it unless she opened her doors, or her mouth, very wide. Rose had learnt more about London society during these lonely months with her mother than she had ever picked up in Hill Street. The younger Mrs Tramore was a mine of *commérages*, and she had no need to go out to bring home the latest intelligence. At any rate Mrs Bray might serve as the end of a wedge. "Oh, I dare say we might think of that," Rose said. "It would be very kind of your sister."

"Guy'll think of it, won't you, Guy?" asked Lady Maresfield.

"Rather!" Guy responded, with an intonation as fine as if he had learnt it at a music hall; while at the same moment the name of his mother's carriage was bawled through the place. Mrs Tramore had parted with her old gentleman; she turned again to her daughter. Nothing occurred but what always occurred, which was exactly this absence of everything—a universal lapse. She didn't exist, even for a second, to any recognising eye. The people who looked at her—of course there were plenty of those—were only the people who didn't exist for hers. Lady Maresfield surged away on her son's arm.

It was this noble matron herself who wrote, the next day, inclosing a card of invitation from Mrs Bray and expressing the hope that Rose would come and dine and let her ladyship take her. She should have only one of her own girls; Gwendolen Vesey was to take the other. Rose handed both the note and the card in silence to her mother; the latter exhibited only the name of Miss Tramore. "You had much better go, dear," her mother said; in answer to which Miss Tramore slowly tore up the documents, looking with clear, meditative eyes out of the window. Her mother always said "You had better go"— there had been other incidents—and Rose had never even once taken account of the observation. She would make no first advances, only plenty of second ones, and, condoning no discrimination, would treat no omission as venial. She would keep all concessions till afterwards; then she would make them one by one. Fighting society was quite as hard as her grandmother had said it would be; but there was a tension in it which made the dreariness vibrate—the dreariness of such a winter as she had just passed. Her companion had cried at the end of it, and she had cried all through; only her tears had been private, while her mother's had fallen once for all, at luncheon on the bleak Easter Monday—produced by the way a silent survey of the deadly square brought home to her that every creature but themselves was out of town and having tremendous fun. Rose felt that it was useless to attempt to explain simply by her mourning this severity of solitude; for if people didn't go to parties (at least a few didn't) for six months after their father died, this was the very time other people took for coming to see them. It was not too much to say that during this first winter of Rose's period with her mother she had no communication whatever with the world. It had the effect of making her take to reading the new American books: she wanted to see how girls got on by themselves. She had never read so much before, and there was a legitimate indifference in it when topics failed with her mother. They often failed after the first days, and then, while she bent over instructive volumes, this lady, dressed as if for an impending function, sat on the sofa and watched her. Rose was not embarrassed by such an appearance, for she could reflect that, a little before, her companion had not even a girl who had taken refuge in queer researches to look at. She was moreover used to her mother's attitude by this time. She had her own description of it: it was the attitude of waiting for the carriage. If they didn't go out it was not that Mrs Tramore was not ready in time, and Rose had even an alarmed prevision of their some day always arriving first. Mrs Tramore's conversation at such moments was abrupt, inconsequent and personal. She sat on the edge of sofas and chairs and glanced occasionally at the fit of her gloves (she was perpetually gloved, and the fit was a thing it was melancholy to see wasted), as people do who are expecting guests to dinner. Rose used almost to fancy herself at times a perfunctory husband on the other side of the fire.

What she was not yet used to—there was still a charm in it—was her mother's extraordinary tact. During the years they lived together they never had a discussion; a circumstance all the more remarkable since if the girl had a reason for sparing her companion (that of being sorry for her) Mrs Tramore had none for sparing her child. She only showed in doing so a happy instinct—the happiest thing about her. She took in perfection a course which represented everything and covered everything; she utterly abjured all authority. She testified to her abjuration in hourly ingenious, touching ways. In this manner nothing had to be talked over, which was a mercy all round. The tears on Easter Monday were merely a nervous gust, to help show she was not a Christmas doll from the Burlington Arcade; and there was no lifting up of the repentant Magdalen, no uttered remorse for the former abandonment of children. Of the way she could treat her children her demeanour to this one was an example; it was an uninterrupted appeal to her eldest daughter for direction. She took the law from Rose in every circumstance, and if you had noticed these ladies without knowing their history you would have wondered what tie was fine enough to make maturity so respectful to youth. No mother was ever so filial as Mrs Tramore, and there had never been such a difference of position between sisters. Not that the elder one fawned, which would have been fearful; she only renounced—whatever she had to renounce. If the amount was not much she at any rate made no scene over it. Her hand was so light that Rose said of her secretly, in vague glances at the past, "No wonder people liked her!" She never characterised the old element of interference with her mother's respectability more definitely than as "people." They were people, it was true, for whom gentleness must have been everything and who didn't demand a variety of interests. The desire to "go out" was the one passion that even a closer acquaintance with her parent revealed to Rose Tramore. She marvelled at its strength, in the light of the poor lady's history: there was comedy enough in this unquenchable flame on the part of a woman who had known such misery. She had drunk deep of every dishonour, but the bitter cup had left her with a taste for lighted candles, for squeezing up staircases and hooking herself to the human elbow. Rose had a vision of the future years in which this taste would grow with restored exercise—of her mother, in a long-tailed dress, jogging on and on and on, jogging further and further from her sins, through a century of the "Morning Post" and down the fashionable avenue of time. She herself would then be very old—she herself would be dead. Mrs Tramore would cover a span of life for which such an allowance of sin was small. The girl could laugh indeed now at that theory of her being dragged down. If one thing were more present to her than another it was the very desolation of their propriety. As she glanced at her companion, it sometimes seemed to her that if she had been a bad woman she would have been worse than that. There were compensations for being "cut" which Mrs Tramore too much neglected.

The lonely old lady in Hill Street—Rose thought of her that way now—was the one person to whom she was ready to say that she would come to her on any terms. She wrote this to her three times over, and she knocked still oftener at her door. But the old lady answered no letters; if Rose had remained in Hill Street it would have been her own function to answer them; and at the door, the butler, whom the girl had known for ten years, considered her, when he told her his mistress was not at home, quite as he might have considered a young person who had come about a place and of whose eligibility he took a negative view. That was Rose's one pang, that she probably appeared rather heartless. Her aunt Julia had gone to Florence with Edith for the winter, on purpose to make her appear more so; for Miss Tramore was still the person most scandalised by her secession. Edith and she, doubtless, often talked over in Florence the destitution of the aged victim in Hill Street. Eric never came to see his sister, because, being full both of family and of personal feeling, he thought she really ought to have stayed with his grandmother. If she had had such an appurtenance all to herself she might have done what she liked with it; but he couldn't forgive such a want of consideration for anything of his. There were moments when Rose would have been ready to take her hand from the plough and insist upon reintegration, if only the fierce voice of the old house had allowed people to look her up. But she read, ever so clearly, that her grandmother had made this a question of loyalty to seventy years of virtue. Mrs Tramore's forlornness didn't prevent her

drawing-room from being a very public place, in which Rose
could hear certain words reverberate: "Leave her alone; it's
the only way to see how long she'll hold out." The old
woman's visitors were people who didn't wish to quarrel, and
the girl was conscious that if they had not let her alone—that is
if they had come to her from her grandmother—she might
perhaps not have held out. She had no friends quite of her
own; she had not been brought up to have them, and it would
not have been easy in a house which two such persons as her
father and his mother divided between them. Her father disapproved of crude intimacies, and all the intimacies of youth
were crude. He had married at five-and-twenty and could
testify to such a truth. Rose felt that she shared even Captain
Jay with her grandmother; she had seen what *he* was worth.
Moreover, she had spoken to him at that last moment in Hill
Street in a way which, taken with her former refusal, made it
impossible that he should come near her again. She hoped he
went to see his protectress: he could be a kind of substitute
and administer comfort.

It so happened, however, that the day after she threw Lady
Maresfield's invitation into the waste-paper basket she received a visit from a certain Mrs Donovan, whom she had
occasionally seen in Hill Street. She vaguely knew this lady
for a busybody, but she was in a situation which even busy-
bodies might alleviate. Mrs Donovan was poor, but honest—
so scrupulously honest that she was perpetually returning
visits she had never received. She was always clad in weather-
beaten sealskin, and had an odd air of being prepared for the
worst, which was borne out by her denying that she was
Irish. She was of the English Donovans.

"Dear child, won't you go out with me?" she asked.

Rose looked at her a moment and then rang the bell. She
spoke of something else, without answering the question, and
when the servant came she said: "Please tell Mrs Tramore that
Mrs Donovan has come to see her."

"Oh, that'll be delightful; only you mustn't tell your grandmother!" the visitor exclaimed.

"Tell her what?"

"That I come to see your mamma."

"You don't," said Rose.

"Sure I hoped you'd introduce me!" cried Mrs Donovan, compromising herself in her embarrassment.

"It's not necessary; you knew her once."

"Indeed and I've known every one once," the visitor confessed.

Mrs Tramore, when she came in, was charming and exactly right; she greeted Mrs Donovan as if she had met her the week before last, giving her daughter such a new illustration of her tact that Rose again had the idea that it was no wonder "people" had liked her. The girl grudged Mrs Donovan so fresh a morsel as a description of her mother at home, rejoicing that she would be inconvenienced by having to keep the story out of Hill Street. Her mother went away before Mrs Donovan departed, and Rose was touched by guessing her reason—the thought that since even this circuitous personage had been moved to come, the two might, if left together, invent some remedy. Rose waited to see what Mrs Donovan had in fact invented.

"You won't come out with me then?"

"Come out with you?"

"My daughters are married. You know I'm a lone woman. It would be an immense pleasure to me to have so charming a creature as yourself to present to the world."

"I go out with my mother," said Rose, after a moment.

"Yes, but sometimes when she's not inclined?"

"She goes everywhere she wants to go," Rose continued, uttering the biggest fib of her life and only regretting it should be wasted on Mrs Donovan.

"Ah, but do you go everywhere *you* want?" the lady asked sociably.

"One goes even to places one hates. Every one does that."

"Oh, what *I* go through!" this social martyr cried. Then she laid a persuasive hand on the girl's arm. "Let me show you at a few places first, and then we'll see. I'll bring them all here."

"I don't think I understand you," replied Rose, though in Mrs Donovan's words she perfectly saw her own theory of the case reflected. For a quarter of a minute she asked herself whether she might not, after all, do so much evil that good might come. Mrs Donovan would take her out the next day, and be thankful enough to annex such an attraction as a pretty girl. Various consequences would ensue and the long delay would be shortened; her mother's drawing-room would resound with the clatter of teacups.

"Mrs Bray's having some big thing next week; come with me there and I'll show you what I mane," Mrs Donovan pleaded.

"I see what you mane," Rose answered, brushing away her temptation and getting up. "I'm much obliged to you."

"You know you're wrong, my dear," said her interlocutress, with angry little eyes.

"I'm not going to Mrs Bray's."

"I'll get you a kyard; it'll only cost me a penny stamp."

"I've got one," said the girl, smiling.

"Do you mean a penny stamp?" Mrs Donovan, especially at departure, always observed all the forms of amity. "You can't do it alone, my darling," she declared.

"Shall they call you a cab?" Rose asked.

"I'll pick one up. I choose my horse. You know you require your start," her visitor went on.

"Excuse my mother," was Rose's only reply.

"Don't mention it. Come to me when you need me. You'll find me in the Red Book."

"It's awfully kind of you."

Mrs Donovan lingered a moment on the threshold. "Who will you *have* now, my child?" she appealed.

"I won't have any one!" Rose turned away, blushing for

her. "She came on speculation," she said afterwards to Mrs Tramore.

Her mother looked at her a moment in silence. "You can do it if you like, you know."

Rose made no direct answer to this observation; she remarked instead: "See what our quiet life allows us to escape."

"We don't escape it. She has been here an hour."

"Once in twenty years! We might meet her three times a day."

"Oh, I'd take her with the rest!" sighed Mrs Tramore; while her daughter recognised that what her companion wanted to do was just what Mrs Donovan was doing. Mrs Donovan's life was her ideal.

On a Sunday, ten days later, Rose went to see one of her old governesses, of whom she had lost sight for some time and who had written to her that she was in London, unoccupied and ill. This was just the sort of relation into which she could throw herself now with inordinate zeal; the idea of it, however, not preventing a foretaste of the queer expression in the excellent lady's face when she should mention with whom she was living. While she smiled at this picture she threw in another joke, asking herself if Miss Hack could be held in any degree to constitute the nucleus of a circle. She would come to see her, in any event—come the more the further she was dragged down. Sunday was always a difficult day with the two ladies—the afternoons made it so apparent that they were not frequented. Her mother, it is true, was comprised in the habits of two or three old gentlemen—she had for a long time avoided male friends of less than seventy —who disliked each other enough to make the room, when they were there at once, crack with pressure. Rose sat for a long time with Miss Hack, doing conscientious justice to the conception that there could be troubles in the world worse than her own; and when she came back her mother was alone, but with a story to tell of a long visit from Mr Guy

Mangler, who had waited and waited for her return. "He's in love with you; he's coming again on Tuesday," Mrs Tramore announced.

"Did he say so?"

"That he's coming back on Tuesday?"

"No, that he's in love with me."

"He didn't need, when he stayed two hours."

"With you? It's you he's in love with, mamma!"

"That will do as well," laughed Mrs Tramore. "For all the use we shall make of him!" she added in a moment.

"We shall make great use of him. His mother sent him."

"Oh, she'll never come!"

"Then *he* sha'n't," said Rose. Yet he was admitted on the Tuesday, and after she had given him his tea Mrs Tramore left the young people alone. Rose wished she hadn't—she herself had another view. At any rate she disliked her mother's view, which she had easily guessed. Mr Mangler did nothing but say how charming he thought his hostess of the Sunday, and what a tremendously jolly visit he had had. He didn't remark in so many words "I had no idea your mother was such a good sort"; but this was the spirit of his simple discourse. Rose liked it at first—a little of it gratified her; then she thought there was too much of it for good taste. She had to reflect that one does what one can and that Mr Mangler probably thought he was delicate. He wished to convey that he desired to make up to her for the injustice of society. Why shouldn't her mother receive gracefully, she asked (not audibly) and who had ever said she didn't? Mr Mangler had a great deal to say about the disappointment of his own parent over Miss Tramore's not having come to dine with them the night of his aunt's ball.

"Lady Maresfield knows why I didn't come," Rose answered at last.

"Ah, now, but *I* don't, you know; can't you tell *me?*" asked the young man.

"It doesn't matter, if your mother's clear about it."

"Oh, but why make such an awful mystery of it, when I'm dying to know?"

He talked about this, he chaffed her about it for the rest of his visit: he had at last found a topic after his own heart. If her mother considered that he might be the emblem of their redemption he was an engine of the most primitive construction. He stayed and stayed; he struck Rose as on the point of bringing out something for which he had not quite, as he would have said, the cheek. Sometimes she thought he was going to begin: "By the way, my mother told me to propose to you." At other moments he seemed charged with the admission: "I say, of course I really know what you're trying to do for her," nodding at the door: "therefore hadn't we better speak of it frankly, so that I can help you with my mother, and more particularly with my sister Gwendolen, who's the difficult one? The fact is, you see, they won't do anything for nothing. If you'll accept me they'll call, but they won't call without something 'down.'" Mr Mangler departed without their speaking frankly, and Rose Tramore had a hot hour during which she almost entertained, vindictively, the project of "accepting" the limpid youth until after she should have got her mother into circulation. The cream of the vision was that she might break with him later. She could read that this was what her mother would have liked, but the next time he came the door was closed to him, and the next and the next.

In August there was nothing to do but to go abroad, with the sense on Rose's part that the battle was still all to fight; for a round of country visits was not in prospect, and English watering-places constituted one of the few subjects on which the girl had heard her mother express herself with disgust. Continental autumns had been indeed for years, one of the various forms of Mrs Tramore's atonement, but Rose could only infer that such fruit as they had borne was bitter. The stony stare of Belgravia could be practised at Homburg; and somehow it was inveterately only gentlemen who sat next to her at the *table d'hôte* at Cadenabbia. Gentlemen had never been of any use to Mrs Tramore for getting back into society; they had only helped her effectually to get out of it. She once dropped, to her daughter, in a moralising mood, the remark that it was astonishing how many of them one could know without its doing one any good. Fifty of them—even very clever ones—represented a value inferior to that of one stupid woman. Rose wondered at the offhand way in which her mother could talk of fifty clever men; it seemed to her that the whole world couldn't contain such a number. She had a sombre sense that mankind must be dull and mean. These cogitations took place in a cold hotel, in an eternal Swiss rain, and they had a flat echo in the transalpine valleys, as the lonely ladies went vaguely down to the Italian lakes and cities. Rose guided their course, at moments, with a kind of aimless ferocity; she moved abruptly, feeling vulgar and hating their life, though destitute of any definite vision of another life that would have been open to her. She had set herself a task and she clung to it; but she appeared to herself despicably idle. She had succeeded in not going to Homburg waters, where London was trying to wash away some of its stains; that would be too staring an advertisement of their situation. The main difference in situations to her now was the difference of being more or less pitied, at the best an intolerable danger; so that the places she preferred were the unsuspicious ones. She wanted to triumph with contempt, not with submission.

One morning in September, coming with her mother out of the marble church at Milan, she perceived that a gentleman who had just passed her on his way into the cathedral and whose face she had not noticed, had quickly raised his hat, with a suppressed ejaculation. She involuntarily glanced back; the gentleman had paused, again uncovering, and Captain Jay stood saluting her in the Italian sunshine. "Oh, good-morning!" she said, and walked on, pursuing her course; her mother was a little in front. She overtook her in a moment, with an unreasonable sense, like a gust of cold air, that men were worse than ever, for Captain Jay had apparently moved into the church. Her mother turned as they met, and suddenly, as she looked back, an expression of peculiar sweetness came into this lady's eyes. It made Rose's take the same direction and rest a second time on Captain Jay, who was planted just where he had stood a minute before. He immediately came forward, asking Rose with great gravity if he might speak to her a moment, while Mrs Tramore went her way again. He had the expression of a man who wished to say something very important; yet his next words were simple enough and consisted of the remark that he had not seen her for a year.

"Is it really so much as that?" asked Rose.

"Very nearly. I would have looked you up, but in the first place I have been very little in London, and in the second I believed it wouldn't have done any good."

"You should have put that first," said the girl. "It wouldn't have done any good."

He was silent over this a moment, in his customary deciphering way; but the view he took of it did not prevent him from inquiring, as she slowly followed her mother, if he mightn't walk with her now. She answered with a laugh that it wouldn't do any good but that he might do as he liked. He replied without the slightest manifestation of levity that it would do more good than if he didn't, and they strolled together, with Mrs Tramore well before them, across the big, amusing piazza, where the front of the cathedral makes a sort of builded light. He asked a question or two and he explained his own presence: having a month's holiday, the first clear time for several years, he had just popped over the Alps. He inquired if Rose had recent news of the old lady in Hill Street, and it was the only tortuous thing she had ever heard him say.

"I have had no communication of any kind from her since

I parted with you under her roof. Hasn't she mentioned that?" said Rose.

"I haven't seen her."

"I thought you were such great friends."

Bertram Jay hesitated a moment. "Well, not so much now."

"What has she done to you?" Rose demanded.

He fidgeted a little, as if he were thinking of something that made him unconscious of her question; then, with mild violence, he brought out the inquiry: "Miss Tramore, are you happy?"

She was startled by the words, for she on her side had been reflecting—reflecting that he had broken with her grandmother and that this pointed to a reason. It suggested at least that he wouldn't now be so much like a mouthpiece for that cold ancestral tone. She turned off his question—said it never was a fair one, as you gave yourself away however you answered it. When he repeated "You give yourself away?" as if he didn't understand, she remembered that he had not read the funny American books. This brought them to a silence, for she had enlightened him only by another laugh, and he was evidently preparing another question, which he wished carefully to disconnect from the former. Presently, just as they were coming near Mrs Tramore, it arrived in the words "Is this lady your mother?" On Rose's assenting, with the addition that she was travelling with her, he said: "Will you be so kind as to introduce me to her?" They were so close to Mrs Tramore that she probably heard, but she floated away with a single stroke of her paddle and an inattentive poise of her head. It was a striking exhibition of the famous tact, for Rose delayed to answer, which was exactly what might have made her mother wish to turn; and indeed when at last the girl spoke she only said to her companion:

"Why do you ask me that?"

"Because I desire the pleasure of making her acquaintance."

Rose had stopped, and in the middle of the square they stood looking at each other. "Do you remember what you said to me the last time I saw you?"

"Oh, don't speak of that!"

"It's better to speak of it now than to speak of it later."

Bertram Jay looked round him, as if to see whether any one would hear; but the bright foreignness gave him a sense of safety, and he unexpectedly exclaimed:

"Miss Tramore, I love you more than ever!"

"Then you ought to have come to see us," declared the girl, quickly walking on.

"You treated me the last time as if I were positively offensive to you."

"So I did, but you know my reason."

"Because I protested against the course you were taking? I did, I did!" the young man rang out, as if he still, a little, stuck to that.

His tone made Rose say gaily: "Perhaps you do so yet?"

"I can't tell till I've seen more of your circumstances," he replied with eminent honesty.

The girl stared; her light laugh filled the air. "And it's in order to see more of them and judge that you wish to make my mother's acquaintance?"

He coloured at this and he evaded; then he broke out with a confused "Miss Tramore, let me stay with you a little!" which made her stop again.

"Your company will do us great honour, but there must be a rigid condition attached to our acceptance of it."

"Kindly mention it," said Captain Jay, staring at the façade of the cathedral.

"You don't take us on trial."

"On trial?"

"You don't make an observation to me—not a single one, ever, ever!—on the matter that, in Hill Street, we had our last words about."

Captain Jay appeared to be counting the thousand pin-
nacles of the church. "I think you really must be right," he
remarked at last.

"There you are!" cried Rose Tramore, and walked
rapidly away.

He caught up with her, he laid his hand upon her arm to
stay her. "If you're going to Venice, let me go to Venice
with you!"

"You don't even understand my condition."

"I'm sure you're right, then: you must be right about
everything."

"That's not in the least true, and I don't care a fig whether
you're sure or not. Please let me go."

He had barred her way, he kept her longer. "I'll go and
speak to your mother myself!"

Even in the midst of another emotion she was amused at
the air of audacity accompanying this declaration. Poor Captain Jay might have been on the point of marching up to a
battery. She looked at him a moment; then she said: "You'll
be disappointed!"

"Disappointed?"

"She's much more proper than grandmamma, because she's
much more amiable!"

"Dear Miss Tramore—dear Miss Tramore!" the young
man murmured helplessly.

"You'll see for yourself. Only there's another condition,"
Rose went on.

"Another?" he cried, with discouragement and alarm.

"You must understand thoroughly, before you throw in
your lot with us even for a few days, what our position
really is."

"Is it very bad?" asked Bertram Jay artlessly.

"No one has anything to do with us, no one speaks to us,
no one looks at us."

"Really?" stared the young man.

"We've no social existence, we're utterly despised."

"Oh, Miss Tramore!" Captain Jay interposed. He added quickly, vaguely, and with a want of presence of mind of which he as quickly felt ashamed: "Do none of your family—?" The question collapsed; the brilliant girl was looking at him.

"We're extraordinarily happy," she threw out.

"Now that's all I wanted to know!" he exclaimed, with a kind of exaggerated cheery reproach, walking on with her briskly to overtake her mother.

He was not dining at their inn, but he insisted on coming that evening to their *table d'hôte*. He sat next Mrs Tramore, and in the evening he accompanied them gallantly to the opera, at a third-rate theatre where they were almost the only ladies in the boxes. The next day they went together by rail to the Charterhouse of Pavia, and while he strolled with the girl, as they waited for the homeward train, he said to her candidly: "Your mother's remarkably pretty." She remembered the words and the feeling they gave her: they were the first note of a new era. The feeling was somewhat that of an anxious, gratified matron who has "presented" her child and is thinking of the matrimonial market. Men might be of no use, as Mrs Tramore said, yet it was from this moment Rose dated the rosy dawn of her confidence that her *protégée* would go off; and when later, in crowded assemblies, the phrase, or something like it behind a hat or a fan, fell repeatedly on her anxious ear, "Your mother *is* in beauty!" or "I've never seen her look better!" she had a faint vision of the yellow sunshine and the afternoon shadows on the dusty Italian platform.

Mrs Tramore's behaviour at this period was a revelation of her native understanding of delicate situations. She needed no account of this one from her daughter—it was one of the things for which she had a scent; and there was a kind of loyalty to the rules of a game in the silent sweetness with which she smoothed the path of Bertram Jay. It was clear that she was in her element in fostering the exercise of the affections, and if she ever spoke without thinking twice it is probable that she would have exclaimed, with some gaiety, "Oh, I know all about *love!*" Rose could see that she thought their companion would be a help, in spite of his being no dispenser of patronage. The key to the gates of fashion had not been placed in his hand, and no one had ever heard of the ladies of his family, who lived in some vague hollow of the Yorkshire moors; but none the less he might administer a muscular push. Yes indeed, men in general were broken reeds, but Captain Jay was peculiarly representative. Respectability was the woman's maximum, as honour was the man's, but this distinguished young soldier inspired more than one kind of confidence. Rose had a great deal of attention for the use to which his respectability was put; and there mingled with this attention some amusement and much compassion. She saw that after a couple of days he decidedly liked her mother, and that he was yet not in the least aware of it. He took for granted that he believed in her but little; notwithstanding which he would have trusted her with anything except Rose herself. His trusting her with Rose would come very soon. He never spoke to her daughter about her qualities of character, but two or three of them (and indeed these were all the poor lady had, and they made the best show) were what he had in mind in praising her appearance. When he remarked: "What attention Mrs Tramore seems to attract everywhere!" he meant: "What a beautifully simple nature it is!" and when he said: "There's something extraordinarily harmonious in the colours she wears," it signified: "Upon my word, I never saw such a sweet temper in my life!" She lost one of her boxes at Verona, and made the prettiest joke of it to Captain Jay. When Rose saw this she said to herself, "Next season we shall have only to choose." Rose knew what was in the box.

By the time they reached Venice (they had stopped at half a dozen little old romantic cities in the most frolicsome æsthetic way) she liked their companion better than she had

ever liked him before. She did him the justice to recognise that
if he was not quite honest with himself he was at least wholly
honest with *her*. She reckoned up everything he had been
since he joined them, and put upon it all an interpretation so
favourable to his devotion that, catching herself in the act of
glossing over one or two episodes that had not struck her at
the time as disinterested she exclaimed, beneath her breath,
"Look out—you're falling in love!" But if he liked correctness wasn't he quite right? Could any one possibly like it more
than *she* did? And if he had protested against her throwing in
her lot with her mother, this was not because of the benefit
conferred but because of the injury received. He exaggerated
that injury, but this was the privilege of a lover perfectly
willing to be selfish on behalf of his mistress. He might have
wanted her grandmother's money for her, but if he had given
her up on first discovering that she was throwing away her
chance of it (oh, this was *her* doing too!) he had given up her
grandmother as much: not keeping well with the old woman,
as some men would have done; not waiting to see how the
perverse experiment would turn out and appeasing her, if it
should promise tolerably, with a view to future operations.
He had had a simple-minded, evangelical, lurid view of what
the girl he loved would find herself in for. She could see this
now—she could see it from his present bewilderment and
mystification, and she liked him and pitied him, with the
kindest smile, for the original *naïveté* as well as for the actual
meekness. No wonder he hadn't known what she was in for,
since he now didn't even know what he was in for himself.
Were there not moments when he thought his companions
almost unnaturally good, almost suspiciously safe? He had
lost all power to verify that sketch of their isolation and
déclassement to which she had treated him on the great square
at Milan. The last thing he noticed was that they were
neglected, and he had never, for himself, had such an impression of society.

It could scarcely be enhanced even by the apparition of a large, fair, hot, red-haired young man, carrying a lady's fan in his hand, who suddenly stood before their little party as, on the third evening after their arrival in Venice, it partook of ices at one of the tables before the celebrated Café Florian. The lamplit Venetian dusk appeared to have revealed them to this gentleman as he sat with other friends at a neighbouring table, and he had sprung up, with unsophisticated glee, to shake hands with Mrs Tramore and her daughter. Rose recalled him to her mother, who looked at first as though she didn't remember him but presently bestowed a sufficiently gracious smile on Mr Guy Mangler. He gave with youthful candour the history of his movements and indicated the whereabouts of his family: he was with his mother and sisters; they had met the Bob Veseys, who had taken Lord Whiteroy's yacht and were going to Constantinople. His mother and the girls, poor things, were at the Grand Hotel, but he was on the yacht with the Veseys, where they had Lord Whiteroy's cook. Wasn't the food in Venice filthy, and wouldn't they come and look at the yacht? She wasn't very fast, but she was awfully jolly. His mother might have come if she would, but she wouldn't at first, and now, when she wanted to, there were other people, who naturally wouldn't turn out for her. Mr Mangler sat down; he alluded with artless resentment to the way, in July, the door of his friends had been closed to him. He was going to Constantinople, but he didn't care—if *they* were going anywhere; meanwhile his mother hoped awfully they would look her up.

Lady Maresfield, if she had given her son any such message, which Rose disbelieved, entertained her hope in a manner compatible with her sitting for half an hour, surrounded by her little retinue, without glancing in the direction of Mrs Tramore. The girl, however, was aware that this was not a good enough instance of their humiliation; inasmuch as it was rather she who, on the occasion of their last contact, had held

off from Lady Maresfield. She was a little ashamed now of not
having answered the note in which this affable personage
ignored her mother. She couldn't help perceiving indeed a
dim movement on the part of some of the other members of
the group; she made out an attitude of observation in the
high-plumed head of Mrs Vaughan-Vesey. Mrs Vesey, perhaps, might have been looking at Captain Jay, for as this
gentleman walked back to the hotel with our young lady
(they were at the "Britannia," and young Mangler, who clung
to them, went in front with Mrs Tramore) he revealed to Rose
that he had some acquaintance with Lady Maresfield's eldest
daughter, though he didn't know and didn't particularly want
to know, her ladyship. He expressed himself with more
acerbity than she had ever heard him use (Christian charity
so generally governed his speech) about the young donkey
who had been prattling to them. They separated at the door
of the hotel. Mrs Tramore had got rid of Mr Mangler, and
Bertram Jay was in other quarters.

"If you know Mrs Vesey, why didn't you go and speak to
her? I'm sure she saw you," Rose said.

Captain Jay replied even more circumspectly than usual.
"Because I didn't want to leave you."

"Well, you can go now; you're free," Rose rejoined.

"Thank you. I shall never go again."

"That won't be civil," said Rose.

"I don't care to be civil. I don't like her."

"Why don't you like her?"

"You ask too many questions."

"I know I do," the girl acknowledged.

Captain Jay had already shaken hands with her, but at this
he put out his hand again. "She's too worldly," he murmured, while he held Rose Tramore's a moment.

"Ah, you dear!" Rose exclaimed almost audibly as, with
her mother, she turned away.

The next morning, upon the Grand Canal, the gondola of

our three friends encountered a stately barge which, though it contained several persons, seemed pervaded mainly by one majestic presence. During the instant the gondolas were passing each other it was impossible either for Rose Tramore or for her companions not to become conscious that this distinguished identity had markedly inclined itself—a circumstance commemorated the next moment, almost within earshot of the other boat, by the most spontaneous cry that had issued for many a day from the lips of Mrs Tramore. "Fancy, my dear, Lady Maresfield has bowed to us!"

"We ought to have returned it," Rose answered; but she looked at Bertram Jay, who was opposite to her. He blushed, and she blushed, and during this moment was born a deeper understanding than had yet existed between these associated spirits. It had something to do with their going together that afternoon, without her mother, to look at certain out-of-the-way pictures as to which Ruskin had inspired her with a desire to see sincerely. Mrs Tramore expressed the wish to stay at home, and the motive of this wish—a finer shade than any that even Ruskin had ever found a phrase for—was not translated into misrepresenting words by either the mother or the daughter. At San Giovanni in Bragora the girl and her companion came upon Mrs Vaughan-Vesey, who, with one of her sisters, was also endeavouring to do the earnest thing. She did it to Rose, she did it to Captain Jay, as well as to Gianbellini; she was a handsome, long-necked, aquiline person, of a different type from the rest of her family, and she did it remarkably well. She secured our friends—it was her own expression—for luncheon, on the morrow, on the yacht, and she made it public to Rose that she would come that afternoon to invite her mother. When the girl returned to the hotel, Mrs Tramore mentioned, before Captain Jay, who had come up to their sitting-room, that Lady Maresfield had called. "She stayed a long time—at least it seemed long!" laughed Mrs Tramore.

The poor lady could laugh freely now; yet there was some grimness in a colloquy that she had with her daughter after Bertram Jay had departed. Before this happened Mrs Vesey's card, scrawled over in pencil and referring to the morrow's luncheon, was brought up to Mrs Tramore.

"They mean it all as a bribe," said the principal recipient of these civilities.

"As a bribe?" Rose repeated.

"She wants to marry you to that boy; they've seen Captain Jay and they're frightened."

"Well, dear mamma, I can't take Mr Mangler for a husband."

"Of course not. But oughtn't we to go to the luncheon?"

"Certainly we'll go to the luncheon," Rose said; and when the affair took place, on the morrow, she could feel for the first time that she was taking her mother out. This appearance was somehow brought home to every one else, and it was really the agent of her success. For it is of the essence of this simple history that, in the first place, her success dated from Mrs Vesey's Venetian *déjeuner*, and in the second reposed, by a subtle social logic, on the very anomaly that had made it dubious. There is always a chance in things, and Rose Tramore's chance was in the fact that Gwendolen Vesey was, as some one had said, awfully modern, an immense improvement on the exploded science of her mother, and capable of seeing what a "draw" there would be in the comedy, if properly brought out, of the reversed positions of Mrs Tramore and Mrs Tramore's diplomatic daughter. With a first-rate managerial eye she perceived that people would flock into any room—and all the more into one of hers—to see Rose bring in her dreadful mother. She treated the cream of English society to this thrilling spectacle later in the autumn, when she once more "secured" both the performers for a week at Brimble. It made a hit on the spot, the very first evening—the girl was felt to play her part so well. The rumour of the

performance spread; every one wanted to see it. It was an entertainment of which, that winter in the country, and the next
season in town, persons of taste desired to give their friends
the freshness. The thing was to make the Tramores come
late, after every one had arrived. They were engaged for a
fixed hour, like the American imitator and the Patagonian
contralto. Mrs Vesey had been the first to say the girl was
awfully original, but that became the general view.

Gwendolen Vesey had with her mother one of the few
quarrels in which Lady Maresfield had really stood up to such
an antagonist (the elder woman had to recognise in general
in whose veins it was that the blood of the Manglers flowed)
on account of this very circumstance of her attaching more
importance to Miss Tramore's originality ("Her originality
be hanged!" her ladyship had gone so far as unintelligently
to exclaim) than to the prospects of the unfortunate Guy.
Mrs Vesey actually lost sight of these pressing problems in
her admiration of the way the mother and the daughter, or
rather the daughter and the mother (it was slightly confus-
ing) "drew." It was Lady Maresfield's version of the case that
the brazen girl (she was shockingly coarse) had treated poor
Guy abominably. At any rate it was made known, just after
Easter, that Miss Tramore was to be married to Captain Jay.
The marriage was not to take place till the summer; but Rose
felt that before this the field would practically be won. There
had been some bad moments, there had been several warm
corners and a certain number of cold shoulders and closed
doors and stony stares; but the breach was effectually made—
the rest was only a question of time. Mrs Tramore could be
trusted to keep what she had gained, and it was the dowagers,
the old dragons with prominent fangs and glittering scales,
whom the trick had already mainly caught. By this time there
were several houses into which the liberated lady had crept
alone. Her daughter had been expected with her, but they
couldn't turn her out because the girl had stayed behind, and

she was fast acquiring a new identity, that of a parental connection with the heroine of such a romantic story. She was at
least the next best thing to her daughter, and Rose foresaw
the day when she would be valued principally as a memento
of one of the prettiest episodes in the annals of London. At
a big official party, in June, Rose had the joy of introducing
Eric to his mother. She was a little sorry it was an official
party—there were some other such queer people there; but
Eric called, observing the shade, the next day but one.

No observer, probably, would have been acute enough to
fix exactly the moment at which the girl ceased to take out her
mother and began to be taken out by her. A later phase was
more distinguishable—that at which Rose forbore to inflict
on her companion a duality that might become oppressive.
She began to economise her force, she went only when the
particular effect was required. Her marriage was delayed by
the period of mourning consequent upon the death of her
grandmother, who, the younger Mrs Tramore averred, was
killed by the rumour of her own new birth. She was the only
one of the dragons who had not been tamed. Julia Tramore
knew the truth about this—she was determined such things
should not kill *her*. She would live to do something—she
hardly knew what. The provisions of her mother's will were
published in the "Illustrated News"; from which it appeared
that everything that was not to go to Eric and to Julia was to
go to the fortunate Edith. Miss Tramore makes no secret of
her own intentions as regards this favourite. Edith is not
pretty, but Lady Maresfield is waiting for her; she is determined Gwendolen Vesey shall not get hold of her. Mrs Vesey
however takes no interest in her at all. She is whimsical, as
befits a woman of her fashion; but there are two persons she
is still very fond of, the delightful Bertram Jays. The fondness
of this pair, it must be added, is not wholly expended in
return. They are extremely united, but their life is more
domestic than might have been expected from the preliminary

signs. It owes a portion of its concentration to the fact that Mrs Tramore has now so many places to go to that she has almost no time to come to her daughter's. She is, under her son-in-law's roof, a brilliant but a rare apparition, and the other day he remarked upon the circumstance to his wife.

"If it hadn't been for you," she replied, smiling, "she might have had her regular place at our fireside."

"Good heavens, how did I prevent it?" cried Captain Jay, with all the consciousness of virtue.

"You ordered it otherwise, you goose!" And she says, in the same spirit, whenever her husband commends her (which he does, sometimes, extravagantly) for the way she launched her mother: "Nonsense, my dear—practically it was *you!*"

SIR EDMUND ORME

THE statement appears to have been written, though the frag-
ment is undated, long after the death of his wife, whom I
take to have been one of the persons referred to. There is,
however, nothing in the strange story to establish this point,
which is, perhaps, not of importance. When I took possession
of his effects I found these pages, in a locked drawer, among
papers relating to the unfortunate lady's too brief career (she
died in childbirth a year after her marriage), letters, memoranda, accounts, faded photographs, cards of invitation. That
is the only connection I can point to, and you may easily and
will probably say that the tale is too extravagant to have had
a demonstrable origin. I cannot, I admit, vouch for his having
intended it as a report of real occurrence—I can only vouch
for his general veracity. In any case it was written for himself, not for others. I offer it to others—having full option—
precisely because it is so singular. Let them, in respect to the
form of the thing, bear in mind that it was written quite for
himself. I have altered nothing but the names.

IF there's a story in the matter I recognise the exact moment
at which it began. This was on a soft, still Sunday noon in
November, just after church, on the sunny Parade. Brighton
was full of people; it was the height of the season, and the day
was even more respectable than lovely—which helped to
account for the multitude of walkers. The blue sea itself was
decorous; it seemed to doze, with a gentle snore (if that *be*
decorum), as if nature were preaching a sermon. After writing
letters all the morning I had come out to take a look at it

before luncheon. I was leaning over the rail which separates the King's Road from the beach, and I think I was smoking a cigarette, when I became conscious of an intended joke in the shape of a light walking-stick laid across my shoulders. The idea, I found, had been thrown off by Teddy Bostwick, of the Rifles, and was intended as a contribution to talk. Our talk came off as we strolled together—he always took your arm to show you he forgave your obtuseness about his humour— and looked at the people, and bowed to some of them, and wondered who others were, and differed in opinion as to the prettiness of the girls. About Charlotte Marden we agreed, however, as we saw her coming toward us with her mother; and there surely could have been no one who wouldn't have agreed with us. The Brighton air, of old, used to make plain girls pretty and pretty girls prettier still—I don't know whether it works the spell now. The place, at any rate, was rare for complexions, and Miss Marden's was one that made people turn round. It made *us* stop, heaven knows—at least, it was one of the things, for we already knew the ladies.

We turned with them, we joined them, we went where they were going. They were only going to the end and back— they had just come out of church. It was another manifestation of Teddy's humour that he got immediate possession of Charlotte, leaving me to walk with her mother. However, I was not unhappy; the girl was before me and I had her to talk about. We prolonged our walk, Mrs Marden kept me, and presently she said she was tired and must sit down. We found a place on a sheltered bench—we gossiped as the people passed. It had already struck me, in this pair, that the resemblance between the mother and the daughter was wonderful even among such resemblances—the more so that it took so little account of a difference of nature. One often hears mature mothers spoken of as warnings—signposts, more or less discouraging, of the way daughters may go. But there was nothing deterrent in the idea that Charlotte, at fifty-five, should be as beautiful, even though it were conditioned on her being as pale and preoccupied, as Mrs Marden. At twenty-two she had a kind of rosy blankness and she was admirably handsome. Her head had the charming shape of her mother's, and her features the same fine order. Then there were looks and movements and tones (moments when you could scarcely say whether it were aspect or sound), which, between the two personalities, were a reflection, a recall.

These ladies had a small fortune and a cheerful little house at Brighton, full of portraits and tokens and trophies (stuffed animals on the top of bookcases, and sallow, varnished fish under glass), to which Mrs Marden professed herself attached by pious memories. Her husband had been "ordered" there in ill-health, to spend the last years of his life, and she had already mentioned to me that it was a place in which she felt herself still under the protection of his goodness. His goodness appeared to have been great, and she sometimes had the air of defending it against mysterious imputations. Some sense of protection, of an influence invoked and cherished, was evidently necessary to her; she had a dim wistfulness, a longing for security. She wanted friends and she had a good many. She was kind to me on our first meeting, and I never suspected her of the vulgar purpose of "making up" to me—a suspicion, of course, unduly frequent in conceited young men. It never struck me that she wanted me for her daughter, nor yet, like some unnatural mammas, for herself. It was as if they had had a common deep, shy need and had been ready to say: "Oh, be friendly to us and be trustful! Don't be afraid, you won't be expected to marry us." "Of course there's something about mamma; that's really what makes her such a dear!" Charlotte said to me, confidentially, at an early stage of our acquaintance. She worshipped her mother's appearance. It was the only thing she was vain of; she accepted the raised eyebrows as a charming ultimate fact. "She looks as if she were waiting for the doctor, dear mamma," she said on another occasion. "Perhaps *you're* the doctor; do you think you are?" It appeared in the event that I had some healing power. At any rate when I learned, for she once dropped the remark, that Mrs Marden also thought there was something "awfully strange" about Charlotte, the relation between the two ladies became extremely interesting. It was happy enough, at bottom; each had the other so much on her mind.

On the Parade the stream of strollers held its course, and Charlotte presently went by with Teddy Bostwick. She smiled and nodded and continued, but when she came back she stopped and spoke to us. Captain Bostwick positively declined to go in, he said the occasion was too jolly: might they therefore take another turn? Her mother dropped a "Do as you like," and the girl gave me an impertinent smile over her shoulder as they quitted us. Teddy looked at me with his glass in one eye; but I didn't mind that; it was only of Miss Marden I was thinking as I observed to my companion, laughing:

"She's a bit of a coquette, you know."

"Don't say that—don't say that!" Mrs Marden murmured.

"The nicest girls always are—just a little," I was magnanimous enough to plead.

"Then why are they always punished?"

The intensity of the question startled me—it had come out in such a vivid flash. Therefore I had to think a moment before I inquired: "What do you know about it?"

"I was a bad girl myself."

"And were you punished?"

"I carry it through life," said Mrs Marden, looking away from me. "Ah!" she suddenly panted, in the next breath, rising to her feet and staring at her daughter, who had reappeared again with Captain Bostwick. She stood a few seconds, with the queerest expression in her face; then she sank upon the seat again and I saw that she had blushed crimson. Charlotte, who had observed her movement, came straight up to her and, taking her hand with quick tenderness, seated herself on the other side of her. The girl had turned pale—she gave her mother a fixed, frightened look. Mrs Marden, who had had some shock which escaped our detection, recovered herself; that is she sat quiet and inexpressive, gazing at the indifferent crowd, the sunny air, the slumbering sea. My eye happened to fall, however, on the interlocked hands of the two ladies, and I quickly guessed that the grasp of the elder one was violent. Bostwick stood before them, wondering what was the matter and asking me from his little vacant disk if *I* knew; which led Charlotte to say to him after a moment, with a certain irritation:

"Don't stand there that way, Captain Bostwick; go away —*please* go away."

I got up at this, hoping that Mrs Marden wasn't ill; but she immediately begged that we would *not* go away, that we would particularly stay and that we would presently come home to lunch. She drew me down beside her and for a moment I felt her hand pressing my arm in a way that might have been an involuntary betrayal of distress and might have been a private signal. What she might have wished to point out to me I couldn't divine: perhaps she had seen somebody or something abnormal in the crowd. She explained to us in a few minutes that she was all right; that she was only liable to palpitations—they came as quickly as they went. It was time to move, and we moved. The incident was felt to be closed. Bostwick and I lunched with our sociable friends, and when I walked away with him he declared that he had never seen such dear kind creatures.

Mrs Marden had made us promise to come back the next day to tea, and had exhorted us in general to come as often as we could. Yet the next day, when at five o'clock I knocked at the door of the pretty house, it was to learn that the ladies had gone up to town. They had left a message for us with the butler: he was to say that they had suddenly been called—

were very sorry. They would be absent a few days. This was all I could extract from the dumb domestic. I went again three days later, but they were still away; and it was not till the end of a week that I got a note from Mrs Marden, saying "We are back; do come and forgive us." It was on this occasion, I remember (the occasion of my going just after getting the note), that she told me she had intuitions. I don't know how many people there were in England at that time in that predicament, but there were very few who would have mentioned it; so that the announcement struck me as original, especially as her point was that some of these uncanny promptings were connected with me. There were other people present—idle Brighton folk, old women with frightened eyes and irrelevant interjections—and I had but a few minutes' talk with Charlotte; but the day after this I met them both at dinner and had the satisfaction of sitting next to Miss Marden. I recall that hour as the hour on which it first completely came over me that she was a beautiful, liberal creature. I had seen her personality in patches and gleams, like a song sung in snatches, but now it was before me in a large rosy glow, as if it had been a full volume of sound—I heard the whole of the air. It was sweet, fresh music—I was often to hum it over.

After dinner I had a few words with Mrs Marden; it was at the moment, late in the evening, when tea was handed about. A servant passed near us with a tray, I asked her if she would have a cup, and, on her assenting, took one and handed it to her. She put out her hand for it and I gave it to her, safely as I supposed; but as she was in the act of receiving it she started and faltered, so that the cup and saucer dropped with a crash of porcelain and without, on the part of my interlocutress, the usual woman's movement to save her dress. I stooped to pick up the fragments and when I raised myself Mrs Marden was looking across the room at her daughter, who looked back at her smiling, but with an anxious light in her eyes. "Dear mamma, what on earth *is* the matter with you?" the silent question seemed to say. Mrs Marden coloured, just as she had done after her strange movement on the Parade the other week, and I was therefore surprised when she said to me with unexpected assurance: "You should really have a steadier hand!" I had begun to stammer a defence of my hand when I became aware that she had fixed her eyes upon me with an intense appeal. It was ambiguous at first and only added to my confusion; then suddenly I understood, as plainly as if she had murmured "Make believe it was you—make believe it was you." The servant came back to take the morsels of the cup and wipe up the spilt tea, and while I was in the midst of making believe Mrs Marden abruptly brushed away from me and from her daughter's attention and went into another room. I noticed that she gave no heed to the state of her dress.

I saw nothing more of either of them that evening, but the next morning, in the King's Road, I met Miss Marden with a roll of music in her muff. She told me she had been a little way alone, to practice duets with a friend, and I asked her if she would go a little way further in company. She gave me leave to attend her to her door, and as we stood before it I inquired if I might go in. "No, not to-day—I don't want you," she said, candidly, though not roughly; while the words caused me to direct a wistful, disconcerted gaze at one of the windows of the house. It fell upon the white face of Mrs Marden, who was looking out at us from the drawing-room. She stood there long enough for me to see that it *was* she and not an apparition, as I had thought for a second, and then she vanished before her daughter had observed her. The girl, during our walk, had said nothing about her. As I had been told they didn't want me I left them alone a little, after which circumstances supervened that kept us still longer apart. I finally went up to London, and while there I received a pressing invitation to come immediately down to Tranton, a pretty old place in Sussex belonging to a couple whose acquaintance I had lately made.

I went to Tranton from town, and on arriving found the Mardens, with a dozen other people, in the house. The first thing Mrs Marden said was: "Will you forgive me?" and when I asked what I had to forgive she answered: "My throwing my tea over you." I replied that it had gone over herself; whereupon she said: "At any rate I was very rude; but some day I think you'll understand, and then you'll make allowances for me." The first day I was there she dropped two or three of these references (she had already indulged in more than one), to the mystic initiation that was in store for me; so that I began, as the phrase is, to chaff her about it, to say I would rather it were less wonderful and take it out at once. She answered that when it should come to me I would have to take it out—there would be little enough option. That it *would* come was privately clear to her, a deep presentiment, which was the only reason she had ever mentioned the matter. Didn't I remember she had told me she had intuitions? From the first time of her seeing me she had been sure there were things I should not escape knowing. Meanwhile there was nothing to do but wait and keep cool, not to be precipitate. She particularly wished not to be any more nervous than she was. And I was above all not to be nervous myself—one got used to everything. I declared that though I couldn't make out what she was talking about I was terribly frightened; the absence of a clue gave such a range to one's imagination. I exaggerated on purpose; for if Mrs Marden was mystifying I can scarcely say she was alarming. I couldn't imagine what she meant, but I wondered more than I shuddered. I might have said to myself that she was a little wrong in the upper story; but that never occurred to me. She struck me as hopelessly right.

There were other girls in the house, but Charlotte Marden was the most charming; which was so generally felt to be the case that she really interfered with the slaughter of ground game. There were two or three men, and I was of the number, who actually preferred her to the society of the beaters. In short she was recognised as a form of sport superior and exquisite. She was kind to all of us—she made us go out late and come in early. I don't know whether she flirted, but several other members of the party thought *they* did. Indeed, as regards himself, Teddy Bostwick, who had come over from Brighton, was visibly sure.

The third day I was at Tranton was a Sunday, and there was a very pretty walk to morning service over the fields. It was grey, windless weather, and the bell of the little old church that nestled in the hollow of the Sussex down sounded near and domestic. We were a straggling procession, in the mild damp air (which, as always at that season, gave one the feeling that after the trees were bare there was more of it—a larger sky), and I managed to fall a good way behind with Miss Marden. I remember entertaining, as we moved together over the turf, a strong impulse to say something intensely personal, something violent and important—important for *me*, such as that I had never seen her so lovely, or that that particular moment was the sweetest of my life. But always, in youth, such words have been on the lips many times before they are spoken; and I had the sense, not that I didn't know her well enough (I cared little for that), but that she didn't know *me* well enough. In the church, where there were old Tranton tombs and brasses, the big Tranton pew was full. Several of us were scattered, and I found a seat for Miss Marden, and another for myself beside it, at a distance from her mother and from most of our friends. There were two or three decent rustics on the bench, who moved in further to make room for us, and I took my place first, to cut off my companion from our neighbours. After she was seated there was still a space left, which remained empty till service was about half over.

This at least was the moment at which I became aware that another person had entered and had taken the seat. When I noticed him he had apparently been for some minutes in the pew, for he had settled himself and put down his hat beside him, and, with his hands crossed on the nob of his cane, was gazing before him at the altar. He was a pale young man in black, with the air of a gentleman. I was slightly startled on perceiving him, for Miss Marden had not attracted my attention to his entrance by moving to make room for him. After a few minutes, observing that he had no prayer-book, I reached across my neighbour and placed mine before him, on the ledge of the pew; a manœuvre the motive of which was not unconnected with the possibility that, in my own destitution, Miss Marden would give me one side of *her* velvet volume to hold. The pretext, however, was destined to fail, for at the moment I offered him the book the intruder—whose intrusion I had so condoned—rose from his place without thanking me, stepped noiselessly out of the pew (it had no door), and, so discreetly as to attract no attention, passed down the centre of the church. A few minutes had sufficed for his devotions. His behaviour was unbecoming, his early departure even more than his late arrival; but he managed so quietly that we were not incommoded, and I perceived, on turning a little to glance after him, that nobody was disturbed by his withdrawal. I only noticed, and with surprise, that Mrs Marden had been so affected by it as to rise, involuntarily, an instant, in her place. She stared at him as he passed, but he passed very quickly, and she as quickly dropped down again, though not too soon to catch my eye across the church. Five minutes later I asked Miss Marden, in a low voice, if she would kindly pass me back my prayer-book—I had waited to see if she would spontaneously perform the act. She restored this aid to devotion, but had been so far from troubling herself about it that she could say to me as she did so: "Why on earth did you put it there?" I was on the point of answering her when she dropped on her knees, and I held my tongue. I had only been going to say: "To be decently civil."

After the benediction, as we were leaving our places, I was slightly surprised, again, to see that Mrs Marden, instead of going out with her companions, had come up the aisle to join us, having apparently something to say to her daughter. She said it, but in an instant I observed that it was only a pretext—her real business was with me. She pushed Charlotte forward and suddenly murmured to me: "Did you see him?"

"The gentleman who sat down here? How could I help seeing him?"

"Hush!" she said, with the intensest excitement; "don't *speak* to her—don't tell her!" She slipped her hand into my arm, to keep me near her, to keep me, it seemed, away from her daughter. The precaution was unnecessary, for Teddy Bostwick had already taken possession of Miss Marden, and as they passed out of church in front of me I saw one of the other men close up on her other hand. It appeared to be considered that I had had my turn. Mrs Marden withdrew her hand from my arm as soon as we got out, but not before I felt that she had really needed the support. "Don't speak to any one—don't tell any one!" she went on.

"I don't understand. Tell them what?"

"Why, that you saw him."

"Surely they saw him for themselves."

"Not one of them, not one of them." She spoke in a tone of such passionate decision that I glanced at her—she was staring straight before her. But she felt the challenge of my eyes and she stopped short, in the old brown timber porch of the church, with the others well in advance of us, and said, looking at me now and in a quite extraordinary manner: "You're the only person, the only person in the world."

"But *you*, dear madam?"

"Oh me—of course. That's my curse!" And with this she moved rapidly away from me to join the body of the party. I hovered on its outskirts on the way home, for I had food for

rumination. Whom had I seen and why was the apparition—
it rose before my mind's eye very vividly again—invisible to
the others? If an exception had been made for Mrs Marden,
why did it constitute a curse, and why was I to share so questionable an advantage? This inquiry, carried on in my own
locked breast, kept me doubtless silent enough during luncheon. After luncheon I went out on the old terrace to smoke
a cigarette, but I had only taken a couple of turns when I
perceived Mrs Marden's moulded mask at the window of one
of the rooms which opened on the crooked flags. It reminded
me of the same flitting presence at the window at Brighton the
day I met Charlotte and walked home with her. But this time
my ambiguous friend didn't vanish; she tapped on the pane
and motioned me to come in. She was in a queer little apartment, one of the many reception-rooms of which the ground-
floor at Tranton consisted; it was known as the Indian room
and had a decoration vaguely Oriental—bamboo lounges,
lacquered screens, lanterns with long fringes and strange idols
in cabinets, objects not held to conduce to sociability. The
place was little used, and when I went round to her we had
it to ourselves. As soon as I entered she said to me: "Please
tell me this; are you in love with my daughter?"

I hesitated a moment. "Before I answer your question will
you kindly tell me what gives you the idea? I don't consider
that I have been very forward."

Mrs Marden, contradicting me with her beautiful anxious
eyes, gave me no satisfaction on the point I mentioned; she
only went on strenuously:

"Did you say nothing to her on the way to church?"

"What makes you think I said anything?"

"The fact that you saw him."

"Saw whom, dear Mrs Marden?"

"Oh, you know," she answered, gravely, even a little
reproachfully, as if I were trying to humiliate her by making
her phrase the unphraseable.

"Do you mean the gentleman who formed the subject of your strange statement in church—the one who came into the pew?"

"You saw him, you saw him!" Mrs Marden panted, with a strange mixture of dismay and relief.

"Of course I saw him; and so did you."

"It didn't follow. Did you feel it to be inevitable?"

I was puzzled again. "Inevitable?"

"That you *should* see him?"

"Certainly, since I'm not blind."

"You might have been; every one else is." I was wonderfully at sea, and I frankly confessed it to my interlocutress; but the case was not made clearer by her presently exclaiming: "I knew you would, from the moment you should be really in love with her! I knew it would be the test—what do I mean?—the proof."

"Are there such strange bewilderments attached to that high state?" I asked, smiling.

"You perceive there are. You see him, you see him!" Mrs Marden announced, with tremendous exaltation. "You'll see him again."

"I've no objection; but I shall take more interest in him if you'll kindly tell me who he is."

She hesitated, looking down a moment; then she said, raising her eyes: "I'll tell you if you'll tell me first what you said to her on the way to church."

"Has she told you I said anything?"

"Do I need that?" smiled Mrs Marden.

"Oh yes, I remember—your intuitions! But I'm sorry to see they're at fault this time; because I really said nothing to your daughter that was the least out of the way."

"Are you very sure?"

"On my honour, Mrs Marden."

"Then you consider that you're not in love with her?"

"That's another affair!" I laughed.

"You are—you *are!* You wouldn't have seen him if you hadn't been."

"Who the deuce *is* he, then, madam?" I inquired with some irritation.

She would still only answer me with another question. "Didn't you at least *want* to say something to her—didn't you come very near it?"

The question was much to the point; it justified the famous intuitions. "Very near it—it was the turn of a hair. I don't know what kept me quiet."

"That was quite enough," said Mrs Marden. "It isn't what you say that determines it; it's what you feel. *That's* what he goes by."

I was annoyed, at last, by her reiterated reference to an identity yet to be established, and I clasped my hands with an air of supplication which covered much real impatience, a sharper curiosity and even the first short throbs of a certain sacred dread. "I entreat you to tell me whom you're talking about."

She threw up her arms, looking away from me, as if to shake off both reserve and responsibility. "Sir Edmund Orme."

"And who is Sir Edmund Orme?"

At the moment I spoke she gave a start. "Hush, here they come." Then as, following the direction of her eyes, I saw Charlotte Marden on the terrace, at the window, she added, with an intensity of warning: "Don't notice him—*never!*"

Charlotte, who had had her hands beside her eyes, peering into the room and smiling, made a sign that she was to be admitted, on which I went and opened the long window. Her mother turned away, and the girl came in with a laughing challenge: "What plot, in the world are you two hatching here?" Some plan—I forget what—was in prospect for the afternoon, as to which Mrs Marden's participation or consent was solicited—*my* adhesion was taken for granted—and she had been half over the place in her quest. I was flurried, because I saw that Mrs Marden was flurried (when she turned round to meet her daughter she covered it by a kind of extravagance, throwing herself on the girl's neck and embracing her), and to pass it off I said, fancifully, to Charlotte:

"I've been asking your mother for your hand."

"Oh, indeed, and has she given it?" Miss Marden answered, gayly.

"She was just going to when you appeared there."

"Well, it's only for a moment—I'll leave you free."

"Do you like him, Charlotte?" Mrs Marden asked, with a candour I scarcely expected.

"It's difficult to say it *before* him isn't it?" the girl replied, entering into the humour of the thing, but looking at me as if she didn't like me.

She would have had to say it before another person as well, for at that moment there stepped into the room from the terrace (the window had been left open), a gentleman who had come into sight, at least into mine, only within the instant. Mrs Marden had said "Here *they* come," but he appeared to have followed her daughter at a certain distance. I immediately recognised him as the personage who had sat beside us in church. This time I saw him better, saw that his face and his whole air were strange. I speak of him as a personage, because one felt, indescribably, as if a reigning prince had come into the room. He held himself with a kind of habitual majesty, as if he were different from us. Yet he looked fixedly and gravely at me, till I wondered what he expected of me. Did he consider that I should bend my knee or kiss his hand? He turned his eyes in the same way on Mrs Marden, but she knew what to do. After the first agitation produced by his approach she took no notice of him whatever; it made me remember her passionate adjuration to me. I had to achieve a great effort to imitate her, for though I knew nothing about him but that he was Sir Edmund Orme I felt his presence as a strong appeal, almost as an oppression. He stood there without speaking—young, pale, handsome, clean-shaven, decorous, with extraordinary light blue eyes and something old-fashioned, like a portrait of years ago, in his head, his manner of wearing his hair. He was in complete mourning (one immediately felt that he was very well dressed), and he carried his hat in his hand. He looked again strangely hard at me, harder than any one in the world had ever looked before; and I remember feeling rather cold and wishing he would say something. No silence had ever seemed to me so soundless. All this was of course an impression intensely rapid; but that it had consumed some instants was proved to me suddenly by the aspect of Charlotte Marden, who stared from her mother to me and back again (he never looked at her, and she had no appearance of looking at him), and then broke out with: "What on earth is the matter with you? You've such odd faces!" I felt the colour come back to mine, and when she went on in the same tone: "One would think you had seen a ghost!" I was conscious that I had turned very red. Sir Edmund Orme never blushed, and I could see that he had no capacity for embarrassment. One had met people of that sort, but never any one with such a grand indifference.

"Don't be impertinent; and go and tell them all that I'll join them," said Mrs Marden with much dignity, but with a quaver in her voice.

"And will you come—*you?*" the girl asked, turning away. I made no answer, taking the question, somehow, as meant for her companion. But he was more silent than I, and when she reached the door (she was going out that way), she stopped, with her hand on the knob, and looked at me, repeating it. I assented, springing forward to open the door for her, and as she passed out she exclaimed to me mockingly: "You haven't got your wits about you—you sha'n't have my hand!"

I closed the door and turned round to find that Sir Edmund Orme had during the moment my back was presented to him retired by the window. Mrs Marden stood there and we looked at each other long. It had only then—as the girl flitted away—come home to me that her daughter was unconscious of what had happened. It was *that*, oddly enough, that gave me a sudden, sharp shake, and not my own perception of our visitor, which appeared perfectly natural. It made the fact vivid to me that she had been equally unaware of him in church, and the two facts together—now that they were over—set my heart more sensibly beating. I wiped my forehead, and Mrs Marden broke out with a low distressful wail: "Now you know my life—now you know my life!"

"In God's name who is he—*what* is he?"

"He's a man I wronged."

"How did you wrong him?"

"Oh, awfully—years ago."

"Years ago? Why, he's very young."

"Young—young?" cried Mrs Marden. "He was born before *I* was!"

"Then why does he look so?"

She came nearer to me, she laid her hand on my arm, and there was something in her face that made me shrink a little. "Don't you understand—don't you *feel?*" she murmured, reproachfully.

"I feel very queer!" I laughed; and I was conscious that my laugh betrayed it.

"He's dead!" said Mrs Marden, from her white face.

"Dead?" I panted. "Then that gentleman was—?" I couldn't even say the word.

"Call him what you like—there are twenty vulgar names. He's a perfect presence."

"He's a splendid presence!" I cried. "The place is haunted —*haunted!*" I exulted in the word as if it represented the fulfilment of my dearest dream.

"It isn't the place—more's the pity! That has nothing to do with it!"

"Then it's you, dear lady?" I said, as if this were still better.

"No, nor me either—I wish it were!"

"Perhaps it's me," I suggested with a sickly smile.

"It's nobody but my child—my innocent, innocent child!" And with this Mrs Marden broke down—she dropped into a chair and burst into tears. I stammered some question—I pressed on her some bewildered appeal, but she waved me off, unexpectedly and passionately. I persisted—couldn't I help her, couldn't I intervene? "You *have* intervened," she sobbed; "you're *in* it, you're *in* it."

"I'm very glad to be in anything so curious," I boldly declared.

"Glad or not, you can't get out of it."

"I don't want to get out of it—it's too interesting."

"I'm glad you like it. Go away."

"But I want to know more about it."

"You'll see all you want—go away!"

"But I want to understand what I see."

"How can you—when I don't understand myself?"

"We'll do so together—we'll make it out."

At this she got up, doing what she could to obliterate her tears. "Yes, it will be better together—that's why I've liked you."

"Oh, we'll see it through!" I declared.

"Then you must control yourself better."

"I will, I will—with practice."

"You'll get used to it," said Mrs Marden, in a tone I never forgot. "But go and join them—I'll come in a moment."

I passed out to the terrace and I felt that I had a part to play. So far from dreading another encounter with the "perfect presence," as Mrs Marden called it, I was filled with an excitement that was positively joyous. I desired a renewal of the sensation—I opened myself wide to the impression, I went round the house as quickly as if I expected to overtake Sir Edmund Orme. I didn't overtake him just then, but the day was not to close without my recognising that, as Mrs Marden had said, I should see all I wanted of him.

We took, or most of us took, the collective sociable walk which, in the English country-house, is the consecrated pastime on Sunday afternoons. We were restricted to such a regulated ramble as the ladies were good for; the afternoons, moreover, were short, and by five o'clock we were restored to the fireside in the hall, with a sense, on my part at least, that we might have done a little more for our tea. Mrs Marden had said she would join us, but she had not appeared; her daughter, who had seen her again before we went out, only explained that she was tired. She remained invisible all the afternoon, but this was a detail to which I gave as little heed as I had given to the circumstance of my not having Miss Marden to myself during all our walk. I was too much taken up with another emotion to care; I felt beneath my feet the threshold of the strange door, in my life, which had suddenly been thrown open and out of which unspeakable vibrations played up through me like a fountain. I had heard all my days of apparitions, but it was a different thing to have seen one and to know that I should in all probability see it familiarly, as it were, again. I was on the look-out for it, as a pilot for the flash of a revolving light, and I was ready to generalise on the sinister subject, to declare that ghosts were much less alarming and much more amusing than was commonly supposed. There is no doubt that I was extremely nervous. I couldn't get over the distinction conferred upon me—the exception (in the way of mystic enlargement of vision), made in my favour. At the same time I think I did justice to Mrs Marden's absence; it was a commentary on what she had said to me— "Now you know my life." She had probably been seeing Sir Edmund Orme for years, and, not having my firm fibre, she had broken down under him. Her nerve was gone, though she had also been able to attest that, in a degree, one got used to him. She had got used to breaking down.

Afternoon tea, when the dusk fell early, was a friendly hour at Tranton; the firelight played into the wide, white last-century hall; sympathies almost confessed themselves, lingering together, before dressing, on deep sofas, in muddy boots, for last words, after walks; and even solitary absorption in the third volume of a novel that was wanted by some one else seemed a form of geniality. I watched my moment and went over to Charlotte Marden when I saw she was about to withdraw. The ladies had left the place one by one, and after I had addressed myself particularly to Miss Marden the three men who were near her gradually dispersed. We had a little vague talk—she appeared preoccupied, and heaven knows *I* was—after which she said she must go: she should be late for dinner. I proved to her by book that she had plenty of time, and she objected that she must at any rate go up to see her mother: she was afraid she was unwell.

"On the contrary, she's better than she has been for a long time—I'll guarantee that," I said. "She has found out that she can have confidence in me, and that has done her good." Miss Marden had dropped into her chair again. I was standing before her, and she looked up at me without a smile—with a dim distress in her beautiful eyes; not exactly as if I were hurting her, but as if she were no longer disposed to treat as a joke what had passed (whatever it was, it was at the same time difficult to be serious about it), between her mother and myself. But I could answer her inquiry in all kindness and candour, for I was really conscious that the poor lady had put off a part of her burden on me and was proportionately relieved and eased. "I'm sure she has slept all the afternoon as she hasn't slept for years," I went on. "You have only to ask her."

Charlotte got up again. "You make yourself out very useful."

"You've a good quarter of an hour," I said. "Haven't I a right to talk to you a little this way, alone, when your mother has given me your hand?"

"And is it *your* mother who has given me yours? I'm much obliged to her, but I don't want it. I think our hands are not our mothers'—they happen to be our own!" laughed the girl.

"Sit down, sit down and let me tell you!" I pleaded.

I still stood before her, urgently, to see if she wouldn't oblige me. She hesitated a moment, looking vaguely this way and that, as if under a compulsion that was slightly painful. The empty hall was quiet—we heard the loud ticking of the great clock. Then she slowly sank down and I drew a chair close to her. This made me face round to the fire again, and with the movement I perceived, disconcertedly, that we were not alone. The next instant, more strangely than I can say, my discomposure, instead of increasing, dropped, for the person before the fire was Sir Edmund Orme. He stood there as I had seen him in the Indian room, looking at me with the expressionless attention which borrowed its sternness from his sombre distinction. I knew so much more about him now that I had to check a movement of recognition, an acknowledgment of his presence. When once I was aware of it, and that it lasted, the sense that we had company, Charlotte and I, quitted me; it was impressed on me on the contrary that I was more intensely alone with Miss Marden. She evidently saw nothing to look at, and I made a tremendous and very nearly successful effort to conceal from her that my own situation was different. I say "very nearly," because she watched me an instant—while my words were arrested—in a way that made me fear she was going to say again, as she had said in the Indian room: "What on earth is the matter with you?"

What the matter with me was I quickly told her, for the full knowledge of it rolled over me with the touching spectacle of her unconsciousness. It was touching that she became, in the presence of this extraordinary portent. What was portended, danger or sorrow, bliss or bane, was a minor question; all I saw, as she sat there, was that, innocent and charming, she was close to a horror, as she might have thought it, that happened to be veiled from her but that might at any moment be disclosed. I didn't mind it now, as I found, but nothing was more possible than she should, and if it wasn't curious and interesting it might easily be very dreadful. If I didn't mind it for myself, as I afterwards saw, this was largely because I was so taken up with the idea of protecting *her*. My heart beat high with this idea, on the spot; I determined to do everything I could to keep her sense sealed. What I could do might have been very obscure to me if I had not, in all this, become more aware than of anything else that I loved her. The way to save her was to love her, and the way to love her was to tell her, now and here, that I did so. Sir Edmund Orme didn't prevent me, especially as after a moment he turned his back to us and stood looking discreetly at the fire. At the end of another moment he leaned his head on his arm, against the chimney-piece, with an air of gradual dejection, like a spirit still more weary than discreet. Charlotte Marden was startled by what I said to her, and she jumped up to escape it; but she took no offence—my tenderness was too real. She only moved about the room with a deprecating murmur, and I was so busy following up any little advantage that I might have obtained that I didn't notice in what manner Sir Edmund Orme disappeared. I only observed presently that he had gone. This made no difference—he had been so small a hindrance; I only remember being struck, suddenly, with something inexorable in the slow, sweet, sad headshake that Miss Marden gave me.

"I don't ask for an answer now," I said; "I only want you to be sure—to know how much depends on it."

"Oh, I don't want to give it to you, now or ever!" she replied. "I hate the subject, please—I wish one could be let alone." And then, as if I might have found something harsh in this irrepressible, artless cry of beauty beset, she added quickly, vaguely, kindly, as she left the room: "Thank you, thank you—thank you so much!"

At dinner I could be generous enough to be glad, for her, that I was placed on the same side of the table with her, where she couldn't see me. Her mother was nearly opposite to me, and just after we had sat down Mrs Marden gave me one long, deep look, in which all our strange communion was expressed. It meant of course "She has told me," but it meant other things beside. At any rate I know what my answering look to her conveyed: "I've seen him again—I've seen him again!" This didn't prevent Mrs Marden from treating her neighbours with her usual scrupulous blandness. After dinner, when, in the drawing-room, the men joined the ladies and I went straight up to her to tell her how I wished we could have some private conversation, she said immediately, in a low tone, looking down at her fan while she opened and shut it:

"He's here—he's here."

"Here?" I looked round the room, but I was disappointed.

"Look where *she* is," said Mrs Marden, with just the faintest asperity. Charlotte was in fact not in the main saloon, but in an apartment into which it opened and which was known as the morning-room. I took a few steps and saw her, through a doorway, upright in the middle of the room, talking with three gentlemen whose backs were practically turned to me. For a moment my quest seemed vain; then I recognised that one of the gentlemen—the middle one—was Sir Edmund Orme. This time it *was* surprising that the others didn't see him. Charlotte seemed to be looking straight at him, addressing her conversation to him. She saw me after an instant, however, and immediately turned her eyes away. I went back to her mother with an annoyed sense that the girl would think I was watching *her*, which would be unjust. Mrs Marden had found a small sofa—a little apart—and I sat down beside her. There were some questions I had so wanted to go into that I wished we were once more in the Indian room. I presently gathered, however, that our privacy was all-sufficient. We communicated so closely and completely now, and with such silent reciprocities, that it would in every circumstance be adequate.

"Oh, yes, he's there," I said; "and at about a quarter-past seven he was in the hall."

"I knew it at the time, and I was so glad!"

"So glad?"

"That it was your affair, this time, and not mine. It's a rest for me."

"Did you sleep all the afternoon?" I asked.

"As I haven't done for months. But how did you know that?"

"As *you* knew, I take it, that Sir Edmund was in the hall. We shall evidently each of us know things now—where the other is concerned."

"Where *he* is concerned," Mrs Marden amended. "It's a blessing, the way you take it," she added, with a long, mild sigh.

"I take it as a man who's in love with your daughter."

"Of course—of course." Intense as I now felt my desire for the girl to be, I couldn't help laughing a little at the tone of these words; and it led my companion immediately to say: "Otherwise you wouldn't have seen him."

"But every one doesn't see him who's in love with her, or there would be dozens."

"They're not in love with her as you are."

"I can, of course, only speak for myself; and I found a moment, before dinner, to do so."

"She told me immediately."

"And have I any hope—any chance?"

"That's what *I* long for, what I pray for."

"Ah, how can I thank you enough?" I murmured.

"I believe it will all pass—if she loves you," Mrs Marden continued.

"It will all pass?"

"We shall never see him again."

"Oh, if she loves me I don't care how often I see him!"

"Ah, you take it better than I could," said my companion. "You have the happiness not to know—not to understand."

"I don't indeed. What on earth does he want?"

"He wants to make me suffer." She turned her wan face upon me with this, and I saw now for the first time, fully, how perfectly, if this had been Sir Edmund Orme's purpose, he had succeeded. "For what I did to him," Mrs Marden explained.

"And what did you do to him?"

She looked at me a moment. "I killed him." As I had seen him fifty yards away only five minutes before the words gave me a start. "Yes, I make you jump; be careful. He's there still, but he killed himself. I broke his heart—he thought me awfully bad. We were to have been married, but I broke it off —just at the last. I saw some one I liked better; I had no reason but that. It wasn't for interest, or money, or position, or anything of that sort. All *those* things were his. It was simply that I fell in love with Captain Marden. When I saw him I felt that I couldn't marry any one else. I wasn't in love with Edmund Orme—my mother, my elder sister had brought it about. But he did love me. I told him I didn't care —that I couldn't, that I *wouldn't*. I threw him over, and he took something, some abominable drug or draught that proved fatal. It was dreadful, it was horrible, he was found that way—he died in agony. I married Captain Marden, but not for five years. I was happy, perfectly happy; time obliterates. But when my husband died I began to see him."

I had listened intently, but I wondered. "To see your husband?"

"Never, never *that* way, thank God! To see *him*, with Chartie—always with Chartie. The first time it nearly killed me—about seven years ago, when she first came out. Never when I'm by myself—only with her. Sometimes not for months, then every day for a week. I've tried everything to break the spell—doctors and *régimes* and climates; I've prayed to God on my knees. That day at Brighton, on the Parade with you, when you thought I was ill, that was the first for an age. And then, in the evening, when I knocked my tea over you, and the day you were at the door with Charlotte and I saw you from the window—each time he was there."

"I see, I see." I was more thrilled than I could say. "It's an apparition like another."

"Like another? Have you ever seen another?"

"No, I mean the sort of thing one has heard of. It's tremendously interesting to encounter a case."

"Do you call me a 'case'?" Mrs Marden asked, with exquisite resentment.

"I mean myself."

"Oh, you're the right one!" she exclaimed. "I was right when I trusted you."

"I'm devoutly grateful you did; but what made you do it?"

"I had thought the whole thing out—I had had time to in those dreadful years, while he was punishing me in my daughter."

"Hardly that," I objected, "if she never knew."

"That has been my terror, that she *will*, from one occasion to another. I've an unspeakable dread of the effect on her."

"She sha'n't, she sha'n't!" I declared, so loud that several people looked round. Mrs Marden made me get up, and I had no more talk with her that evening. The next day I told her I must take my departure from Tranton—it was neither comfortable nor considerate to remain as a rejected suitor. She was disconcerted, but she accepted my reasons, only saying to me out of her mournful eyes: "You'll leave me alone then with my burden?" It was of course understood between us that for many weeks to come there would be no discretion in "worrying poor Charlotte": such were the terms in which, with odd feminine and maternal inconsistency, she alluded to an attitude on my part that she favoured. I was prepared to be heroically considerate, but it seemed to me that even this delicacy permitted me to say a word to Miss Marden before I went. I begged her, after breakfast, to take a turn with me on the terrace, and as she hesitated, looking at me distantly, I informed her that it was only to ask her a question and to say good-bye—I was leaving Tranton for *her*.

She came out with me, and we passed slowly round the house three or four times. Nothing is finer than this great airy platform, from which every look is a sweep of the country, with the sea on the furthest edge. It might have been that as we passed the windows we were conspicuous to our friends in the house, who would divine, sarcastically, why I was so significantly bolting. But I didn't care; I only wondered whether they wouldn't really this time make out Sir Edmund Orme, who joined us on one of our turns and strolled slowly on the other side of my companion. Of what transcendent essence he was composed I knew not; I have no theory about him (leaving that to others), any more than I have one about such or such another of my fellow-mortals whom I have elbowed in life. He was as positive, as individual, as ultimate a fact as any of these. Above all he was as respectable, as sensitive a fact; so that I should no more have thought of taking a liberty, of practicing an experiment with him, of touching him, for instance, or speaking to him, since he set the example of silence, than I should have thought of committing any other social grossness. He had always, as I saw more fully later, the perfect propriety of his position—had always the appearance of being dressed and, in attitude and aspect, of comporting himself, as the occasion demanded. He looked strange, incontestably, but somehow he always looked *right*. I very soon came to attach an idea of beauty to his unmentionable presence, the beauty of an old story of love and pain. What I ended by feeling was that he was on my side, that he was watching over my interest, that he was looking to it that my heart shouldn't be broken. Oh, he had taken it seriously, his own catastrophe—he had certainly proved that in his day. If poor Mrs Marden, as she told me, had thought it out, I also subjected the case to the finest analysis of which my intellect was capable. It was a case of retributive justice. The mother was to pay, in suffering, for the suffering she had inflicted, and as the disposition to jilt a lover might have been transmitted to the daughter, the daughter was to be watched, so that *she* might be made to suffer should she do an equal wrong. She might reproduce her mother in character as vividly as she did in face. On the day she should transgress, in other words, her eyes would be opened suddenly and unpitiedly to the "perfect presence," which she would have to work as she could into her conception of a young lady's universe. I had no great fear for her, because I didn't believe she was, in any cruel degree, a coquette. We should have a good deal of ground to get over before I, at least, should be in a position to be sacrificed by her. She couldn't throw me over before she had made a little more of me.

The question I asked her on the terrace that morning was whether I might continue, during the winter, to come to Mrs Marden's house. I promised not to come too often and not to speak to her for three months of the question I had raised the day before. She replied that I might do as I liked, and on this we parted.

I carried out the vow I had made her; I held my tongue for my three months. Unexpectedly to myself there were moments of this time when she struck me as capable of playing with a man. I wanted so to make her like me that I became subtle and ingenious, wonderfully alert, patiently diplomatic. Sometimes I thought I had earned my reward, brought her to the point of saying: "Well, well, you're the best of them all— you may speak to me now." Then there was a greater blankness than ever in her beauty, and on certain days a mocking light in her eyes, of which the meaning seemed to be: "If you don't take care, I *will* accept you, to have done with you the more effectually." Mrs Marden was a great help to me simply by believing in me, and I valued her faith all the more that it continued even though there was a sudden intermission of the miracle that had been wrought for me. After our visit to Tranton Sir Edmund Orme gave us a holiday, and I confess it was at first a disappointment to me. I felt less designated, less connected with Charlotte. "Oh, don't cry till you're out of the wood," her mother said; "he has let me off sometimes for six months. He'll break out again when you least expect it—he knows what he's about." For her these weeks were happy, and she was wise enough not to talk about me to the girl. She was so good as to assure me that I was taking the right way, that I looked as if I felt secure and that in the long run women give way to that. She had known them do it even when the man was a fool for looking so—or was a fool on any terms. For herself she felt it to be a good time, a sort of St Martin's summer of the soul. She was better than she had been for years, and she had me to thank for it. The sense of visitation was light upon her—she wasn't in anguish every time she looked round. Charlotte contradicted me very often, but she contradicted herself still more. That winter was a wonder of mildness, and we often sat out in the sun. I walked up and down with Charlotte, and Mrs Marden, sometimes on a bench, sometimes in a bath-chair, waited for us and smiled at us as we passed. I always looked out for a sign in her face—"He's with you, he's with you" (she would see him before I should), but nothing came; the season had brought us also a sort of spiritual softness. Toward the end of April the air was so like June that, meeting my two friends one night at some Brighton sociability—an evening party with amateur music—I drew Miss Marden unresistingly out upon a balcony to which a window in one of the rooms stood open. The night was close and thick, the stars were dim, and below us, under the cliff, we heard the regular rumble of the sea. We listened to it a little and we heard mixed with it, from within the house, the sound of a violin accompanied by a piano—a performance which had been our pretext for passing out.

"Do you like me a little better?" I asked, abruptly, after a minute. "Could you listen to me again?"

I had no sooner spoken than she laid her hand quickly, with a certain force, on my arm. "Hush!—isn't there some one there?" She was looking into the gloom of the far end of the balcony. This balcony ran the whole width of the house, a width very great in the best of the old houses at Brighton. We were lighted a little by the open window behind us, but the other windows, curtained within, left the darkness undiminished, so that I made out but dimly the figure of a gentleman standing there and looking at us. He was in evening dress, like a guest—I saw the vague shine of his white shirt and the pale oval of his face—and he might perfectly have been a guest who had stepped out in advance of us to take the air. Miss Marden took him for one at first—then evidently, even in a few seconds, she saw that the intensity of his gaze was unconventional. What else she saw I couldn't determine; I was too taken up with my own impression to do more than feel the quick contact of her uneasiness. My own impression was in fact the strongest of sensations, a sensation of horror; for what could the thing mean but that the girl at last *saw?* I heard her give a sudden, gasping "Ah!" and move quickly into the house. It was only afterwards that I knew that I myself had had a totally new emotion—my horror passing into anger, and my anger into a stride along the balcony with a gesture of reprobation. The case was simplified to the vision of a frightened girl whom I loved. I advanced to vindicate her security, but I found nothing there to meet me. It was either all a mistake or Sir Edmund Orme had vanished.

I followed Miss Marden immediately, but there were symptoms of confusion in the drawing-room when I passed in. A lady had fainted, the music had stopped; there was a shuffling of chairs and a pressing forward. The lady was not Charlotte, as I feared, but Mrs Marden, who had suddenly been taken ill. I remember the relief with which I learned this, for to see Charlotte stricken would have been anguish, and her mother's condition gave a channel to her agitation. It was of course all a matter for the people of the house and for the ladies, and I could have no share in attending to my friends or in conducting them to their carriage. Mrs Marden revived and insisted on going home, after which I uneasily withdrew.

I called the next morning to ask about her and was informed that she was better, but when I asked if Miss Marden would see me the message sent down was that it was impossible. There was nothing for me to do all day but to roam about with a beating heart. But toward evening I received a line in pencil, brought by hand—"Please come; mother wishes you." Five minutes afterward I was at the door again and ushered into the drawing-room. Mrs Marden lay upon the sofa, and as soon as I looked at her I saw the shadow of death in her face. But the first thing she said was that she was better, ever so much better; her poor old heart had been behaving queerly again, but now it was quiet. She gave me her hand and I bent over her with my eyes in hers, and in this way I was able to read what she didn't speak—"I'm really very ill, but appear to take what I say exactly as I say it." Charlotte stood there beside her, looking not frightened now, but intensely grave, and not meeting my eyes. "She has told me—she has told me!" her mother went on.

"She has told you?" I stared from one of them to the other, wondering if Mrs Marden meant that the girl had spoken to her of the circumstances on the balcony.

"That you spoke to her again—that you're admirably faithful."

I felt a thrill of joy at this; it showed me that that memory had been uppermost, and also that Charlotte had wished to say the thing that would soothe her mother most, not the thing that would alarm her. Yet I now knew, myself, as well as if Mrs Marden had told me, that she knew and had known at the moment what her daughter had seen. "I spoke—I spoke, but she gave me no answer," I said.

"She will now, won't you, Chartie? I want it so, I want it!" the poor lady murmured, with ineffable wistfulness.

"You're very good to me," Charlotte said to me, seriously and sweetly, looking fixedly on the carpet. There was something different in her, different from all the past. She had recognised something, she felt a coercion. I could see that she was trembling.

"Ah, if you would let me show you *how* good I can be!" I exclaimed, holding out my hands to her. As I uttered the words I was touched with the knowledge that something had happened. A form had constituted itself on the other side of the bed, and the form leaned over Mrs Marden. My whole being went forth into a mute prayer that Charlotte shouldn't see it and that I should be able to betray nothing. The impulse to glance toward Mrs Marden was even stronger than the involuntary movement of taking in Sir Edmund Orme; but I could resist even that, and Mrs Marden was perfectly still. Charlotte got up to give me her hand, and with the definite act she saw. She gave, with a shriek, one stare of dismay, and another sound, like a wail of one of the lost, fell at the same instant on my ear. But I had already sprung toward the girl to cover her, to veil her face. She had already thrown herself into my arms. I held her there a moment—bending over her, given up to her, feeling each of her throbs with my own and not knowing which was which; then, all of a sudden, coldly, I gathered that we were alone. She released herself. The figure beside the sofa had vanished; but Mrs Marden lay in her place with closed eyes, with something in her stillness that gave us both another terror. Charlotte expressed it in the cry of "Mother, mother!" with which she

flung herself down. I fell on my knees beside her. Mrs Marden
had passed away.

Was the sound I heard when Chartie shrieked—the other
and still more tragic sound I mean—the despairing cry of the
poor lady's death-shock or the articulate sob (it was like a
waft from a great tempest), of the exorcised and pacified
spirit? Possibly the latter, for that was, mercifully, the last of
Sir Edmund Orme.

NONA VINCENT

I

"I WONDERED whether you wouldn't read it to me," said
Mrs Alsager, as they lingered a little near the fire before he
took leave. She looked down at the fire sideways, drawing her
dress away from it and making her proposal with a shy sincerity that added to her charm. Her charm was always great
for Allan Wayworth, and the whole air of her house, which
was simply a sort of distillation of herself, so soothing, so
beguiling that he always made several false starts before
departure. He had spent some such good hours there, had
forgotten, in her warm, golden drawing-room, so much of the
loneliness and so many of the worries of his life, that it had
come to be the immediate answer to his longings, the cure for
his aches, the harbour of refuge from his storms. His tribulations were not unprecedented, and some of his advantages, if
of a usual kind, were marked in degree, inasmuch as he was
very clever for one so young, and very independent for one so
poor. He was eight-and-twenty, but he had lived a good deal
and was full of ambitions and curiosities and disappointments.
The opportunity to talk of some of these in Grosvenor Place
corrected perceptibly the immense inconvenience of London.
This inconvenience took for him principally the line of insensibility to Allan Wayworth's literary form. He had a
literary form, or he thought he had, and her intelligent recognition of the circumstance was the sweetest consolation Mrs
Alsager could have administered. She was even more literary
and more artistic than he, inasmuch as he could often work off
his overflow (this was his occupation, his profession), while
the generous woman, abounding in happy thoughts, but

inedited and unpublished, stood there in the rising tide like the nymph of a fountain in the plash of the marble basin.

The year before, in a big newspapery house, he had found himself next her at dinner, and they had converted the intensely material hour into a feast of reason. There was no motive for her asking him to come to see her but that she liked him, which it was the more agreeable to him to perceive as he perceived at the same time that she was exquisite. She was enviably free to act upon her likings, and it made Wayworth feel less unsuccessful to infer that for the moment he happened to be one of them. He kept the revelation to himself, and indeed there was nothing to turn his head in the kindness of a kind woman. Mrs Alsager occupied so completely the ground of possession that she would have been condemned to inaction had it not been for the principle of giving. Her husband, who was twenty years her senior, a massive personality in the City and a heavy one at home (wherever he stood, or even sat, he was monumental), owned half a big newspaper and the whole of a great many other things. He admired his wife, though she bore no children, and liked her to have other tastes than his, as that seemed to give a greater acreage to their life. His own appetites went so far he could scarcely see the boundary, and his theory was to trust her to push the limits of hers, so that between them the pair should astound by their consumption. His ideas were prodigiously vulgar, but some of them had the good fortune to be carried out by a person of perfect delicacy. Her delicacy made her play strange tricks with them, but he never found this out. She attenuated him without his knowing it, for what he mainly thought was that he had aggrandised *her*. Without her he really would have been bigger still, and society, breathing more freely, was practically under an obligation to her which, to do it justice, it acknowledged by an attitude of mystified respect. She felt a tremulous need to throw her liberty and her leisure into the things of the soul—the most beautiful things she knew. She found them, when she gave time to seeking, in a hundred places, and particularly in a dim and sacred region—the region of active pity—over her entrance into which she dropped curtains so thick that it would have been an impertinence to lift them. But she cultivated other beneficent passions, and if she cherished the dream of something fine the moments at which it most seemed to her to come true were when she saw beauty plucked flower-like in the garden of art. She loved the perfect work—she had the artistic chord. This chord could vibrate only to the touch of another, so that appreciation, in her spirit, had the added intensity of regret. She could understand the joy of creation, and she thought it scarcely enough to be told that she herself created happiness. She would have liked, at any rate, to choose her way; but it was just here that her liberty failed her. She had not the voice —she had only the vision. The only envy she was capable of was directed to those who, as she said, could do something.

As everything in her, however, turned to gentleness, she was admirably hospitable to such people as a class. She believed Allan Wayworth could do something, and she liked to hear him talk of the ways in which he meant to show it. He talked of them almost to no one else—she spoiled him for other listeners. With her fair bloom and her quiet grace she was indeed an ideal public, and if she had ever confided to him that she would have liked to scribble (she had in fact not mentioned it to a creature), he would have been in a perfect position for asking her why a woman whose face had so much expression should not have felt that she achieved. How in the world could she express better? There was less than that in Shakespeare and Beethoven. She had never been more generous than when, in compliance with her invitation, which I have recorded, he brought his play to read to her. He had spoken of it to her before, and one dark November afternoon, when her red fireside was more than ever an escape from the place and the season, he had broken out as he came in—"I've done it, I've done it!" She made him tell her all about it—she took an interest really minute and asked questions delightfully apt. She had spoken from the first as if he were on the point of being acted, making him jump, with her participation, all sorts of dreary intervals. She liked the theatre as she liked all the arts of expression, and he had known her to go all the way to Paris for a particular performance. Once he had gone with her—the time she took that stupid Mrs Mostyn. She had been struck, when he sketched it, with the subject of his drama, and had spoken words that helped him to believe in it. As soon as he had rung down his curtain on the last act he rushed off to see her, but after that he kept the thing for repeated last touches. Finally, on Christmas day, by arrangement, she sat there and listened to it. It was in three acts and in prose, but rather of the romantic order, though dealing with contemporary English life, and he fondly believed that it showed the hand if not of the master, at least of the prize pupil.

Allan Wayworth had returned to England, at two-and-twenty, after a miscellaneous continental education; his father, the correspondent, for years, in several foreign countries successively, of a conspicuous London journal, had died just after this, leaving his mother and her two other children, portionless girls, to subsist on a very small income in a very dull German town. The young man's beginnings in London were difficult, and he had aggravated them by his dislike of journalism. His father's connection with it would have helped him, but he was (insanely, most of his friends judged— the great exception was always Mrs Alsager) *intraitable* on the question of form. Form—in his sense—was not demanded by English newspapers, and he couldn't give it to them in *their* sense. The demand for it was not great anywhere, and Wayworth spent costly weeks in polishing little compositions for magazines that didn't pay for style. The only person who paid for it was really Mrs Alsager: she had an infallible instinct for the perfect. She paid in her own way, and if Allan Wayworth

had been a wage-earning person it would have made him feel
that if he didn't receive his legal dues his palm was at least
occasionally conscious of a gratuity. He had his limitations, his
perversities, but the finest parts of him were the most alive,
and he was restless and sincere. It is however the impression
he produced on Mrs Alsager that most concerns us: she
thought him not only remarkably good-looking but altogether original. There were some usual bad things he would
never do—too many prohibitive puddles for him in the short
cut to success.

For himself, he had never been so happy as since he had
seen his way, as he fondly believed, to some sort of mastery of
the scenic idea, which struck him as a very different matter
now that he looked at it from within. He had had his early
days of contempt for it, when it seemed to him a jewel, dim at
the best, hidden in a dunghill, a taper burning low in an air
thick with vulgarity. It was hedged about with sordid
approaches, it was not worth sacrifice and suffering. The man
of letters, in dealing with it, would have to put off all literature, which was like asking the bearer of a noble name to
forego his immemorial heritage. Aspects change, however,
with the point of view: Wayworth had waked up one morning in a different bed altogether. It is needless here to trace this
accident to its source; it would have been much more interesting to a spectator of the young man's life to follow some of
the consequences. He had been made (as he felt) the subject of
a special revelation, and he wore his hat like a man in love. An
angel had taken him by the hand and guided him to the shabby
door which opens, it appears, into an interior both splendid
and austere. The scenic idea was magnificent when once you
had embraced it—the dramatic form had a purity which
made some others look ingloriously rough. It had the high
dignity of the exact sciences, it was mathematical and archi-
tectural. It was full of the refreshment of calculation and construction, the incorruptibility of line and law. It was bare, but

it was erect, it was poor, but it was noble; it reminded him of some sovereign famed for justice who should have lived in a palace despoiled. There was a fearful amount of concession in it, but what you kept had a rare intensity. You were perpetually throwing over the cargo to save the ship, but what a motion you gave her when you made her ride the waves—a motion as rhythmic as the dance of a goddess! Wayworth took long London walks and thought of these things—London poured into his ears the mighty hum of its suggestion. His imagination glowed and melted down material, his intentions multiplied and made the air a golden haze. He saw not only the thing he should do, but the next and the next and the next; the future opened before him and he seemed to walk on marble slabs. The more he tried the dramatic form the more he loved it, the more he looked at it the more he perceived in it. What he perceived in it indeed he now perceived everywhere; if he stopped, in the London dusk, before some flaring shop-window, the place immediately constituted itself behind footlights, became a framed stage for his figures. He hammered at these figures in his lonely lodging, he shaped them and he shaped their tabernacle; he was like a goldsmith chiselling a casket, bent over with the passion for perfection. When he was neither roaming the streets with his vision nor worrying his problem at his table, he was exchanging ideas on the general question with Mrs Alsager, to whom he promised details that would amuse her in later and still happier hours. Her eyes were full of tears when he read her the last words of the finished work, and she murmured, divinely—

"And now—to get it done, to get it done!"

"Yes, indeed—to get it done!" Wayworth stared at the fire, slowly rolling up his type-copy. "But that's a totally different part of the business, and altogether secondary."

"But of course you want to be acted?"

"Of course I do—but it's a sudden descent. I want to intensely, but I'm sorry I want to."

"It's there indeed that the difficulties begin," said Mrs Alsager, a little off her guard.

"How can you say that? It's there that they end!"

"Ah, wait to see where they end!"

"I mean they'll now be of a totally different order," Wayworth explained. "It seems to me there can be nothing in the world more difficult than to write a play that will stand an all-round test, and that in comparison with them the complications that spring up at this point are of an altogether smaller kind."

"Yes, they're not inspiring," said Mrs Alsager; "they're discouraging, because they're vulgar. The other problem, the working out of the thing itself, is pure art."

"How well you understand everything!" The young man had got up, nervously, and was leaning against the chimney-piece with his back to the fire and his arms folded. The roll of his copy, in his fist, was squeezed into the hollow of one of them. He looked down at Mrs Alsager, smiling gratefully, and she answered him with a smile from eyes still charmed and suffused. "Yes, the vulgarity will begin now," he presently added.

"You'll suffer dreadfully."

"I shall suffer in a good cause."

"Yes, giving *that* to the world! You must leave it with me, I must read it over and over," Mrs Alsager pleaded, rising to come nearer and draw the copy, in its cover of greenish-grey paper, which had a generic identity now to him, out of his grasp. "Who in the world will do it?—who in the world *can?*" she went on, close to him, turning over the leaves. Before he could answer she had stopped at one of the pages; she turned the book round to him, pointing out a speech. "That's the most beautiful place—those lines are a perfection." He glanced at the spot she indicated, and she begged him to read them again—he had read them admirably before. He knew them by heart, and, closing the book while she held the other end of it, he murmured them over to her—they had indeed a cadence that pleased him—watching, with a facetious complacency which he hoped was pardonable, the applause in her face. "Ah, who can utter such lines as *that?*" Mrs Alsager broke out; "whom can you find to do *her?*"

"We'll find people to do them all!"

"But not people who are worthy."

"They'll be worthy enough if they're willing enough. I'll work with them—I'll grind it into them." He spoke as if he had produced twenty plays.

"Oh, it will be interesting!" she echoed.

"But I shall have to find my theatre first. I shall have to get a manager to believe in me."

"Yes—they're so stupid!"

"But fancy the patience I shall want, and how I shall have to watch and wait," said Allan Wayworth. "Do you see me hawking it about London?"

"Indeed I don't—it would be sickening."

"It's what I shall have to do. I shall be old before it's produced."

"I shall be old very soon if it isn't!" Mrs Alsager cried. "I know one or two of them," she mused.

"Do you mean you would speak to them?"

"The thing is to get them to read it. I could do that."

"That's the utmost I ask. But it's even for that I shall have to wait."

She looked at him with kind sisterly eyes. "You sha'n't wait."

"Ah, you dear lady!" Wayworth murmured.

"That is *you* may, but *I* won't! Will you leave me your copy?" she went on, turning the pages again.

"Certainly; I have another." Standing near him she read to herself a passage here and there; then, in her sweet voice, she read some of them out. "Oh, if *you* were only an actress!" the young man exclaimed.

"That's the last thing I am. There's no comedy in *me!*"

She had never appeared to Wayworth so much his good
genius. "Is there any tragedy?" he asked, with the levity of
complete confidence.

She turned away from him, at this, with a strange and
charming laugh and a "Perhaps that will be for you to determine!" But before he could disclaim such a responsibility she
had faced him again and was talking about Nona Vincent as
if she had been the most interesting of their friends and her
situation at that moment an irresistible appeal to their sympathy. Nona Vincent was the heroine of the play, and Mrs
Alsager had taken a tremendous fancy to her. "I can't *tell* you
how I like that woman!" she exclaimed in a pensive rapture
of credulity which could only be balm to the artistic spirit.

"I'm awfully glad she lives a bit. What I feel about her is
that she's a good deal like *you*," Wayworth observed.

Mrs Alsager stared an instant and turned faintly red. This
was evidently a view that failed to strike her; she didn't, however, treat it as a joke. "I'm not impressed with the resemblance. I don't see myself doing what she does."

"It isn't so much what she *does*," the young man argued,
drawing out his moustache.

"But what she does is the whole point. She simply tells
her love—I should never do that."

"If you repudiate such a proceeding with such energy, why
do you like her for it?"

"It isn't what I like her for."

"What else, then? That's intensely characteristic."

Mrs Alsager reflected, looking down at the fire; she had the
air of having half-a-dozen reasons to choose from. But the
one she produced was unexpectedly simple; it might even
have been prompted by despair at not finding others. "I like
her because *you* made her!" she exclaimed with a laugh,
moving again away from her companion.

Wayworth laughed still louder. "You made her a little
yourself. I've thought of her as looking like you."

"She ought to look much better," said Mrs Alsager. "No, certainly, I shouldn't do what *she* does."

"Not even in the same circumstances?"

"I should never find myself in such circumstances. They're exactly your play, and have nothing in common with such a life as mine. However," Mrs Alsager went on, "her behaviour was natural for *her*, and not only natural, but, it seems to me, thoroughly beautiful and noble. I can't sufficiently admire the talent and tact with which you make one accept it, and I tell you frankly that it's evident to me there must be a brilliant future before a young man who, at the start, has been capable of such a stroke as that. Thank heaven I can admire Nona Vincent as intensely as I feel that I don't resemble her!"

"Don't exaggerate that," said Allan Wayworth.

"My admiration?"

"Your dissimilarity. She has your face, your air, your voice, your motion; she has many elements of your being."

"Then she'll damn your play!" Mrs Alsager replied. They joked a little over this, though it was not in the tone of pleasantry that Wayworth's hostess soon remarked: "You've got your remedy, however: have her done by the right woman."

"Oh, have her 'done'—have her 'done'!" the young man gently wailed.

"I see what you mean, my poor friend. What a pity, when it's such a magnificent part—such a chance for a clever serious girl! Nona Vincent is practically your play—it will be open to her to carry it far or to drop it at the first corner."

"It's a charming prospect," said Allan Wayworth, with sudden scepticism. They looked at each other with eyes that, for a lurid moment, saw the worst of the worst; but before they parted they had exchanged vows and confidences that were dedicated wholly to the ideal. It is not to be supposed, however, that the knowledge that Mrs Alsager would help him made Wayworth less eager to help himself. He did what he could and felt that she, on her side, was doing no less; but at the end of a year he was obliged to recognise that their united effort had mainly produced the fine flower of discouragement. At the end of a year the lustre had, to his own eyes, quite faded from his unappreciated masterpiece, and he found himself writing for a biographical dictionary little lives of celebrities he had never heard of. To be printed, anywhere and anyhow, was a form of glory for a man so unable to be acted, and to be paid, even at encyclopædic rates, had the consequence of making one resigned and verbose. He couldn't smuggle style into a dictionary, but he could at least reflect that he had done his best to learn from the drama that it is a gross impertinence almost anywhere. He had knocked at the door of every theatre in London, and, at a ruinous expense, had multiplied type-copies of *Nona Vincent* to replace the neat transcripts that had descended into the managerial abyss. His play was not even declined—no such flattering intimation was given him that it had been read. What the managers would do for Mrs Alsager concerned him little today; the thing that was relevant was that they would do nothing for *him*. That charming woman felt humbled to the earth, so little response had she had from the powers on which she counted. The two never talked about the play now, but he tried to show her a still finer friendship, that she might not think he felt she had failed him. He still walked about London with his dreams, but as months succeeded months and he left the year behind him they were dreams not so much of success as of revenge. Success seemed a colourless name for the reward of his patience; something fiercely florid, something sanguinolent was more to the point. His best consolation however was still in the scenic idea; it was not till now that he discovered how incurably he was in love with it. By the time a vain second year had chafed itself away he cherished his fruitless faculty the more for the obloquy it seemed to suffer. He lived, in his best hours, in a world of subjects and situations; he wrote another play and made it as different from its predecessor as such a very good thing could be. It might be a very good thing, but when he had committed it to the theatrical limbo indiscriminating fate took no account of the difference. He was at last able to leave England for three or four months; he went to Germany to pay a visit long deferred to his mother and sisters.

Shortly before the time he had fixed for his return he received from Mrs Alsager a telegram consisting of the words: "Loder wishes see you—putting *Nona* instant rehearsal." He spent the few hours before his departure in kissing his mother and sisters, who knew enough about Mrs Alsager to judge it lucky this respectable married lady was not there—a relief, however, accompanied with speculative glances at London and the morrow. Loder, as our young man was aware, meant the new "Renaissance," but though he reached home in the evening it was not to this convenient modern theatre that Wayworth first proceeded. He spent a late hour with Mrs Alsager, an hour that throbbed with calculation. She told him that Mr Loder was charming, he had simply taken up the play in its turn; he had hopes of it, moreover, that on the part of a professional pessimist might almost be qualified as ecstatic. It had been cast, with a margin for objections, and Violet Grey was to do the heroine. She had been capable, while he was away, of a good piece of work at that foggy old playhouse the "Legitimate;" the piece was a clumsy *réchauffé*, but she at least had been fresh. Wayworth remembered Violet Grey—hadn't he, for two years, on a fond policy of "looking out," kept dipping into the London theatres to pick up prospective interpreters? He had not picked up many as yet, and this young lady at all events had never wriggled in his net. She was pretty and she was odd, but he had never prefigured her as Nona Vincent, nor indeed found himself attracted by what he already felt sufficiently launched in the profession to speak

of as her artistic personality. Mrs Alsager was different—she
declared that she had been struck not a little by some of her
tones. The girl was interesting in the thing at the "Legitimate," and Mr Loder, who had his eye on her, described her
as ambitious and intelligent. She wanted awfully to get on—
and some of those ladies were so lazy! Wayworth was sceptical—he had seen Miss Violet Grey, who was terribly
itinerant, in a dozen theatres but only in one aspect. Nona
Vincent had a dozen aspects, but only one theatre; yet with
what a feverish curiosity the young man promised himself to
watch the actress on the morrow! Talking the matter over
with Mrs Alsager now seemed the very stuff that rehearsal was
made of. The near prospect of being acted laid a finger even
on the lip of inquiry; he wanted to go on tiptoe till the first
night, to make no condition but that they should speak his
lines, and he felt that he wouldn't so much as raise an eye-
brow at the scene-painter if he should give him an old oak
chamber.

He became conscious, the next day, that his danger would
be other than this, and yet he couldn't have expressed to himself what it would be. Danger was there, doubtless—danger
was everywhere, in the world of art, and still more in the
world of commerce; but what he really seemed to catch, for
the hour, was the beating of the wings of victory. Nothing
could undermine that, since it was victory simply to be acted.
It would be victory even to be acted badly; a reflection that
didn't prevent him, however, from banishing, in his politic
optimism, the word "bad" from his vocabulary. It had no
application, in the compromise of practice; it didn't apply
even to his play, which he was conscious he had already out-
lived and as to which he foresaw that, in the coming weeks,
frequent alarm would alternate, in his spirit, with frequent
esteem. When he went down to the dusky daylit theatre (it
arched over him like the temple of fame) Mr Loder, who was
as charming as Mrs Alsager had announced, struck him as the

genius of hospitality. The manager began to explain why, for so long, he had given no sign; but that was the last thing that interested Wayworth now, and he could never remember afterwards what reasons Mr Loder had enumerated. He liked, in the whole business of discussion and preparation, even the things he had thought he should probably dislike, and he revelled in those he had thought he should like. He watched Miss Violet Grey that evening with eyes that sought to penetrate her possibilities. She certainly had a few; they were qualities of voice and face, qualities perhaps even of intelligence; he sat there at any rate with a fostering, coaxing attention, repeating over to himself as convincingly as he could that she was not common—a circumstance all the more creditable as the part she was playing seemed to him desperately so. He perceived that this was why it pleased the audience; he divined that it was the part they enjoyed rather than the actress. He had a private panic, wondering how, if they liked *that* form, they could possibly like his. His form had now become quite an ultimate idea to him. By the time the evening was over some of Miss Violet Grey's features, several of the turns of her head, a certain vibration of her voice, had taken their place in the same category. She *was* interesting, she was distinguished; at any rate he had accepted her: it came to the same thing. But he left the theatre that night without speaking to her—moved (a little even to his own mystification) by an odd procrastinating impulse. On the morrow he was to read his three acts to the company, and then he should have a good deal to say; what he felt for the moment was a vague indisposition to commit himself. Moreover he found a slight confusion of annoyance in the fact that though he had been trying all the evening to look at Nona Vincent in Violet Grey's person, what subsisted in his vision was simply Violet Grey in Nona's. He didn't wish to see the actress so directly, or even so simply as that; and it had been very fatiguing, the effort to focus Nona both through the performer and through the "Legitimate." Before he went to bed that night he posted three words to Mrs Alsager—"She's not a bit like it, but I dare say I can make her do."

He was pleased with the way the actress listened, the next day, at the reading; he was pleased indeed with many things, at the reading, and most of all with the reading itself. The whole affair loomed large to him and he magnified it and mapped it out. He enjoyed his occupation of the big, dim, hollow theatre, full of the echoes of "effect" and of a queer smell of gas and success—it all seemed such a passive canvas for his picture. For the first time in his life he was in command of resources; he was acquainted with the phrase, but had never thought he should know the feeling. He was surprised at what Loder appeared ready to do, though he reminded himself that he must never show it. He foresaw that there would be two distinct concomitants to the artistic effort of producing a play, one consisting of a great deal of anguish and the other of a great deal of amusement. He looked back upon the reading, afterwards, as the best hour in the business, because it was then that the piece had most struck him as represented. What came later was the doing of others; but this, with its imperfections and failures, was all his own. The drama lived, at any rate, for that hour, with an intensity that it was promptly to lose in the poverty and patchiness of rehearsal; he could see its life reflected, in a way that was sweet to him, in the stillness of the little semi-circle of attentive and inscrutable, of water-proofed and muddy-booted, actors. Miss Violet Grey was the auditor he had most to say to, and he tried on the spot, across the shabby stage, to let her have the soul of her part. Her attitude was graceful, but though she appeared to listen with all her faculties her face remained perfectly blank; a fact, however, not discouraging to Wayworth, who liked her better for not being premature. Her companions gave discernible signs of recognising the passages of comedy; yet Wayworth forgave her even then for being inexpressive. She evidently wished before everything else to be simply sure of what it was all about.

He was more surprised even than at the revelation of the scale on which Mr Loder was ready to proceed by the discovery that some of the actors didn't like their parts, and his heart sank as he asked himself what he could possibly do with them if they were going to be so stupid. This was the first of his disappointments; somehow he had expected every individual to become instantly and gratefully conscious of a rare opportunity, and from the moment such a calculation failed he was at sea, or mindful at any rate that more disappointments would come. It was impossible to make out what the manager liked or disliked; no judgment, no comment escaped him; his acceptance of the play and his views about the way it should be mounted had apparently converted him into a veiled and shrouded figure. Wayworth was able to grasp the idea that they would all move now in a higher and sharper air than that of compliment and confidence. When he talked with Violet Grey after the reading he gathered that she was really rather crude: what better proof of it could there be than her failure to break out instantly with an expression of delight about her great chance? This reserve, however, had evidently nothing to do with high pretensions; she had no wish to make him feel that a person of her eminence was superior to easy raptures. He guessed, after a little, that she was puzzled and even somewhat frightened—to a certain extent she had not understood. Nothing could appeal to him more than the opportunity to clear up her difficulties, in the course of the examination of which he quickly discovered that, so far as she *had* understood, she had understood wrong. If she was crude it was only a reason the more for talking to her; he kept saying to her "Ask me—ask me: ask me everything you can think of."

She asked him, she was perpetually asking him, and at the first rehearsals, which were without form and void to a degree that made them strike him much more as the death of an experiment than as the dawn of a success, they threshed things out immensely in a corner of the stage, with the effect of his coming to feel that at any rate she was in earnest. He felt more and more that his heroine was the keystone of his arch, for which indeed the actress was very ready to take her. But when he reminded this young lady of the way the whole thing practically depended on her she was alarmed and even slightly scandalised: she spoke more than once as if that could scarcely be the right way to construct a play—make it stand or fall by one poor nervous girl. She was almost morbidly conscientious, and in theory he liked her for this, though he lost patience three or four times with the things she couldn't do and the things she could. At such times the tears came to her eyes; but they were produced by her own stupidity, she hastened to assure him, not by the way he spoke, which was awfully kind under the circumstances. Her sincerity made her beautiful, and he wished to heaven (and made a point of telling her so) that she could sprinkle a little of it over Nona. Once, however, she was so touched and troubled that the sight of it brought the tears for an instant to his own eyes; and it so happened that, turning at this moment, he found himself face to face with Mr Loder. The manager stared, glanced at the actress, who turned in the other direction, and then smiling at Wayworth, exclaimed, with the humour of a man who heard the gallery laugh every night:

"I say—I say!"

"What's the matter?" Wayworth asked.

"I'm glad to see Miss Grey is taking such pains with you."

"Oh, yes—she'll turn me out!" said the young man, gaily. He was quite aware that it was apparent he was not superficial about Nona, and abundantly determined, into the bargain, that the rehearsal of the piece should not sacrifice a shade of thoroughness to any extrinsic consideration.

Mrs Alsager, whom, late in the afternoon, he used often to

go and ask for a cup of tea, thanking her in advance for the
rest she gave him and telling her how he found that rehearsal
(as *they* were doing it—it was a caution!) took it out of one—
Mrs Alsager, more and more his good genius and, as he repeatedly assured her, his ministering angel, confirmed him in
this superior policy and urged him on to every form of artistic
devotion. She had, naturally, never been more interested than
now in his work; she wanted to hear everything about everything. She treated him as heroically fatigued, plied him with
luxurious restoratives, made him stretch himself on cushions
and rose-leaves. They gossipped more than ever, by her fire,
about the artistic life; he confided to her, for instance, all his
hopes and fears, all his experiments and anxieties, on the subject of the representative of Nona. She was immensely interested in this young lady and showed it by taking a box again
and again (she had seen her half-a-dozen times already), to
study her capacity through the veil of her present part. Like
Allan Wayworth she found her encouraging only by fits, for
she had fine flashes of badness. She was intelligent, but she
cried aloud for training, and the training was so absent that
the intelligence had only a fraction of its effect. She was like
a knife without an edge—good steel that had never been
sharpened; she hacked away at her hard dramatic loaf, she
couldn't cut it smooth.

II

"Certainly my leading lady won't make Nona much like
you!" Wayworth one day gloomily remarked to Mrs Alsager.
There were days when the prospect seemed to him awful.

"So much the better. There's no necessity for that."

"I wish you'd train her a little—you could so easily," the
young man went on; in response to which Mrs Alsager requested him not to make such cruel fun of her. But she was

curious about the girl, wanted to hear of her character, her private situation, how she lived and where, seemed indeed desirous to befriend her. Wayworth might not have known much about the private situation of Miss Violet Grey, but, as it happened, he was able, by the time his play had been three weeks in rehearsal, to supply information on such points. She was a charming, exemplary person, educated, cultivated, with highly modern tastes, an excellent musician. She had lost her parents and was very much alone in the world, her only two relations being a sister, who was married to a civil servant (in a highly responsible post) in India, and a dear little old-fashioned aunt (really a great-aunt) with whom she lived at Notting Hill, who wrote children's books and who, it appeared, had once written a Christmas pantomime. It was quite an artistic home—not on the scale of Mrs Alsager's (to compare the smallest things with the greatest!) but intensely refined and honourable. Wayworth went so far as to hint that it would be rather nice and human on Mrs Alsager's part to go there—they would take it so kindly if she should call on them. She had acted so often on his hints that he had formed a pleasant habit of expecting it: it made him feel so wisely responsible about giving them. But this one appeared to fall to the ground, so that he let the subject drop. Mrs Alsager, however, went yet once more to the "Legitimate," as he found by her saying to him abruptly, on the morrow: "Oh, she'll be very good—she'll be very good." When they said "she," in these days, they always meant Violet Grey, though they pretended, for the most part, that they meant Nona Vincent.

"Oh yes," Wayworth assented, "she wants so to!"

Mrs Alsager was silent a moment; then she asked, a little inconsequently, as if she had come back from a reverie: "Does she want to *very* much?"

"Tremendously—and it appears she has been fascinated by the part from the first."

"Why then didn't she say so?"

"Oh, because she's so funny."

"She *is* funny," said Mrs Alsager, musingly; and presently she added: "She's in love with you."

Wayworth stared, blushed very red, then laughed out. "What is there funny in that?" he demanded; but before his interlocutress could satisfy him on this point he inquired, further, how she knew anything about it. After a little graceful evasion she explained that the night before, at the "Legitimate," Mrs Beaumont, the wife of the actor-manager, had paid her a visit in her box; which had happened, in the course of their brief gossip, to lead to her remarking that she had never been "behind." Mrs Beaumont offered on the spot to take her round, and the fancy had seized her to accept the invitation. She had been amused for the moment, and in this way it befell that her conductress, at her request, had introduced her to Miss Violet Grey, who was waiting in the wing for one of her scenes. Mrs Beaumont had been called away for three minutes, and during this scrap of time, face to face with the actress, she had discovered the poor girl's secret. Wayworth qualified it as a senseless thing, but wished to know what had led to the discovery. She characterised this inquiry as superficial for a painter of the ways of women; and he doubtless didn't improve it by remarking profanely that a cat might look at a king and that such things were convenient to know. Even on this ground, however, he was threatened by Mrs Alsager, who contended that it might not be a joking matter to the poor girl. To this Wayworth, who now professed to hate talking about the passions he might have inspired, could only reply that he meant it couldn't make a difference to Mrs Alsager.

"How in the world do you know what makes a difference to *me?*" this lady asked, with incongruous coldness, with a haughtiness indeed remarkable in so gentle a spirit.

He saw Violet Grey that night at the theatre, and it was

she who spoke first of her having lately met a friend of his.

"She's in love with you," the actress said, after he had made a show of ignorance; "doesn't that tell you anything?"

He blushed redder still than Mrs Alsager had made him blush, but replied, quickly enough and very adequately, that hundreds of women were naturally dying for him.

"Oh, I don't care, for you're not in love with *her!*" the girl continued.

"Did she tell you that too?" Wayworth asked; but she had at that moment to go on.

Standing where he could see her he thought that on this occasion she threw into her scene, which was the best she had in the play, a brighter art than ever before, a talent that could play with its problem. She was perpetually doing things out of rehearsal (she did two or three to-night, in the other man's piece), that he as often wished to heaven Nona Vincent might have the benefit of. She appeared to be able to do them for every one but him—that is for every one but Nona. He was conscious, in these days, of an odd new feeling, which mixed (this was a part of its oddity) with a very natural and comparatively old one and which in its most definite form was a dull ache of regret that this young lady's unlucky star should have placed her on the stage. He wished in his worst uneasiness that, without going further, she would give it up; and yet it soothed that uneasiness to remind himself that he saw grounds to hope she would go far enough to make a marked success of Nona. There were strange and painful moments when, as the interpretress of Nona, he almost hated her; after which, however, he always assured himself that he exaggerated, inasmuch as what made this aversion seem great, when he was nervous, was simply its contrast with the growing sense that there *were* grounds—totally different—on which she pleased him. She pleased him as a charming creature—by her sincerities and her perversities, by the varieties and surprises of her character and by certain happy facts of her person. In private her eyes were sad to him and her voice was rare. He detested the idea that she should have a disappointment or an humiliation, and he wanted to rescue her altogether, to save and transplant her. One way to save her was to see to it, to the best of his ability, that the production of his play should be a triumph; and the other way—it was really too queer to express—was almost to wish that it shouldn't be. Then, for the future, there would be safety and peace, and not the peace of death—the peace of a different life. It is to be added that our young man clung to the former of these ways in proportion as the latter perversely tempted him. He was nervous at the best, increasingly and intolerably nervous; but the immediate remedy was to rehearse harder and harder, and above all to work it out with Violet Grey. Some of her comrades reproached him with working it out only with her, as if she were the whole affair; to which he replied that they could afford to be neglected, they were all so tremendously good. She was the only person concerned whom he didn't flatter.

The author and the actress stuck so to the business in hand that she had very little time to speak to him again of Mrs Alsager, of whom indeed her imagination appeared adequately to have disposed. Wayworth once remarked to her that Nona Vincent was supposed to be a good deal like his charming friend; but she gave a blank "Supposed by whom?" in consequence of which he never returned to the subject. He confided his nervousness as freely as usual to Mrs Alsager, who easily understood that he had a peculiar complication of anxieties. His suspense varied in degree from hour to hour, but any relief there might have been in this was made up for by its being of several different kinds. One afternoon, as the first performance drew near, Mrs Alsager said to him, in giving him his cup of tea and on his having mentioned that he had not closed his eyes the night before:

"You must indeed be in a dreadful state. Anxiety for another is still worse than anxiety for one's self."

"For another?" Wayworth repeated, looking at her over the rim of his cup.

"My poor friend, you're nervous about Nona Vincent, but you're infinitely more nervous about Violet Grey."

"She *is* Nona Vincent!"

"No, she isn't—not a bit!" said Mrs Alsager, abruptly.

"Do you really think so?" Wayworth cried, spilling his tea in his alarm.

"What I think doesn't signify—I mean what I think about that. What I meant to say was that great as is your suspense about your play, your suspense about your actress is greater still."

"I can only repeat that my actress *is* my play."

Mrs Alsager looked thoughtfully into the teapot.

"Your actress is your—"

"My what?" the young man asked, with a little tremor in his voice, as his hostess paused.

"Your very dear friend. You're in love with her—at present." And with a sharp click Mrs Alsager dropped the lid on the fragrant receptacle.

"Not yet—not yet!" laughed her visitor.

"You will be if she pulls you through."

"You declare that she *won't* pull me through."

Mrs Alsager was silent a moment, after which she softly murmured: "I'll pray for her."

"You're the most generous of women!" Wayworth cried; then coloured as if the words had not been happy. They would have done indeed little honour to a man of tact.

The next morning he received five hurried lines from Mrs Alsager. She had suddenly been called to Torquay, to see a relation who was seriously ill; she should be detained there several days, but she had an earnest hope of being able to return in time for his first night. In any event he had her unrestricted good wishes. He missed her extremely, for these last days were a great strain and there was little comfort to be derived from Violet Grey. She was even more nervous than himself, and so pale and altered that he was afraid she would be too ill to act. It was settled between them that they made each other worse and that he had now much better leave her alone. They had pulled Nona so to pieecs that nothing seemed left of her—she must at least have time to grow together again. He left Violet Grey alone, to the best of his ability, but she carried out imperfectly her own side of the bargain. She came to him with new questions—she waited for him with old doubts, and half an hour before the last dress-rehearsal, on the eve of production, she proposed to him a totally fresh rendering of his heroine. This incident gave him such a sense of insecurity that he turned his back on her without a word, bolted out of the theatre, dashed along the Strand and walked as far as the Bank. Then he jumped into a hansom and came westward, and when he reached the theatre again the business was nearly over. It appeared, almost to his disappointment, not bad enough to give him the consolation of the old playhouse adage that the worst dress-rehearsals make the best first nights.

The morrow, which was a Wednesday, was the dreadful day; the theatre had been closed on the Monday and the Tuesday. Every one, on the Wednesday, did his best to let every one else alone, and every one signally failed in the attempt. The day, till seven o'clock, was understood to be consecrated to rest, but every one except Violet Grey turned up at the theatre. Wayworth looked at Mr Loder, and Mr Loder looked in another direction, which was as near as they came to conversation. Wayworth was in a fidget, unable to eat or sleep or sit still, at times almost in terror. He kept quiet by keeping, as usual, in motion; he tried to walk away from his nervousness. He walked in the afternoon toward Notting Hill, but he succeeded in not breaking the vow he had taken not to meddle with his actress. She was like an acrobat poised on a slippery ball—if he should touch her she would topple over. He passed her door three times and he thought of her three hundred. This was the hour at which he most regretted that Mrs Alsager had not come back—for he had called at her house only to learn that she was still at Torquay. This was probably queer, and it was probably queerer still that she hadn't written to him; but even of these things he wasn't sure, for in losing, as he had now completely lost, his judgment of his play, he seemed to himself to have lost his judgment of everything. When he went home, however, he found a telegram from the lady of Grosvenor Place—"Shall be able to come—reach town by seven." At half-past eight o'clock, through a little aperture in the curtain of the "Renaissance," he saw her in her box with a cluster of friends—completely beautiful and beneficent. The house was magnificent—too good for his play, he felt; too good for any play. Everything now seemed too good—the scenery, the furniture, the dresses, the very programmes. He seized upon the idea that this was probably what was the matter with the representative of Nona—she was only too good. He had completely arranged with this young lady the plan of their relations during the evening; and though they had altered everything else that they had arranged they had promised each other not to alter this. It was wonderful the number of things they had promised each other. He would start her, he would see her off—then he would quit the theatre and stay away till just before the end. She besought him to stay away—it would make her infinitely easier. He saw that she was exquisitely dressed—she had made one or two changes for the better since the night before, and that seemed something definite to turn over and over in his mind as he rumbled foggily home in the four-wheeler in which, a few steps from the stage-door, he had taken refuge as soon as he knew that the curtain was up. He lived a couple of miles off, and he had chosen a four-wheeler to drag out the time.

When he got home his fire was out, his room was cold, and he lay down on his sofa in his overcoat. He had sent his landlady to the dress-circle, on purpose; she would overflow with words and mistakes. The house seemed a black void, just as the streets had done—every one was, formidably, at his play. He was quieter at last than he had been for a fortnight, and he felt too weak even to wonder how the thing was going. He believed afterwards that he had slept an hour; but even if he had he felt it to be still too early to return to the theatre. He sat down by his lamp and tried to read—to read a little compendious life of a great English statesman, out of a "series." It struck him as brilliantly clever, and he asked himself whether that perhaps were not rather the sort of thing he ought to have taken up; not the statesmanship, but the art of brief biography. Suddenly he became aware that he must hurry if he was to reach the theatre at all—it was a quarter to eleven o'clock. He scrambled out and, this time, found a hansom—he had lately spent enough money in cabs to add to his hope that the profits of his new profession would be great. His anxiety, his suspense flamed up again, and as he rattled eastward—he went fast now—he was almost sick with alternations. As he passed into the theatre the first man—some underling—who met him, cried to him, breathlessly: "You're wanted, sir—you're wanted!" He thought his tone very ominous—he devoured the man's eyes with his own, for a betrayal: did he mean that he was wanted for execution? Some one else pressed him, almost pushed him, forward; he was already on the stage. Then he became conscious of a sound more or less continuous, but seemingly faint and far, which he took at first for the voice of the actors heard through their canvas walls, the beautiful built-in room of the last act. But the actors were in the wing, they surrounded him; the curtain was down and they were coming off from before it. They had been called, and *he* was called—they all greeted him with "Go on—go on!" He was terrified—he couldn't go on—he didn't

believe in the applause, which seemed to him only audible
enough to sound half-hearted.

"Has it gone?—*has* it gone?" he gasped to the people
round him; and he heard them say "Rather—rather!" per-
functorily, mendaciously too, as it struck him, and even with
mocking laughter, the laughter of defeat and despair. Suddenly, though all this must have taken but a moment, Loder
burst upon him from somewhere with a "For God's sake
don't keep them, or they'll *stop!*" "But I can't go on for
that!" Wayworth cried, in anguish; the sound seemed to him
already to have ceased. Loder had hold of him and was
shoving him; he resisted and looked round frantically for
Violet Grey, who perhaps would tell him the truth. There was
by this time a crowd in the wing, all with strange grimacing
painted faces, but Violet was not among them and her very
absence frightened him. He uttered her name with an accent
that he afterwards regretted—it gave them, as he thought,
both away; and while Loder hustled him before the curtain he
heard some one say "She took her call and disappeared." She
had had a call, then—this was what was most present to the
young man as he stood for an instant in the glare of the footlights, looking blindly at the great vaguely-peopled horse-
shoe and greeted with plaudits which now seemed to him at
once louder than he deserved and feebler than he desired. They
sank to rest quickly, but he felt it to be long before he could
back away, before he could, in his turn, seize the manager by
the arm and cry huskily—"Has it really gone—*really?*"

Mr Loder looked at him hard and replied after an instant:
"The play's all right!"

Wayworth hung upon his lips. "Then what's all wrong?"

"We must do something to Miss Grey."

"What's the matter with her?"

"She isn't *in* it!"

"Do you mean she has failed?"

"Yes, damn it—she has failed."

Wayworth stared. "Then how can the play be all right?"

"Oh, we'll save it—we'll save it."

"Where's Miss Grey—where *is* she?" the young man asked.

Loder caught his arm as he was turning away again to look for his heroine. "Never mind her now—she knows it!"

Wayworth was approached at the same moment by a gentleman he knew as one of Mrs Alsager's friends—he had perceived him in that lady's box. Mrs Alsager was waiting there for the successful author; she desired very earnestly that he would come round and speak to her. Wayworth assured himself first that Violet had left the theatre—one of the actresses could tell him that she had seen her throw on a cloak, without changing her dress, and had learnt afterwards that she had, the next moment, flung herself, after flinging her aunt, into a cab. He had wished to invite half a dozen persons, of whom Miss Grey and her elderly relative were two, to come home to supper with him; but she had refused to make any engagement beforehand (it would be so dreadful to have to keep it if she shouldn't have made a hit), and this attitude had blighted the pleasant plan, which fell to the ground. He had called her morbid, but she was immovable. Mrs Alsager's messenger let him know that he was expected to supper in Grosvenor Place, and half an hour afterwards he was seated there among complimentary people and flowers and popping corks, eating the first orderly meal he had partaken of for a week. Mrs Alsager had carried him off in her brougham—the other people who were coming got into things of their own. He stopped her short as soon as she began to tell him how tremendously every one had been struck by the piece; he nailed her down to the question of Violet Grey. Had she spoilt the play, had she jeopardised or compromised it—had she been utterly bad, had she been good in any degree?

"Certainly the performance would have seemed better if *she* had been better," Mrs Alsager confessed.

"And the play would have seemed better if the performance had been better," Wayworth said, gloomily, from the corner of the brougham.

"She does what she can, and she has talent, and she looked lovely. But she doesn't *see* Nona Vincent. She doesn't see the type—she doesn't see the individual—she doesn't see the woman you meant. She's out of it—she gives you a different person."

"Oh, the woman I meant!" the young man exclaimed, looking at the London lamps as he rolled by them. "I wish to God she had known *you!*" he added, as the carriage stopped. After they had passed into the house he said to his companion: "You see she *won't* pull me through."

"Forgive her—be kind to her!" Mrs Alsager pleaded.

"I shall only thank her. The play may go to the dogs."

"If it does—if it does," Mrs Alsager began, with her pure eyes on him.

"Well, what if it does?"

She couldn't tell him, for the rest of her guests came in together; she only had time to say: "It *sha'n't* go to the dogs!"

He came away before the others, restless with the desire to go to Notting Hill even that night, late as it was, haunted with the sense that Violet Grey had measured her fall. When he got into the street, however, he allowed second thoughts to counsel another course; the effect of knocking her up at two o'clock in the morning would hardly be to soothe her. He looked at six newspapers the next day and found in them never a good word for her. They were well enough about the piece, but they were unanimous as to the disappointment caused by the young actress whose former efforts had excited such hopes and on whom, on this occasion, such pressing responsibilities rested. They asked in chorus what was the matter with her, and they declared in chorus that the play, which was not without promise, was handicapped (they all used the same word) by the odd want of correspondence between the heroine and her interpreter. Wayworth drove early to Notting Hill, but he didn't take the newspapers with him; Violet Grey could be trusted to have sent out for them by the peep of dawn and to have fed her anguish full. She declined to see him—she only sent down word by her aunt that she was extremely unwell and should be unable to act that night unless she were suffered to spend the day unmolested and in bed. Wayworth sat for an hour with the old lady, who understood everything and to whom he could speak frankly. She gave him a touching picture of her niece's condition, which was all the more vivid for the simple words in which it was expressed: "She feels she isn't right, you know—she feels she isn't right!"

"Tell her it doesn't matter—it doesn't matter a straw!" said Wayworth.

"And she's so proud—you know how proud she is!" the old lady went on.

"Tell her I'm more than satisfied, that I accept her gratefully as she is."

"She says she injures your play, that she ruins it," said his interlocutress.

"She'll improve, immensely—she'll grow into the part," the young man continued.

"She'd improve if she knew how—but she says she doesn't. She has given all she has got, and she doesn't know what's wanted."

"What's wanted is simply that she should go straight on and trust me."

"How can she trust you when she feels she's losing you?"

"Losing me?" Wayworth cried.

"You'll never forgive her if your play is taken off!"

"It will run six months," said the author of the piece.

The old lady laid her hand on his arm. "What will you do for her if it does?"

He looked at Violet Grey's aunt a moment. "Do you say your niece is very proud?"

"Too proud for her dreadful profession."

"Then she wouldn't wish you to ask me that," Wayworth answered, getting up.

When he reached home he was very tired, and for a person to whom it was open to consider that he had scored a success he spent a remarkably dismal day. All his restlessness had gone, and fatigue and depression possessed him. He sank into his old chair by the fire and sat there for hours with his eyes closed. His landlady came in to bring his luncheon and mend the fire, but he feigned to be asleep, so as not to be spoken to. It is to be supposed that sleep at last overtook him, for about the hour that dusk began to gather he had an extraordinary impression, a visit that, it would seem, could have belonged to no waking consciousness. Nona Vincent, in face and form, the living heroine of his play, rose before him in his little silent room, sat down with him at his dingy fireside. She was not Violet Grey, she was not Mrs Alsager, she was not any woman he had seen upon earth, nor was it any masquerade of friendship or of penitence. Yet she was more familiar to him than the women he had known best, and she was in-effably beautiful and consoling. She filled the poor room with her presence, the effect of which was as soothing as some odour of incense. She was as quiet as an affectionate sister, and there was no surprise in her being there. Nothing more real had ever befallen him, and nothing, somehow, more reassur-ing. He felt her hand rest upon his own, and all his senses seemed to open to her message. She struck him, in the stran-gest way, both as his creation and as his inspirer, and she gave him the happiest consciousness of success. If she was so charming, in the red firelight, in her vague, clear-coloured garments, it was because he had made her so, and yet if the weight seemed lifted from his spirit it was because she drew it away. When she bent her deep eyes upon him they seemed to speak of safety and freedom and to make a green garden of the future. From time to time she smiled and said: "I live—I live —I live." How long she stayed he couldn't have told, but when his landlady blundered in with the lamp Nona Vincent was no longer there. He rubbed his eyes, but no dream had ever been so intense; and as he slowly got out of his chair it was with a deep still joy—the joy of the artist—in the thought of how right he had been, how exactly like herself he had made her. She had come to show him that. At the end of five minutes, however, he felt sufficiently mystified to call his landlady back—he wanted to ask her a question. When the good woman reappeared the question hung fire an instant; then it shaped itself as the inquiry: "Has any lady been here?"

"No, sir—no lady at all."

The woman seemed slightly scandalised.

"Not Miss Vincent?"

"Miss Vincent, sir?"

"The young lady of my play, don't you know?"

"Oh, sir, you mean Miss Violet Grey!"

"No I don't, at all. I think I mean Mrs Alsager."

"There has been no Mrs Alsager, sir."

"Nor anybody at all like her?"

The woman looked at him as if she wondered what had suddenly taken him. Then she asked in an injured tone: "Why shouldn't I have told you if you'd 'ad callers, sir?"

"I thought you might have thought I was asleep."

"Indeed you were, sir, when I came in with the lamp—and well you'd earned it, Mr Wayworth!"

The landlady came back an hour later to bring him a telegram; it was just as he had begun to dress to dine at his club and go down to the theatre.

"See me to-night in front, and don't come near me till it's over."

It was in these words that Violet communicated her wishes

for the evening. He obeyed them to the letter; he watched
her from the depths of a box. He was in no position to say
how she might have struck him the night before, but what he
saw during these charmed hours filled him with admiration
and gratitude. She *was* in it, this time; she had pulled herself
together, she had taken possession, she was felicitous at every
turn. Fresh from his revelation of Nona he was in a position
to judge, and as he judged he exulted. He was thrilled and
carried away, and he was moreover intensely curious to know
what had happened to her, by what unfathomable art she had
managed in a few hours to effect such a change of base. It was
as if *she* had had a revelation of Nona, so convincing a clearness had been breathed upon the picture. He kept himself
quiet in the *entr'actes*—he would speak to her only at the end;
but before the play was half over the manager burst into his box.

"It's prodigious, what she's up to!" cried Mr Loder,
almost more bewildered than gratified. "She has gone in for
a new reading—a blessed somersault in the air!"

"Is it quite different?" Wayworth asked, sharing his mystification.

"Different? Hyperion to a satyr! It's devilish good, my
boy!"

"It's devilish good," said Wayworth, "and it's in a different key altogether from the key of her rehearsal."

"I'll run you six months!" the manager declared; and he
rushed round again to the actress, leaving Wayworth with a
sense that she had already pulled him through. She had with
the audience an immense personal success.

When he went behind, at the end, he had to wait for her;
she only showed herself when she was ready to leave the
theatre. Her aunt had been in her dressing-room with her, and
the two ladies appeared together. The girl passed him quickly,
motioning him to say nothing till they should have got out of
the place. He saw that she was immensely excited, lifted altogether above her common artistic level. The old lady said to

him: "You must come home to supper with us: it has been all arranged." They had a brougham, with a little third seat, and he got into it with them. It was a long time before the actress would speak. She leaned back in her corner, giving no sign but still heaving a little, like a subsiding sea, and with all her triumph in the eyes that shone through the darkness. The old lady was hushed to awe, or at least to discretion, and Wayworth was happy enough to wait. He had really to wait till they had alighted at Notting Hill, where the elder of his companions went to see that supper had been attended to.

"I was better—I was better," said Violet Grey, throwing off her cloak in the little drawing-room.

"You were perfection. You'll be like that every night, won't you?"

She smiled at him. "Every night? There can scarcely be a miracle every day."

"What do you mean by a miracle?"

"I've had a revelation."

Wayworth stared. "At what hour?"

"The right hour—this afternoon. Just in time to save me—and to save *you*."

"At five o'clock? Do you mean you had a visit?"

"She came to me—she stayed two hours."

"Two hours? Nona Vincent?"

"Mrs Alsager." Violet Grey smiled more deeply. "It's the same thing."

"And how did Mrs Alsager save you?"

"By letting me look at her. By letting me hear her speak. By letting me know her."

"And what did she say to you?"

"Kind things—encouraging, intelligent things."

"Ah, the dear woman!" Wayworth cried.

"You ought to like her—she likes *you*. She was just what I wanted," the actress added.

"Do you mean she talked to you about Nona?"

"She said you thought she was like her. She *is*—she's exquisite."

"She's exquisite," Wayworth repeated. "Do you mean she tried to coach you?"

"Oh, no—she only said she would be so glad if it would help me to see her. And I felt it did help me. I don't know what took place—she only sat there, and she held my hand and smiled at me, and she had tact and grace, and she had goodness and beauty, and she soothed my nerves and lighted up my imagination. Somehow she seemed to *give* it all to me. I took it—I took it. I kept her before me, I drank her in. For the first time, in the whole study of the part, I had my model—I could make my copy. All my courage came back to me, and other things came that I hadn't felt before. She was different—she was delightful; as I've said, she was a revelation. She kissed me when she went away—and you may guess if I kissed *her*. We were awfully affectionate, but it's *you* she likes!" said Violet Grey.

Wayworth had never been more interested in his life, and he had rarely been more mystified. "Did she wear vague, clear-coloured garments?" he asked, after a moment.

Violet Grey stared, laughed, then bade him go in to supper. "*You* know how she dresses!"

He was very well pleased at supper, but he was silent and a little solemn. He said he would go to see Mrs Alsager the next day. He did so, but he was told at her door that she had returned to Torquay. She remained there all winter, all spring, and the next time he saw her his play had run two hundred nights and he had married Violet Grey. His plays sometimes succeed, but his wife is not in them now, nor in any others. At these representations Mrs Alsager continues frequently to be present.

THE PRIVATE LIFE

WE talked of London, face to face with a great bristling, primeval glacier. The hour and the scene were one of those impressions which make up a little, in Switzerland, for the modern indignity of travel—the promiscuities and vulgarities, the station and the hotel, the gregarious patience, the struggle for a scrappy attention, the reduction to a numbered state. The high valley was pink with the mountain rose, the cool air as fresh as if the world were young. There was a faint flush of afternoon on undiminished snows, and the fraternizing tinkle of the unseen cattle came to us with a cropped and sun-warmed odour. The balconied inn stood on the very neck of the sweetest pass in the Oberland, and for a week we had had company and weather. This was felt to be great luck, for one would have made up for the other had either been bad.

The weather certainly would have made up for the company; but it was not subjected to this tax, for we had by a happy chance the *fleur des pois:* Lord and Lady Mellifont, Clare Vawdrey, the greatest (in the opinion of many) of our literary glories, and Blanche Adney, the greatest (in the opinion of all) of our theatrical. I mention these first, because they were just the people whom in London, at that time, people tried to "get." People endeavoured to "book" them six weeks ahead, yet on this occasion we had come in for them, we had all come in for each other, without the least wire-pulling. A turn of the game had pitched us together, the last of August, and we recognized our luck by remaining so, under protection of the barometer. When the golden days were over —that would come soon enough—we should wind down opposite sides of the pass and disappear over the crest of surrounding heights. We were of the same general communion, we participated in the same miscellaneous publicity. We met, in London, with irregular frequency; we were more or less governed by the laws and the language, the traditions and the shibboleths of the same dense social state. I think all of us, even the ladies, "did" something, though we pretended we didn't when it was mentioned. Such things are not mentioned indeed in London, but it was our innocent pleasure to be different here. There had to be some way to show the difference, inasmuch as we were under the impression that this was our annual holiday. We felt at any rate that the conditions were more human than in London, or that at least we ourselves were. We were frank about this, we talked about it: it was what we were talking about as we looked at the flushing glacier, just as some one called attention to the prolonged absence of Lord Mellifont and Mrs Adney. We were seated on the terrace of the inn, where there were benches and little tables, and those of us who were most bent on proving that we had returned to nature were, in the queer Germanic fashion, having coffee before meat.

The remark about the absence of our two companions was not taken up, not even by Lady Mellifont, not even by little Adney, the fond composer; for it had been dropped only in the briefest intermission of Clare Vawdrey's talk. (This celebrity was "Clarence" only on the title-page.) It was just that revelation of our being after all human that was his theme. He asked the company whether, candidly, every one hadn't been tempted to say to every one else: "I had no idea you were really so nice." I had had, for my part, an idea that *he* was, and even a good deal nicer, but that was too complicated to go into then; besides it is exactly my story. There was a general understanding among us that when Vawdrey talked we should be silent, and not, oddly enough, because he at all expected it. He didn't, for of all abundant talkers he was the most unconscious, the least greedy and professional. It was rather the religion of the host, of the hostess, that prevailed among us: it was their own idea, but they always looked for a listening circle when the great novelist dined with them. On the occasion I allude to there was probably no one present with whom, in London, he had not dined, and we felt the force of this habit. He had dined even with me; and on the evening of that dinner, as on this Alpine afternoon, I had been at no pains to hold my tongue, absorbed as I inveterately was in a study of the question which always rose before me, to such a height, in his fair, square, strong stature.

This question was all the more tormenting that he never suspected himself (I am sure) of imposing it, any more than he had ever observed that every day of his life every one listened to him at dinner. He used to be called "subjective" in the weekly papers, but in society no distinguished man could have been less so. He never talked about himself; and this was a topic on which, though it would have been tremendously worthy of him, he apparently never even reflected. He had his hours and his habits, his tailor and his hatter, his hygiene and his particular wine, but all these things together never made up an attitude. Yet they constituted the only attitude he ever adopted, and it was easy for him to refer to our being "nicer" abroad than at home. *He* was exempt from variations, and not a shade either less or more nice in one place than in another. He differed from other people, but never from himself (save in the extraordinary sense which I will presently explain), and struck me as having neither moods nor sensibilities nor preferences. He might have been always in the same company, so far as he recognized any influence from age or condition or sex: he addressed himself to women exactly as he addressed himself to men, and gossiped with all men alike, talking no better to clever folk than to dull. I used to feel a despair at his way of liking one subject—so far as I could tell—precisely as much as another: there were some I hated so myself. I never found him anything but loud and cheerful and copious, and I never heard him utter a paradox or express a shade or play with an idea. That fancy about our being "human" was, in his conversation, quite an exceptional flight. His opinions were sound and second-rate, and of his perceptions it was too mystifying to think. I envied him his magnificent health.

Vawdrey had marched, with his even pace and his perfectly good conscience, into the flat country of anecdote, where stories are visible from afar like windmills and signposts; but I observed after a little that Lady Mellifont's attention wandered. I happened to be sitting next her. I noticed that her eyes rambled a little anxiously over the lower slopes of the mountains. At last, after looking at her watch, she said to me: "Do you know where they went?"

"Do you mean Mrs Adney and Lord Mellifont?"

"Lord Mellifont and Mrs Adney." Her ladyship's speech seemed—unconsciously indeed—to correct me, but it didn't occur to me that this was because she was jealous. I imputed to her no such vulgar sentiment: in the first place, because I liked her, and in the second because it would always occur to one quickly that it was right, in any connection, to put Lord Mellifont first. He *was* first—extraordinarily first. I don't say greatest or wisest or most renowned, but essentially at the top of the list and the head of the table. That is a position by itself, and his wife was naturally accustomed to see him in it. My phrase had sounded as if Mrs Adney had taken him; but it was not possible for him to be taken—he only took. No one, in the nature of things, could know this better than Lady Mellifont. I had originally been rather afraid of her, thinking her, with her stiff silences and the extreme blackness of almost everything that made up her person, somewhat hard, even a little saturnine. Her paleness seemed slightly grey, and her glossy black hair metallic, like the brooches and bands and combs with which it was inveterately adorned. She was in perpetual mourning, and wore numberless ornaments of jet and onyx, a thousand clicking chains and bugles and beads. I had heard Mrs Adney call her the queen of night, and the term was descriptive if you understood that the night was cloudy. She had a secret, and if you didn't find it out as you knew her better you at least perceived that she was gentle and unaffected and limited, and also rather submissively sad. She was like a woman with a painless malady. I told her that I had merely seen her husband and his companion stroll down the glen together about an hour before, and suggested that Mr Adney would perhaps know something of their intentions.

Vincent Adney, who, though he was fifty years old, looked like a good little boy on whom it had been impressed that children should not talk before company, acquitted himself with remarkable simplicity and taste of the position of husband of a great exponent of comedy. When all was said about her making it easy for him, one couldn't help admiring the charmed affection with which he took everything for granted. It is difficult for a husband who is not on the stage, or at least in the theatre, to be graceful about a wife who is; but Adney was more than graceful—he was exquisite, he was inspired. He set his beloved to music; and you remember how genuine his music could be—the only English compositions I ever saw a foreigner take an interest in. His wife was in them, somewhere, always; they were like a free, rich translation of the impression she produced. She seemed, as one listened, to pass laughing, with loosened hair, across the scene. He had been only a little fiddler at her theatre, always in his place during the acts; but she had made him something rare and misunderstood. Their superiority had become a kind of partnership, and their happiness was a part of the happiness of their friends. Adney's one discomfort was that he couldn't write a play for his wife, and the only way he meddled with her affairs was by asking impossible people if *they* couldn't.

Lady Mellifont, after looking across at him a moment, remarked to me that she would rather not put any question to him. She added the next minute: "I had rather people shouldn't see I'm nervous."

"*Are* you nervous?"

"I always become so if my husband is away from me for any time."

"Do you imagine something has happened to him?"

"Yes, always. Of course I'm used to it."

"Do you mean his tumbling over precipices—that sort of thing?"

"I don't know exactly what it is: it's the general sense that he'll never come back."

She said so much and kept back so much that the only way to treat the condition she referred to seemed the jocular. "Surely he'll never forsake you!" I laughed.

She looked at the ground a moment. "Oh, at bottom I'm easy."

"Nothing can ever happen to a man so accomplished, so infallible, so armed at all points," I went on, encouragingly.

"Oh, you don't know how he's armed!" she exclaimed, with such an odd quaver that I could account for it only by her being nervous. This idea was confirmed by her moving just afterwards, changing her seat rather pointlessly, not as if to cut our conversation short, but because she was in a fidget. I couldn't know what was the matter with her, but I was presently relieved to see Mrs Adney come toward us. She had in her hand a big bunch of wild flowers, but she was not closely attended by Lord Mellifont. I quickly saw, however, that she had no disaster to announce; yet as I knew there was a question Lady Mellifont would like to hear answered, but did not wish to ask, I expressed to her immediately the hope that his lordship had not remained in a crevasse.

"Oh, no; he left me but three minutes ago. He has gone into the house." Blanche Adney rested her eyes on mine an instant—a mode of intercourse to which no man, for himself, could ever object. The interest, on this occasion, was quickened by the particular thing the eyes happened to say. What they usually said was only: "Oh, yes, I'm charming, I know, but don't make a fuss about it. I only want a new part—I do, I do!" At present they added, dimly, surreptitiously, and of course sweetly—for that was the way they did everything: "It's all right, but something did happen. Perhaps I'll tell you later." She turned to Lady Mellifont, and the transition to simple gaiety suggested her mastery of her profession. "I've brought him safe. We had a charming walk."

"I'm so very glad," returned Lady Mellifont, with her faint smile; continuing vaguely, as she got up: "He must have gone to dress for dinner. Isn't it rather near?" She moved away, to the hotel, in her leave-taking, simplifying fashion, and the rest of us, at the mention of dinner, looked at each other's watches, as if to shift the responsibility of such grossness. The head-waiter, essentially, like all head-waiters, a man of the world, allowed us hours and places of our own, so that in the evening, apart under the lamp, we formed a compact, an indulged little circle. But it was only the Mellifonts who "dressed" and as to whom it was recognized that they naturally *would* dress: she in exactly the same manner as on any other evening of her ceremonious existence (she was not a woman whose habits could take account of anything so mutable as fitness); and he, on the other hand, with remarkable adjustment and suitability. He was almost as much a man of the world as the head-waiter, and spoke almost as many languages; but he abstained from courting a comparison of dress-coats and white waistcoats, analyzing the occasion in a much finer way—into black velvet and blue velvet and brown velvet, for instance, into delicate harmonies of necktie and subtle informalities of shirt. He had a costume for every function and a moral for every costume; and his functions and costumes and morals were ever a part of the amusement of life —a part at any rate of its beauty and romance—for an immense circle of spectators. For his particular friends indeed these things were more than an amusement; they were a topic, a social support and of course, in addition, a subject of perpetual suspense. If his wife had not been present before dinner they were what the rest of us probably would have been putting our heads together about.

Clare Vawdrey had a fund of anecdote on the whole question: he had known Lord Mellifont almost from the beginning. It was a peculiarity of this nobleman that there could be no conversation about him that didn't instantly take the form of anecdote, and a still further distinction that there could apparently be no anecdote that was not on the whole to his honour. If he had come into a room at any moment, people might have said frankly: "Of course we were telling stories about you!" As consciences go, in London, the general conscience would have been good. Moreover it would have been impossible to imagine his taking such a tribute otherwise than amiably, for he was always as unperturbed as an actor with the right cue. He had never in his life needed the prompter—his very embarrassments had been rehearsed. For myself, when he was talked about I always had an odd impression that we were speaking of the dead—it was with that peculiar accumulation of relish. His reputation was a kind of gilded obelisk, as if he had been buried beneath it; the body of legend and reminiscence of which he was to be the subject had crystallized in advance.

This ambiguity sprang, I suppose, from the fact that the mere sound of his name and air of his person, the general expectation he created, were, somehow, too exalted to be verified. The experience of his urbanity alwavs came later; the prefigurement, the legend paled before the reality. I remember that on the evening I refer to the reality was particularly operative. The handsomest man of his period could never have looked better, and he sat among us like a bland conductor controlling by an harmonious play of arm an orchestra still a little rough. He directed the conversation by gestures as irresistible as they were vague; one felt as if without him it wouldn't have had anything to call a tone. This was essentially what he contributed to any occasion—what he contributed above all to English public life. He pervaded it, he coloured it, he embellished it, and without him it would scarcely have had a vocabulary. Certainly it would not have had a style; for a style was what it had in having Lord Mellifont. He *was* a style. I was freshly struck with it as, in the *salle à manger* of the little Swiss inn, we resigned ourselves to inevitable veal. Confronted with his form (I must parenthesize that it was not confronted much), Clare Vawdrey's talk suggested the reporter contrasted with the bard. It was interesting to watch the shock of characters from which, of an evening, so much would be expected. There was however no concussion—it was all muffled and minimized in Lord Mellifont's tact. It was rudimentary with him to find the solution of such a problem in playing the host, assuming responsibilities which carried with them their sacrifice. He had indeed never been a guest in his life; he was the host, the patron, the moderator at every board. If there was a defect in his manner (and I suggest it under my breath), it was that he had a little more art than any conjunction—even the most complicated—could possibly require. At any rate one made one's reflections in noticing how the accomplished peer handled the situation and how the sturdy man of letters was unconscious that the situation (and least of all he himself as part of it), was handled. Lord Mellifont poured forth treasures of tact, and Clare Vawdrey never dreamed he was doing it.

Vawdrey had no suspicion of any such precaution even when Blanche Adney asked him if he saw yet their third act—an inquiry into which she introduced a subtlety of her own. She had a theory that he was to write her a play and that the heroine, if he would only do his duty, would be the part for which she had immemorially longed. She was forty years old (this could be no secret to those who had admired her from the first), and she could now reach out her hand and touch her uttermost goal. This gave a kind of tragic passion—perfect actress of comedy as she was—to her desire not to miss the great thing. The years had passed, and still she had missed it; none of the things she had done was the thing she had dreamed of, so that at present there was no more time to lose. This was the canker in the rose, the ache beneath the smile. It made her touching—made her sadness even sweeter than her laughter. She had done the old English and the new French, and had charmed her generation; but she was haunted by the vision of a bigger chance, of something truer to the conditions that lay near her. She was tired of Sheridan and she hated Bowdler; she called for a canvas of a finer grain. The worst of it, to my sense, was that she would never extract her modern comedy from the great mature novelist, who was as incapable of producing it as he was of threading a needle. She coddled him, she talked to him, she made love to him, as she frankly proclaimed; but she dwelt in illusions—she would have to live and die with Bowdler.

It is difficult to be cursory over this charming woman, who was beautiful without beauty and complete with a dozen deficiencies. The perspective of the stage made her over, and in society she was like the model off the pedestal. She was the picture walking about, which to the artless social mind was a perpetual surprise—a miracle. People thought she told them the secrets of the pictorial nature, in return for which they gave her relaxation and tea. She told them nothing and she drank the tea; but they had, all the same, the best of the bargain. Vawdrey was really at work on a play; but if he had begun it because he liked her I think he let it drag for the same reason. He secretly felt the atrocious difficulty—knew that from his hand the finished piece would have received no active life. At the same time nothing could be more agreeable than to have such a question open with Blanche Adney, and from time to time he put something very good into the play.

If he deceived Mrs Adney it was only because in her despair she was determined to be deceived. To her question about their third act he replied that, before dinner, he had written a magnificent passage.

"Before dinner?" I said. "Why, *cher maître*, before dinner you were holding us all spellbound on the terrace."

My words were a joke, because I thought his had been; but for the first time that I could remember I perceived a certain confusion in his face. He looked at me hard, throwing back his head quickly, the least bit like a horse who has been pulled up short. "Oh, it was before that," he replied, naturally enough.

"Before that you were playing billiards with *me*," Lord Mellifont intimated.

"Then it must have been yesterday," said Vawdrey.

But he was in a tight place. "You told me this morning you did nothing yesterday," the actress objected.

"I don't think I really know when I do things." Vawdrey looked vaguely, without helping himself, at a dish that was offered him.

"It's enough if *we* know," smiled Lord Mellifont.

"I don't believe you've written a line," said Blanche Adney.

"I think I could repeat you the scene." Vawdrey helped himself to *haricots verts*.

"Oh, do—oh, do!" two or three of us cried.

"After dinner, in the salon; it will be an immense *régal*," Lord Mellifont declared.

"I'm not sure, but I'll try," Vawdrey went on.

"Oh, you lovely man!" exclaimed the actress, who was practising Americanisms, being resigned even to an American comedy.

"But there must be this condition," said Vawdrey: "you must make your husband play."

"Play while you're reading? Never!"

"I've too much vanity," said Adney.

Lord Mellifont distinguished him. "You must give us the overture, before the curtain rises. That's a peculiarly delightful moment."

"I sha'n't read—I shall just speak," said Vawdrey.

"Better still, let me go and get your manuscript," the actress suggested.

Vawdrey replied that the manuscript didn't matter; but an hour later, in the salon, we wished he might have had it. We sat expectant, still under the spell of Adney's violin. His wife, in the foreground, on an ottoman, was all impatience and profile, and Lord Mellifont, in the chair—it was always *the* chair, Lord Mellifont's—made our grateful little group feel like a social science congress or a distribution of prizes. Suddenly, instead of beginning, our tame lion began to roar out of tune—he had clean forgotten every word. He was very sorry, but the lines absolutely wouldn't come to him; he was utterly ashamed, but his memory was a blank. He didn't look in the least ashamed—Vawdrey had never looked ashamed in his life; he was only imperturbably and merrily natural. He protested that he had never expected to make such a fool of himself, but we felt that this wouldn't prevent the incident from taking its place among his jolliest reminiscences. It was only *we* who were humiliated, as if he had played us a premeditated trick. This was an occasion, if ever, for Lord Mellifont's tact, which descended on us all like balm: he told us, in his charming artistic way, his way of bridging over arid intervals (he had a *débit*—there was nothing to approach it in England—like the actors of the Comédie Française), of his own collapse on a momentous occasion, the delivery of an address to a mighty multitude, when, finding he had forgotten his memoranda, he fumbled, on the terrible platform, the cynosure of every eye, fumbled vainly in irreproachable pockets for indispensable notes. But the point of his story was finer than that of Vawdrey's pleasantry; for he sketched with a few light gestures the brilliancy of a performance which had risen superior to embarrassment, had resolved itself, we were left to divine, into an effort recognised at the moment as not absolutely a blot on what the public was so good as to call his reputation.

"Play up—play up!" cried Blanche Adney, tapping her husband and remembering how, on the stage, a *contretemps* is always drowned in music. Adney threw himself upon his fiddle, and I said to Clare Vawdrey that his mistake could easily be corrected by his sending for the manuscript. If he would tell me where it was I would immediately fetch it from his room. To this he replied: "My dear fellow, I'm afraid there *is* no manuscript."

"Then you've not written anything?"

"I'll write it to-morrow."

"Ah, you trifle with us," I said, in much mystification.

Vawdrey hesitated an instant. "If there *is* anything, you'll find it on my table."

At this moment one of the others spoke to him, and Lady Mellifont remarked audibly, as if to correct gently our want of consideration, that Mr Adney was playing something very beautiful. I had noticed before that she appeared extremely fond of music; she always listened to it in a hushed transport. Vawdrey's attention was drawn away, but it didn't seem to me that the words he had just dropped constituted a definite permission to go to his room. Moreover I wanted to speak to Blanche Adney; I had something to ask her. I had to await my chance, however, as we remained silent awhile for her husband, after which the conversation became general. It was our habit to go to bed early, but there was still a little of the evening left. Before it quite waned I found an opportunity to tell the actress that Vawdrey had given me leave to put my hand on his manuscript. She adjured me, by all I held sacred, to bring it immediately, to give it to her; and her insistence was proof against my suggestion that it would now be too late for

him to begin to read; besides which the charm was broken—
the others wouldn't care. It was not too late for *her* to begin;
therefore I was to possess myself, without more delay, of the
precious pages. I told her she should be obeyed in a moment,
but I wanted her first to satisfy my just curiosity. What had
happened before dinner, while she was on the hills with Lord
Mellifont?

"How do you know anything happened?"

"I saw it in your face when you came back."

"And they call me an actress!" cried Mrs Adney.

"What do they call *me*?" I inquired.

"You're a searcher of hearts—that frivolous thing an
observer."

"I wish you'd let an observer write you a play!" I broke out.

"People don't care for what you write: you'd break any
run of luck."

"Well, I see plays all round me," I declared; "the air is full
of them to-night."

"The air? Thank you for nothing! I only wish my table-
drawers were."

"Did he make love to you on the glacier?" I went on.

She stared; then broke into the graduated ecstasy of her
laugh. "Lord Mellifont, poor dear? What a funny place! It
would indeed be the place for *our* love!"

"Did he fall into a crevasse?" I continued.

Blanche Adney looked at me again as she had done for an
instant when she came up, before dinner, with her hands full
of flowers. "I don't know into what he fell. I'll tell you to-
morrow."

"He did come down, then?"

"Perhaps he went up," she laughed. "It's really strange."

"All the more reason you should tell me to-night."

"I must think it over; I must puzzle it out."

"Oh, if you want conundrums I'll throw in another," I
said. "What's the matter with the master?"

"The master of what?"

"Of every form of dissimulation. Vawdrey hasn't written a line."

"Go and get his papers and we'll see."

"I don't like to expose him," I said.

"Why not, if I expose Lord Mellifont?"

"Oh, I'd do anything for that," I conceded. "But why should Vawdrey have made a false statement? It's very curious."

"It's very curious," Blanche Adney repeated, with a musing air and her eyes on Lord Mellifont. Then, rousing herself, she added: "Go and look in his room."

"In Lord Mellifont's?"

She turned to me quickly. "*That* would be a way!"

"A way to what?"

"To find out—to find out!" She spoke gaily and excitedly, but suddenly checked herself. "We're talking nonsense," she said.

"We're mixing things up, but I'm struck with your idea. Get Lady Mellifont to let you."

"Oh, *she* has looked!" Mrs Adney murmured, with the oddest dramatic expression. Then, after a movement of her beautiful uplifted hand, as if to brush away a fantastic vision, she exclaimed imperiously: "Bring me the scene—bring me the scene!"

"I go for it," I answered; "but don't tell me I can't write a play."

She left me, but my errand was arrested by the approach of a lady who had produced a birthday-book—we had been threatened with it for several evenings—and who did me the honour to solicit my autograph. She had been asking the others, and she couldn't decently leave me out. I could usually remember my name, but it always took me some time to recall my date, and even when I had done so I was never very sure. I hesitated between two days and I remarked to my petitioner that I would sign on both if it would give her any satisfaction. She said that surely I had been born only once; and I replied of course that on the day I made her acquaintance I had been born again. I mention the feeble joke only to show that, with the obligatory inspection of the other autographs, we gave some minutes to this transaction. The lady departed with her book, and then I became aware that the company had dispersed. I was alone in the little salon that had been appropriated to our use. My first impression was one of disappointment: if Vawdrey had gone to bed I didn't wish to disturb him. While I hesitated, however, I recognised that Vawdrey had not gone to bed. A window was open, and the sound of voices outside came in to me: Blanche was on the terrace with her dramatist, and they were talking about the stars. I went to the window for a glimpse—the Alpine night was splendid. My friends had stepped out together; the actress had picked up a cloak; she looked as I had seen her look in the wing of the theatre. They were silent awhile, and I heard the roar of a neighbouring torrent. I turned back into the room, and its quiet lamplight gave me an idea. Our companions had dispersed—it was late for a pastoral country— and we three should have the place to ourselves. Clare Vawdrey had written his scene—it was magnificent; and his reading it to us there, at such an hour, would be an episode intensely memorable. I would bring down his manuscript and meet the two with it as they came in.

I quitted the salon for this purpose; I had been in Vawdrey's room and knew it was on the second floor, the last in a long corridor. A minute later my hand was on the knob of his door, which I naturally pushed open without knocking. It was equally natural that in the absence of its occupant the room should be dark; the more so as, the end of the corridor being at that hour unlighted, the obscurity was not immediately diminished by the opening of the door. I was only aware at first that I had made no mistake and that, the window-curtains not being drawn, I was confronted with a couple of vague starlighted apertures. Their aid, however, was not sufficient to enable me to find what I had come for, and my hand, in my pocket, was already on the little box of matches that I always carried for cigarettes. Suddenly I withdrew it with a start, uttering an ejaculation, an apology. I had entered the wrong room; a glance prolonged for three seconds showed me a figure seated at a table near one of the windows—a figure I had at first taken for a travelling-rug thrown over a chair. I retreated, with a sense of intrusion; but as I did so I became aware, more rapidly than it takes me to express it, in the first place that this was Vawdrey's room and in the second that, most singularly, Vawdrey himself sat before me. Checking myself on the threshold I had a momentary feeling of bewilderment, but before I knew it I had exclaimed: "Hullo! is that you, Vawdrey?"

He neither turned nor answered me, but my question received an immediate and practical reply in the opening of a door on the other side of the passage. A servant, with a candle, had come out of the opposite room, and in this flitting illumination I definitely recognised the man whom, an instant before, I had to the best of my belief left below in conversation with Mrs Adney. His back was half turned to me, and he bent over the table in the attitude of writing, but I was conscious that I was in no sort of error about his identity. "I beg your pardon—I thought you were downstairs," I said; and as the personage gave no sign of hearing me I added: "If you're busy I won't disturb you." I backed out, closing the door—I had been in the place, I suppose, less than a minute. I had a sense of mystification, which however deepened infinitely the next instant. I stood there with my hand still on the knob of the door, overtaken by the oddest impression of my life. Vawdrey was at his table, writing, and it was a very natural place for him to be; but why was he writing in the dark and why hadn't he answered me? I waited a few seconds for the sound of some movement, to see if he wouldn't rouse himself from his abstraction—a fit conceivable in a great writer—and call out: "Oh, my dear fellow, is it you?" But I heard only the stillness, I felt only the starlighted dusk of the room, with the unexpected presence it enclosed. I turned away, slowly retracing my steps, and came confusedly downstairs. The lamp was still burning in the salon, but the room was empty. I passed round to the door of the hotel and stepped out. Empty too was the terrace. Blanche Adney and the gentleman with her had apparently come in. I hung about five minutes; then I went to bed.

I slept badly, for I was agitated. On looking back at these queer occurrences (you will see presently that they were queer), I perhaps suppose myself more agitated than I was; for great anomalies are never so great at first as after we have reflected upon them. It takes us some time to exhaust explanations. I was vaguely nervous—I had been sharply startled; but there was nothing I could not clear up by asking Blanche Adney, the first thing in the morning, who had been with her on the terrace. Oddly enough, however, when the morning dawned—it dawned admirably—I felt less desire to satisfy myself on this point than to escape, to brush away the shadow of my stupefaction. I saw the day would be splendid, and the fancy took me to spend it, as I had spent happy days of youth, in a lonely mountain ramble. I dressed early, partook of conventional coffee, put a big roll into one pocket and a small flask into the other, and, with a stout stick in my hand, went forth into the high places. My story is not closely concerned with the charming hours I passed there—hours of the kind that make intense memories. If I roamed away half of them on the shoulders of the hills, I lay on the sloping grass for the other half and, with my cap pulled over my eyes (save a peep for immensities of view), listened, in the bright stillness, to the mountain bee and felt most things sink and dwindle. Clare Vawdrey grew small, Blanche Adney grew dim, Lord Mellifont grew old, and before the day was over I forgot that I had ever been puzzled. When in the late afternoon I made my way down to the inn there was nothing I wanted so much to find out as whether dinner would not soon be ready. To-night I dressed, in a manner, and by the time I was presentable they were all at table.

In their company again my little problem came back to me, so that I was curious to see if Vawdrey wouldn't look at me the least bit queerly. But he didn't look at me at all; which gave me a chance both to be patient and to wonder why I should hesitate to ask him my question across the table. I did hesitate, and with the consciousness of doing so came back a little of the agitation I had left behind me, or below me, during the day. I wasn't ashamed of my scruple, however: it was only a fine discretion. What I vaguely felt was that a public inquiry wouldn't have been fair. Lord Mellifont was there, of course, to mitigate with his perfect manner all consequences; but I think it was present to me that with these particular elements his lordship would not be at home. The moment we got up, therefore, I approached Mrs Adney, asking her whether, as the evening was lovely, she wouldn't take a turn with me outside.

"You've walked a hundred miles; had you not better be quiet?" she replied.

"I'd walk a hundred miles more to get you to tell me something."

She looked at me an instant, with a little of the queerness that I had sought, but had not found, in Clare Vawdrey's eyes. "Do you mean what became of Lord Mellifont?"

"Of Lord Mellifont?" With my new speculation I had lost that thread.

"Where's your memory, foolish man? We talked of it last evening."

"Ah, yes!" I cried, recalling; "we shall have lots to discuss." I drew her out to the terrace, and before we had gone three steps I said to her: "Who was with you here last night?"

"Last night?" she repeated, as wide of the mark as I had been.

"At ten o'clock—just after our company broke up. You came out here with a gentleman; you talked about the stars."

She stared a moment; then she gave her laugh. "Are you jealous of dear Vawdrey?"

"Then it was he?"

"Certainly it was."

"And how long did he stay?"

"You have it badly. He stayed about a quarter of an hour —perhaps rather more. We walked some distance; he talked about his play. There you have it all; that is the only witchcraft I have used."

"And what did Vawdrey do afterwards?"

"I haven't the least idea. I left him and went to bed."

"At what time did you go to bed?"

"At what time did *you*? I happen to remember that I parted from Mr Vawdrey at ten twenty-five," said Mrs Adney. "I came back into the salon to pick up a book, and I noticed the clock."

"In other words you and Vawdrey distinctly lingered here from about five minutes past ten till the hour you mention?"

"I don't know how distinct we were, but we were very jolly. *Où voulez-vous en venir?*" Blanche Adney asked.

"Simply to this, dear lady: that at the time your companion was occupied in the manner you describe, he was also engaged in literary composition in his own room."

She stopped short at this, and her eyes had an expression in the darkness. She wanted to know if I challenged her veracity; and I replied that, on the contrary, I backed it up—it made the case so interesting. She returned that this would only be if she should back up mine; which, however, I had no difficulty in persuading her to do, after I had related to her circumstantially the incident of my quest of the manuscript—the manuscript which, at the time, for a reason I could now understand, appeared to have passed so completely out of her own head.

"His talk made me forget it—I forgot I sent you for it. He made up for his fiasco in the salon: he declaimed me the scene," said my companion. She had dropped on a bench to listen to me and, as we sat there, had briefly cross-examined me. Then she broke out into fresh laughter "Oh, the eccentricities of genius!"

"They seem greater even than I supposed."

"Oh, the mysteries of greatness!"

"You ought to know all about them, but they take me by surprise."

"Are you absolutely certain it was Mr Vawdrey?" my companion asked.

"If it wasn't he, who in the world was it? That a strange gentleman, looking exactly like him, should be sitting in his room at that hour of the night and writing at his table *in the dark*," I insisted, "would be practically as wonderful as my own contention."

"Yes, why in the dark?" mused Mrs Adney.

"Cats can see in the dark," I said.

She smiled at me dimly. "Did it look like a cat?"

"No, dear lady, but I'll tell you what it did look like—it looked like the author of Vawdrey's admirable works. It looked infinitely more like him than our friend does himself," I declared.

"Do you mean it was somebody he gets to do them?"

"Yes, while he dines out and disappoints you."

"Disappoints me?" murmured Mrs Adney artlessly.

"Disappoints *me*—disappoints every one who looks in him for the genius that created the pages they adore. Where is it in his talk?"

"Ah, last night he was splendid," said the actress.

"He's always splendid, as your morning bath is splendid,

or a sirloin of beef, or the railway service to Brighton. But he's never rare."

"I see what you mean."

"That's what makes you such a comfort to talk to. I've often wondered—now I know. There are two of them."

"What a delightful idea!"

"One goes out, the other stays at home. One is the genius, the other's the bourgeois, and it's only the bourgeois whom we personally know. He talks, he circulates, he's awfully popular, he flirts with you—"

"Whereas it's the genius *you* are privileged to see!" Mrs Adney broke in. "I'm much obliged to you for the distinction."

I laid my hand on her arm. "See him yourself. Try it, test it, go to his room."

"Go to his room? It wouldn't be proper!" she exclaimed, in the tone of her best comedy.

"Anything is proper in such an inquiry. If you see him, it settles it."

"How charming—to settle it!" She thought a moment, then she sprang up. "Do you mean *now*?"

"Whenever you like."

"But suppose I should find the wrong one?" said Blanche Adney, with an exquisite effect.

"The wrong one? Which one do you call the right?"

"The wrong one for a lady to go and see. Suppose I shouldn't find—the genius?"

"Oh, I'll look after the other," I replied. Then, as I had happened to glance about me, I added: "Take care—here comes Lord Mellifont."

"I wish you'd look after *him*," my interlocutress murmured.

"What's the matter with him?"

"That's just what I was going to tell you."

"Tell me now; he's not coming."

Blanche Adney looked a moment. Lord Mellifont, who appeared to have emerged from the hotel to smoke a meditative cigar, had paused, at a distance from us, and stood admiring the wonders of the prospect, discernible even in the dusk. We strolled slowly in another direction, and she presently said: "My idea is almost as droll as yours."

"I don't call mine droll: it's beautiful."

"There's nothing so beautiful as the droll,": Mrs Adney declared.

"You take a professional view. But I'm all ears." My curiosity was indeed alive again.

"Well then, my dear friend, if Clare Vawdrey is double (and I'm bound to say I think that the more of him the better), his lordship there has the opposite complaint: he isn't even whole."

We stopped once more, simultaneously. "I don't understand."

"No more do I. But I have a fancy that if there are two of Mr Vawdrey, there isn't so much as one, all told, of Lord Mellifont."

I considered a moment, then I laughed out. "I think I see what you mean!"

"That's what makes *you* a comfort. Did you ever see him alone?"

I tried to remember. "Oh, yes; he has been to see me."

"Ah, then he wasn't alone."

"And I've been to see him, in his study."

"Did he know you were there?"

"Naturally—I was announced."

Blanche Adney glanced at me like a lovely conspirator. "You mustn't be announced!" With this she walked on.

I rejoined her, breathless. "Do you mean one must come upon him when he doesn't know it?"

"You must take him unawares. You must go to his room—that's what you must do."

If I was elated by the way our mystery opened out, I was also, pardonably, a little confused. "When I know he's not there?"

"When you know he *is*."

"And what shall I see?"

"You won't see anything!" Mrs Adney cried as we turned round.

We had reached the end of the terrace, and our movement brought us face to face with Lord Mellifont, who, resuming his walk, had now, without indiscretion, overtaken us. The sight of him at that moment was illuminating, and it kindled a great backward train, connecting itself with one's general impression of the personage. As he stood there smiling at us and waving a practised hand into the transparent night (he introduced the view as if it had been a candidate and "supported" the very Alps), as he rose before us in the delicate fragrance of his cigar and all his other delicacies and fragrances, with more perfections, somehow, heaped upon his handsome head than one had ever seen accumulated before, he struck me as so essentially, so conspicuously and uniformly the public character that I read in a flash the answer to Blanche Adney's riddle. He was all public and had no corresponding private life, just as Clare Vawdrey was all private and had no corresponding public one. I had heard only half my companion's story, yet as we joined Lord Mellifont (he had followed us—he liked Mrs Adney; but it was always to be conceived of him that he accepted society rather than sought it), as we participated for half an hour in the distributed wealth of his conversation, I felt with unabashed duplicity that we had, as it were, found him out. I was even more deeply diverted by that whisk of the curtain to which the actress had just treated me than I had been by my own discovery; and if I was not ashamed of my share of her secret any more than of having divided my own with her (though my own was, of the two mysteries, the more glorious for the personage involved), this was because there was no cruelty in my advantage, but on the contrary an extreme tenderness and a positive compassion. Oh, he was safe with me, and I felt moreover rich and enlightened, as if I had suddenly put the universe into my pocket. I had learned what an affair of the spot and the moment a great appearance may be. It would doubtless be too much to say that I had always suspected the possibility, in the background of his lordship's being, of some such beautiful instance; but it is at least a fact that, patronising as it sounds, I had been conscious of a certain reserve of indulgence for him. I had secretly pitied him for the perfection of his performance, had wondered what blank face such a mask had to cover, what was left to him for the immitigable hours in which a man sits down with himself, or, more serious still, with that intenser self, his lawful wife. How was he at home and what did he do when he was alone? There was something in Lady Mellifont that gave a point to these researches—something that suggested that even to her he was still the public character and that she was haunted by similar questionings. She had never cleared them up: that was her eternal trouble. We therefore knew more than she did, Blanche Adney and I; but we wouldn't tell her for the world, nor would she probably thank us for doing so. She preferred the relative grandeur of uncertainty. She was not at home with him, so she couldn't say; and with her he was not alone, so he couldn't show her. He represented to his wife and he was a hero to his servants, and what one wanted to arrive at was what really became of him when no eye could see. He rested, presumably; but what form of rest could repair such a plenitude of presence? Lady Mellifont was too proud to pry, and as she had never looked through a keyhole she remained dignified and unassuaged.

It may have been a fancy of mine that Blanche Adney drew out our companion, or it may be that the practical irony of our relation to him at such a moment made me see him more vividly: at any rate he never had struck me as so dissimilar from what he would have been if we had not offered him a reflection of his image. We were only a concourse of two, but he had never been more public. His perfect manner had never been more perfect, his remarkable tact had never been more remarkable. I had a tacit sense that it would all be in the morning papers, with a leader, and also a secretly exhilarating one that I knew something that wouldn't be, that never could be, though any enterprising journal would give one a fortune for it. I must add, however, that in spite of my enjoyment—it was almost sensual, like that of a consummate dish—I was eager to be alone again with Mrs Adney, who owed me an anecdote. It proved impossible, that evening, for some of the others came out to see what we found so absorbing; and then Lord Mellifont bespoke a little music from the fiddler, who produced his violin and played to us divinely, on our plat-form of echoes, face to face with the ghosts of the moun-tains. Before the concert was over I missed our actress and, glancing into the window of the salon, saw that she was established with Vawdrey, who was reading to her from a manuscript. The great scene had apparently been achieved and was doubtless the more interesting to Blanche from the new lights she had gathered about its author. I judged it dis-creet not to disturb them, and I went to bed without seeing her again. I looked out for her betimes the next morning and, as the promise of the day was fair, proposed to her that we should take to the hills, reminding her of the high obligation she had incurred. She recognised the obligation and gratified me with her company; but before we had strolled ten yards up the pass she broke out with intensity: "My dear friend, you've no idea how it works in me! I can think of nothing else."

"Than your theory about Lord Mellifont?"

"Oh, bother Lord Mellifont! I allude to yours about Mr Vawdrey, who is much the more interesting person of the two. I'm fascinated by that vision of his—what-do-you-call-it?"

"His alternative identity?"

"His other self: that's easier to say."

"You accept it, then, you adopt it?"

"Adopt it? I rejoice in it! It became tremendously vivid to me last evening."

"While he read to you there?"

"Yes, as I listened to him, watched him. It simplified everything, explained everything."

"That's indeed the blessing of it. Is the scene very fine?"

"Magnificent, and he reads beautifully."

"Almost as well as the other one writes!" I laughed.

This made my companion stop a moment, laying her hand on my arm. "You utter my very impression. I felt that he was reading me the work of another man."

"What a service to the other man!"

"Such a totally different person," said Mrs Adney. We talked of this difference as we went on, and of what a wealth it constituted, what a resource for life, such a duplication of character.

"It ought to make him live twice as long as other people," I observed.

"Ought to make which of them?"

"Well, both; for after all they're members of a firm, and one of them couldn't carry on the business without the other. Moreover mere survival would be dreadful for either."

Blanche Adney was silent a little; then she exclaimed: "I don't know—I wish he *would* survive!"

"May I, on my side, inquire which?"

"If you can't guess I won't tell you."

"I know the heart of woman. You always prefer the other."

She halted again, looking round her. "Off here, away from my husband, I *can* tell you. I'm in love with him!"

"Unhappy woman, he has no passions," I answered.

"That's exactly why I adore him. Doesn't a woman with my history know that the passions of others are insupportable? An actress, poor thing, can't care for any love that's not all on *her* side; she can't afford to be repaid. My marriage proves that: marriage is ruinous. Do you know what was in my mind last night, all the while Mr Vawdrey was reading me those beautiful speeches? An insane desire to see the author." And dramatically, as if to hide her shame, Blanche Adney passed on.

"We'll manage that," I returned. "I want another glimpse of him myself. But meanwhile please remember that I've been waiting more than forty-eight hours for the evidence that supports your sketch, intensely suggestive and plausible, of Lord Mellifont's private life."

"Oh, Lord Mellifont doesn't interest me."

"He did yesterday," I said.

"Yes, but that was before I fell in love. You blotted him out with your story."

"You'll make me sorry I told it. Come," I pleaded, "if you don't let me know how your idea came into your head I shall imagine you simply made it up."

"Let me recollect then, while we wander in this grassy valley."

We stood at the entrance of a charming crooked gorge, a portion of whose level floor formed the bed of a stream that was smooth with swiftness. We turned into it, and the soft walk beside the clear torrent drew us on and on; till suddenly, as we continued and I waited for my companion to remember, a bend of the valley showed us Lady Mellifont coming toward us. She was alone, under the canopy of her parasol, drawing her sable train over the turf; and in this form, on the devious ways, she was a sufficiently rare apparition. She usually took a footman, who marched behind her on the highroads and whose livery was strange to the mountaineers. She blushed on seeing us, as if she ought somehow to justify herself; she laughed vaguely and said she had come out for a little early stroll. We stood together a moment, exchanging platitudes, and then she remarked that she had thought she might find her husband.

"Is he in this quarter?" I inquired.

"I supposed he would be. He came out an hour ago to sketch."

"Have you been looking for him?" Mrs Adney asked.

"A little; not very much," said Lady Mellifont.

Each of the women rested her eyes with some intensity, as it seemed to me, on the eyes of the other.

"We'll look for him *for* you, if you like," said Mrs Adney.

"Oh, it doesn't matter. I thought I'd join him."

"He won't make his sketch if you don't," my companion hinted.

"Perhaps he will if *you* do," said Lady Mellifont.

"Oh, I dare say he'll turn up," I interposed.

"He certainly will if he knows we're here!" Blanche Adney retorted.

"Will you wait while we search?" I asked of Lady Mellifont.

She repeated that it was of no consequence; upon which Mrs Adney went on: "We'll go into the matter for our own pleasure."

"I wish you a pleasant expedition," said her ladyship, and was turning away when I sought to know if we should inform her husband that she had followed him. She hesitated a moment; then she jerked out oddly: "I think you had better not." With this she took leave of us, floating a little stiffly down the gorge.

My companion and I watched her retreat, then we exchanged a stare, while a light ghost of a laugh rippled from the actress's lips. "She might be walking in the shrubberies at Mellifont!"

"She suspects it, you know," I replied.

"And she doesn't want him to know it. There won't be any sketch."

"Unless we overtake him," I subjoined. "In that case we shall find him producing one, in the most graceful attitude, and the queer thing is that it will be brilliant."

"Let us leave him alone—he'll have to come home without it."

"He'd rather never come home. Oh, he'll find a public!"

"Perhaps he'll do it for the cows," Blanche Adney suggested; and as I was on the point of rebuking her profanity she went on: "That's simply what I happened to discover."

"What are you speaking of?"

"The incident of day before yesterday."

"Ah, let's have it at last!"

"That's all it was—that I was like Lady Mellifont: I couldn't find him."

"Did you lose him?"

"He lost *me*—that appears to be the way of it. He thought I was gone."

"But you did find him, since you came home with him."

"It was he who found *me*. That again is what must happen. He's there from the moment he knows somebody else is."

"I understand his intermissions," I said after a short reflection, "but I don't quite seize the law that governs them."

"Oh, it's a fine shade, but I caught it at that moment. I had started to come home. I was tired, and I had insisted on his not coming back with me. We had found some rare flowers—those I brought home—and it was he who had discovered almost all of them. It amused him very much, and I knew he wanted to get more; but I was weary and I quitted him. He let me go—where else would have been his tact?—and I was too stupid then to have guessed that from the moment I was not there no flower would be gathered. I started homeward, but at the end of three minutes I found I had brought away his penknife—he had lent it to me to trim a branch—and I knew he would need it. I turned back a few steps, to call him, but before I spoke I looked about for him. You can't understand what happened then without having the place before you."

"You must take me there," I said.

"We may see the wonder here. The place was simply one that offered no chance for concealment—a great gradual hillside, without obstructions or trees. There were some rocks below me, behind which I myself had disappeared, but from which on coming back I immediately emerged again."

"Then he must have seen you."

"He was too utterly gone, for some reason best known to himself. It was probably some moment of fatigue—he's getting on, you know, so that, with the sense of returning solitude, the reaction had been proportionately great, the extinction proportionately complete. At any rate the stage was as bare as your hand."

"Could he have been somewhere else?"

"He couldn't have been, in the time, anywhere but where I had left him. Yet the place was utterly empty—as empty as this stretch of valley before us. He had vanished—he had ceased to be. But as soon as my voice rang out (I uttered his name), he rose before me like the rising sun."

"And where did the sun rise?"

"Just where it ought to—just where he would have been and where I should have seen him had he been like other people."

I had listened with the deepest interest, but it was my duty to think of objections. "How long a time elapsed between the moment you perceived his absence and the moment you called?"

"Oh, only an instant. I don't pretend it was long."

"Long enough for you to be sure?" I said.

"Sure he wasn't there?"

"Yes, and that you were not mistaken, not the victim of some hocus-pocus of your eyesight."

"I may have been mistaken, but I don't believe it. At any rate, that's just why I want you to look in his room."

I thought a moment. "How *can* I, when even his wife doesn't dare to?"

"She *wants* to; propose it to her. It wouldn't take much to make her. She does suspect."

I thought another moment. "Did he seem to know?"

"That I had missed him? So it struck me, but he thought he had been quick enough."

"Did you speak of his disappearance?"

"Heaven forbid! It seemed to me too strange."

"Quite right. And how did he look?"

Trying to think it out again and reconstitute her miracle, Blanche Adney gazed abstractedly up the valley. Suddenly she exclaimed: "Just as he looks now!" and I saw Lord Mellifont stand before us with his sketch-block. I perceived, as we met him, that he looked neither suspicious nor blank: he looked simply, as he did always, everywhere, the principal feature of the scene. Naturally he had no sketch to show us, but nothing could better have rounded off our actual conception of him than the way he fell into position as we approached. He had been selecting his point of view; he took possession of it with a flourish of the pencil. He leaned against a rock; his beautiful little box of water-colours reposed on a natural table beside him, a ledge of the bank which showed how inveterately nature ministered to his convenience. He painted while he talked and he talked while he painted; and if the painting was as miscellaneous as the talk, the talk would equally have graced an album. We waited while the exhibition went on, and it seemed indeed as if the conscious profiles of the peaks were interested in his success. They grew as black as silhouettes in paper, sharp against a livid sky from which, however, there would be nothing to fear till Lord Mellifont's sketch should be finished. Blanche Adney communed with me dumbly, and I could read the language of her eyes: "Oh, if *we* could only do it as well as that! He fills the stage in a way that beats us." We could no more have left him than we could have quitted the theatre till the play was over; but in due time we turned round with him and strolled back to the inn, before the door of which his lordship, glancing again at his picture, tore the fresh leaf from the block and presented it with a few happy words to Mrs Adney. Then he went into the house; and a moment later, looking up from where we stood, we saw him, above, at the window of his sitting-room (he had the best apartments), watching the signs of the weather.

"He'll have to rest after this," Blanche said, dropping her eyes on her water-colour.

"Indeed he will!" I raised mine to the window: Lord Mellifont had vanished. "He's already reabsorbed."

"Reabsorbed?" I could see the actress was now thinking of something else.

"Into the immensity of things. He has lapsed again; there's an *entr'acte*."

"It ought to be long." Mrs Adney looked up and down the terrace, and at that moment the head-waiter appeared in the doorway. Suddenly she turned to this functionary with the question: "Have you seen Mr Vawdrey lately?"

The man immediately approached. "He left the house five minutes ago—for a walk, I think. He went down the pass; he had a book."

I was watching the ominous clouds. "He had better have had an umbrella."

The waiter smiled. "I recommended him to take one."

"Thank you," said Mrs Adney; and the Oberkellner withdrew. Then she went on, abruptly: "Will you do me a favour?"

"Yes, if you'll do *me* one. Let me see if your picture is signed."

She glanced at the sketch before giving it to me. "For a wonder it isn't."

"It ought to be, for full value. May I keep it awhile?"

"Yes, if you'll do what I ask. Take an umbrella and go after Mr Vawdrey."

"To bring him to Mrs Adney?"

"To keep him out—as long as you can."

"I'll keep him as long as the rain holds off."

"Oh, never mind the rain!" my companion exclaimed.

"Would you have us drenched?"

"Without remorse." Then with a strange light in her eyes she added: "I'm going to try."

"To try?"

"To see the real one. Oh, if I can get at him!" she broke out with passion.

"Try, try!" I replied. "I'll keep our friend all day."

"If I can get at the one who does it"—and she paused, with shining eyes—"if I can have it out with him I shall get my part!"

"I'll keep Vawdrey for ever!" I called after her as she passed quickly into the house.

Her audacity was communicative, and I stood there in a glow of excitement. I looked at Lord Mellifont's water-colour and I looked at the gathering storm; I turned my eyes again to his lordship's windows and then I bent them on my watch. Vawdrey had so little the start of me that I should have time to overtake him—time even if I should take five minutes to go up to Lord Mellifont's sitting-room (where we had all been hospitably received), and say to him, as a messenger, that Mrs Adney begged he would bestow upon his sketch the high consecration of his signature. As I again considered this work of art I perceived there was something it certainly did lack: what else then but so noble an autograph? It was my duty to supply the deficiency without delay, and in accordance with this conviction I instantly re-entered the hotel. I went up to Lord Mellifont's apartments; I reached the door of his salon. Here, however, I was met by a difficulty of which my extravagance had not taken account. If I were to knock I should spoil everything; yet was I prepared to dispense with this ceremony? I asked myself the question, and it embarrassed me; I turned my little picture round and round, but it didn't give me the answer I wanted. I wanted it to say: "Open the door gently, gently, without a sound, yet very quickly: then you will see what you will see." I had gone so far as to lay my hand upon the knob when I became aware (having my wits so about me), that exactly in the manner I was thinking of— gently, gently, without a sound—another door had moved, on the opposite side of the hall. At the same instant I found myself smiling rather constrainedly upon Lady Mellifont, who, on seeing me, had checked herself on the threshold of her room. For a moment, as she stood there, we exchanged two or three ideas that were the more singular for being unspoken. We had caught each other hovering, and we understood each other; but as I stepped over to her (so that we were separated from the sitting-room by the width of the hall), her lips formed the almost soundless entreaty: "Don't!" I could see in her conscious eyes everything that the word expressed —the confession of her own curiosity and the dread of the consequences of mine. "*Don't!*" she repeated, as I stood before her. From the moment my experiment could strike her as an act of violence I was ready to renounce it; yet I thought I detected in her frightened face a still deeper betrayal—a possibility of disappointment if I should give way. It was as if she had said: "I'll let you do it if you'll take the responsibility. Yes, with some one else I'd surprise him. But it would never do for him to think it was I."

"We soon found Lord Mellifont," I observed, in allusion to our encounter with her an hour before, "and he was so good as to give this lovely sketch to Mrs Adney, who has asked me to come up and beg him to put in the omitted signature."

Lady Mellifont took the drawing from me, and I could guess the struggle that went on in her while she looked at it. She was silent for some time; then I felt that all her delicacies and dignities, all her old timidities and pieties were fighting against her opportunity. She turned away from me and, with the drawing, went back to her room. She was absent for a couple of minutes, and when she reappeared I could see that she had vanquished her temptation; that even, with a kind of resurgent horror, she had shrunk from it. She had deposited the sketch in the room. "If you will kindly leave the picture with me, I will see that Mrs Adney's request is attended to," she said, with great courtesy and sweetness, but in a manner that put an end to our colloquy.

I assented, with a somewhat artificial enthusiasm perhaps, and then, to ease off our separation, remarked that we were going to have a change of weather.

"In that case we shall go—we shall go immediately," said Lady Mellifont. I was amused at the eagerness with which she made this declaration: it appeared to represent a coveted flight into safety, an escape with her threatened secret. I was the more surprised therefore when, as I was turning away, she put out her hand to take mine. She had the pretext of bidding me farewell, but as I shook hands with her on this supposition I felt that what the movement really conveyed was: "I thank you for the help you would have given me, but it's better as it is. If I should know, who would help me then?" As I went to my room to get my umbrella I said to myself: "She's sure, but she won't put it to the proof."

A quarter of an hour later I had overtaken Clare Vawdrey in the pass, and shortly after this we found ourselves looking for refuge. The storm had not only completely gathered, but it had broken at the last with extraordinary rapidity. We scrambled up a hillside to an empty cabin, a rough structure that was hardly more than a shed for the protection of cattle. It was a tolerable shelter however, and it had fissures through which we could watch the splendid spectacle of the tempest. This entertainment lasted an hour—an hour that has remained with me as full of odd disparities. While the lightning played with the thunder and the rain gushed in on our umbrellas, I said to myself that Clare Vawdrey was disappointing. I don't know exactly what I should have predicated of a great author exposed to the fury of the elements, I can't say what particular Manfred attitude I should have expected my companion to assume, but it seemed to me somehow that I shouldn't have looked to him to regale me in such a situation with stories (which I had already heard), about the celebrated Lady Ringrose. Her ladyship formed the subject of Vawdrey's conversation during this prodigious scene, though before it was quite over he had launched out on Mr Chafer, the scarcely less notorious reviewer. It broke my heart to hear a man like Vawdrey talk of reviewers. The lightning projected a hard clearness upon the truth, familiar to me for years, to which the last day or two had added transcendent support—the irritating certitude that for personal relations this admirable genius thought his second-best good enough. It *was*, no doubt, as society was made, but there was a contempt in the distinction which could not fail to be galling to an admirer. The world was vulgar and stupid, and the real man would have been a fool to come out for it when he could gossip and dine by deputy. None the less my heart sank as I felt my companion practice this economy. I don't know exactly what I wanted; I suppose I wanted him to make an exception for *me*. I almost believed he would, if he had known how I worshipped his talent. But I had never been able to translate this to him, and his application of his principle was relentless. At any rate I was more than ever sure that at such an hour his chair at home was not empty: *there* was the Manfred attitude, *there* were the responsive flashes. I could only envy Mrs Adney her presumable enjoyment of them.

The weather drew off at last, and the rain abated sufficiently to allow us to emerge from our asylum and make our way back to the inn, where we found on our arrival that our prolonged absence had produced some agitation. It was judged apparently that the fury of the elements might have placed us in a predicament. Several of our friends were at the door, and they seemed a little disconcerted when it was perceived that we were only drenched. Clare Vawdrey, for some reason, was wetter than I, and he took his course to his room. Blanche Adney was among the persons collected to look out for us, but as Vawdrey came toward her she shrank from him, without a greeting; with a movement that I observed as almost one of estrangement she turned her back on him and went quickly into the salon. Wet as I was I went in after her; on which she immediately flung round and faced me. The first thing I saw was that she had never been so beautiful. There was a light of inspiration in her face, and she broke out to me in the quickest whisper, which was at the same time the loudest cry, I have ever heard: "I've got my *part!*"

"You went to his room—I was right?"

"Right?" Blanche Adney repeated. "Ah, my dear fellow!" she murmured.

"He was there—you saw him?"

"He saw me. It was the hour of my life!"

"It must have been the hour of his, if you were half as lovely as you are at this moment."

"He's splendid," she pursued, as if she didn't hear me. "He *is* the one who does it!" I listened, immensely impressed, and she added: "We understood each other."

"By flashes of lightning?"

"Oh, I didn't see the lightning then!"

"How long were you there?" I asked with admiration.

"Long enough to tell him I adore him."

"Ah, that's what I've never been able to tell him!" I exclaimed ruefully.

"I shall have my part—I shall have my part!" she continued, with triumphant indifference; and she flung round the room with the joy of a girl, only checking herself to say: "Go and change your clothes."

"You shall have Lord Mellifont's signature," I said.

"Oh, bother Lord Mellifont's signature! He's far nicer than Mr Vawdrey," she went on irrelevantly.

"Lord Mellifont?" I pretended to inquire.

"Confound Lord Mellifont!" And Blanche Adney, in her elation, brushed by me, whisking again through the open door. Just outside of it she came upon her husband; whereupon, with a charming cry of "We're talking of you, my love!" she threw herself upon him and kissed him.

I went to my room and changed my clothes, but I remained there till the evening. The violence of the storm had passed over us, but the rain had settled down to a drizzle. On descending to dinner I found that the change in the weather had already broken up our party. The Mellifonts had departed in a carriage and four, they had been followed by others, and several vehicles had been bespoken for the morning. Blanche Adney's was one of them, and on the pretext that she had preparations to make she quitted us directly after dinner. Clare Vawdrey asked me what was the matter with her—she suddenly appeared to dislike him. I forget what answer I gave, but I did my best to comfort him by driving away with him the next day. Mrs Adney had vanished when we came down; but they made up their quarrel in London, for he finished his play, which she produced. I must add that she is still, nevertheless, in want of the great part. I have a beautiful one in my head, but she doesn't come to see me to stir me up about it. Lady Mellifont always drops me a kind word when we meet, but that doesn't console me.

THE REAL THING

I

WHEN the porter's wife (she used to answer the house-bell) announced "A gentleman—with a lady, sir," I had, as I often had in those days, for the wish was father to the thought, an immediate vision of sitters. Sitters my visitors in this case proved to be; but not in the sense I should have preferred. However, there was nothing at first to indicate that they might not have come for a portrait. The gentleman, a man of fifty, very high and very straight, with a moustache slightly grizzled and a dark grey walking-coat admirably fitted, both of which I noted professionally—I don't mean as a barber or yet as a tailor—would have struck me as a celebrity if celebrities often were striking. It was a truth of which I had for some time been conscious that a figure with a good deal of frontage was, as one might say, almost never a public institution. A glance at the lady helped to remind me of this paradoxical law: she also looked too distinguished to be a "personality." Moreover one would scarcely come across two variations together.

Neither of the pair spoke immediately—they only prolonged the preliminary gaze which suggested that each wished to give the other a chance. They were visibly shy; they stood there letting me take them in—which, as I afterwards perceived, was the most practical thing they could have done. In this way their embarrassment served their cause. I had seen people painfully reluctant to mention that they desired anything so gross as to be represented on canvas; but the scruples of my new friends appeared almost insurmountable. Yet the gentleman might have said "I should like a portrait of my wife," and the lady might have said "I should like a portrait of my husband." Perhaps they were not husband and wife—this naturally would make the matter more delicate. Perhaps they wished to be done together—in which case they ought to have brought a third person to break the news.

"We come from Mr Rivet," the lady said at last, with a dim smile which had the effect of a moist sponge passed over a "sunk" piece of painting, as well as of a vague allusion to vanished beauty. She was as tall and straight, in her degree, as her companion, and with ten years less to carry. She looked as sad as a woman could look whose face was not charged with expression; that is her tinted oval mask showed friction as an exposed surface shows it. The hand of time had played over her freely, but only to simplify. She was slim and stiff, and so well-dressed, in dark blue cloth, with lappets and pockets and buttons, that it was clear she employed the same tailor as her husband. The couple had an indefinable air of prosperous thrift—they evidently got a good deal of luxury for their money. If I was to be one of their luxuries it would behove me to consider my terms.

"Ah, Claude Rivet recommended me?" I inquired; and I added that it was very kind of him, though I could reflect that, as he only painted landscape, this was not a sacrifice.

The lady looked very hard at the gentleman, and the gentleman looked round the room. Then staring at the floor a moment and stroking his moustache, he rested his pleasant eyes on me with the remark: "He said you were the right one."

"I try to be, when people want to sit."

"Yes, we should like to," said the lady anxiously.

"Do you mean together?"

My visitors exchanged a glance. "If you could do anything with *me*, I suppose it would be double," the gentleman stammered.

"Oh yes, there's naturally a higher charge for two figures than for one."

"We should like to make it pay," the husband confessed.

"That's very good of you," I returned, appreciating so unwonted a sympathy—for I supposed he meant pay the artist.

A sense of strangeness seemed to dawn on the lady. "We mean for the illustrations—Mr Rivet said you might put one in."

"Put one in—an illustration?" I was equally confused.

"Sketch her off, you know," said the gentleman, colouring.

It was only then that I understood the service Claude Rivet had rendered me; he had told them that I worked in black and white, for magazines, for story-books, for sketches of contemporary life, and consequently had frequent employment for models. These things were true, but it was not less true (I may confess it now—whether because the aspiration was to lead to everything or to nothing I leave the reader to guess), that I couldn't get the honours, to say nothing of the emoluments, of a great painter of portraits out of my head. My "illustrations" were my pot-boilers; I looked to a different branch of art (far and away the most interesting it had always seemed to me), to perpetuate my fame. There was no shame in looking to it also to make my fortune; but that fortune was by so much further from being made from the moment my visitors wished to be "done" for nothing. I was disappointed; for in the pictorial sense I had immediately *seen* them. I had seized their type—I had already settled what I would do with it. Something that wouldn't absolutely have pleased them, I afterwards reflected.

"Ah, you're—you're—a—?" I began, as soon as I had mastered my surprise. I couldn't bring out the dingy word "models"; it seemed to fit the case so little.

"We haven't had much practice," said the lady.

"We've got to *do* something, and we've thought that an artist in your line might perhaps make something of us," her husband threw off. He further mentioned that they didn't know many artists and that they had gone first, on the off-chance (he painted views of course, but sometimes put in figures—perhaps I remembered), to Mr Rivet, whom they had met a few years before at a place in Norfolk where he was sketching.

"We used to sketch a little ourselves," the lady hinted.

"It's very awkward, but we absolutely *must* do something," her husband went on.

"Of course, we're not so *very* young," she admitted, with a wan smile.

With the remark that I might as well know something more about them, the husband had handed me a card extracted from a neat new pocket-book (their appurtenances were all of the freshest) and inscribed with the words "Major Monarch." Impressive as these words were they didn't carry my knowledge much further; but my visitor presently added: "I've left the army, and we've had the misfortune to lose our money. In fact our means are dreadfully small."

"It's an awful bore," said Mrs Monarch.

They evidently wished to be discreet—to take care not to swagger because they were gentlefolks. I perceived they would have been willing to recognise this as something of a drawback, at the same time that I guessed at an underlying sense—their consolation in adversity—that they *had* their points. They certainly had; but these advantages struck me as preponderantly social; such for instance as would help to make a drawing-room look well. However, a drawing-room was always, or ought to be, a picture.

In consequence of his wife's allusion to their age Major Monarch observed: "Naturally, it's more for the figure that we thought of going in. We can still hold ourselves up." On the instant I saw that the figure was indeed their strong point. His "naturally" didn't sound vain, but it lighted up the question. "*She* has got the best," he continued, nodding at his wife, with a pleasant after-dinner absence of circumlocution. I could only reply, as if we were in fact sitting over our wine, that this didn't prevent his own from being very good; which led him in turn to rejoin: "We thought that if you ever have to do people like us, we might be something like it. *She*, particularly—for a lady in a book, you know."

I was so amused by them that, to get more of it, I did my best to take their point of view; and though it was an embarrassment to find myself appraising physically, as if they were animals on hire or useful blacks, a pair whom I should have expected to meet only in one of the relations in which criticism is tacit, I looked at Mrs Monarch judicially enough to be able to exclaim, after a moment, with conviction: "Oh yes, a lady in a book!" She was singularly like a bad illustration.

"We'll stand up, if you like," said the Major; and he raised himself before me with a really grand air.

I could take his measure at a glance—he was six feet two and a perfect gentleman. It would have paid any club in process of formation and in want of a stamp to engage him at a salary to stand in the principal window. What struck me immediately was that in coming to me they had rather missed their vocation; they could surely have been turned to better account for advertising purposes. I couldn't of course see the thing in detail, but I could see them make someone's fortune—I don't mean their own. There was something in them for a waistcoat-maker, an hotel-keeper or a soap-vendor. I could imagine "We always use it" pinned on their bosoms with the greatest effect; I had a vision of the promptitude with which they would launch a table d'hôte.

Mrs Monarch sat still, not from pride but from shyness, and presently her husband said to her: "Get up my dear and show how smart you are." She obeyed, but she had no need to get up to show it. She walked to the end of the studio, and then she came back blushing, with her fluttered eyes on her husband. I was reminded of an incident I had accidentally had a glimpse of in Paris—being with a friend there, a dramatist about to produce a play—when an actress came to him to ask to be intrusted with a part. She went through her paces before him, walked up and down as Mrs Monarch was doing. Mrs Monarch did it quite as well, but I abstained from applauding. It was very odd to see such people apply for such poor pay. She looked as if she had ten thousand a year. Her husband had used the word that described her: she was, in the London current jargon, essentially and typically "smart." Her figure was, in the same order of ideas, conspicuously and irreproachably "good." For a woman of her age her waist was surprisingly small; her elbow moreover had the orthodox crook. She held her head at the conventional angle; but why did she come to *me?* She ought to have tried on jackets at a big shop. I feared my visitors were not only destitute, but "artistic"—which would be a great complication. When she sat down again I thanked her, observing that what a draughts-man most valued in his model was the faculty of keeping quiet.

"Oh, *she* can keep quiet," said Major Monarch. Then he added, jocosely: "I've always kept her quiet."

"I'm not a nasty fidget, am I?" Mrs Monarch appealed to her husband.

He addressed his answer to me. "Perhaps it isn't out of place to mention—because we ought to be quite business-like, oughtn't we?—that when I married her she was known as the Beautiful Statue."

"Oh dear!" said Mrs Monarch, ruefully.

"Of course I should want a certain amount of expression," I rejoined.

"Of *course!*" they both exclaimed.

"And then I suppose you know that you'll get awfully tired."

"Oh, we *never* get tired!" they eagerly cried.

"Have you had any kind of practice?"

They hesitated—they looked at each other. "We've been photographed, *immensely*," said Mrs Monarch.

"She means the fellows have asked us," added the Major.

"I see—because you're so good-looking."

"I don't know what they thought, but they were always after us."

"We always got our photographs for nothing," smiled Mrs Monarch.

"We might have brought some, my dear," her husband remarked.

"I'm not sure we have any left. We've given quantities away," she explained to me.

"With our autographs and that sort of thing," said the Major.

"Are they to be got in the shops?" I inquired, as a harmless pleasantry.

"Oh, yes; *hers*—they used to be."

"Not now," said Mrs Monarch, with her eyes on the floor.

II

I COULD fancy the "sort of thing" they put on the presentation-copies of their photographs, and I was sure they wrote a beautiful hand. It was odd how quickly I was sure of everything that concerned them. If they were now so poor as to have to earn shillings and pence, they never had had much of a margin. Their good looks had been their capital, and they had good-humouredly made the most of the career that this resource marked out for them. It was in their faces, the blankness, the deep intellectual repose of the twenty years of country-house visiting which had given them pleasant intonations. I could see the sunny drawing-rooms, sprinkled with periodicals she didn't read, in which Mrs Monarch had continuously sat; I could see the wet shrubberies in which she had walked, equipped to admiration for either exercise. I could see the rich covers the Major had helped to shoot and the wonderful garments in which, late at night, he repaired to the smoking-room to talk about them. I could imagine their leggings and waterproofs, their knowing tweeds and rugs, their rolls of sticks and cases of tackle and neat umbrellas; and I could evoke the exact appearance of their servants and the compact variety of their luggage on the platforms of country stations.

They gave small tips, but they were liked; they didn't do anything themselves, but they were welcome. They looked so well everywhere; they gratified the general relish for stature, complexion and "form." They knew it without fatuity or vulgarity, and they respected themselves in consequence. They were not superficial; they were thorough and kept themselves up—it had been their line. People with such a taste for activity had to have some line. I could feel how, even in a dull house, they could have been counted upon for cheerfulness. At present something had happened—it didn't matter what, their little income had grown less, it had grown least—and they had to do something for pocket-money. Their friends liked them, but didn't like to support them. There was something about them that represented credit—their clothes, their manners, their type; but if credit is a large empty pocket in which an occasional chink reverberates, the chink at least must be audible. What they wanted of me was to help to make it so. Fortunately they had no children—I soon divined that. They would also perhaps wish our relations to be kept secret: this was why it was "for the figure"—the reproduction of the face would betray them.

I liked them—they were so simple; and I had no objection to them if they would suit. But, somehow, with all their perfections I didn't easily believe in them. After all they were amateurs, and the ruling passion of my life was the detestation of the amateur. Combined with this was another perversity—an innate preference for the represented subject over the real one: the defect of the real one was so apt to be a lack of representation. I liked things that appeared; then one was sure. Whether they *were* or not was a subordinate and almost always a profitless question. There were other considerations, the first of which was that I already had two or three people in use, notably a young person with big feet, in alpaca, from Kilburn, who for a couple of years had come to me regularly for my illustrations and with whom I was still—perhaps ignobly—satisfied. I frankly explained to my visitors how the case stood; but they had taken more precautions than I supposed. They had reasoned out their opportunity, for Claude Rivet had told them of the projected *édition de luxe* of one of the writers of our day—the rarest of the novelists—who, long neglected by the multitudinous vulgar and dearly prized by the attentive (need I mention Philip Vincent?) had had the happy fortune of seeing, late in life, the dawn and then the full light of a higher criticism—an estimate in which, on the part of the public, there was something really of expiation. The edition in question, planned by a publisher of taste, was practically an act of high reparation; the woodcuts with which it was to be enriched were the homage of English art to one of the most independent representatives of English letters. Major and Mrs Monarch confessed to me that they had hoped I might be able to work *them* into my share of the enterprise. They knew I was to do the first of the books, "Rutland Ramsay," but I had to make clear to them that my participation in the rest of the affair—this first book was to be a test—was to depend on the satisfaction I should give. If this should be limited my employers would drop me without a scruple. It was therefore a crisis for me, and naturally I was making special preparations, looking about for new people, if they should be necessary, and securing the best types. I admitted however that I should like to settle down to two or three good models who would do for everything.

"Should we have often to—a—put on special clothes?" Mrs Monarch timidly demanded.

"Dear, yes—that's half the business."

"And should we be expected to supply our own costumes?"

"Oh, no; I've got a lot of things. A painter's models put on—or put off—anything he likes."

"And do you mean—a—the same?"

"The same?"

Mrs Monarch looked at her husband again.

"Oh, she was just wondering," he explained, "if the costumes are in *general* use." I had to confess that they were, and I mentioned further that some of them (I had a lot of genuine, greasy last-century things), had served their time, a hundred years ago, on living, world-stained men and women. "We'll put on anything that *fits*," said the Major.

"Oh, I arrange that—they fit in the pictures."

"I'm afraid I should do better for the modern books. I would come as you like," said Mrs Monarch.

"She has got a lot of clothes at home: they might do for contemporary life," her husband continued.

"Oh, I can fancy scenes in which you'd be quite natural." And indeed I could see the slipshod rearrangements of stale properties—the stories I tried to produce pictures for without the exasperation of reading them—whose sandy tracts the good lady might help to people. But I had to return to the fact that for this sort of work—the daily mechanical grind—I was already equipped; the people I was working with were fully adequate.

"We only thought we might be more like *some* characters," said Mrs Monarch mildly, getting up.

Her husband also rose; he stood looking at me with a dim wistfulness that was touching in so fine a man. "Wouldn't it be rather a pull sometimes to have—a—to have—?" He hung fire; he wanted me to help him by phrasing what he meant. But I couldn't—I didn't know. So he brought it out, awkwardly: "The *real* thing; a gentleman, you know, or a lady." I was quite ready to give a general assent—I admitted that there was a great deal in that. This encouraged Major Monarch to say, following up his appeal with an unacted gulp: "It's awfully hard—we've tried everything." The gulp was communicative; it proved too much for his wife. Before I knew it Mrs Monarch had dropped again upon a divan and burst into tears. Her husband sat down beside her, holding one of her hands; whereupon she quickly dried her eyes with the other, while I felt embarrassed as she looked up at me. "There isn't a confounded job I haven't applied for—waited for—prayed for. You can fancy we'd be pretty bad first. Secretaryships and that sort of thing? You might as well ask for a peerage. I'd be *anything*—I'm strong; a messenger or a coalheaver. I'd put on a gold-laced cap and open carriage-doors in front of the haberdasher's; I'd hang about a station, to carry portmanteaus; I'd be a postman. But they won't *look* at you; there are thousands, as good as yourself, already on the ground. *Gentlemen*, poor beggars, who have drunk their wine, who have kept their hunters!"

I was as reassuring as I knew how to be, and my visitors were presently on their feet again while, for the experiment, we agreed on an hour. We were discussing it when the door opened and Miss Churm came in with a wet umbrella. Miss Churm had to take the omnibus to Maida Vale and then walk half-a-mile. She looked a trifle blowsy and slightly splashed. I scarcely ever saw her come in without thinking afresh how odd it was that, being so little in herself, she should yet be so much in others. She was a meagre little Miss Churm, but she was an ample heroine of romance. She was only a freckled cockney, but she could represent everything, from a fine lady to a shepherdess; she had the faculty, as she might have had a fine voice or long hair. She couldn't spell, and she loved beer, but she had two or three "points," and practice, and a knack, and mother-wit, and a kind of whimsical sensibility, and a love of the theatre, and seven sisters, and not an ounce of respect, especially for the *h*. The first thing my visitors saw was that her umbrella was wet, and in their spotless perfection they visibly winced at it. The rain had come on since their arrival.

"I'm all in a soak; there *was* a mess of people in the 'bus. I wish you lived near a stytion," said Miss Churm. I requested her to get ready as quickly as possible, and she passed into the room in which she always changed her dress. But before going out she asked me what she was to get into this time.

"It's the Russian princess, don't you know?" I answered; "the one with the 'golden eyes,' in black velvet, for the long thing in the *Cheapside*."

"Golden eyes? I *say!*" cried Miss Churm, while my companions watched her with intensity as she withdrew. She always arranged herself, when she was late, before I could turn round; and I kept my visitors a little, on purpose, so that they might get an idea, from seeing her, what would be expected of themselves. I mentioned that she was quite my notion of an excellent model—she was really very clever.

"Do you think she looks like a Russian princess?" Major Monarch asked, with lurking alarm.

"When I make her, yes."

"Oh, if you have to *make* her—!" he reasoned, acutely.

"That's the most you can ask. There are so many that are not makeable."

"Well now, *here's* a lady"—and with a persuasive smile he passed his arm into his wife's—"who's already made!"

"Oh, I'm not a Russian princess," Mrs Monarch protested, a little coldly. I could see that she had known some and didn't like them. There, immediately, was a complication of a kind that I never had to fear with Miss Churm.

This young lady came back in black velvet—the gown was rather rusty and very low on her lean shoulders—and with a Japanese fan in her red hands. I reminded her that in the scene I was doing she had to look over someone's head. "I forget whose it is; but it doesn't matter. Just look over a head."

"I'd rather look over a stove," said Miss Churm; and she took her station near the fire. She fell into position, settled herself into a tall attitude, gave a certain backward inclination to her head and a certain forward droop to her fan, and looked, at least to my prejudiced sense, distinguished and charming, foreign and dangerous. We left her looking so, while I went down-stairs with Major and Mrs Monarch.

"I think I could come about as near it as that," said Mrs Monarch.

"Oh, you think she's shabby, but you must allow for the alchemy of art."

However, they went off with an evident increase of comfort, founded on their demonstrable advantage in being the real thing. I could fancy them shuddering over Miss Churm. She was very droll about them when I went back, for I told her what they wanted.

"Well, if *she* can sit I'll tyke to bookkeeping," said my model.

"She's very lady-like," I replied, as an innocent form of aggravation.

"So much the worse for *you*. That means she can't turn round."

"She'll do for the fashionable novels."

"Oh yes, she'll *do* for them!" my model humorously declared. "Ain't they bad enough without her?" I had often sociably denounced them to Miss Churm.

III

IT was for the elucidation of a mystery in one of these works that I first tried Mrs Monarch. Her husband came with her, to be useful if necessary—it was sufficiently clear that as a general thing he would prefer to come with her. At first I wondered if this were for "propriety's" sake—if he were going to be jealous and meddling. The idea was too tiresome, and if it had been confirmed it would speedily have brought our acquaintance to a close. But I soon saw there was nothing in it and that if he accompanied Mrs Monarch it was (in addition to the chance of being wanted), simply because he had nothing else to do. When she was away from him his occupation was gone —she never *had* been away from him. I judged, rightly, that in their awkward situation their close union was their main comfort and that this union had no weak spot. It was a real marriage, an encouragement to the hesitating, a nut for pessimists to crack. Their address was humble (I remember afterwards thinking it had been the only thing about them that was really professional), and I could fancy the lamentable lodgings in which the Major would have been left alone. He could bear them with his wife—he couldn't bear them without her.

He had too much tact to try and make himself agreeable when he couldn't be useful; so he simply sat and waited, when I was too absorbed in my work to talk. But I liked to make him talk—it made my work, when it didn't interrupt it, less sordid, less special. To listen to him was to combine the excitement of going out with the economy of staying at home. There was only one hindrance: that I seemed not to know any of the people he and his wife had known. I think he wondered extremely, during the term of our intercourse, whom the deuce I *did* know. He hadn't a stray sixpence of an idea to fumble for; so we didn't spin it very fine—we confined ourselves to questions of leather and even of liquor (saddlers and breeches-makers and how to get good claret cheap), and matters like "good trains" and the habits of small game. His lore on these last subjects was astonishing, he managed to interweave the stationmaster with the ornithologist. When he couldn't talk about greater things he could talk cheerfully about smaller, and since I couldn't accompany him into reminiscences of the fashionable world he could lower the conversation without a visible effort to my level.

So earnest a desire to please was touching in a man who could so easily have knocked one down. He looked after the fire and had an opinion on the draught of the stove, without my asking him, and I could see that he thought many of my arrangements not half clever enough. I remember telling him that if I were only rich I would offer him a salary to come and teach me how to live. Sometimes he gave a random sigh, of which the essence was: "Give me even such a bare old barrack as *this*, and I'd do something with it!" When I wanted to use him he came alone; which was an illustration of the superior courage of women. His wife could bear her solitary second floor, and she was in general more discreet; showing by various small reserves that she was alive to the propriety of keeping our relations markedly professional—not letting them slide into sociability. She wished it to remain clear that she and the Major were employed, not cultivated, and if she approved of me as a superior, who could be kept in his place, she never thought me quite good enough for an equal.

She sat with great intensity, giving the whole of her mind to it, and was capable of remaining for an hour almost as motionless as if she were before a photographer's lens. I could see she had been photographed often, but somehow the very habit that made her good for that purpose unfitted her for mine. At first I was extremely pleased with her lady-like air, and it was a satisfaction, on coming to follow her lines, to see how good they were and how far they could lead the pencil. But after a few times I began to find her too insurmountably stiff; do what I would with it my drawing looked like a photograph or a copy of a photograph. Her figure had no variety of expression—she herself had no sense of variety. You may say that this was my business, was only a question of placing her. I placed her in every conceivable position, but she managed to obliterate their differences. She was always a lady certainly, and into the bargain was always the same lady. She was the real thing, but always the same thing. There were moments when I was oppressed by the serenity of her confidence that she *was* the real thing. All her dealings with me and all her husband's were an implication that this was lucky for *me*. Meanwhile I found myself trying to invent types that approached her own, instead of making her own transform itself—in the clever way that was not impossible, for instance, to poor Miss Churm. Arrange as I would and take the precautions I would, she always, in my pictures, came out too tall—landing me in the dilemma of having represented a fascinating woman as seven feet high, which, out of respect perhaps to my own very much scantier inches, was far from my idea of such a personage.

The case was worse with the Major—nothing I could do would keep *him* down, so that he became useful only for the representation of brawny giants. I adored variety and range, I cherished human accidents, the illustrative note; I wanted to characterise closely, and the thing in the world I most hated was the danger of being ridden by a type. I had quarrelled with some of my friends about it—I had parted company with them for maintaining that one *had* to be, and that if the type was beautiful (witness Raphael and Leonardo), the servitude was only a gain. I was neither Leonardo nor Raphael; I might only be a presumptuous young modern searcher, but I held that everything was to be sacrificed sooner than character. When they averred that the haunting type in question could easily *be* character, I retorted, perhaps superficially: "Whose?" It couldn't be everybody's—it might end in being nobody's.

After I had drawn Mrs Monarch a dozen times I perceived more clearly than before that the value of such a model as Miss Churm resided precisely in the fact that she had no positive stamp, combined of course with the other fact that what she did have was a curious and inexplicable talent for imitation. Her usual appearance was like a curtain which she could draw up at request for a capital performance. This performance was simply suggestive; but it was a word to the wise— it was vivid and pretty. Sometimes, even, I thought it, though she was plain herself, too insipidly pretty; I made it a reproach to her that the figures drawn from her were monotonously (*bêtement*, as we used to say) graceful. Nothing made her more angry; it was so much her pride to feel that she could sit for characters that had nothing in common with each other. She would accuse me at such moments of taking away her "reputytion."

It suffered a certain shrinkage, this queer quantity, from the repeated visits of my new friends. Miss Churm was greatly in demand, never in want of employment, so I had no scruple in putting her off occasionally, to try them more at my ease. It was certainly amusing at first to do the real thing—it was amusing to do Major Monarch's trousers. They *were* the real thing, even if he did come out colossal. It was amusing to do his wife's back hair (it was so mathematically neat,) and the particular "smart" tension of her tight stays. She lent herself especially to positions in which the face was somewhat averted or blurred; she abounded in lady-like back views and *profils perdus*. When she stood erect she took naturally one of the attitudes in which court-painters represent queens and princesses; so that I found myself wondering whether, to draw out this accomplishment, I couldn't get the editor of the *Cheapside* to publish a really royal romance, "A Tale of Buckingham Palace." Sometimes, however, the real thing and the make-believe came into contact; by which I mean that Miss Churm, keeping an appointment or coming to make one on days when I had much work in hand, encountered her invidious rivals. The encounter was not on their part, for they noticed her no more than if she had been the housemaid; not from intentional loftiness, but simply because, as yet, professionally, they didn't know how to fraternise, as I could guess that they would have liked—or at least that the Major would. They couldn't talk about the omnibus—they always walked; and they didn't know what else to try—she wasn't interested in good trains or cheap claret. Besides, they must have felt—in the air—that she was amused at them, secretly derisive of their ever knowing how. She was not a person to conceal her scepticism if she had had a chance to show it. On the other hand Mrs Monarch didn't think her tidy; for why else did she take pains to say to me (it was going out of the way, for Mrs Monarch), that she didn't like dirty women?

One day when my young lady happened to be present with my other sitters (she even dropped in, when it was convenient, for a chat), I asked her to be so good as to lend a hand in getting tea—a service with which she was familiar and which was one of a class that, living as I did in a small way, with slender domestic resources, I often appealed to my models to render. They liked to lay hands on my property, to break the sitting, and sometimes the china—I made them feel Bohemian. The next time I saw Miss Churm after this incident she surprised me greatly by making a scene about it— she accused me of having wished to humiliate her. She had not resented the outrage at the time, but had seemed obliging and amused, enjoying the comedy of asking Mrs Monarch, who sat vague and silent, whether she would have cream and sugar, and putting an exaggerated simper into the question. She had tried intonations—as if she too wished to pass for the real thing; till I was afraid my other visitors would take offence.

Oh, *they* were determined not to do this; and their touching patience was the measure of their great need. They would sit by the hour, uncomplaining, till I was ready to use them; they would come back on the chance of being wanted and would walk away cheerfully if they were not. I used to go to the door with them to see in what magnificent order they retreated. I tried to find other employment for them—I introduced them to several artists. But they didn't "take," for reasons I could appreciate, and I became conscious, rather anxiously, that after such disappointments they fell back upon me with a heavier weight. They did me the honour to think that it was I who was most *their* form. They were not picturesque enough for the painters, and in those days there were not so many serious workers in black and white. Besides, they had an eye to the great job I had mentioned to them—they had secretly set their hearts on supplying the right essence for my pictorial vindication of our fine novelist. They knew that for this undertaking I should want no costume-effects, none of the frippery of past ages—that it was a case in which everything would be contemporary and satirical and, presumably, genteel. If I could work them into it their future would be assured, for the labour would of course be long and the occupation steady.

One day Mrs Monarch came without her husband—she explained his absence by his having had to go to the City. While she sat there in her usual anxious stiffness there came, at the door, a knock which I immediately recognised as the subdued appeal of a model out of work. It was followed by the entrance of a young man whom I easily perceived to be a foreigner and who proved in fact an Italian acquainted with no English word but my name, which he uttered in a way that made it seem to include all others. I had not then visited his country, nor was I proficient in his tongue; but as he was not so meanly constituted—what Italian is?—as to depend only on that member for expression he conveyed to me, in familiar but graceful mimicry, that he was in search of exactly the employment in which the lady before me was engaged. I was not struck with him at first, and while I continued to draw I emitted rough sounds of discouragement and dismissal. He stood his ground, however, not importunately, but with a dumb, dog-like fidelity in his eyes which amounted to innocent impudence—the manner of a devoted servant (he might have been in the house for years), unjustly suspected. Suddenly I saw that this very attitude and expression made a picture, whereupon I told him to sit down and wait till I should be free. There was another picture in the way he obeyed me, and I observed as I worked that there were others still in the way he looked wonderingly, with his head thrown back, about the high studio. He might have been crossing himself in St Peter's. Before I finished I said to myself: "The fellow's a bankrupt orange-monger, but he's a treasure."

When Mrs Monarch withdrew he passed across the room like a flash to open the door for her, standing there with the rapt, pure gaze of the young Dante spellbound by the young Beatrice. As I never insisted, in such situations, on the blankness of the British domestic, I reflected that he had the making of a servant (and I needed one, but couldn't pay him to be only that), as well as of a model; in short I made up my mind to adopt my bright adventurer if he would agree to officiate in the double capacity. He jumped at my offer, and in the event my rashness (for I had known nothing about him), was not brought home to me. He proved a sympathetic though a desultory ministrant, and had in a wonderful degree the *sentiment de la pose*. It was uncultivated, instinctive; a part of the happy instinct which had guided him to my door and helped him to spell out my name on the card nailed to it. He had had no other introduction to me than a guess, from the shape of my high north window, seen outside, that my place was a studio, and that as a studio it would contain an artist. He had wandered to England in search of fortune, like other itinerants, and had embarked, with a partner and a small green handcart, on the sale of penny ices. The ices had melted away and the partner had dissolved in their train. My young man wore tight yellow trousers with reddish stripes and his name was Oronte. He was sallow but fair, and when I put him into some old clothes of my own he looked like an Englishman. He was as good as Miss Churm, who could look, when required, like an Italian.

IV

I THOUGHT Mrs Monarch's face slightly convulsed when, on her coming back with her husband, she found Oronte installed. It was strange to have to recognise in a scrap of a lazzarone a competitor to her magnificent Major. It was she who scented danger first, for the Major was anecdotically unconscious. But Oronte gave us tea, with a hundred eager confusions (he had never seen such a queer process), and I think she thought better of me for having at last an "establishment." They saw a couple of drawings that I had made of the establishment, and Mrs Monarch hinted that it never would have struck her that he had sat for them. "Now the drawings you make from *us*, they look exactly like us," she reminded me, smiling in triumph; and I recognised that this was indeed just their defect. When I drew the Monarchs I couldn't, somehow, get away from them—get into the character I wanted to represent; and I had not the least desire my model should be discoverable in my picture. Miss Churm never was, and Mrs Monarch thought I hid her, very properly, because she was vulgar; whereas if she was lost it was only as the dead who go to heaven are lost—in the gain of an angel the more.

By this time I had got a certain start with "Rutland Ramsay," the first novel in the great projected series; that is I had produced a dozen drawings, several with the help of the Major and his wife, and I had sent them in for approval. My understanding with the publishers, as I have already hinted, had been that I was to be left to do my work, in this particular case, as I liked, with the whole book committed to me; but my connection with the rest of the series was only contingent. There were moments when, frankly, it *was* a comfort to have the real thing under one's hand; for there were characters in "Rutland Ramsay" that were very much like it. There were people presumably as straight as the Major and women of as good a fashion as Mrs Monarch. There was a great deal of country-house life—treated, it is true, in a fine, fanciful, ironical, generalised way—and there was a considerable implication of knickerbockers and kilts. There were certain things I had to settle at the outset; such things for instance as the exact appearance of the hero, the particular bloom of the heroine. The author of course gave me a lead, but there was a margin for interpretation. I took the Monarchs into my confidence, I told them frankly what I was about, I mentioned my embarrassments and alternatives. "Oh, take *him!*" Mrs Monarch murmured sweetly, looking at her husband; and "What could you want better than my wife?" the Major inquired, with the comfortable candour that now prevailed between us.

I was not obliged to answer these remarks—I was only obliged to place my sitters. I was not easy in mind, and I postponed, a little timidly perhaps, the solution of the question. The book was a large canvas, the other figures were numerous, and I worked off at first some of the episodes in which the hero and the heroine were not concerned. When once I had set *them* up I should have to stick to them—I couldn't make my young man seven feet high in one place and five feet nine in another. I inclined on the whole to the latter measurement, though the Major more than once reminded me that *he* looked about as young as anyone. It was indeed quite possible to arrange him, for the figure, so that it would have been difficult to detect his age. After the spontaneous Oronte had been with me a month, and after I had given him to understand several different times that his native exuberance would presently constitute an insurmountable barrier to our further intercourse, I waked to a sense of his heroic capacity. He was only five feet seven, but the remaining inches were latent. I tried him almost secretly at first, for I was really rather afraid of the judgment my other models would pass on such a choice. If they regarded Miss Churm as little better than a snare, what would they think of the representation by a person so little the real thing as an Italian street-vendor of a protagonist formed by a public school?

If I went a little in fear of them it was not because they bullied me, because they had got an oppressive foothold, but because in their really pathetic decorum and mysteriously permanent newness they counted on me so intensely. I was therefore very glad when Jack Hawley came home: he was always of such good counsel. He painted badly himself, but there was no one like him for putting his finger on the place. He had been absent from England for a year; he had been somewhere —I don't remember where—to get a fresh eye. I was in a good deal of dread of any such organ, but we were old friends; he had been away for months and a sense of emptiness was creeping into my life. I hadn't dodged a missile for a year.

He came back with a fresh eye, but with the same old black velvet blouse, and the first evening he spent in my studio we smoked cigarettes till the small hours. He had done no work himself, he had only got the eye; so the field was clear for the production of my little things. He wanted to see what I had done for the *Cheapside*, but he was disappointed in the exhibition. That at least seemed the meaning of two or three comprehensive groans which, as he lounged on my big divan, on a folded leg, looking at my latest drawings, issued from his lips with the smoke of the cigarette.

"What's the matter with you?" I asked.

"What's the matter with *you?*"

"Nothing save that I'm mystified."

"You are indeed. You're quite off the hinge. What's the meaning of this new fad?" And he tossed me, with visible irreverence, a drawing in which I happened to have depicted both my majestic models. I asked if he didn't think it good, and he replied that it struck him as execrable, given the sort of thing I had always represented myself to him as wishing to arrive at; but I let that pass, I was so anxious to see exactly what he meant. The two figures in the picture looked colossal, but I supposed this was *not* what he meant, inasmuch as, for aught he knew to the contrary, I might have been trying for that. I maintained that I was working exactly in the same way as when he last had done me the honour to commend me. "Well, there's a big hole somewhere," he answered; "wait a bit and I'll discover it." I depended upon him to do so: where else was the fresh eye? But he produced at last nothing more luminous than "I don't know—I don't like your types." This was lame, for a critic who had never consented to discuss with me anything but the question of execution, the direction of strokes and the mystery of values.

"In the drawings you've been looking at I think my types are very handsome."

"Oh, they won't do!"

"I've had a couple of new models."

"I see you have. *They* won't do."

"Are you very sure of that?"

"Absolutely—they're stupid."

"You mean *I* am—for I ought to get round that."

"You *can't*—with such people. Who are they?"

I told him, as far as was necessary, and he declared, heartlessly: "*Ce sont des gens qu'il faut mettre à la porte.*"

"You've never seen them; they're awfully good," I compassionately objected.

"Not seen them? Why, all this recent work of yours drops to pieces with them. It's all I want to see of them."

"No one else has said anything against it—the *Cheapside* people are pleased."

"Everyone else is an ass, and the *Cheapside* people the biggest asses of all. Come, don't pretend, at this time of day, to have pretty illusions about the public, especially about publishers and editors. It's not for *such* animals you work—it's for those who know, *coloro che sanno;* so keep straight for *me* if you can't keep straight for yourself. There's a certain sort of thing you tried for from the first—and a very good thing it is. But this twaddle isn't *in* it." When I talked with Hawley later about "Rutland Ramsay" and its possible successors he declared that I must get back into my boat again or I would go to the bottom. His voice in short was the voice of warning.

I noted the warning, but I didn't turn my friends out of doors. They bored me a good deal; but the very fact that they bored me admonished me not to sacrifice them—if there was anything to be done with them—simply to irritation. As I look back at this phase they seem to me to have pervaded my life not a little. I have a vision of them as most of the time in my studio, seated, against the wall, on an old velvet bench to be out of the way, and looking like a pair of patient courtiers in a royal ante-chamber. I am convinced that during the coldest weeks of the winter they held their ground because it saved them fire. Their newness was losing its gloss, and it was impossible not to feel that they were objects of charity. Whenever Miss Churm arrived they went away, and after I was fairly launched in "Rutland Ramsay" Miss Churm arrived pretty often. They managed to express to me tacitly that they supposed I wanted her for the low life of the book, and I let them suppose it, since they had attempted to study the work —it was lying about the studio—without discovering that it dealt only with the highest circles. They had dipped into the most brilliant of our novelists without deciphering many passages. I still took an hour from them, now and again, in spite of Jack Hawley's warning: it would be time enough to dismiss them, if dismissal should be necessary, when the rigour of the season was over. Hawley had made their acquaintance—he had met them at my fireside—and thought them a ridiculous pair. Learning that he was a painter they tried to approach him, to show him too that they were the real thing; but he looked at them, across the big room, as if they were miles away: they were a compendium of everything that he most objected to in the social system of his country. Such people as that, all convention and patent-leather, with ejaculations that stopped conversation, had no business in a studio. A studio was a place to learn to see, and how could you see through a pair of feather beds?

The main inconvenience I suffered at their hands was that, at first, I was shy of letting them discover how my artful little servant had begun to sit to me for "Rutland Ramsay." They knew that I had been odd enough (they were prepared by this time to allow oddity to artists,) to pick a foreign vagabond out of the streets, when I might have had a person with whiskers and credentials; but it was some time before they learned how high I rated his accomplishments. They found him in an attitude more than once, but they never doubted I was doing him as an organ-grinder. There were several things they never guessed, and one of them was that for a striking scene in the novel, in which a footman briefly figured, it occurred to me to make use of Major Monarch as the menial. I kept putting this off, I didn't like to ask him to don the livery—besides the difficulty of finding a livery to fit him. At last, one day late in the winter, when I was at work on the despised Oronte (he caught one's idea in an instant), and was in the glow of feeling that I was going very straight, they came in, the Major and his wife, with their society laugh about nothing (there was less and less to laugh at), like country-callers—they always re-minded me of that—who have walked across the park after church and are presently persuaded to stay to luncheon. Luncheon was over, but they could stay to tea—I knew they wanted it. The fit was on me, however, and I couldn't let my ardour cool and my work wait, with the fading daylight, while my model prepared it. So I asked Mrs Monarch if she would mind laying it out—a request which, for an instant, brought all the blood to her face. Her eyes were on her husband's for a second, and some mute telegraphy passed between them. Their folly was over the next instant; his cheerful shrewdness put an end to it. So far from pitying their wounded pride, I must add, I was moved to give it as complete a lesson as I could. They bustled about together and got out the cups and saucers and made the kettle boil. I know they felt as if they were waiting on my servant, and when the tea was prepared I said: "He'll have a cup, please—he's tired." Mrs Monarch brought him one where he stood, and he took it from her as if he had been a gentleman at a party, squeezing a crush-hat with an elbow.

Then it came over me that she had made a great effort for me—made it with a kind of nobleness—and that I owed her a compensation. Each time I saw her after this I wondered what the compensation could be. I couldn't go on doing the wrong thing to oblige them. Oh, it *was* the wrong thing, the stamp of the work for which they sat—Hawley was not the only person to say it now. I sent in a large number of the drawings I had made for "Rutland Ramsay," and I received a warning that was more to the point than Hawley's. The artistic adviser of the house for which I was working was of opinion that many of my illustrations were not what had been looked for. Most of these illustrations were the subjects in which the Monarchs had figured. Without going into the question of what *had* been looked for, I saw at this rate I shouldn't get the other books to do. I hurled myself in despair upon Miss Churm, I put her through all her paces. I not only adopted Oronte publicly as my hero, but one morning when the Major looked in to see if I didn't require him to finish a figure for the *Cheapside*, for which he had begun to sit the week before, I told him that I had changed my mind—I would do the drawing from my man. At this my visitor turned pale and stood looking at me. "Is *he* your idea of an English gentleman?" he asked.

I was disappointed, I was nervous, I wanted to get on with my work; so I replied with irritation: "Oh, my dear Major— I can't be ruined for *you!*"

He stood another moment; then, without a word, he quitted the studio. I drew a long breath when he was gone, for I said to myself that I shouldn't see him again. I had not told him definitely that I was in danger of having my work rejected, but I was vexed at his not having felt the catastrophe in the air, read with me the moral of our fruitless collaboration, the lesson that, in the deceptive atmosphere of art, even the highest respectability may fail of being plastic.

I didn't owe my friends money, but I did see them again. They re-appeared together, three days later, and under the circumstances there was something tragic in the fact. It was a proof to me that they could find nothing else in life to do. They had threshed the matter out in a dismal conference— they had digested the bad news that they were not in for the series. If they were not useful to me even for the *Cheapside* their function seemed difficult to determine, and I could only judge at first that they had come, forgivingly, decorously, to take a last leave. This made me rejoice in secret that I had little leisure for a scene; for I had placed both my other models in position together and I was pegging away at a drawing from which I hoped to derive glory. It had been suggested by the passage in which Rutland Ramsay, drawing up a chair to Artemisia's piano-stool, says extraordinary things to her while she ostensibly fingers out a difficult piece of music. I had done Miss Churm at the piano before—it was an attitude in which she knew how to take on an absolutely poetic grace. I wished the two figures to "compose" together, intensely, and my little Italian had entered perfectly into my conception. The pair were vividly before me, the piano had been pulled out; it was a charming picture of blended youth and murmured love, which I had only to catch and keep. My visitors stood and looked at it, and I was friendly to them over my shoulder.

They made no response, but I was used to silent company and went on with my work, only a little disconcerted (even though exhilarated by the sense that *this* was at least the ideal thing), at not having got rid of them after all. Presently I heard Mrs Monarch's sweet voice beside, or rather above me: "I wish her hair was a little better done." I looked up and she was staring with a strange fixedness at Miss Churm, whose back was turned to her. "Do you mind my just touching it?" she went on—a question which made me spring up for an instant, as with the instinctive fear that she might do the young lady a harm. But she quieted me with a glance I shall never forget—I confess I should like to have been able to paint *that*—and went for a moment to my model. She spoke to her softly, laying a hand upon her shoulder and bending over her; and as the girl, understanding, gratefully assented, she disposed her rough curls, with a few quick passes, in such a way as to make Miss Churm's head twice as charming. It was one of the most heroic personal services I have ever seen rendered. Then Mrs Monarch turned away with a low sigh and, looking about her as if for something to do, stooped to the floor with a noble humility and picked up a dirty rag that had dropped out of my paint-box.

The Major meanwhile had also been looking for something to do and, wandering to the other end of the studio, saw before him my breakfast things, neglected, unremoved. "I say, can't I be useful *here?*" he called out to me with an irrepressible quaver. I assented with a laugh that I fear was awkward and for the next ten minutes, while I worked, I heard the light clatter of china and the tinkle of spoons and glass. Mrs Monarch assisted her husband—they washed up my crockery, they put it away. They wandered off into my little scullery, and I afterwards found that they had cleaned my knives and that my slender stock of plate had an unprecedented surface. When it came over me, the latent eloquence of what they were doing, I confess that my drawing was blurred for a moment—the picture swam. They had accepted their failure, but they couldn't accept their fate. They had bowed their heads in bewilderment to the perverse and cruel law in virtue of which the real thing could be so much less precious than the unreal; but they didn't want to starve. If my servants were my models, my models might be my servants. They would reverse the parts—the others would sit for the ladies and gentlemen, and *they* would do the work. They would still be in the studio—it was an intense dumb appeal to me not to turn them out. "Take us on," they wanted to say—"we'll do *anything*."

When all this hung before me the *afflatus* vanished—my pencil dropped from my hand. My sitting was spoiled and I got rid of my sitters, who were also evidently rather mystified and awestruck. Then, alone with the Major and his wife, I had a most uncomfortable moment. He put their prayer into a single sentence: "I say, you know—just let *us* do for you, can't you?" I couldn't—it was dreadful to see them emptying my slops; but I pretended I could, to oblige them, for about a week. Then I gave them a sum of money to go away; and I never saw them again. I obtained the remaining books, but my friend Hawley repeats that Major and Mrs Monarch did me a permanent harm, got me into a second-rate trick. If it be true I am content to have paid the price—for the memory.

LORD BEAUPRÉ

I

SOME reference had been made to Northerley, which was within an easy drive, and Firminger described how he had dined there the night before and had found a lot of people. Mrs Ashbury, one of the two visitors, inquired who these people might be, and he mentioned half-a-dozen names, among which was that of young Raddle, which had been a good deal on people's lips, and even in the newspapers, on the occasion, still recent, of his stepping into the fortune, exceptionally vast even as the product of a patent-glue, left him by a father whose ugly name on all the vacant spaces of the world had exasperated generations of men.

"Oh, is he there?" asked Mrs Ashbury, in a tone which might have been taken as a vocal rendering of the act of pricking up one's ears. She didn't hand on the information to her daughter, who was talking—if a beauty of so few phrases could have been said to talk—with Mary Gosselin, but in the course of a few moments she put down her teacup with a failure of suavity and, getting up, gave the girl a poke with her parasol. "Come, Maud, we must be stirring."

"You pay us a very short visit," said Mrs Gosselin, intensely demure over the fine web of her knitting. Mrs Ashbury looked hard for an instant into her bland eyes, then she gave poor Maud another poke. She alluded to a reason and expressed regrets; but she got her daughter into motion, and Guy Firminger passed through the garden with the two ladies to put them into their carriage. Mrs Ashbury protested particularly against any further escort. While he was absent the other parent and child, sitting together on their pretty lawn in

the yellow light of the August afternoon, talked of the frightful way Maud Ashbury had "gone off," and of something
else as to which there was more to say when their third visitor
came back.

"Don't think me grossly inquisitive if I ask you where they
told the coachman to drive," said Mary Gosselin as the young
man dropped, near her, into a low wicker chair, stretching his
long legs as if he had been one of the family.

Firminger stared. "Upon my word I didn't particularly
notice, but I think the old lady said 'Home.'"

"There, mamma dear!" the girl exclaimed triumphantly.

But Mrs Gosselin only knitted on, persisting in profundity.
She replied that "Home" was a feint, that Mrs Ashbury
would already have given another order, and that it was her
wish to hurry off to Northerley that had made her keep them
from going with her to the carriage, in which they would have
seen her take a suspected direction. Mary explained to Guy
Firminger that her mother had perceived poor Mrs Ashbury
to be frantic to reach the house at which she had heard that
Mr Raddle was staying. The young man stared again and
wanted to know what she desired to do with Mr Raddle. Mary
replied that her mother would tell him what Mrs Ashbury
desired to do with poor Maud.

"What all Christian mothers desire," said Mrs Gosselin.
"Only she doesn't know how."

"To marry the dear child to Mr Raddle," Mary added,
smiling.

Firminger's vagueness expanded with the subject. "Do
you mean you want to marry *your* dear child to that little
cad?" he asked of the elder lady.

"I speak of the general duty—not of the particular case,"
said Mrs Gosselin.

"Mamma *does* know how," Mary went on.

"Then why ain't you married?"

"Because we're not acting, like the Ashburys, with injudicious precipitation. Is that correct?" the girl demanded, laughing, of her mother.

"Laugh at me, my dear, as much as you like—it's very lucky you've got me," Mrs Gosselin declared.

"She means I can't manage for myself," said Mary to the visitor.

"What nonsense you talk!" Mrs Gosselin murmured, counting stitches.

"I can't, mamma, I can't; I admit it," Mary continued.

"But injudicious precipitation and—what's the other thing? —creeping prudence, seem to come out in very much the same place," the young man objected.

"Do you mean since I too wither on the tree?"

"It only comes back to saying how hard it is nowadays to marry one's daughters," said the lucid Mrs Gosselin, saving Firminger, however, the trouble of an ingenious answer. "I don't contend that, at the best, it's easy."

But Guy Firminger would not have struck you as capable of much conversational effort as he lounged there in the summer softness, with ironic familiarities, like one of the old friends who rarely deviate into sincerity. He was a robust but loose-limbed young man, with a well-shaped head and a face smooth, fair and kind. He was in knickerbockers, and his clothes, which had seen service, were composed of articles that didn't match. His laced boots were dusty—he had evidently walked a certain distance; an indication confirmed by the lingering, sociable way in which, in his basket-seat, he tilted himself towards Mary Gosselin. It pointed to a pleasant reason for a long walk. This young lady, of five-and-twenty, had black hair and blue eyes; a combination often associated with the effect of beauty. The beauty in this case, however, was dim and latent, not vulgarly obvious; and if her height and slenderness gave that impression of length of line which, as we know, is the fashion, Mary Gosselin had on the other hand too much expression to be generally admired. Every one thought her intellectual; a few of the most simple-minded even thought her plain. What Guy Firminger thought—or rather what he took for granted, for he was not built up on depths of reflection—will probably appear from this narrative.

"Yes indeed; things have come to a pass that's awful for *us*," the girl announced.

"For *us*, you mean," said Firminger. "We're hunted like the ostrich; we're trapped and stalked and run to earth. We go in fear—I assure you we do."

"Are *you* hunted, Guy?" Mrs Gosselin asked with an inflection of her own.

"Yes, Mrs Gosselin, even *moi qui vous parle*, the ordinary male of commerce, inconceivable as it may appear. I know something about it."

"And of whom do you go in fear?" Mary Gosselin took up an uncut book and a paper-knife which she had laid down on the advent of the other visitors.

"My dear child, of Diana and her nymphs, of the spinster at large. She's always out with her rifle. And it isn't only that; you know there's always a second gun, a walking arsenal, at her heels. I forget, for the moment, who Diana's mother was, and the genealogy of the nymphs; but not only do the old ladies know the younger ones are out, they distinctly go *with* them."

"Who was Diana's mother, my dear?" Mrs Gosselin inquired of her daughter.

"She was a beautiful old lady with pink ribbons in her cap and a genius for knitting," the girl replied, cutting her book.

"Oh, I'm not speaking of you two dears; you're not like anyone else; you're an immense comfort," said Guy Firminger. "But they've reduced it to a science, and I assure you that if one were any one in particular, if one were not protected by one's obscurity, one's life would be a burden. Upon my honour one wouldn't escape. I've seen it, I've watched them. Look at poor Beaupré—look at little Raddle over there. I object to him, but I bleed for him."

"Lord Beaupré won't marry again," said Mrs Gosselin with an air of conviction.

"So much the worse for him!"

"Come—that's a concession to our charms!" Mary laughed.

But the ruthless young man explained away his concession. "I mean that to be married's the only protection—or else to be engaged."

"To be permanently engaged,—wouldn't that do?" Mary Gosselin asked.

"Beautifully—I would try it if I were a *parti*."

"And how's the little boy?" Mrs Gosselin presently inquired.

"What little boy?"

"Your little cousin—Lord Beaupré's child: isn't it a boy?"

"Oh, poor little beggar, he isn't up to much. He was awfully cut up by scarlet fever."

"You're not the rose indeed, but you're tolerably near it," the elder lady presently continued.

"What do you call near it? Not even in the same garden—not in any garden at all, alas!"

"There are three lives—but after all!"

"Dear lady, don't be homicidal!"

"What do you call the 'rose'?" Mary asked of her mother.

"The title," said Mrs Gosselin, promptly but softly.

Something in her tone made Firminger laugh aloud. "You don't mention the property."

"Oh, I mean the whole thing."

"Is the property very large?" said Mary Gosselin.

"Fifty thousand a year," her mother responded; at which the young man laughed out again.

"Take care, mamma, or we shall be thought to be out with

our guns!" the girl interposed; a recommendation that drew from Guy Firminger the just remark that there would be time enough for this when his prospects should be worth speaking of. He leaned over to pick up his hat and stick, as if it were his time to go, but he didn't go for another quarter of an hour, and during these minutes his prospects received some frank consideration. He was Lord Beaupré's first cousin, and the three intervening lives were his lordship's own, that of his little sickly son, and that of his uncle the Major, who was also Guy's uncle and with whom the young man was at present staying. It was from homely Trist, the Major's house, that he had walked over to Mrs Gosselin's. Frank Firminger, who had married in youth a woman with something of her own and eventually left the army, had nothing but girls, but he was only of middle age and might possibly still have a son. At any rate his life was a very good one. Beaupré might marry again, and, marry or not, he was barely thirty-three and might live to a great age. The child moreover, poor little devil, would doubtless, with the growing consciousness of an incentive (there was none like feeling you were in people's way), develop a capacity for duration; so that altogether Guy professed himself, with the best will in the world, unable to take a rosy view of the disappearance of obstacles. He treated the subject with a jocularity that, in view of the remoteness of his chance, was not wholly tasteless, and the discussion, between old friends and in the light of this extravagance, was less crude than perhaps it sounds. The young man quite declined to see any latent brilliancy in his future. They had all been lashing him up, his poor dear mother, his uncle Frank, and Beaupré as well, to make that future political; but even if he should get in (he was nursing—oh, so languidly!—a possible opening), it would only be into the shallow edge of the stream. He would stand there like a tall idiot with the water up to his ankles. He didn't know how to swim—in that element; he didn't know how to do anything.

"I think you're very perverse, my dear," said Mrs Gosselin. "I'm sure you have great dispositions."

"For what—except for sitting here and talking with you and Mary? I revel in this sort of thing, but I scarcely like anything else."

"You'd do very well if you weren't so lazy," Mary said. "I believe you're the very laziest person in the world."

"So do I—the very laziest in the world," the young man contentedly replied. "But how can I regret it, when it keeps me so quiet, when (I might even say) it makes me so amiable?"

"You'll have, one of these days, to get over your quietness, and perhaps even a little over your amiability," Mrs Gosselin sagaciously stated.

"I devoutly hope not."

"You'll have to perform the duties of your position."

"Do you mean keep my stump of a broom in order and my crossing irreproachable?"

"You may say what you like; you will be a *parti*," Mrs Gosselin continued.

"Well, then, if the worst comes to the worst I shall do what I said just now: I shall get some good plausible girl to see me through."

"The proper way to 'get' her will be to marry her. After you're married you won't be a *parti*."

"Dear mamma, he'll think you're already levelling your rifle!" Mary Gosselin laughingly wailed.

Guy Firminger looked at her a moment. "I say, Mary, wouldn't *you* do?"

"For the good plausible girl? Should I be plausible enough?"

"Surely—what could be more natural? Everything would seem to contribute to the suitability of our alliance. I should be known to have known you for years—from childhood's sunny hour; I should be known to have bullied you, and even to have been bullied *by* you, in the period of pinafores. My relations from a tender age with your brother, which led to our schoolroom romps in holidays and to the happy footing on which your mother has always been so good as to receive me here, would add to all the presumptions of intimacy. People would accept such a conclusion as inevitable."

"Among all your reasons you don't mention the young lady's attractions," said Mary Gosselin.

Firminger stared a moment, his clear eye lighted by his happy thought. "I don't mention the young man's. They would be so obvious, on one side and the other, as to be taken for granted."

"And is it your idea that one should pretend to be engaged to you all one's life?"

"Oh no, simply till I should have had time to look round. I'm determined not to be hustled and bewildered into matrimony—to be dragged to the shambles before I know where I am. With such an arrangement as the one I speak of I should be able to take my time, to keep my head, to make my choice."

"And how would the young lady make hers?"

"How do you mean, hers?"

"The selfishness of men is something exquisite. Suppose the young lady—if it's conceivable that you should find one idiotic enough to be a party to such a transaction—suppose the poor girl herself should happen to wish to be *really* engaged?"

Guy Firminger thought a moment, with his slow but not stupid smile. "Do you mean to *me?*"

"To you—or to some one else."

"Oh, if she'd give me notice I'd let her off."

"Let her off till you could find a substitute?"

"Yes—but I confess it would be a great inconvenience. People wouldn't take the second one so seriously."

"She would have to make a sacrifice; she would have to

wait till you should know where you were," Mrs Gosselin suggested.

"Yes, but where would *her* advantage come in?" Mary persisted.

"Only in the pleasure of charity; the moral satisfaction of doing a fellow a good turn," said Firminger.

"You must think people are keen to oblige you!"

"Ah, but surely I could count on *you*, couldn't I?" the young man asked.

Mary had finished cutting her book; she got up and flung it down on the tea-table. "What a preposterous conversation!" she exclaimed with force, tossing the words from her as she tossed her book; and, looking round her vaguely a moment, without meeting Guy Firminger's eye, she walked away to the house.

Firminger sat watching her; then he said serenely to her mother: "Why has our Mary left us?"

"She has gone to get something, I suppose."

"What has she gone to get?"

"A little stick to beat you perhaps."

"You don't mean I've been objectionable?"

"Dear, no—I'm joking. One thing is very certain," pursued Mrs Gosselin; "that you ought to work—to try to get on exactly as if nothing could ever happen. Oughtn't you?" She threw off the question mechanically as her visitor continued silent.

"I'm sure she doesn't like it!" he exclaimed, without heeding her appeal.

"Doesn't like what?"

"My free play of mind. It's perhaps too much in the key of our old romps."

"You're very clever; she always likes *that*," said Mrs Gosselin. "You ought to go in for something serious, for something honourable," she continued, "just as much as if you had nothing at all to look to."

"Words of wisdom, dear Mrs Gosselin," Firminger replied, rising slowly from his relaxed attitude. "But what *have* I to look to?"

She raised her mild, deep eyes to him as he stood before her—she might have been a fairy godmother. "Everything!"

"But you know I can't poison them!"

"That won't be necessary."

He looked at her an instant; then with a laugh: "One might think *you* would undertake it!"

"I almost would—for *you*. Good-bye."

"Take care,—if they *should* be carried off!" But Mrs Gosselin only repeated her good-bye, and the young man departed before Mary had come back.

II

NEARLY two years after Guy Firminger had spent that friendly hour in Mrs Gosselin's little garden in Hampshire this far-seeing woman was enabled (by the return of her son, who at New York, in an English bank, occupied a position they all rejoiced over—to such great things might it duly lead), to resume possession, for the season, of the little London house which her husband had left her to inhabit, but which her native thrift, in determining her to let it for a term, had converted into a source of income. Hugh Gosselin, who was thirty years old and at twenty-three, before his father's death, had been dispatched to America to exert himself, was understood to be doing very well—so well that his devotion to the interests of his employers had been rewarded, for the first time, with a real holiday. He was to remain in England from May to August, undertaking, as he said, to make it all right if during this time his mother should occupy (to contribute to his entertainment), the habitation in Chester Street. He was a small, preoccupied young man, with a sharpness as acquired as a new hat; he struck his mother and sister as intensely American. For the first few days after his arrival they were startled by his intonations, though they admitted that they had had an escape when he reminded them that he might have brought with him an accent embodied in a wife.

"When you do take one," said Mrs Gosselin, who regarded such an accident, over there, as inevitable, "you must charge her high for it."

It was not with this question, however, that the little family in Chester Street was mainly engaged, but with the last incident in the extraordinary succession of events which, like a chapter of romance, had in the course of a few months converted their vague and impecunious friend into a personage envied and honoured. It was as if a blight had been cast on all Guy Firminger's hindrances. On the day Hugh Gosselin sailed from New York the delicate little boy at Bosco had succumbed to an attack of diphtheria. His father had died of typhoid the previous winter at Naples; his uncle, a few weeks later, had had a fatal accident in the hunting-field. So strangely, so rapidly had the situation cleared up, had his fate and theirs worked for him. Guy had opened his eyes one morning to an earldom which carried with it a fortune not alone nominally but really great. Mrs Gosselin and Mary had not written to him, but they knew he was at Bosco; he had remained there after the funeral of the late little lord. Mrs Gosselin, who heard everything, had heard somehow that he was behaving with the greatest consideration, giving the guardians, the trustees, whatever they were called, plenty of time to do everything. Everything was comparatively simple; in the absence of collaterals there were so few other people concerned. The principal relatives were poor Frank Firminger's widow and her girls, who had seen themselves so near to new honours and comforts. Probably the girls would expect their cousin Guy to marry one of them, and think it the least he could decently do; a view the young man himself (if he were very magnanimous) might possibly embrace. The question would be whether he would be very magnanimous. These young ladies exhausted in their three persons the numerous varieties of plainness. On the other hand Guy Firminger—or Lord Beaupré, as one would have to begin to call him now—was unmistakably kind. Mrs Gosselin appealed to her son as to whether their noble friend were not unmistakably kind.

"Of course I've known him always, and that time he came out to America—when was it? four years ago—I saw him every day. I like him awfully and all that, but since you push me, you know," said Hugh Gosselin, "I'm bound to say that the first thing to mention in any description of him would be—if you wanted to be quite correct—that he's unmistakably selfish."

"I see—I see," Mrs Gosselin unblushingly replied. "Of course I know what you mean," she added in a moment. "But is he any more so than any one else? Every one's unmistakably selfish."

"Every one but you and Mary," said the young man.

"And *you*, dear!" his mother smiled. "But a person may be kind, you know—mayn't he?—at the same time that he *is* selfish. There are different sorts."

"Different sorts of kindness?" Hugh Gosselin asked with a laugh; and the inquiry undertaken by his mother occupied them for the moment, demanding a subtlety of treatment from which they were not conscious of shrinking, of which rather they had an idea that they were perhaps exceptionally capable. They came back to the temperate view that Guy would never put himself out, would probably never do anything great, but might show himself all the same a delightful member of society. Yes, he was probably selfish, like other people; but unlike most of them he was, somehow, amiably, attachingly, sociably, almost lovably selfish. Without doing anything great he would yet be a great success—a big, pleasant, gossiping, lounging and, in its way doubtless very splendid, presence. He would have no ambition, and it was ambition that made selfishness ugly. Hugh and his mother were sure of this last point until Mary, before whom the discussion, when it reached this stage, happened to be carried on, checked them by asking whether that, on the contrary, were not just what was supposed to make it fine.

"Oh, he only wants to be comfortable," said her brother; "but he *does* want it!"

"There'll be a tremendous rush for him," Mrs Gosselin prophesied to her son.

"Oh, he'll never marry. It will be too much trouble."

"It's done here without any trouble—for the men. One sees how long you've been out of the country."

"There was a girl in New York whom he might have married—he really liked her. But he wouldn't turn round for her."

"Perhaps she wouldn't turn round for *him*," said Mary.

"I daresay she'll turn round *now*," Mrs Gosselin rejoined; on which Hugh mentioned that there was nothing to be feared from her, all her revolutions had been accomplished. He added that nothing would make any difference—so intimate was his conviction that Beaupré would preserve his independence.

"Then I think he's not so selfish as you say," Mary declared. "Or at any rate one will never know whether he is. Isn't married life the great chance to show it?"

"Your father never showed it," said Mrs Gosselin; and as her children were silent in presence of this tribute to the departed she added, smiling: "Perhaps you think that *I* did!" They embraced her, to indicate what they thought, and the conversation ended, when she had remarked that Lord Beaupré was a man who would be perfectly easy to manage *after* marriage, with Hugh's exclaiming that this was doubtless exactly why he wished to keep out of it.

Such was evidently his wish, as they were able to judge in Chester Street when he came up to town. He appeared there oftener than was to have been expected, not taking himself in his new character at all too seriously to find stray half-hours for old friends. It was plain that he was going to do just as he liked, that he was not a bit excited or uplifted by his change of fortune. Mary Gosselin observed that he had no imagination —she even reproached him with the deficiency to his face; an incident which showed indeed how little seriously *she* took him. He had no idea of playing a part, and yet he would have been clever enough. He wasn't even systematic about being simple; his simplicity was a series of accidents and indifferences. Never was a man more conscientiously superficial. There were matters on which he valued Mrs Gosselin's judgment and asked her advice—without, as usually appeared later, ever taking it; such questions, mainly, as the claims of a predecessor's servants, and those, in respect to social intercourse, of the clergyman's family. He didn't like his parson— what was a fellow to do when he didn't like his parson? What he did like was to talk with Hugh about American investments, and it was amusing to Hugh, though he tried not to show his amusement, to find himself looking at Guy Firminger in the light of capital. To Mary he addressed from the first the oddest snatches of confidential discourse, rendered in fact, however, by the levity of his tone, considerably less confidential than in intention. He had something to tell her that he joked about, yet without admitting that it was any less important for being laughable. It was neither more nor less than that Charlotte Firminger, the eldest of his late uncle's four girls, had designated to him in the clearest manner the person she considered he ought to marry. She appealed to his sense of justice, she spoke and wrote, or at any rate she looked and moved, she sighed and sang, in the name of common honesty. He had had four letters from her that week, and to his knowledge there were a series of people in London, people she could bully, whom she had got to promise to take her in for the season. She was going to be on the spot, she was going to follow him up. He took his stand on common honesty, but he had a mortal horror of Charlotte. At the same time, when a girl had a jaw like that and had marked you—really *marked* you, mind, you felt your safety oozing away. He had given them during the past three months, all those terrible girls, every sort of present that Bond Street could supply: but these demonstrations had only been held to constitute another pledge. Therefore what was a fellow to do? Besides, there were other portents; the air was thick with them, as the sky over battlefields was darkened by the flight of vultures. They were flocking, the birds of prey, from every quarter, and every girl in England, by Jove! was going to be thrown at his head. What had he done to deserve such a fate? He wanted to stop in England and see all sorts of things through; but how could he stand there and face such a charge? Yet what good would it do to bolt? Wherever he should go there would be fifty of them there first. On his honour he could say that he didn't deserve it; he had never, to his own sense, been a flirt, such a flirt at least as to have given anyone a handle. He appealed candidly to Mary Gosselin to know whether his past conduct justified such penalties. "*Have* I been a flirt?—have I given anyone a handle?" he inquired with pathetic intensity.

She met his appeal by declaring that he had been awful, committing himself right and left; and this manner of treating his affliction contributed to the sarcastic publicity (as regarded the little house in Chester Street) which presently became its natural element. Lord Beaupré's comical and yet thoroughly grounded view of his danger was soon a frequent theme among the Gosselins, who however had their own reasons for not communicating the alarm. They had no motive for concealing their interest in their old friend, but their allusions to him among their other friends may be said on the whole to have been studied. His state of mind recalled of course to

Mary and her mother the queer talk about his prospects that they had had, in the country, that afternoon on which Mrs Gosselin had been so strangely prophetic (she confessed that she had had a flash of divination: the future had been mysteriously revealed to her), and poor Guy too had seen himself quite as he was to be. He had seen his nervousness, under inevitable pressure, deepen to a panic, and he now, in intimate hours, made no attempt to disguise that a panic had become his portion. It was a fixed idea with him that he should fall a victim to woven toils, be caught in a trap constructed with superior science. The science evolved in an enterprising age by this branch of industry, the manufacture of the trap matrimonial, he had terrible anecdotes to illustrate; and what had he on his lips but a scientific term when he declared, as he perpetually did, that it was his fate to be hypnotised?

Mary Gosselin reminded him, they each in turn reminded him that his safeguard was to fall in love: were he once to put himself under that protection all the mothers and maids in Mayfair would not prevail against him. He replied that this was just the impossibility; it took leisure and calmness and opportunity and a free mind to fall in love, and never was a man less open to such experiences. He was literally fighting his way. He reminded the girl of his old fancy for pretending already to have disposed of his hand if he could put that hand on a young person who should like him well enough to be willing to participate in the fraud. She would have to place herself in rather a false position of course— have to take a certain amount of trouble; but there would after all be a good deal of fun in it (there was always fun in duping the world,) between the pair themselves, the two happy comedians.

"Why should they both be happy?" Mary Gosselin asked. "I understand why you should; but, frankly, I don't quite grasp the reason of *her* pleasure."

Lord Beaupré, with his sunny human eyes, thought a

moment. "Why, for the lark, as they say, and that sort of thing. I should be awfully nice to her."

"She would require indeed to be in want of recreation!"

"Ah, but I should want a good sort—a quiet, reasonable one, you know!" he somewhat eagerly interposed.

"You're too delightful!" Mary Gosselin exclaimed, continuing to laugh. He thanked her for this appreciation, and she returned to her point—that she didn't really see the advantage his accomplice could hope to enjoy as her compensation for extreme disturbance.

Guy Firminger stared. "But what extreme disturbance?"

"Why, it would take a lot of time; it might become intolerable."

"You mean I ought to pay her—to hire her for the season?"

Mary Gosselin considered him a moment. "Wouldn't marriage come cheaper at once?" she asked with a quieter smile.

"You *are* chaffing me!" he sighed forgivingly. "Of course she would have to be good-natured enough to pity me."

"Pity's akin to love. If she were good-natured enough to want so to help you she'd be good-natured enough to want to marry you. That would be *her* idea of help."

"Would it be *yours?*" Lord Beaupré asked rather eagerly.

"You're too absurd! You must sail your own boat!" the girl answered, turning away.

That evening at dinner she stated to her companions that she had never seen a fatuity so dense, so serene, so preposterous as his lordship's.

"Fatuity, my dear! what do you mean?" her mother inquired.

"Oh, mamma, you know perfectly." Mary Gosselin spoke with a certain impatience.

"If you mean he's conceited I'm bound to say I don't agree with you," her brother observed. "He's too indifferent to everyone's opinion for that."

"He's not vain, he's not proud, he's not pompous," said Mrs Gosselin.

Mary was silent a moment. "He takes more things for granted than anyone I ever saw."

"What sort of things?"

"Well, one's interest in his affairs."

"With old friends surely a gentleman may."

"Of course," said Hugh Gosselin, "old friends have in turn the right to take for granted a corresponding interest on *his* part."

"Well, who could be nicer to us than he is or come to see us oftener?" his mother asked.

"He comes exactly for the purpose I speak of—to talk about himself," said Mary.

"There are thousands of girls who would be delighted with his talk," Mrs Gosselin returned.

"We agreed long ago that he's intensely selfish," the girl went on; "and if I speak of it to-day it's not because that in itself is anything of a novelty. What I'm freshly struck with is simply that he more shamelessly shows it."

"He shows it, exactly," said Hugh; "he shows all there is. There it is, on the surface; there are not depths of it underneath."

"He's not hard," Mrs Gosselin contended; "he's not impervious."

"Do you mean he's soft?" Mary asked.

"I mean he's yielding." And Mrs Gosselin, with considerable expression, looked across at her daughter. She added, before they rose from dinner, that poor Beaupré had plenty of difficulties and that she thought, for her part, they ought in common loyalty to do what they could to assist him.

For a week nothing more passed between the two ladies on the subject of their noble friend, and in the course of this week they had the amusement of receiving in Chester Street a member of Hugh's American circle, Mr Bolton-Brown, a young man from New York. He was a person engaged in large affairs, for whom Hugh Gosselin professed the highest regard, from whom in New York he had received much hospitality, and for whose advent he had from the first prepared his companions. Mrs Gosselin begged the amiable stranger to stay with them, and if she failed to overcome his hesitation it was because his hotel was near at hand and he should be able to see them often. It became evident that he would do so, and, to the two ladies, as the days went by, equally evident that no objection to such a relation was likely to arise. Mr Bolton-Brown was delightfully fresh; the most usual expressions acquired on his lips a wellnigh comical novelty, the most superficial sentiments, in the look with which he accompanied them, a really touching sincerity. He was unmarried and good-looking, clever and natural, and if he was not very rich was at least very free-handed. He literally strewed the path of the ladies in Chester Street with flowers, he choked them with French confectionery. Hugh, however, who was often rather mysterious on monetary questions, placed in a light sufficiently clear the fact that his friend had in Wall Street (they knew all about Wall Street), improved each shining hour. They introduced him to Lord Beaupré, who thought him "tremendous fun," as Hugh said, and who immediately declared that the four must spend a Sunday at Bosco a week or two later. The date of this visit was fixed—Mrs Gosselin had uttered a comprehensive acceptance; but after Guy Firminger had taken leave of them (this had been his first appearance since the odd conversation with Mary), our young lady confided to her mother that she should not be able to join the little party. She expressed the conviction that it would be all that was essential if Mrs Gosselin should go with the two others. On being pressed to communicate the reason of this aloofness Mary was able to give no better one than that she never had cared for Bosco.

"What makes you hate him so?" her mother presently

broke out in a tone which brought the red to the girl's cheek.
Mary denied that she entertained for Lord Beaupré any sentiment so intense; to which Mrs Gosselin rejoined with some
sternness and, no doubt, considerable wisdom: "Look out
what you do then, or you'll be thought by everyone to be in
love with him!"

III

I KNOW not whether it was this danger—that of appearing
to be moved to extremes—that weighed with Mary Gosselin;
at any rate when the day arrived she had decided to be
perfectly colourless and take her share of Lord Beaupré's
hospitality. On perceiving that the house, when with her companions she reached it, was full of visitors, she consoled herself with the sense that such a share would be of the smallest.
She even wondered whether its smallness might not be caused
in some degree by the sufficiently startling presence, in this
stronghold of the single life, of Maud Ashbury and her
mother. It was true that during the Saturday evening she
never saw their host address an observation to them; but she
was struck, as she had been struck before, with the girl's cold
and magnificent beauty. It was very well to say she had "gone
off"; she was still handsomer than anyone else. She had failed
in everything she had tried; the campaign undertaken with so
much energy against young Raddle had been conspicuously
disastrous. Young Raddle had married his grandmother, or
a person who might have filled such an office, and Maud was
a year older, a year more disappointed and a year more
ridiculous. Nevertheless one could scarcely believe that a
creature with such advantages would always fail, though indeed the poor girl was stupid enough to be a warning. Perhaps it would be at Bosco, or with the master of Bosco, that

fate had appointed her to succeed. Except Mary herself she was the only young unmarried woman on the scene, and Mary glowed with the generous sense of not being a competitor. She felt as much out of the question as the blooming wives, the heavy matrons, who formed the rest of the female contingent. Before the evening closed, however, her host, who, she saw, was delightful in his own house, mentioned to her that he had a couple of guests who had not been invited.

"Not invited?"

"They drove up to my door as they might have done to an inn. They asked for rooms and complained of those that were given them. Don't pretend not to know who they are."

"Do you mean the Ashburys? How amusing!"

"Don't laugh; it freezes my blood."

"Do you really mean you're afraid of them?"

"I tremble like a leaf. Some monstrous ineluctable fate seems to look at me out of their eyes."

"That's because you secretly admire Maud. How can you help it? She's extremely good-looking, and if you get rid of her mother she'll become a very nice girl."

"It's an odious thing, no doubt, to say about a young person under one's own roof, but I don't think I ever saw any one who happened to be less to my taste," said Guy Firminger. "I don't know why I don't turn them out even now."

Mary persisted in sarcasm. "Perhaps you can make her have a worse time by letting her stay."

"*Please* don't laugh," her interlocutor repeated. "Such a fact as I have mentioned to you seems to me to speak volumes —to show you what my life is."

"Oh, your life, your life!" Mary Gosselin murmured, with her mocking note.

"Don't you agree that at such a rate it may easily become impossible?"

"Many people would change with you. I don't see what there is for you to do but to bear your cross!"

"That's easy talk!" Lord Beaupré sighed.

"Especially from me, do you mean? How do you know I don't bear mine?"

"Yours?" he asked vaguely.

"How do you know that *I'm* not persecuted, that *my* footsteps are not dogged, that *my* life isn't a burden?"

They were walking in the old gardens, the proprietor of which, at this, stopped short. "Do you mean by fellows who want to marry you?"

His tone produced on his companion's part an irrepressible peal of hilarity; but she walked on as she exclaimed: "You speak as if there couldn't *be* such madmen!"

"Of course such a charming girl must be made up to," Guy Firminger conceded as he overtook her.

"I don't speak of it; I keep quiet about it."

"You realise then, at any rate, that it's all horrid when you don't care for them."

"I suffer in silence, because I know there are worse tribulations. It seems to me you ought to remember that," Mary continued. "Your cross is small compared with your crown. You've everything in the world that most people most desire, and I'm bound to say I think your life is made very comfortable for you. If you're oppressed by the quantity of interest and affection you inspire you ought simply to make up your mind to bear up and be cheerful under it."

Lord Beaupré received this admonition with perfect good humour; he professed himself able to do it full justice. He remarked that he would gladly give up some of his material advantages to be a little less badgered, and that he had been quite content with his former insignificance. No doubt, however, such annoyances were the essential drawbacks of ponderous promotions; one had to pay for everything. Mary was quite right to rebuke him; her own attitude, as a young woman much admired, was a lesson to his irritability. She cut this appreciation short, speaking of something else; but a few minutes later he broke out irrelevantly: "Why, if you are hunted as well as I, that dodge I proposed to you would be just the thing for us *both!*" He had evidently been reasoning it out.

Mary Gosselin was silent at first; she only paused gradually in their walk at a point where four long alleys met. In the centre of the circle, on a massive pedestal, rose in Italian bronze a florid, complicated image, so that the place made a charming old-world picture. The grounds of Bosco were stately without stiffness and full of marble terraces and misty avenues. The fountains in particular were royal. The girl had told her mother in London that she disliked this fine residence, but she now looked round her with a vague pleased sigh, holding up her glass (she had been condemned to wear one, with a long handle, since she was fifteen), to consider the weather-stained garden group. "What a perfect place of its kind!" she musingly exclaimed.

"Wouldn't it really be just the thing?" Lord Beaupré went on, with the eagerness of his idea.

"Wouldn't what be just the thing?"

"Why, the defensive alliance we've already talked of. You wanted to know the good it would do *you*. Now you see the good it would do you!"

"I don't like practical jokes," said Mary. "The remedy's worse than the disease," she added; and she began to follow one of the paths that took the direction of the house.

Poor Lord Beaupré was absurdly in love with his invention; he had all an inventor's importunity. He kept up his attempt to place his "dodge" in a favourable light, in spite of a further objection from his companion, who assured him that it was one of those contrivances which break down in practice in just the proportion in which they make a figure in theory. At last she said: "I was not sincere just now when I told you I'm worried. I'm *not* worried!"

"They *don't* buzz about you?" Guy Firminger asked.

She hesitated an instant. "They buzz about me; but at bottom it's flattering and I don't mind it. Now please drop the subject."

He dropped the subject, though not without congratulating her on the fact that, unlike his infirm self, she could keep her head and her temper. His infirmity found a trap laid for it before they had proceeded twenty yards, as was proved by his sudden exclamation of horror. "Good Heavens—if there isn't Lottie!"

Mary perceived, in effect, in the distance a female figure coming towards them over a stretch of lawn, and she simultaneously saw, as a gentleman passed from behind a clump of shrubbery, that it was not unattended. She recognized Charlotte Firminger, and she also distinguished the gentleman. She was moved to larger mirth at the dismay expressed by poor Firminger, but she was able to articulate: "Walking with Mr Brown."

Lord Beaupré stopped again before they were joined by the pair. "Does *he* buzz about you?"

"Mercy, what questions you ask!" his companion exclaimed.

"Does he—*please?*" the young man repeated with odd intensity.

Mary looked at him an instant; she was puzzled by the deep annoyance that had flushed through the essential good-humour of his face. Then she saw that this annoyance had exclusive reference to poor Charlotte; so that it left her free to reply, with another laugh: "Well, yes—he does. But you know I like it!"

"I don't, then!" Before she could have asked him, even had she wished to, in what manner such a circumstance concerned him, he added with his droll agitation: "I never invited *her*, either! Don't let her get at me!"

"What can I do?" Mary demanded as the others advanced.

"Please take her away; keep her yourself! I'll take the

American, I'll keep *him*," he murmured, inconsequently, as a bribe.

"But I don't object to him."

"Do you like him so much?"

"Very much indeed," the girl replied.

The reply was perhaps lost upon her interlocutor, whose eye now fixed itself gloomily on the dauntless Charlotte. As Miss Firminger came nearer he exclaimed almost loud enough for her to hear: "I think I shall *murder* her some day!"

Mary Gosselin's first impression had been that, in his panic, under the empire of that fixed idea to which he confessed himself subject, he attributed to his kinswoman machinations and aggressions of which she was incapable; an impression that might have been confirmed by this young lady's decorous placidity, her passionless eyes, her expressionless cheeks and colourless tones. She was ugly, yet she was orthodox; she was not what writers of books called intense. But after Mary, to oblige their host, had tried, successfully enough, to be crafty, had drawn her on to stroll a little in advance of the two gentlemen, she became promptly aware, by the mystical influence of propinquity, that Miss Firminger was indeed full of views, of a purpose single, simple and strong, which gave her the effect of a person carrying with a stiff, steady hand, with eyes fixed and lips compressed, a cup charged to the brim. She had driven over to lunch, driven from somewhere in the neighbourhood; she had picked up some weak woman as an escort. Mary, though she knew the neighbourhood, failed to recognize her base of operations, and, as Charlotte was not specific, ended by suspecting that, far from being entertained by friends, she had put up at an inn and hired a fly. This suspicion startled her; it gave her for the first time something of the measure of the passions engaged, and she wondered to what the insecurity complained of by Guy might lead. Charlotte, on arriving, had gone through a part of the house in quest of its master (the servants being unable to tell her where he was), and she had finally come upon Mr Bolton-Brown, who was looking at old books in the library. He had placed himself at her service, as if he had been trained immediately to recognize in such a case his duty, and informing her that he believed Lord Beaupré to be in the grounds, had come out with her to help to find him. Lottie Firminger questioned her companion about this accommodating person; she intimated that he was rather odd but rather nice. Mary mentioned to her that Lord Beaupré thought highly of him; she believed they were going somewhere together. At this Miss Firminger turned round to look for them, but they had already disappeared, and the girl became ominously dumb.

Mary wondered afterwards what profit she could hope to derive from such proceedings; they struck her own sense, naturally, as disreputable and desperate. She was equally unable to discover the compensation they offered, in another variety, to poor Maud Ashbury, whom Lord Beaupré, the greater part of the day, neglected as conscientiously as he neglected his cousin. She asked herself if he should be blamed, and replied that the others should be blamed first. He got rid of Charlotte somehow after tea; she had to fall back to her mysterious lines. Mary knew this method would have been detestable to him—he hated to force his friendly nature; she was sorry for him and wished to lose sight of him. She wished not to be mixed up even indirectly with his tribulations, and the fevered faces of the Ashburys were particularly dreadful to her. She spent as much of the long summer afternoon as possible out of the house, which indeed on such an occasion emptied itself of most of its inmates. Mary Gosselin asked her brother to join her in a devious ramble; she might have had other society, but she was in a mood to prefer his. These two were "great chums," and they had been separated so long that they had arrears of talk to make up. They had been at Bosco more than once, and though Hugh Gosselin said that the land of the free (which he had assured his sister was even more enslaved than dear old England) made one forget there were such spots on earth, they both remembered, a couple of miles away, a little ancient church to which the walk across the fields would be the right thing. They talked of other things as they went, and among them they talked of Mr Bolton-Brown, in regard to whom Hugh, as scantily addicted to enthusiasm as to bursts of song (he was determined not to be taken in), became, in commendation, almost lyrical. Mary asked what he had done with his paragon, and he replied that he believed him to have gone out stealthily to sketch: they might come across him. He was extraordinarily clever at water-colours, but haunted with the fear that the public practice of such an art on Sunday was viewed with disfavour in England. Mary exclaimed that this was the respectable fact, and when her brother ridiculed the idea she told him she had already noticed he had lost all sense of things at home, so that Mr Bolton-Brown was apparently a better Englishman than he. "He is indeed—he's awfully artificial!" Hugh returned; but it must be added that in spite of this rigour their American friend, when they reached the goal of their walk, was to be perceived in an irregular attitude in the very churchyard. He was perched on an old flat tomb, with a box of colours beside him and a sketch half completed. Hugh asserted that this exercise was the only thing that Mr Bolton-Brown really cared for, but the young man protested against the imputation in the face of an achievement so modest. He showed his sketch to Mary however, and it consoled her for not having kept up her own experiments; she never could make her trees so leafy. He had found a lovely bit on the other side of the hill, a bit he should like to come back to, and he offered to show it to his friends. They were on the point of starting with him to look at it when Hugh Gosselin, taking out his watch, remembered the hour at which he had promised to be at the house again to give his mother, who wanted a little mild exercise, his arm. His sister, at this, said she would go back with him; but

Bolton-Brown interposed an earnest inquiry. Mightn't she let Hugh keep his appointment and let *him* take her over the hill and bring her home?

"Happy thought—*do* that!" said Hugh, with a crudity that showed the girl how completely he had lost his English sense. He perceived however in an instant that she was embarrassed, whereupon he went on: "My dear child, I've walked with girls so often in America that we really ought to let poor Brown walk with one in England." I know not if it was the effect of this plea or that of some further eloquence of their friend; at any rate Mary Gosselin in the course of another minute had accepted the accident of Hugh's secession, had seen him depart with an injunction to her to render it clear to poor Brown that he had made quite a monstrous request. As she went over the hill with her companion she reflected that since she had granted the request it was not in her interest to pretend she had gone out of her way. She wondered moreover whether her brother had wished to throw them together: it suddenly occurred to her that the whole incident might have been prearranged. The idea made her a little angry with Hugh; it led her however to entertain no resentment against the other party (if party Mr Brown had been) to the transaction. He told her all the delight that certain sweet old corners of rural England excited in his mind, and she liked him for hovering near some of her own secrets.

Hugh Gosselin meanwhile, at Bosco, strolling on the terrace with his mother, who preferred walks that were as slow as conspiracies and had had much to say to him about his extraordinary indiscretion, repeated over and over (it ended by irritating her), that as he himself had been out for hours with American girls it was only fair to let their friend have a turn with an English one.

"Pay as much as you like, but don't pay with your sister!" Mrs Gosselin replied; while Hugh submitted that it was just his sister who was required to make the payment *his*. She turned his logic to easy scorn and she waited on the terrace till she had seen the two explorers reappear. When the ladies went to dress for dinner she expressed to her daughter her extreme disapproval of such conduct, and Mary did nothing more to justify herself than to exclaim at first "Poor dear man!" and then to say "I was afraid you wouldn't like it." There were reservations in her silence that made Mrs Gosselin uneasy, and she was glad that at dinner Mr Bolton-Brown had to take in Mrs Ashbury: it served him so right. This arrangement had in Mrs Gosselin's eyes the added merit of serving Mrs Ashbury right. She was more uneasy than ever when after dinner, in the drawing-room, she saw Mary sit for a period on the same small sofa with the culpable American. This young couple leaned back together familiarly, and their conversation had the air of being desultory without being in the least difficult. At last she quitted her place and went over to them, remarking to Mr Bolton-Brown that she wanted him to come and talk a bit to *her*. She conducted him to another part of the room, which was vast and animated by scattered groups, and held him there very persuasively, quite maternally, till the approach of the hour at which the ladies would exchange looks and murmur good-nights. She made him talk about America, though he wanted to talk about England, and she judged that she gave him an impression of the kindest attention, though she was really thinking, in alternation, of three important things. One of these was a circumstance of which she had become conscious only just after sitting down with him—the prolonged absence of Lord Beaupré from the drawing-room; the second was the absence, equally marked (to her imagination) of Maud Ashbury; the third was a matter different altogether. "England gives one such a sense of immemorial continuity, something that drops like a plummet-line into the past," said the young American, ingeniously exerting himself while Mrs Gosselin, rigidly contemporaneous, strayed into deserts of conjecture. Had the fact that their host was out of the room any connection with the fact that the most beautiful, even though the most suicidal, of his satellites had quitted it? Yet if poor Guy was taking a turn by starlight on the terrace with the misguided girl, what had he done with his resentment at her invasion and by what inspiration of despair had Maud achieved such a triumph? The good lady studied Mrs Ashbury's face across the room; she decided that triumph, accompanied perhaps with a shade of nervousness, looked out of her insincere eyes. An intelligent consciousness of ridicule was at any rate less present in them than ever. While Mrs Gosselin had her infallible finger on the pulse of the occasion one of the doors opened to readmit Lord Beaupré, who struck her as pale and who immediately approached Mrs Ashbury with a remark evidently intended for herself alone. It led this lady to rise with a movement of dismay and, after a question or two, leave the room. Lord Beaupré left it again in her company. Mr Bolton-Brown had also noticed the incident; his conversation languished and he asked Mrs Gosselin if she supposed anything had happened. She turned it over a moment and then she said: "Yes, something will have happened to Miss Ashbury."

"What do you suppose? Is she ill?"

"I don't know; we shall see. They're capable of anything."

"Capable of anything?"

"I've guessed it,—she wants to have a grievance."

"A grievance?" Mr Bolton-Brown was mystified.

"Of course you don't understand; how should you? Moreover it doesn't signify. But I'm so vexed with them (he's a very old friend of ours) that really, though I dare say I'm indiscreet, I can't speak civilly of them."

"Miss Ashbury's a wonderful type," said the young American.

This remark appeared to irritate his companion. "I see perfectly what has happened; she has made a scene."

"A scene?" Mr Bolton-Brown was terribly out of it.

"She has tried to be injured—to provoke him, I mean, to some act of impatience, to some failure of temper, of courtesy. She has asked him if he wishes her to leave the house at midnight, and he may have answered—But no, he wouldn't!" Mrs Gosselin suppressed the wild supposition.

"How you read it! She looks so quiet."

"Her mother has coached her, and (I won't pretend to say *exactly* what has happened) they've done, somehow, what they wanted; they've got him to do something to them that he'll have to make up for."

"What an evolution of ingenuity!" the young man laughed.

"It often answers."

"Will it in this case?"

Mrs Gosselin was silent a moment. "It *may*."

"Really, you think?"

"I mean it might if it weren't for something else."

"I'm too judicious to ask what that is."

"I'll tell you when we're back in town," said Mrs Gosselin, getting up.

Lord Beaupré was restored to them, and the ladies prepared to withdraw. Before she went to bed Mrs Gosselin asked him if there had been anything the matter with Maud; to which he replied with abysmal blankness (she had never seen him wear just that face) that he was afraid Miss Ashbury was ill. She proved in fact in the morning too unwell to return to London: a piece of news communicated to Mrs Gosselin at breakfast.

"She'll have to stay; I can't turn her out of the house," said Guy Firminger.

"Very well; let her stay her fill!"

"I wish you would stay too," the young man went on.

"Do you mean to nurse her?"

"No, her mother must do that. I mean to keep me company."

"*You?* You're not going up?"

"I think I had better wait over to-day, or long enough to see what's the matter."

"Don't you *know* what's the matter?"

He was silent a moment. "I may have been nasty last night."

"You have compunctions? You're too good-natured."

"I dare say I hit rather wild. It will look better for me to stop over twenty-four hours."

Mrs Gosselin fixed her eyes on a distant object. "Let no one ever say you're selfish!"

"*Does* anyone ever say it?"

"You're too generous, you're too soft, you're too foolish. But if it will give you any pleasure Mary and I will wait till to-morrow."

"And Hugh, too, won't he, and Bolton-Brown?"

"Hugh will do as he pleases. But don't keep the American."

"Why not? He's all right."

"That's why I want him to go," said Mrs Gosselin, who could treat a matter with candour, just as she could treat it with humour, at the right moment.

The party at Bosco broke up and there was a general retreat to town. Hugh Gosselin pleaded pressing business, he accompanied the young American to London. His mother and sister came back on the morrow, and Bolton-Brown went in to see them, as he often did, at tea-time. He found Mrs Gosselin alone in the drawing-room, and she took such a convenient occasion to mention to him, what she had withheld on the eve of their departure from Bosco, the reason why poor Maud Ashbury's frantic assault on the master of that property would be vain. He was greatly surprised, the more so that Hugh hadn't told him. Mrs Gosselin replied that Hugh didn't know: she had not seen him all day and it had only just come out. Hugh's friend at any rate was deeply interested, and his interest took for several minutes the form of throbbing silence. At last Mrs Gosselin heard a sound below, on which she said quickly: "That's Hugh—I'll tell him now!" She left the room with the request that their visitor would wait for

Mary, who would be down in a moment. During the instants that he spent alone the visitor lurched, as if he had been on a deck in a blow, to the window, and stood there with his hands in his pockets, staring vacantly into Chester Street; then, turning away, he gave himself, with an odd ejaculation, an impatient shake which had the effect of enabling him to meet Mary Gosselin composedly enough when she came in. It took her mother apparently some time to communicate the news to Hugh, so that Bolton-Brown had a considerable margin for nervousness and hesitation before he could say to the girl, abruptly, but with an attempt at a voice properly gay: "You must let me very heartily congratulate you!"

Mary stared. "On what?"

"On your engagement."

"My engagement?"

"To Lord Beaupré."

Mary Gosselin looked strange; she coloured. "Who told you I'm engaged?"

"Your mother—just now."

"Oh!" the girl exclaimed, turning away. She went and rang the bell for fresh tea, rang it with noticeable force. But she said "Thank you very much!" before the servant came.

IV

BOLTON-BROWN did something that evening toward disseminating the news: he told it to the first people he met socially after leaving Chester Street; and this although he had to do himself a certain violence in speaking. He would have preferred to hold his peace; therefore if he resisted his inclination it was for an urgent purpose. This purpose was to prove to himself that he didn't mind. A perfect indifference could be for him the only result of any understanding Mary Gosselin might arrive at with anyone, and he wanted to be more and more conscious of his indifference. He was aware indeed that it required demonstration, and this was why he was almost feverishly active. He could mentally concede at least that he had been surprised, for he had suspected nothing at Bosco. When a fellow was attentive in America everyone knew it, and judged by this standard Lord Beaupré made no show: how otherwise should *he* have achieved that sweet accompanied ramble? Everything at any rate was lucid now, except perhaps a certain ambiguity in Hugh Gosselin, who on coming into the drawing-room with his mother had looked flushed and grave and had stayed only long enough to kiss Mary and go out again. There had been nothing effusive in the scene; but then there was nothing effusive in any English scene. This helped to explain why Miss Gosselin had been so blank during the minutes she spent with him before her mother came back.

He himself wanted to cultivate tranquillity, and he felt that he did so the next day in not going again to Chester Street. He went instead to the British Museum, where he sat quite like an elderly gentleman, with his hands crossed on the top of his stick and his eyes fixed on an Assyrian bull. When he came away, however, it was with the resolution to move briskly; so that he walked westward the whole length of Oxford Street and arrived at the Marble Arch. He stared for some minutes at this monument, as in the national collection he had stared at even less intelligible ones; then brushing away the apprehension that he should meet two persons riding together, he passed into the park. He didn't care a straw whom he met. He got upon the grass and made his way to the southern expanse, and when he reached the Row he dropped into a chair, rather tired, to watch the capering procession of riders. He watched it with a lustreless eye, for what he seemed mainly to extract from it was a vivification of his disappointment. He had had a hope that he should not be

forced to leave London without inducing Mary Gosselin to
ride with him; but that prospect failed, for what he had
accomplished in the British Museum was the determination to
go to Paris. He tried to think of the attractions supposed
to be evoked by that name, and while he was so engaged
he recognised that a gentleman on horseback, close to the
barrier of the Row, was making a sign to him. The gentleman
was Lord Beaupré, who had pulled up his horse and whose
sign the young American lost no time in obeying. He went
forward to speak to his late host, but during the instant of
the transit he was able both to observe that Mary Gosselin was
not in sight and to ask himself why she was not. She rode with
her brother; why then didn't she ride with her future husband? It was singular at such a moment to see her future
husband disporting himself alone. This personage conversed
a few moments with Bolton-Brown, said it was too hot to
ride, but that he ought to be mounted (*he* would give him a
mount if he liked) and was on the point of turning away
when his interlocutor succumbed to the temptation to put his
modesty to the test.

"Good-bye, but let me congratulate you first," said
Bolton-Brown.

"Congratulate me? On what?" His look, his tone were
very much what Mary Gosselin's had been.

"Why, on your engagement. Haven't you heard of
it?"

Lord Beaupré stared a moment while his horse shifted uneasily. Then he laughed and said: "Which of them do you
mean?"

"There's only one I know anything about. To Miss
Gosselin," Brown added, after a puzzled pause.

"Oh yes, I see—thanks so much!" With this, letting his
horse go, Lord Beaupré broke off, while Bolton-Brown stood
looking after him and saying to himself that perhaps he *didn't*
know! The chapter of English oddities was long.

But on the morrow the announcement was in "The Morning Post," and that surely made it authentic. It was doubtless only superficially singular that Guy Firminger should have found himself unable to achieve a call in Chester Street until this journal had been for several hours in circulation. He appeared there just before luncheon, and the first person who received him was Mrs Gosselin. He had always liked her, finding her infallible on the question of behaviour; but he was on this occasion more than ever struck with her ripe astuteness, her independent wisdom.

"I knew what you wanted, I knew what you needed, I knew the subject on which you had pressed her," the good lady said; "and after Sunday I found myself really haunted with your dangers. There was danger in the air at Bosco, in your own defended house; it seemed to me too monstrous. I said to myself 'We *can* help him, poor dear, and we *must*. It's the least one can do for so old and so good a friend.' I decided what to do: I simply put this other story about. In London that always answers. I knew that Mary pitied you really as much as I do, and that what she saw at Bosco had been a revelation—had at any rate brought your situation home to her. Yet of course she would be shy about saying out for herself: 'Here I am—I'll do what you want.' The thing was for me to say it *for* her; so I said it first to that chattering American. He repeated it to several others, and there you are! I just forced her hand a little, but it's all right. All she has to do is not to contradict it. It won't be any trouble and you'll be comfortable. That will be our reward!" smiled Mrs Gosselin.

"Yes, all she has to do is not to contradict it," Lord Beaupré replied, musing a moment. "It *won't* be any trouble," he added, "and I *hope* I shall be comfortable." He thanked Mrs Gosselin formally and liberally, and expressed all his impatience to assure Mary herself of his deep obligation to her; upon which his hostess promised to send her daughter to him on the instant: she would go and call her, so that they might be alone. Before Mrs Gosselin left him however she touched on one or two points that had their little importance. Guy Firminger had asked for Hugh, but Hugh had gone to the City, and his mother mentioned candidly that he didn't take part in the game. She even disclosed his reason: he thought there was a want of dignity in it. Lord Beaupré stared at this and after a moment exclaimed: "Dignity? Dignity be hanged! One must save one's life!"

"Yes, but the point poor Hugh makes is that one must save it by the use of one's *own* wits, or one's *own* arms and legs. But do you know what I said to him?" Mrs Gosselin continued.

"Something very clever, I daresay."

"That if *we* were drowning you'd be the very first to jump in. And we may fall overboard yet!" Fidgeting there with his hands in his pockets Lord Beaupré gave a laugh at this, but assured her that there was nothing in the world for which they mightn't count upon him. None the less she just permitted herself another warning, a warning, it is true, that was in his own interest, a reminder of a peril that he ought beforehand to look in the face. Wasn't there always the chance— just the bare chance—that a girl in Mary's position would, in the event, decline to let him off, decline to release him even on the day he should wish to marry? She wasn't speaking of Mary, but there were of course girls who would play him that trick. Guy Firminger considered this contingency; then he declared that it wasn't a question of "girls," it was simply a question of dear old Mary! If *she* should wish to hold him, so much the better: he would do anything in the world that she wanted. "Don't let us dwell on such vulgarities; but I had it on my conscience!" Mrs Gosselin wound up.

She left him, but at the end of three minutes Mary came in, and the first thing she said was: "Before you speak a word, please understand this, that it's wholly mamma's doing. I hadn't dreamed of it, but she suddenly began to tell people."

"It was charming of her, and it's charming of you!" the visitor cried.

"It's not charming of any one, I think," said Mary Gosselin, looking at the carpet. "It's simply idiotic."

"Don't be nasty about it. It will be tremendous fun."

"I've only consented because mamma says we owe it to you," the girl went on.

"Never mind your reason—the end justifies the means. I can never thank you enough nor tell you what a weight it lifts off my shoulders. Do you know I feel the difference already? —a peace that passeth understanding!" Mary replied that this was childish; how could such a feeble fiction last? At the very best it could live but an hour, and then he would be no better off than before. It would bristle moreover with difficulties and absurdities; it would be so much more trouble than it was worth. She reminded him that so ridiculous a service had never been asked of any girl, and at this he seemed a little struck; he said: "Ah, well, if it's positively disagreeable to you we'll instantly drop the idea. But I—I thought you really liked me enough——!" She turned away impatiently, and he went on to argue imperturbably that she had always treated him in the kindest way in the world. He added that the worst was over, the start, they were off: the thing would be in all the evening papers. Wasn't it much simpler to accept it? That was all they would have to do; and all *she* would have to do would be not to gainsay it and to smile and thank people when she was congratulated. She would have to *act* a little, but that would just be part of the fun. Oh, he hadn't the shadow of a scruple about taking the world in; the world deserved it richly, and she couldn't deny that this was what she had felt for him, that she had really been moved to compassion. He grew eloquent and charged her with having recognised in his predicament a genuine motive for charity.

Their little plot would last what it could—it would be a part of their amusement to *make* it last. Even if it should be but a thing of a day there would have been always so much gained. But they would be ingenious, they would find ways, they would have no end of sport.

"*You* must be ingenious; I can't," said Mary. "If people scarcely ever see us together they'll guess we're trying to humbug them."

"But they *will* see us together. We *are* together. We've been together—I mean we've seen a lot of each other—all our lives."

"Ah, not *that* way!"

"Oh, trust me to work it right!" cried the young man, whose imagination had now evidently begun to glow in the air of their pious fraud.

"You'll find it a dreadful bore," said Mary Gosselin.

"Then I'll drop it, don't you see? And *you*'ll drop it, of course, the moment *you*'ve had enough," Lord Beaupré punctually added. "But as soon as you begin to realise what a lot of good you do me you won't *want* to drop it. That is if you're what I take you for!" laughed his lordship.

If a third person had been present at this conversation—and there was nothing in it surely that might not have been spoken before a trusty listener—that person would perhaps have thought, from the immediate expression of Mary Gosselin's face, that she was on the point of exclaiming "You take me for too big a fool!" No such ungracious words in fact however passed her lips; she only said after an instant: "What reason do you propose to give, on the day you need one, for our rupture?"

Her interlocutor stared. "To you, do you mean?"

"*I* sha'n't ask you for one. I mean to other people."

"Oh, I'll tell them you're sick of me. I'll put everything on you, and you'll put everything on me."

"You *have* worked it out!" Mary exclaimed.

"Oh, I shall be intensely considerate."

"Do you call that being considerate—publicly accusing me?"

Guy Firminger stared again. "Why, isn't that the reason *you*'ll give?"

She looked at him an instant. "I won't tell you the reason I shall give."

"Oh, I shall learn it from others."

"I hope you'll like it when you do!" said Mary, with sudden gaiety; and she added frankly though kindly the hope that he might soon light upon some young person who would really meet his requirements. He replied that he shouldn't be in a hurry—that was now just the comfort; and she, as if thinking over to the end the list of arguments against his clumsy contrivance, broke out: "And of course you mustn't dream of giving me anything—any tokens or presents."

"Then it won't look natural."

"That's exactly what I say. You can't make it deceive anybody."

"I *must* give you something—something that people can see. There must be some evidence! You can simply put my offerings away after a little and give them back." But about this Mary was visibly serious; she declared that she wouldn't touch anything that came from his hand, and she spoke in such a tone that he coloured a little and hastened to say: "Oh, all right, I shall be thoroughly careful!" This appeared to complete their understanding; so that after it was settled that for the deluded world they *were* engaged, there was obviously nothing for him to do but to go. He therefore shook hands with her very gratefully and departed.

V

HE was able promptly to assure his accomplice that their little plot was working to a charm; it already made such a difference for the better. Only a week had elapsed, but he felt quite another man; his life was no longer spent in springing to arms and he had ceased to sleep in his boots. The ghost of his great fear was laid, he could follow out his inclinations and attend to his neglected affairs. The news had been a bomb in the enemy's camp, and there were plenty of blank faces to testify to the confusion it had wrought. Every one was "sold" and every one made haste to clap him on the back. Lottie Firminger only had written in terms of which no notice could be taken, though of course he expected, every time he came in, to find her waiting in his hall. Her mother was coming up to town and he should have the family at his ears; but, taking them as a single body, he could manage them, and that was a detail. The Ashburys had remained at Bosco till that establishment was favoured with the tidings that so nearly concerned it (they were communicated to Maud's mother by the housekeeper), and then the beautiful sufferer had found in her defeat strength to seek another asylum. The two ladies had departed for a destination unknown; he didn't think they had turned up in London. Guy Firminger averred that there were precious portable objects which he was sure he should miss on returning to his country home.

He came every day to Chester Street, and was evidently much less bored than Mary had prefigured by this regular tribute to verisimilitude. It was amusement enough to see the progress of their comedy and to invent new touches for some of its scenes. The girl herself was amused; it was an opportunity like another for cleverness such as hers and had much

in common with private theatricals, especially with the rehearsals, the most amusing part. Moreover she was good-
natured enough to be really pleased at the service it was
impossible for her not to acknowledge that she had rendered.
Each of the parties to this queer contract had anecdotes and
suggestions for the other, and each reminded the other duly
that they must at every step keep their story straight. Except
for the exercise of this care Mary Gosselin found her duties
less onerous than she had feared and her part in general much
more passive than active. It consisted indeed largely of murmuring thanks and smiling and looking happy and handsome; as
well as perhaps also in saying in answer to many questions that
nothing as yet was fixed and of trying to remain humble when
people expressed without ceremony that such a match was a
wonder for such a girl. Her mother on the other hand was
devotedly active. She treated the situation with private
humour but with public zeal and, making it both real and
ideal, told so many fibs about it that there were none left for
Mary. The girl had failed to understand Mrs Gosselin's interest in this elaborate pleasantry; the good lady had seen in it
from the first more than she herself had been able to see. Mary
performed her task mechanically, sceptically, but Mrs Gosselin attacked hers with conviction and had really the air at
moments of thinking that their fable had crystallised into fact.
Mary allowed her as little of this attitude as possible and was
ironical about her duplicity; warnings which the elder lady
received with gaiety until one day when repetition had made
them act on her nerves. Then she begged her daughter, with
sudden asperity, not to talk to her as if she were a fool. She
had already had words with Hugh about some aspects of the
affair—so much as this was evident in Chester Street; a
smothered discussion which at the moment had determined
the poor boy to go to Paris with Bolton-Brown. The young
men came back together after Mary had been "engaged"
three weeks, but she remained in ignorance of what passed

between Hugh and his mother the night of his return. She had gone to the opera with Lady Whiteroy, after one of her invariable comments on Mrs Gosselin's invariable remark that of course Guy Firminger would spend his evening in their box. The remedy for his trouble, Lord Beaupré's prospective bride had said, was surely worse than the disease; she was in perfect good faith when she wondered that his lordship's sacrifices, his laborious cultivation of appearances should "pay."

Hugh Gosselin dined with his mother and at dinner talked of Paris and of what he had seen and done there; he kept the conversation superficial and after he had heard how his sister, at the moment, was occupied, asked no question that might have seemed to denote an interest in the success of the experiment for which in going abroad he had declined responsibility. His mother could not help observing that he never mentioned Guy Firminger by either of his names, and it struck her as a part of the same detachment that later, upstairs (she sat with him while he smoked), he should suddenly say as he finished a cigar:

"I return to New York next week."

"Before your time? What for?" Mrs Gosselin was horrified.

"Oh, mamma, you know what for!"

"Because you still resent poor Mary's good-nature?"

"I don't understand it, and I don't like things I don't understand; therefore I'd rather not be here to see it. Besides I really can't tell a pack of lies."

Mrs Gosselin exclaimed and protested; she had arguments to prove that there was no call at present for the least deflection from the truth; all that any one had to reply to any question (and there could be none that was embarrassing save the ostensible determination of the date of the marriage) was that nothing was settled as yet—a form of words in which for the life of her she couldn't see any perjury. "Why, then, go in for anything in such bad taste, to culminate only in something so absurd?" Hugh demanded. "If the essential part of the matter can't be spoken of as fixed nothing is fixed, the deception becomes transparent and they give the whole idea away. It's child's play."

"That's why it's so innocent. All I can tell you is that practically their attitude answers; he's delighted with its success. Those dreadful women have given him up; they've already found some other victim."

"And how is it all to end, please?"

Mrs Gosselin was silent a moment. "Perhaps it won't end."

"Do you mean that the engagement will become real?"

Again the good lady said nothing until she broke out: "My dear boy, can't you trust your poor old mummy?"

"Is *that* your speculation? Is that Mary's? I never heard of anything so odious!" Hugh Gosselin cried. But she defended his sister with eagerness, with a gloss of coaxing, maternal indignation, declaring that Mary's disinterestedness was complete—she had the perfect proof of it. Hugh was conscious as he lighted another cigar that the conversation was more fundamental than any that he had ever had with his mother, who however hung fire but for an instant when he asked her what this "perfect proof" might be. He didn't doubt of his sister, he admitted that; but the perfect proof would make the whole thing more luminous. It took finally the form of a confession from Mrs Gosselin that the girl evidently liked—well, greatly liked—Mr Bolton-Brown. Yes, the good lady had seen for herself at Bosco that the smooth young American was making up to her and that, time and opportunity aiding, something might very well happen which could not be regarded as satisfactory. She had been very frank with Mary, had besought her not to commit herself to a suitor who in the very nature of the case couldn't meet the most legitimate of their views. Mary, who pretended not to know what their "views" were, had denied that she was in danger; but Mrs

Gosselin had assured her that she had all the air of it and had said triumphantly: "Agree to what Lord Beaupré asks of you, and I'll *believe* you." Mary had wished to be believed—so she had agreed. That was all the witchcraft any one had used.

Mrs Gosselin out-talked her son, but there were two or three plain questions that he came back to; and the first of these bore upon the ground of her aversion to poor Bolton-Brown. He told her again, as he had told her before, that his friend was that rare bird a maker of money who was also a man of culture. He was a gentleman to his finger-tips, accomplished, capable, kind, with a charming mother and two lovely sisters (she should see them!) the sort of fellow in short whom it was stupid not to appreciate.

"I believe it all, and if I had three daughters he should be very welcome to one of them."

"You might easily have had three daughters who wouldn't attract him at all! You've had the good fortune to have one who does, and I think you do wrong to interfere with it."

"My eggs are in one basket then, and that's a reason the more for preferring Lord Beaupré," said Mrs Gosselin.

"Then it *is* your calculation—?" stammered Hugh in dismay; on which she coloured and requested that he would be a little less rough with his mother. She would rather part with him immediately, sad as that would be, than that he should attempt to undo what she had done. When Hugh replied that it was not to Mary but to Beaupré himself that he judged it important he should speak, she informed him that a rash remonstrance might do his sister a cruel wrong. Dear Guy was *most* attentive.

"If you mean that he really cares for her there's the less excuse for his taking such a liberty with her. He's either in love with her or he isn't. If he is, let him make her a serious offer; if he isn't, let him leave her alone."

Mrs Gosselin looked at her son with a kind of patient joy. "He's in love with her, but he doesn't know it."

"He ought to know it, and if he's so idiotic I don't see that we ought to consider him."

"Don't worry—he *shall* know it!" Mrs Gosselin cried; and, continuing to struggle with Hugh, she insisted on the delicacy of the situation. She made a certain impression on him, though on confused grounds; she spoke at one moment as if he was to forbear because the matter was a make-believe that happened to contain a convenience for a distressed friend, and at another as if one ought to strain a point because there were great possibilities at stake. She was most lucid when she pictured the social position and other advantages of a peer of the realm. What had those of an American stockbroker, however amiable and with whatever shrill belongings in the background, to compare with them? She was inconsistent, but she was diplomatic, and the result of the discussion was that Hugh Gosselin became conscious of a dread of "injuring" his sister. He became conscious at the same time of a still greater apprehension, that of seeing her arrive at the agreeable in a tortuous, a second-rate manner. He might keep the peace to please his mother, but he couldn't enjoy it, and he actually took his departure, travelling in company with Bolton-Brown, who of course before going waited on the ladies in Chester Street to thank them for the kindness they had shown him. It couldn't be kept from Guy Firminger that Hugh was not happy, though when they met, which was only once or twice before he quitted London, Mary Gosselin's brother flattered himself that he was too proud to show it. He had always liked old loafing Guy and it was disagreeable to him not to like him now; but he was aware that he must either quarrel with him definitely or not at all and that he had passed his word to his mother. Therefore his attitude was strictly negative; he took with the parties to it no notice whatever of the "engagement," and he couldn't help it if to other people he had the air of not being initiated. They doubtless thought him strangely fastidious. Perhaps he was; the tone of London struck him in some respects as very horrid; he had grown in a manner away from it. Mary was impenetrable; tender, gay, charming, but with no patience, as she said, for his premature flight. Except when Lord Beaupré was present you would not have dreamed that he existed for her. In his company—he had to be present more or less of course—she was simply like any other English girl who disliked effusiveness. They had each the same manner, that of persons of rather a shy tradition who were on their guard against public "spooning." They practised their fraud with good taste, a good taste mystifying to Bolton-Brown, who thought their precautions excessive. When he took leave of Mary Gosselin her eyes consented for a moment to look deep down into his. He had been from the first of the opinion that they were beautiful, and he was more mystified than ever.

If Guy Firminger had failed to ask Hugh Gosselin whether he had a fault to find with what they were doing, this was, in spite of old friendship, simply because he was too happy now to care much whom he didn't please, to care at any rate for criticism. He had ceased to be critical himself, and his high prosperity could take his blamelessness for granted. His happiness would have been offensive if people generally hadn't liked him, for it consisted of a kind of monstrous candid comfort. To take all sorts of things for granted was still his great, his delightful characteristic; but it didn't prevent his showing imagination and tact and taste in particular circumstances. He made, in their little comedy, all the right jokes and none of the wrong ones: the girl had an acute sense that there were some jokes that would have been detestable. She gathered that it was universally supposed she was having an unprecedented season, and something of the glory of an enviable future seemed indeed to hang about her. People no doubt thought it odd that she didn't go about more with her future husband; but those who knew anything about her knew that she had never done exactly as other girls did. She had her own ways, her own freedoms and her own scruples. Certainly he made the London weeks much richer than they had ever been for a subordinate young person; he put more things into them, so that they grew dense and complicated. This frightened her at moments, especially when she thought with compunction that she was deceiving her very friends. She didn't mind taking the vulgar world in, but there were people she hated not to enlighten, to reassure. She could undeceive no one now, and indeed she would have been ashamed. There were hours when she wanted to stop—she had such a dread of doing too much; hours when she thought with dismay that the fiction of the rupture was still to come, with its horrid train of new untrue things. She spoke of it repeatedly to her confederate, who only postponed and postponed, told her she would never dream of forsaking him if she measured the good she was doing him. She did measure it however when she met him in the great world; she was of course always meeting him: that was the only way appearances were kept up. There was a certain attitude she could allow him to take on these occasions; it covered and carried off their subterfuge. He could talk to her unmolested; for herself she never spoke of anything but the charming girls, everywhere present, among whom he could freely choose. He didn't protest, because to choose freely was what he wanted, and they discussed these young ladies one by one. Some she recommended, some she disparaged, but it was almost the only subject she tolerated. It was her system in short, and she wondered he didn't get tired of it; she was so tired of it herself.

She tried other things that she thought he might find wearisome, but his good-humour was magnificent. He was now really for the first time enjoying his promotion, his wealth, his insight into the terms on which the world offered itself to the happy few, and these terms made a mixture healing to irritation. Once, at some glittering ball, he asked her if she should be jealous if he were to dance again with Lady Whiteroy, with whom he had danced already, and this was the only occasion on which he had come near making a joke of the wrong sort. She showed him what she thought of it and made him feel that the way to be forgiven was to spend the rest of the evening with that lovely creature. Now that the phalanx of the pressingly nubile was held in check there was accordingly nothing to prevent his passing his time pleasantly. Before he had taken this effective way the diplomatic mother, when she spied him flirting with a married woman, felt that in urging a virgin daughter's superior claims she worked for righteousness as well as for the poor girl. But Mary Gosselin protected these scandals practically by the still greater scandal of her indifference; so that he was in the odd position of having waited to be confined to know what it was to be at large. He had in other words the maximum of security with the minimum of privation. The lovely creatures of Lady Whiteroy's order thought Mary Gosselin charming, but they were the first to see through her falsity.

All this carried our precious pair to the middle of July; but nearly a month before that, one night under the summer stars, on the deck of the steamer that was to reach New York on the morrow, something had passed between Hugh Gosselin and his brooding American friend. The night was warm and splendid; these were their last hours at sea, and Hugh, who had been playing whist in the cabin, came up very late to take an observation before turning in. It was in this way that he chanced on his companion, who was leaning over the stern of the ship and gazing off, beyond its phosphorescent track, at the muffled, moaning ocean, the backward darkness, everything he had relinquished. Hugh stood by him for a moment and then asked him what he was thinking about. Bolton-Brown gave at first no answer; after which he turned round and, with his back against the guard of the deck, looked up at the multiplied stars. "He has it badly," Hugh Gosselin mentally commented. At last his friend replied: "About something you said yesterday."

"I forget what I said yesterday."

"You spoke of your sister's intended marriage; it was the only time you had spoken of it. You seemed to intimate that it might not after all take place."

Hugh hesitated a little. "Well, it *won't* take place. They're not engaged, not really. This is a secret, a preposterous secret. I wouldn't tell any one else, but I'm willing to tell *you*. It may make a difference to you."

Bolton-Brown turned his head; he looked at Hugh a minute through the fresh darkness. "It does make a difference to me. But I don't understand," he added.

"Neither do I. I don't like it. It's a pretence, a temporary make-believe, to help Beaupré through."

"Through what?"

"He's so run after."

The young American stared, ejaculated, mused. "Oh, yes —your mother told me."

"It's a sort of invention of my mother's and a notion of his own (very absurd, I think) till he can see his way. Mary serves as a kind of escort for these first exposed months. It's ridiculous, but I don't know that it hurts her."

"Oh!" said Bolton-Brown.

"I don't know either that it does her any good."

"No!" said Bolton-Brown. Then he added: "It's certainly very kind of her."

"It's a case of old friends," Hugh explained, inadequately as he felt. "He has always been in and out of our house."

"But how will it end?"

"I haven't the least idea."

Bolton-Brown was silent; he faced about to the stern again and stared at the rush of the ship. Then shifting his position once more: "Won't the engagement, before they've done, develop into the regular thing?"

Hugh felt as if his mother were listening. "I daresay not. If there were even a remote chance of that, Mary wouldn't have consented."

"But mayn't *he* easily find that—charming as she is—he's in love with her?"

"He's too much taken up with himself."

"That's just a reason," said Bolton-Brown. "Love is selfish." He considered a moment longer, then he went on: "And mayn't *she* find—?"

"Find what?" said Hugh, as he hesitated.

"Why, that she likes him."

"She likes him of course, else she wouldn't have come to his assistance. But her certainty about herself must have been just what made her not object to lending herself to the arrangement. She could do it decently because she doesn't seriously care for him. If she did—!" Hugh suddenly stopped.

"If she did?" his friend repeated.

"It would have been odious."

"I see," said Bolton-Brown gently. "But how will they break off?"

"It will be Mary who'll break off."

"Perhaps she'll find it difficult."

"She'll require a pretext."

"I see," mused Bolton-Brown, shifting his position again.

"She'll find one," Hugh declared.

"I hope so," his companion responded.

For some minutes neither of them spoke; then Hugh asked: "Are you in love with her?"

"Oh, my dear fellow!" Bolton-Brown wailed. He instantly added: "Will it be any use for me to go back?"

Again Hugh felt as if his mother were listening. But he answered: "*Do* go back."

"It's awfully strange," said Bolton-Brown. "I'll go back."

"You had better wait a couple of months, you know."

"Mayn't I lose her then?"

"No—they'll drop it all."

"I'll go back!" the American repeated, as if he hadn't heard. He was restless, agitated; he had evidently been much affected. He fidgeted away dimly, moved up the level length of the deck. Hugh Gosselin lingered longer at the stern; he fell into the attitude in which he had found the other, leaning over it and looking back at the great vague distance they had come. He thought of his mother.

VI

To remind her fond parent of the vanity of certain expectations which she more than suspected her of entertaining, Mary Gosselin, while she felt herself intensely watched (it had all brought about a horrid new situation at home) produced every day some fresh illustration of the fact that people were no longer imposed upon. Moreover these illustrations were not invented; the girl believed in them, and when once she had begun to note them she saw them multiply fast. Lady Whiteroy, for one, was distinctly suspicious; she had taken the liberty more than once of asking the future Lady Beaupré what in the world was the matter with her. Brilliant figure as she was and occupied with her own pleasures, which were of a very independent nature, she had nevertheless constituted herself Miss Gosselin's social sponsor: she took a particular interest in her marriage, an interest all the greater as it rested not only on a freely-professed regard for her, but on a keen sympathy with the other party to the transaction. Lady White-roy, who was very pretty and very clever and whom Mary secretly but profoundly mistrusted, delighted in them both in short; so much so that Mary judged herself happy to be in a false position, so certain should she have been to be jealous had she been in a true one. This charming woman threw out

inquiries that made the girl not care to meet her eyes; and
Mary ended by forming a theory of the sort of marriage for
Lord Beaupré that Lady Whiteroy really would have appreciated. It would have been a marriage to a fool, a marriage
to Maud Ashbury or to Charlotte Firminger. She would have
her reasons for preferring that; and, as regarded the actual
prospect, she had only discovered that Mary was even more
astute than herself.

It will be understood how much our young lady was on
the crest of the wave when I mention that in spite of this
complicated consciousness she was one of the ornaments (Guy
Firminger was of course another) of the party entertained by
her zealous friend and Lord Whiteroy during the Goodwood
week. She came back to town with the firm intention of putting an end to a comedy which had more than ever become
odious to her; in consequence of which she had on this subject
with her fellow-comedian a scene—the scene she had dreaded
—half-pathetic, half-ridiculous. He appealed to her, wrestled
with her, took his usual ground that she was saving his life
without really lifting a finger. He denied that the public was
not satisfied with their pretexts for postponement, their explanations of delay; what else was expected of a man who
would wish to celebrate his nuptials on a suitable scale, but
who had the misfortune to have had, one after another, three
grievous bereavements? He promised not to molest her for the
next three months, to go away till his "mourning" was over,
to go abroad, to let her do as she liked. He wouldn't come
near her, he wouldn't even write (no one would know it), if
she would let him keep up the mere form of their fiction; and
he would let her off the very first instant he definitely perceived that this expedient had ceased to be effective. She
couldn't judge of that—she must let *him* judge; and it was a
matter in which she could surely trust to his honour.

Mary Gosselin trusted to it, but she insisted on his going
away. When he took such a tone as that she couldn't help

being moved; he breathed with such frank, generous lips on the irritation she had stored up against him. Guy Firminger went to Homburg, and if his confederate consented not to clip the slender thread by which this particular engagement still hung, she made very short work with every other. A dozen invitations, for Cowes, for the country, for Scotland, shimmered there before her, made a pathway of flowers, but she sent barbarous excuses. When her mother, aghast, said to her "What then will you do?" she replied in a very conclusive manner "I'll go home!" Mrs Gosselin was wise enough not to struggle; she saw that the thread was delicate, that it must dangle in quiet air. She therefore travelled back with her daughter to homely Hampshire, feeling that they were people of less importance than they had been for many a week. On the August afternoons they sat again on the little lawn on which Guy Firminger had found them the day he first became eloquent about the perils of the desirable young bachelor; and it was on this very spot that, toward the end of the month, and with some surprise, they beheld Mr Bolton-Brown once more approach. He had come back from America; he had arrived but a few days before; he was staying, of all places in the world, at the inn in the village.

His explanation of this caprice was of all explanations the oddest: he had come three thousand miles for the love of water-colour. There was nothing more sketchable than the sketchability of Hampshire—wasn't it celebrated, classic? and he was so good as to include Mrs Gosselin's charming premises, and even their charming occupants, in his view of the field. He fell to work with speed, with a sort of feverish eagerness; he seemed possessed indeed by the frenzy of the brush. He sketched everything on the place, and when he had represented an object once he went straight at it again. His advent was soothing to Mary Gosselin, in spite of his nervous activity; it must be admitted indeed that at the moment he arrived she had already felt herself in quieter waters. The

August afternoons, the relinquishment of London, the simplified life, had rendered her a service which, if she had freely
qualified it, she would have described as a restoration of her
self-respect. If poor Guy found any profit in such conditions
as these there was no great reason to repudiate him. She had
so completely shaken off responsibility that she took scarcely
more than a languid interest in the fact, communicated to her
by Lady Whiteroy, that Charlotte Firminger had also, as the
newspapers said, "proceeded" to Homburg. Lady Whiteroy knew, for Lady Whiteroy had "proceeded" as well; her
physician had discovered in her constitution a pressing need
for the comfort imbibed in dripping matutinal tumblers. She
chronicled Charlotte's presence, and even to some extent her
behaviour, among the haunters of the spring, but it was not
till some time afterwards that Mary learned how Miss Firminger's pilgrimage had been made under her ladyship's
protection. This was a further sign that, like Mrs Gosselin,
Lady Whiteroy had ceased to struggle; she had, in town, only
shrugged her shoulders ambiguously on being informed that
Lord Beaupré's intended was going down to her stupid home.

The fulness of Mrs Gosselin's renunciation was apparent
during the stay of the young American in the neighbourhood
of that retreat. She occupied herself with her knitting, her
garden and the cares of a punctilious hospitality, but she had
no appearance of any other occupation. When people came to
tea Bolton-Brown was always there, and she had the self-
control to attempt to say nothing that could assuage their
natural surprise. Mrs Ashbury came one day with poor Maud,
and the two elder ladies, as they had done more than once
before, looked for some moments into each other's eyes. This
time it was not a look of defiance, it was rather—or it would
have been for an observer completely in the secret—a look of
reciprocity, of fraternity, a look of arrangement. There was
however no one completely in the secret save perhaps Mary,
and Mary didn't heed. The arrangement at any rate was

ineffectual; Mrs Gosselin might mutely say, over the young American's eager, talkative shoulders, "Yes, you may have him if you can get him:" the most rudimentary experiments demonstrated that he was not to be got. Nothing passed on this subject between Mary and her mother, whom the girl none the less knew to be holding her breath and continuing to watch. She counted it more and more as one unpleasant result of her conspiracy with Guy Firminger that it almost poisoned a relation that had always been sweet. It was to show that she was independent of it that she did as she liked now, which was almost always as Bolton-Brown liked. When in the first days of September—it was in the warm, clear twilight, and they happened, amid the scent of fresh hay, to be leaning side by side on a stile—he gave her a view of the fundamental and esoteric, as distinguished from the convenient and superficial motive of his having come back to England, she of course made no allusion to a prior tie. On the other hand she insisted on his going up to London by the first train the next day. He was to wait—that was distinctly understood—for his satisfaction.

She desired meanwhile to write immediately to Guy Firminger, but as he had kept his promise of not complicating their contract with letters she was uncertain as to his actual whereabouts: she was only sure he would have left Homburg. Lady Whiteroy had become silent, so there were no more sidelights, and she was on the point of telegraphing to London for an address when she received a telegram from Bosco. The proprietor of that seat had arrived there the day before, and he found he could make trains fit if she would on the morrow allow him to come over and see her for a day or two. He had returned sooner than their agreement allowed, but she answered "Come" and she showed his missive to her mother, who at the sight of it wept with strange passion. Mary said to her "For heaven's sake, don't let him see you!" She lost no time; she told him on the morrow as soon as he entered the house that she couldn't keep it up another hour.

"All right—it *is* no use," he conceded; "they're at it again!"

"You see you've gained nothing!" she replied triumphantly. She had instantly recognised that he was different, how much had happened.

"I've gained some of the happiest days of my life."

"Oh, that was not what you tried for!"

"Indeed it was, and I got exactly what I wanted," said Guy Firminger. They were in the cool little drawing-room where the morning light was dim. Guy Firminger had a sunburnt appearance, as in England people returning from other countries are apt to have, and Mary thought he had never looked so well. It was odd, but it was noticeable, that he had grown much handsomer since he had become a personage. He paused a moment, smiling at her while her mysterious eyes rested on him, and then he added: "Nothing ever worked better. It's no use now—people see. But I've got a start. I wanted to turn round and look about, and I *have* turned round and looked about. There are things I've escaped. I'm afraid you'll never understand how deeply I'm indebted to you."

"Oh, it's all right!" said Mary Gosselin.

There was another short silence, after which he went on: "I've come back sooner than I promised, but only to be strictly fair. I began to see that we couldn't hold out and that it was my duty to let you off. From that moment I was bound to put an end to your situation. I might have done so by letter, but that seemed scarcely decent. It's all I came back for, you know, and it's why I wired to you yesterday."

Mary hesitated an instant, she reflected intensely. What had happened, what would happen, was that if she didn't take care the signal for the end of their little arrangement would not have appeared to come from herself. She particularly wished it not to come from anyone else, she had even a horror of that;

so that after an instant she hastened to say: "I was on the very point of wiring to *you*—I was only waiting for your address."

"Wiring to me?" He seemed rather blank.

"To tell you that our absurd affair really, this time, can't go on another day—to put a complete stop to it."

"Oh!" said Guy Firminger.

"So it's all right."

"You've always hated it!" Guy laughed; and his laugh sounded slightly foolish to the girl.

"I found yesterday that I hated it more than ever."

Lord Beaupré showed a quickened attention. "For what reason—yesterday?"

"I would rather not tell you, please. Perhaps some time you'll find it out."

He continued to look at her brightly and fixedly with his confused cheerfulness. Then he said with a vague, courteous alacrity: "I see, I see!" She had an impression that he didn't see; but it didn't matter, she was nervous and quite preferred that he shouldn't. They both got up, and in a moment he exclaimed: "Well, I'm intensely sorry it's over! It has been so charming."

"You've been very good about it; I mean very reasonable," Mary said, to say something. Then she felt in her nervousness that this was just what she ought not to have said: it sounded ironical and provoking, whereas she had meant it as pure good-nature. "Of course you'll stay to luncheon?" she continued. She was bound in common hospitality to speak of that, and he answered that it would give him the greatest pleasure. After this her apprehension increased, and it was confirmed in particular by the manner in which he suddenly asked:

"By the way, what reason shall we give?"

"What reason?"

"For our rupture. Don't let us seem to have quarrelled."

"We can't help that," said Mary. "Nothing else will account for our behaviour."

"Well, I sha'n't say anything about *you*."

"Do you mean you'll let people think it was yourself who were tired of it?"

"I mean I sha'n't *blame* you."

"You ought to behave as if you cared!" said Mary.

Guy Firminger laughed, but he looked worried and he evidently was puzzled. "You must act as if you had jilted me."

"You're not the sort of person unfortunately that people jilt."

Lord Beaupré appeared to accept this statement as incontestable; not with elation however, but with candid regret, the slightly embarrassed recognition of a fundamental obstacle. "Well, it's no one's business, at any rate, is it?"

"No one's, and that's what I shall say if people question me. Besides," Mary added, "they'll see for themselves."

"What will they see?"

"I mean they'll understand. And now we had better join mamma."

It was his evident inclination to linger in the room after he had said this that gave her complete alarm. Mrs Gosselin was in another room, in which she sat in the morning, and Mary moved in that direction, pausing only in the hall for him to accompany her. She wished to get him into the presence of a third person. In the hall he joined her, and in doing so laid his hand gently on her arm. Then looking into her eyes with all the pleasantness of his honesty, he said: "It will be very easy for me to appear to care—for I *shall* care. I shall care immensely!" Lord Beaupré added smiling.

Anything, it struck her, was better than that—than that he should say: "We'll keep on, if you like (*I* should!) only this time it will be serious. Hold me to it—do; don't let me go; lead me on to the altar—really!" Some such words as these, she believed, were rising to his lips, and she had an insurmountable horror of hearing them. It was as if, well enough meant on *his* part, they would do her a sort of dishonour, so that all her impulse was quickly to avert them. That was not the way she wanted to be asked in marriage. "Thank you very much," she said, "but it doesn't in the least matter. You will seem to have been jilted—so it's all right!"

"All right! You mean—?" He hesitated, he had coloured a little: his eyes questioned her.

"I'm engaged to be married—in earnest."

"Oh!" said Lord Beaupré.

"You asked me just now if I had a special reason for having been on the point of telegraphing to you, and I said I had. That was my special reason."

"I see!" said Lord Beaupré. He looked grave for a few seconds, then he gave an awkward smile. But he behaved with perfect tact and discretion, didn't even ask her who the gentleman in the case might be. He congratulated her in the dark, as it were, and if the effect of this was indeed a little odd she liked him for his quick perception of the fine fitness of pulling up short. Besides, he extracted the name of the gentleman soon enough from her mother, in whose company they now immediately found themselves. Mary left Guy Firminger with the good lady for half an hour before luncheon; and when the girl came back it was to observe that she had been crying again. It was dreadful—what she might have been saying. Their guest, however, at luncheon was not lachrymose; he was natural, but he was talkative and gay. Mary liked the way he now behaved, and more particularly the way he departed immediately after the meal. As soon as he was gone Mrs Gosselin broke out suppliantly: "Mary!" But her daughter replied:

"I know, mamma, perfectly what you're going to say, and if you attempt to say it I shall leave the room." With this threat (day after day, for the following time) she kept the terrible appeal unuttered until it was too late for an appeal to be of use. That afternoon she wrote to Bolton-Brown that she accepted his offer of marriage.

Guy Firminger departed altogether; he went abroad again

and to far countries. He was therefore not able to be present at the nuptials of Miss Gosselin and the young American whom he had entertained at Bosco, which took place in the middle of November. Had he been in England however he probably would have felt impelled by a due regard for past verisimilitude to abstain from giving his countenance to such an occasion. His absence from the country contributed to the needed even if astonishing effect of his having been jilted; so, likewise, did the reputed vastness of Bolton-Brown's young income, which in London was grossly exaggerated. Hugh Gosselin had perhaps a little to do with this; as he had sacrificed a part of his summer holiday, he got another month and came out to his sister's wedding. He took public comfort in his brother-in-law; nevertheless he listened with attention to a curious communication made him by his mother after the young couple had started for Italy; even to the point of bringing out the inquiry (in answer to her assertion that poor Guy had been ready to place everything he had at Mary's feet): "Then why the devil didn't he do it?"

"From simple delicacy! He didn't want to make her feel as if she had lent herself to an artifice only on purpose to get hold of him—to treat her as if she too had been at bottom one of the very harpies she helped him to elude."

Hugh thought a moment. "That *was* delicate."

"He's the dearest creature in the world. He's on his guard, he's prudent, he tested himself by separation. Then he came back to England in love with her. She might have had it all!"

"I'm glad she didn't get it *that* way."

"She had only to wait—to put an end to their artifice, harmless as it was, for the present, but still wait. She might have broken off in a way that would have made it come on again better."

"That's exactly what she didn't want."

"I mean as a quite separate incident," said Mrs Gosselin.

"*I* loathed their artifice, harmless as it was!" her son observed.

Mrs Gosselin for a moment made no answer; then she turned away from the fire into which she had been pensively gazing with the ejaculation "Poor dear Guy!"

"I can't for the life of me see that he's to be pitied."

"He'll marry Charlotte Firminger."

"If he's such an ass as that it's his own affair."

"Bessie Whiteroy will bring it about."

"What has *she* to do with it?"

"She wants to get hold of him."

"Then why will she marry him to another woman?"

"Because in that way she can select the other—a woman he won't care for. It will keep him from taking some one that's nicer."

Hugh Gosselin stared—he laughed aloud. "Lord, mamma, you're deep!"

"Indeed I am, I see much more."

"What do you see?"

"Mary won't in the least care for America. Don't tell me she will," Mrs Gosselin added, "for you know perfectly you don't believe it."

"She'll care for her husband, she'll care for everything that concerns him."

"He's very nice, in his little way he's delightful. But as an alternative to Lord Beaupré he's ridiculous!"

"Mary's in a position in which she has nothing to do with alternatives."

"For the present, yes, but not for ever. She'll have enough of your New York; they'll come back here. I see the future dark," Mrs Gosselin pursued, inexorably musing.

"Tell me then all you see."

"She'll find poor Guy wretchedly married, and she'll be very sorry for him."

"Do you mean that he'll make love to her? You give a queer account of your paragon."

"He'll value her sympathy. I see life as it is."

"You give a queer account of your daughter."

"I don't give *any* account. She'll behave perfectly," Mrs Gosselin somewhat inconsequently subjoined.

"Then what are you afraid of?"

"She'll be sorry for him, and it will be all a worry."

"A worry to whom?"

The good lady was silent a moment. "To me," she replied. "And to you as well."

"Then they mustn't come back."

"That will be a greater worry still."

"Surely not a greater—a smaller. We'll put up with the lesser evil."

"Nothing will prevent her coming to a sense, eventually, of what *might* have been. And when they *both* recognize it——"

"It will be very dreadful!" Hugh exclaimed, completing gaily his mother's phrase. "I don't see, however," he added, "what in all this you do with Bessie Whiteroy."

"Oh, he'll be tired of her; she's hard, she'll have become despotic. I see life as it is," the good lady repeated.

"Then all I can say is that it's not very nice! But they sha'n't come back: *I*'ll attend to that!" said Hugh Gosselin, who has attended to it up to this time successfully, though the rest of his mother's prophecy is so far accomplished (it was her second hit) as that Charlotte Firminger is now, strange as it may seem, Lady Beaupré.

THE VISITS

THE other day, after her death, when they were discussing her, someone said in reference to the great number of years she had lived, the people she had seen and the stories she knew: "What a pity no one ever took any notes of her talk!" For a London epitaph that was almost exhaustive, and the subject presently changed. One of the listeners had taken many notes, but he didn't confess it on the spot. The following story is a specimen of my exactitude—I took it down, *verbatim*, having that faculty, the day after I heard it. I choose it, at hazard, among those of her reminiscences that I have preserved; it's not worse than the others. I will give you some of the others too—when occasion offers—so that you may judge.

I met in town that year a dear woman whom I had scarcely seen since I was a girl; she had dropped out of the world; she came up but once in five years. We had been together as very young creatures, and then we had married and gone our ways. It was arranged between us that after I should have paid a certain visit in August in the west of England I would take her—it would be very convenient, she was just over the Cornish border—on the way to my other engagements: I would work her in, as you say nowadays. She wanted immensely to show me her home, and she wanted still more to show me her girl, who had not come up to London, choosing instead, after much deliberation, to go abroad for a month with her brother and her brother's coach—he had been cramming for something—and Mrs Coach of course. All that Mrs Chantry had been able to show me in town was her husband, one of those country gentlemen with a moderate property and an old place who are a part of the essence in their own neighbourhood and not a part of anything anywhere else.

A couple of days before my visit to Chantry Court the people to whom I had gone from town took me over to see some friends of theirs who lived, ten miles away, in a place that was supposed to be fine. As it was a long drive we stayed to luncheon; and then as there were gardens and other things that were more or less on show we struggled along to tea, so as to get home just in time for dinner. There were a good many other people present, and before luncheon a very pretty girl came into the drawing-room, a real maiden in her flower, less than twenty, fresh and fair and charming, with the expression of some one I knew. I asked who she was, and was told she was Miss Chantry, so that in a moment I spoke to her, mentioning that I was an old friend of her mother's and that I was coming to pay them a visit. She looked rather frightened and blank, was apparently unable to say that she had ever heard of me, and hinted at no pleasure in the idea that she was to hear of me again. But this didn't prevent my perceiving that she was lovely, for I was wise enough even then not to think it necessary to measure people by the impression that one makes on them. I saw that any I should make on Louisa Chantry would be much too clumsy a test. She had been staying at the house at which I was calling; she had come alone, as the people were old friends and to a certain extent neighbours, and was going home in a few days. It was a daughterless house, but there was inevitable young life: a couple of girls from the vicarage, a married son and his wife, a young man who had "ridden over" and another young man who was staying.

Louisa Chantry sat opposite to me at luncheon, but too far for conversation, and before we got up I had discovered that if her manner to me had been odd it was not because she was inanimate. She was on the contrary in a state of intense though carefully muffled vibration. There was some fever in her blood, but no one perceived it, no one, that is, with an exception—an exception which was just a part of the very circumstance. This single suspicion was lodged in the breast of the young man whom I have alluded to as staying in the house. He was on the same side of the table as myself and diagonally facing the girl; therefore what I learned about him was for the moment mainly what she told me; meaning by "she" her face, her eyes, her movements, her whole perverted personality. She was extremely on her guard, and I should never have guessed her secret but for an accident. The accident was that the only time she dropped her eyes upon him during the repast I happened to notice it. It might not have been much to notice, but it led to my seeing that there was a little drama going on and that the young man would naturally be the hero. It was equally natural that in this capacity he should be the cause of my asking my left-hand neighbour, who happened to be my host, for some account of him. But "Oh, that fellow? he's my nephew," was a description which, to appear copious, required that I should know more about the uncle.

We had coffee on the terrace of the house; a terrace laid out in one quarter, oddly and charmingly, in grass where the servants who waited upon us seemed to tread, processionally, on soundless velvet. There I had a good look at my host's nephew and a longer talk with my friend's daughter, in regard to whom I had become conscious of a faint, formless anxiety. I remember saying to her, gropingly, instinctively: "My dear child, can I do anything for you? I shall perhaps see your mother before you do. Can I for instance say anything to her *from* you?" This only made her blush and turn away; and it was not till too many days had passed that I guessed that what had looked out at me unwittingly in her little gazing trepidation was something like "Oh, just take me away in spite of myself!" Superficially, conspicuously, there was nothing in the young man to take her away from. He was a person of the middle condition, and save that he didn't look at all humble might have passed for a poor relation. I mean that he had rather a seedy, shabby air, as if he were wearing out old clothes (he had on faded things that didn't match); and I formed vaguely the theory that he was a specimen of the numerous youthful class that goes to seek its fortune in the colonies, keeps strange company there and comes home without a penny. He had a brown, smooth, handsome face, a slightly swaggering, self-conscious ease, and was probably objected to in the house. He hung about, smoking cigarettes on the terrace, and nobody seemed to have much to say to him—a circumstance which, as he managed somehow to convey, left him absolutely indifferent. Louisa Chantry strolled away with one of the girls from the vicarage; the party on the terrace broke up and the nephew disappeared.

It was settled that my friends and I should take leave at half-past five, and I begged to be abandoned in the interval to my devices. I turned into the library and, mounted on ladders, I handled old books and old prints and soiled my gloves. Most of the others had gone to look at the church, and I was left in possession. I wandered into the rooms in which I knew there were pictures; and if the pictures were not good there was some interesting china which I followed from corner to corner and from cabinet to cabinet. At last I found myself on the threshold of a small room which appeared to terminate the series and in which, between the curtains draping the doorways, there appeared to be rows of rare old plates on velvet screens. I was on the point of going in when I became aware that there was something else beside, something which threw me back. Two persons were standing side by side at the window, looking out together with their backs to me—two persons as to whom I immediately felt that they believed themselves to be alone and unwatched. One of them was Louisa Chantry, the other was the young man whom my

host had described as his nephew. They were so placed as not
to see me, and when I recognized them I checked myself
instinctively. I hesitated a moment; then I turned away altogether. I can't tell you why, except that if I had gone in I
should have had somehow the air of discovering them. There
was no visible reason why they should have been embarrassed
by discovery, inasmuch as, so far as I could see, they were
doing no harm, were only standing more or less together,
without touching, and for the moment apparently saying
nothing. Were they watching something out of the window?
I don't know; all I know is that the observation I had made
at luncheon gave me a sense of responsibility. I might have
taken my responsibility the other way and broken up their
communion; but I didn't feel this to be sufficiently my
business. Later on I wished I had.

I passed through the rooms again, and then out of the
house. The gardens were ingenious, but they made me think
(I have always that conceited habit) how much cleverer *I*
should have been about them. Presently I met several of the
rest of the party coming back from the church; on which my
hostess took possession of me, declaring there was a point
of view I must absolutely be treated to. I saw she was a walking woman and that this meant half a mile in the park. But
I was good for that, and we wandered off together while the
others returned to the house. It was present to me that I
ought to ask my companion, for Helen Chantry's sake, a
question about Louisa—whether for instance she had happened to notice the way the girl seemed to be going. But it
was difficult to say anything without saying too much; so that
to begin with I merely risked the observation that our young
friend was remarkably pretty. As the point admitted of no
discussion this didn't take us very far; nor was the subject
much enlarged by our unanimity as to the fact that she was
also remarkably nice. I observed that I had had very little
chance to talk with her, for which I was sorry, having known

her mother for years. My hostess, at this, looked vaguely round, as if she had missed her for the first time. "Sure enough, she has not been about. I daresay she's been writing to her mother—she's always writing to her mother." "Not always," I mentally reflected; but I waited discreetly, admiring everything and rising to the occasion and the views, before I inquired casually who the young man might be who had sat two or three below me at luncheon—the rather good-looking young man, with the regular features and the brownish clothes—not the one with the moustache.

"Oh, poor Jack Brandon," said my companion, in a tone calculated to make him seem no one in particular.

"Is he very poor?" I asked, with a laugh.

"Oh dear, yes. There are nine of them—fancy!—all boys; and there's nothing for anyone but the eldest. He's my husband's nephew—his poor mother's my sister-in-law. He sometimes turns up here when he has nothing better to do; but I don't think he likes us much." I saw she meant that they didn't like *him*; and I exposed myself to suspicion by asking if he had been with them long. But my friend was not very plastic, and she simplified my whole theory of the case by replying after she had thought a moment that she wasn't clear about it—she thought he had come only the morning before. It seemed to me I could safely feel a little further, so I inquired if he were likely to stay many days. "Oh dear, no; he'll go to-morrow!" said my hostess. There was nothing whatever to show that she saw a connection between my odd interest in Mr Brandon and the subject of our former reference; there was only a quick lucidity on the subject of the young man's departure. It reassured me, for no great complications would have arisen in forty-eight hours.

In retracing our steps we passed again through a part of the gardens. Just after we had entered them my hostess, begging me to excuse her, called at a man who was raking leaves to ask him a question about his wife. I heard him reply "Oh, she's very bad, my lady," and I followed my course. Presently my lady turned round with him, as if to go to see his wife, who apparently was ill and on the place. I continued to look about me—there were such charming things; and at the end of five minutes I missed my way—I had not taken the direction of the house. Suddenly at the turn of a walk, the angle of a great clipped hedge, I found myself face to face with Jack Brandon. He was moving rapidly, looking down, with his hands in his pockets, and he started and stared at me a moment. I said "Oh, how d'ye do?" and I was on the point of adding "Won't you kindly show me the right way?" But with a summary salute and a queer expression of face he had already passed me. I looked after him an instant and I all but stopped him; then one of the faintest voices of the air told me that Louisa Chantry would not be far off, that in fact if I were to go on a few steps I should find her. I continued and I passed through an arched aperture of the hedge, a kind of door in the partition. This corner of the place was like an old French garden, a little inclosed apartment, with statues set into the niches of the high walls of verdure. I paused in admiration; then just opposite to me I saw poor Louisa. She was on a bench, with her hands clasped in her lap, her head bent, her eyes staring down before her. I advanced on the grass, attracting her attention; and I was close to her before she looked at me, before she sprang up and showed me a face convulsed with nameless pain. She was so pale that I thought she was ill—I had a vision of her companion's having rushed off for help. She stood gazing at me with expanded eyes and parted lips, and what I was mainly conscious of was that she had become ten years older. Whatever troubled her it was something pitiful—something that prompted me to hold out my two hands to her and exclaim tenderly "My poor child, my poor child!" She wavered a moment, as if she wanted to escape me but couldn't trust herself to run; she looked away from me, turning her head this way and that. Then as I went close to her she covered her face with her two hands, she let me lay mine upon her and draw her to my breast. As she dropped her head upon it she burst into tears, sobbing soundlessly and tragically. I asked her no question, I only held her so long as she would, letting her pour out the passion which I felt at the same time she made a tremendous effort to smother. She couldn't smother it, but she could break away violently; and this she quickly did, hurrying out of the nook where our little scene—and some other greater scene, I judged, just before it—had taken place, and leaving me infinitely mystified. I sat down on the bench a moment and thought it over; then I succeeded in discovering a path to the house.

The carriage was at the door for our drive home, but my companions, who had had tea, were waiting for our hostess, of whom they wished to take leave and who had not yet come in. I reported her as engaged with the wife of one of the gardeners, but we lingered a little in the hall, a largeish group, to give her time to arrive. Two other persons were absent, one of whom was Louisa Chantry and the other the young man whom I had just seen quitting her in the garden. While I sat there, a trifle abstracted, still somewhat agitated by the sequel to that incident and at the same time impatient of our last vague dawdle, one of the footmen presented me with a little folded note. I turned away to open it, and at the very moment our hostess fortunately came in. This diverted the attention of the others from the action of the footman, whom, after I had looked at the note, I immediately followed into the drawing-room. He led me through it and through two or three others to the door of the little retreat in which, nearly an hour before, I had come upon Louisa Chantry and Mr Brandon. The note was from Louisa, it contained the simple words "Would you very kindly speak to me an instant before you go?" She was waiting for me in the most sequestered spot she had been able to select, and there the footman left us. The girl came straight at me and in an instant she had grasped my hands. I became aware that her condition had changed; her tears were gone, she had a concentrated purpose. I could scarcely see her beautiful young face—it was pressed, beseechingly, so close to mine. I only felt, as her dry, shining eyes almost dazzled me, that a strong light had been waved back and forth before me. Her words at first seemed to me incoherent; then I understood that she was asking me for a pledge.

"Excuse me, forgive me for bringing you here—to say something I can't say before all those people. *Do* forgive me —it was so awfully kind of you to come. I couldn't think of any other way—just for two seconds. I want you to swear to me," she went on, with her hands now raised and intensely clasped.

"To swear, dearest child?"

"I'm not your dearest child—I'm not anyone's! But *don't* tell mamma. Promise me—promise me," she insisted.

"Tell her what?—I don't understand."

"Oh, you do—you do!" she kept on; "and if you're going to Chantry you'll see her, you'll be with her, you may see her before I do. On my knees I ask you for a vow!"

She seemed on the point of throwing herself at my feet, but I stopped her, I kept her erect. "When shall *you* see your mother?"

"As soon as I can. I want to get home—I want to get home!" With this I thought she was going to cry again, but she controlled herself and only pressed me with feverish eyes.

"You have some great trouble—for heaven's sake tell me what it is."

"It isn't anything—it will pass. Only don't breathe it to mamma!"

"How can I breathe it if I don't know what it is?"

"You do know—you know what I mean." Then after an instant's pause she added: "What I did in the garden."

"*What* did you do in the garden?"

"I threw myself on your neck and I sobbed—I behaved like a maniac."

"Is that all you mean?"

"It's what I don't want mamma to know—it's what I beseech you to keep silent about. If you don't I'll never, never go home. Have *mercy* on me!" the poor child quavered.

"Dear girl, I only want to be tender to you—to be perfect. But tell me first: has anyone acted wrongly to you?"

"No one—*no* one. I speak the truth."

She looked into my eyes, and I looked far into hers. They were wild with pain and yet they were so pure that they made me confusedly believe her. I hesitated a moment; then I risked the question: "Isn't Mr Brandon responsible for anything?"

"For nothing—for nothing! Don't blame *him!*" the girl passionately cried.

"He hasn't made love to you?"

"Not a word—before God! Oh, it was too awful!" And with this she broke away from me, flung herself on her knees before a sofa, burying her face in it and in her arms. "Promise me, promise me, promise me!" she continued to wail.

I was horribly puzzled but I was immeasurably touched. I stood looking a moment at her extravagant prostration; then I said "I'm dreadfully in the dark, but I promise."

This brought her to her feet again, and again she seized my hands. "Solemnly, sacredly?" she panted.

"Solemnly, sacredly."

"Not a syllable—not a hint?"

"Dear Louisa," I said kindly, "when I promise I perform."

"You see I don't know you. And when do you go to Chantry?"

"Day after to-morrow. And when do you?"

"To-morrow if I can."

"Then you'll see your mother first—it will be all right," I said smiling.

"All right, all right!" she repeated, with her woeful eyes. "Go, go!" she added, hearing a step in the adjoining room.

The footman had come back to announce that my friends were seated in the carriage, and I was careful to say before him in a different tone: "Then there's nothing more I can do for you?"

"Nothing—good-bye," said Louisa, tearing herself away too abruptly to take my kiss, which, to follow the servant again, I left unbestowed. I felt awkward and guilty as I took leave of the company, murmuring something to my entertainers about having had an arrangement to make with Miss Chantry. Most of the people bade us good-bye from the steps, but I didn't see Jack Brandon. On our drive home in the waning afternoon my other friends doubtless found me silent and stupid.

I went to Chantry two days later, and was disappointed to find that the daughter of the house had not returned, though indeed after parting with her I had been definitely of the opinion that she was much more likely to go to bed and be ill. Her mother however had not heard that she was ill, and my inquiry about the young lady was of course full of circumspection. It was a little difficult, for I had to talk about her, Helen being particularly delighted that we had already made acquaintance. No day had been fixed for her return, but it came over my friend that she oughtn't to be absent during too much of my visit. She was the best thing they had to show— she was the flower and the charm of the place. It had other charms as well—it was a sleepy, silvery old home, exquisitely grey and exquisitely green; a house where you could have confidence in your leisure: it would be as genuine as the butter and the claret. The very look of the pleasant, prosaic drawing-room suggested long mornings of fancy work, of Berlin wool and premeditated patterns, new stitches and mild pauses. My good Helen was always in the middle of something eternal, of which the past and the future were rolled up in oilcloth and tissue paper, and the intensest moments of conversation were when it was spread out for pensive opinions. These used to drop sometimes even from Christopher Chantry when he straddled vaguely in with muddy leggings and the raw materials of a joke. He had a mind like a large, full milk-pan, and his wit was as thick as cream.

One evening I came down to dinner a little early and, to my surprise, found my troubled maiden in possession of the drawing-room. She was evidently troubled still, and had been waiting there in the hope of seeing me alone. We were too quickly interrupted by her parents, however, and I had no conversation with her till I sat down to the piano after dinner and beckoned to her to come and stand by it. Her father had gone off to smoke; her mother dozed by one of the crackling little fires of the summer's end.

"Why didn't you come home the day you told me you meant to?"

She fixed her eyes on my hands. "I couldn't, I couldn't!"

"You look to me as if you were very ill."

"I am," the girl said simply.

"You ought to see some one. Something ought to be done."

She shook her head with quiet despair. "It would be no use—no one would know."

"What do you mean—would know?"

"No one would understand."

"You ought to make them!"

"Never—never!" she repeated. "Never!"

"I confess *I* don't," I replied, with a kind of angry renunciation. I played louder, with the passion of my uneasiness and the aggravation of my responsibility.

"No, you don't indeed," said Louisa Chantry.

I had only to accept this disadvantage, and after a moment I went on: "What became of Mr Brandon?"

"I don't know."

THE VISITS

THE VISITS

"Did he go away?"

"That same evening."

"Which same evening?"

"The day you were there. I never saw him again."

I was silent a minute, then I risked: "And you never will, eh?"

"Never—never."

"Then why shouldn't you get better?"

She also hesitated, after which she answered: "Because I'm going to die."

My music ceased, in spite of me, and we sat looking at each other. Helen Chantry woke up with a little start and asked what was the matter. I rose from the piano and I couldn't help saying "Dear Helen, I haven't the least idea." Louisa sprang up, pressing her hand to her left side, and the next instant I cried aloud "She's faint—she's ill—do come to her!" Mrs Chantry bustled over to us, and immediately afterwards the girl had thrown herself on her mother's breast, as she had thrown herself days before on mine; only this time without tears, without cries, in the strangest, most tragic silence. She was not faint, she was only in despair—that at least is the way I really saw her. There was something in her contact that scared poor Helen, that operated a sudden revelation: I can see at this hour the queer frightened look she gave me over Louisa's shoulder. The girl however in a moment disengaged herself, declaring that she was not ill, only tired, very tired, and wanted to go to bed. "Take her, take her—go with her," I said to her mother; and I pushed them, got them out of the room, partly to conceal my own trepidation. A few moments after they had gone Christopher Chantry came in, having finished his cigar, and I had to mention to him—to explain their absence—that his daughter was so fatigued that she had withdrawn under her mother's superintendence. "Didn't she seem done up, awfully done up? What on earth, at that confounded place, did she go in for?" the dear man asked with his pointless kindness. I couldn't tell him this was just what I myself wanted to know; and while I pretended to read I wondered inextinguishably what indeed she had "gone in" for. It had become still more difficult to keep my vow than I had expected; it was also very difficult that evening to converse with Christopher Chantry. His wife's continued absence rendered some conversation necessary; yet it had the advantage of making him remark, after it had lasted an hour, that he must go to see what was the matter. He left me, and soon afterwards I betook myself to my room; bed-time was elastic in the early sense at Chantry. I knew I should only have to wait awhile for Helen to come to me, and in fact by eleven o'clock she arrived.

"She's in a very strange state—something happened there."

"And *what* happened, pray?"

"I can't make out; she won't tell me."

"Then what makes you suppose so?"

"She has broken down utterly; she says there was something."

"Then she does tell you?"

"Not a bit. She only begins and then stops short—she says it's too dreadful."

"Too dreadful?"

"She says it's *horrible*," my poor friend murmured, with tears in her eyes and tragic speculation in her mild maternal face.

"But in what way? Does she give you no facts, no clue?"

"It was something she did."

We looked at each other a moment. "Did?" I echoed. "Did to whom?"

"She won't tell me—she says she *can't*. She tries to bring it out, but it sticks in her throat."

"Nonsense. She did nothing," I said.

"What *could* she do?" Helen asked, gazing at me.

"She's ill, she's in a fever, her mind's wandering."

"So I say to her father."

"And what does *she* say to him?"

"Nothing—she won't speak to him. He's with her now, but she only lies there letting him hold her hand, with her face turned away from him and her eyes closed."

"You must send for the doctor immediately."

"I've already sent for him."

"Should you like me to sit up with her?"

"Oh, I'll do that!" Helen said. Then she asked: "But if you were there the other day, what did *you* see?"

"Nothing whatever," I resolutely answered.

"*Really* nothing?"

"Really, my dear child."

"But was there nobody there who could have made up to her?"

I hesitated a moment. "My poor Helen, you should have seen them!"

"She wouldn't look at anybody that wasn't remarkably nice," Helen mused.

"Well—I don't want to abuse your friends—but nobody was remarkably nice. Believe me, she hasn't looked at anybody, and nothing whatever has occurred. She's ill, and it's a mere morbid fancy."

"It's a mere morbid fancy——!" Mrs Chantry gobbled down this formula. I felt that I was giving her another still more acceptable, and which she as promptly adopted, when I added that Louisa would soon get over it.

I may as well say at once that Louisa never got over it. There followed an extraordinary week, which I look back upon as one of the most uncomfortable of my life. The doctor had something to say about the action of his patient's heart—it was weak and slightly irregular, and he was anxious to learn whether she had lately been exposed to any violent shock or emotion—but he could give no name to the disorder under the influence of which she had begun unmistakably to sink.

She lay on the sofa in her room—she refused to go to bed, and in the absence of complications it was not insisted on— utterly white, weak and abstracted, shaking her head at all suggestion, waving away all nourishment save the infinitesimally little that enabled her to stretch out her hand from time to time (at intervals of very unequal length) and begin "Mother, mother!" as if she were mustering courage for a supreme confession. The courage never came; she was haunted by a strange impulse to speak, which in turn was checked on her lips by some deeper horror or some stranger fear. She seemed to seek relief spasmodically from some unforgettable consciousness and then to find the greatest relief of all in impenetrable silence. I knew these things only from her mother, for before me (I went gently in and out of her room two or three times a day) she gave no sign whatever. The little local doctor, after the first day, acknowledged himself at sea and expressed a desire to consult with a colleague at Exeter. The colleague journeyed down to us and shuffled and stammered: he recommended an appeal to a high authority in London. The high authority was summoned by telegraph and paid us a flying visit. He enunciated the valuable opinion that it was a very curious case and dropped the striking remark that in so charming a home a young lady ought to bloom like a flower. The young lady's late hostess came over, but she could throw no light on anything: all that she had ever noticed was that Louisa had seemed "rather blue" for a day or two before she brought her visit to a close. Our days were dismal enough and our nights were dreadful, for I took turns with Helen in sitting up with the girl. Chantry Court itself seemed conscious of the riddle that made its chambers ache; it bowed its grey old head over the fate of its daughter. The people who had been coming were put off; dinner became a ceremony enacted mainly by the servants. I sat alone with Christopher Chantry, whose honest hair, in his mystification, stuck out as if he had been overhauling accounts. My hours with Louisa were even more intensely silent, for she almost never looked at me. In the watches of the night however I at last saw more clearly into what she was thinking of. Once when I caught her wan eyes resting upon me I took advantage of it to kneel down by her bed and speak to her with the utmost tenderness.

"If you can't say it to your mother, can you say it perhaps to *me?*"

She gazed at me for some time. "What does it matter now —if I'm dying?"

I shook my head and smiled. "You won't die if you get it off your mind."

"You'd be cruel to him," she said. "He's innocent—he's innocent."

"Do you mean *you're* guilty? What trifle are you magnifying?"

"Do you call it a trifle——?" She faltered and paused.

"Certainly I do, my dear." Then I risked a great stroke. "I've often done it myself!"

"*You?* Never, never! I was cruel to him," she added.

This puzzled me; I couldn't work it into my conception. "How were you cruel?"

"In the garden. I changed suddenly, I drove him away, I told him he filled me with horror."

"Why did you do that?"

"Because my shame came over me."

"Your shame?"

"What I had done in the house."

"And what had you done?"

She lay a few moments with her eyes closed, as if she were living it over. "I broke out to him, I told him," she began at last. But she couldn't continue, she was powerless to utter it.

"Yes, I know what you told him. Millions of girls have told young men that before."

"They've been asked, they've been asked! They didn't speak *first!* I didn't even know him, he didn't care for me, I had seen him for the first time the day before. I said strange things to him, and he behaved like a gentleman."

"Well he might!"

"Then before he could turn round, when we had simply walked out of the house together and strolled in the garden— it was as if I were borne along in the air by the wonder of what I had said—it rolled over me that I was lost."

"Lost?"

"That I had been horrible—that I had been mad. Nothing could ever unsay it. I frightened him—I almost struck him."

"Poor fellow!" I smiled.

"Yes—pity him. He was kind. But he'll see me that way— always!"

I hesitated as to the answer it was best to make to this; then I produced: "Don't think he'll remember you—he'll see other girls."

"Ah, he'll *forget* me!" she softly and miserably wailed; and I saw that I had said the wrong thing. I bent over her more closely, to kiss her, and when I raised my head her mother was on the other side of the bed. She fell on her knees there for the same purpose, and when Louisa felt her lips she stretched out her arms to embrace her. She had the strength to draw her close, and I heard her begin again, for the hundredth time, "Mother, mother——"

"Yes, my own darling."

Then for the hundredth time I heard her stop. There was an intensity in her silence. It made me wildly nervous; I got up and turned away.

"Mother, mother," the girl repeated, and poor Helen replied with a sound of passionate solicitation. But her daughter only exhaled in the waiting hush, while I stood at the window where the dawn was faint, the most miserable moan in the world. "I'm dying," she said, articulately; and she died that night, after an hour, unconscious. The doctor arrived almost at the moment; this time he was sure it must have been the heart. The poor parents were in stupefaction, and I gave up half my visits and stayed with them a month. But in spite of their stupefaction I kept my vow.

SIR DOMINICK FERRAND

I

"THERE are several objections to it, but I'll take it if you'll alter it," Mr Locket's rather curt note had said; and there was no waste of words in the postscript in which he had added: "If you'll come in and see me, I'll show you what I mean." This communication had reached Jersey Villas by the first post, and Peter Baron had scarcely swallowed his leathery muffin before he got into motion to obey the editorial behest. He knew that such precipitation looked eager, and he had no desire to look eager—it was not in his interest; but how could he maintain a god-like calm, principled though he was in favour of it, the first time one of the great magazines had accepted, even with a cruel reservation, a specimen of his ardent young genius?

It was not till, like a child with a sea-shell at his ear, he began to be aware of the great roar of the "underground," that, in his third-class carriage, the cruelty of the reservation penetrated, with the taste of acrid smoke, to his inner sense. It was really degrading to be eager in the face of having to "alter." Peter Baron tried to figure to himself at that moment that he was not flying to betray the extremity of his need, but hurrying to fight for some of those passages of superior boldness which were exactly what the conductor of the "Promiscuous Review" would be sure to be down upon. He made believe—as if to the greasy fellow-passenger opposite—that he felt indignant; but he saw that to the small round eye of this still more downtrodden brother he represented selfish success. He would have liked to linger in the conception that he had been "approached" by the Promiscuous; but whatever

343

might be thought in the office of that periodical of some of his flights of fancy, there was no want of vividness in his occasional suspicion that he passed there for a familiar bore. The only thing that was clearly flattering was the fact that the Promiscuous rarely published fiction. He should therefore be associated with a deviation from a solemn habit, and that would more than make up to him for a phrase in one of Mr Locket's inexorable earlier notes, a phrase which still rankled, about his showing no symptom of the faculty really creative. "You don't seem able to keep a character together," this pitiless monitor had somewhere else remarked. Peter Baron, as he sat in his corner while the train stopped, considered, in the befogged gaslight, the bookstall standard of literature and asked himself whose character had fallen to pieces now. Tormenting indeed had always seemed to him such a fate as to have the creative head without the creative hand.

It should be mentioned, however, that before he started on his mission to Mr Locket his attention had been briefly engaged by an incident occurring at Jersey Villas. On leaving the house (he lived at No. 3, the door of which stood open to a small front garden), he encountered the lady who, a week before, had taken possession of the rooms on the ground floor, the "parlours" of Mrs Bundy's terminology. He had heard her, and from his window, two or three times, had even seen her pass in and out, and this observation had created in his mind a vague prejudice in her favour. Such a prejudice, it was true, had been subjected to a violent test; it had been fairly apparent that she had a light step, but it was still less to be overlooked that she had a cottage piano. She had furthermore a little boy and a very sweet voice, of which Peter Baron had caught the accent, not from her singing (for she only played), but from her gay admonitions to her child, whom she occasionally allowed to amuse himself—under restrictions very publicly enforced—in the tiny black patch which, as a forecourt to each house, was held, in the humble row, to be a feature. Jersey Villas stood in pairs, semi-detached, and Mrs Ryves—such was the name under which the new lodger presented herself—had been admitted to the house as confessedly musical. Mrs Bundy, the earnest proprietress of No. 3, who considered her "parlours" (they were a dozen feet square), even more attractive, if possible, than the second floor with which Baron had had to content himself—Mrs Bundy, who reserved the drawing-room for a casual dressmaking business, had threshed out the subject of the new lodger in advance with our young man, reminding him that her affection for his own person was a proof that, other things being equal, she positively preferred tenants who were clever.

This was the case with Mrs Ryves; she had satisfied Mrs Bundy that she was not a simple strummer. Mrs Bundy admitted to Peter Baron that, for herself, she had a weakness for a pretty tune, and Peter could honestly reply that his ear was equally sensitive. Everything would depend on the "touch" of their inmate. Mrs Ryves's piano would blight his existence if her hand should prove heavy or her selections vulgar; but if she played agreeable things and played them in an agreeable way she would render him rather a service while he smoked the pipe of "form." Mrs Bundy, who wanted to let her rooms, guaranteed on the part of the stranger a first-class talent, and Mrs Ryves, who evidently knew thoroughly what she was about, had not falsified this somewhat rash prediction. She never played in the morning, which was Baron's working-time, and he found himself listening with pleasure at other hours to her discreet and melancholy strains. He really knew little about music, and the only criticism he would have made of Mrs Ryves's conception of it was that she seemed devoted to the dismal. It was not, however, that these strains were not pleasant to him; they floated up, on the contrary, as a sort of conscious response to some of his broodings and doubts. Harmony, therefore, would have reigned supreme had it not been for the singularly bad taste of No. 4. Mrs Ryves's piano was on the free side of the house and was regarded by Mrs Bundy as open to no objection but that of their own gentleman, who was so reasonable. As much, however, could not be said of the gentleman of No. 4, who had not even Mr Baron's excuse of being "littery" (he kept a bull-terrier and had five hats—the street could count them), and whom, if you had listened to Mrs Bundy, you would have supposed to be divided from the obnoxious instrument by walls and corridors, obstacles and intervals, of massive structure and fabulous extent. This gentleman had taken up an attitude which had now passed into the phase of correspondence and compromise; but it was the opinion of the immediate neighbourhood that he had not a leg to stand upon, and on whatever subject the sentiment of Jersey Villas might have been vague, it was not so on the rights and the wrongs of landladies.

Mrs Ryves's little boy was in the garden as Peter Baron issued from the house, and his mother appeared to have come out for a moment, bareheaded, to see that he was doing no harm. She was discussing with him the responsibility that he might incur by passing a piece of string round one of the iron palings and pretending he was in command of a "geegee"; but it happened that at the sight of the other lodger the child was seized with a finer perception of the drivable. He rushed at Baron with a flourish of the bridle, shouting, "Ou geegee!" in a manner productive of some refined embarrassment to his mother. Baron met his advance by mounting him on a shoulder and feigning to prance an instant, so that by the time this performance was over—it took but a few seconds—the young man felt introduced to Mrs Ryves. Her smile struck him as charming, and such an impression shortens many steps. She said, "Oh, thank you—you mustn't let him worry you"; and then as, having put down the child and raised his hat, he was turning away, she added: "It's very good of you not to complain of my piano."

"I particularly enjoy it—you play beautifully," said Peter Baron.

"I have to play, you see—it's all I can do. But the people next door don't like it, though my room, you know, is not against their wall. Therefore I thank you for letting me tell them that you, in the house, don't find me a nuisance."

She looked gentle and bright as she spoke, and as the young man's eyes rested on her the tolerance for which she expressed herself indebted seemed to him the least indulgence she might count upon. But he only laughed and said "Oh, no, you're not a nuisance!" and felt more and more introduced.

The little boy, who was handsome, hereupon clamoured for another ride, and she took him up herself, to moderate his transports. She stood a moment with the child in her arms, and he put his fingers exuberantly into her hair, so that while she smiled at Baron she slowly, permittingly shook her head to get rid of them.

"If they really make a fuss I'm afraid I shall have to go," she went on.

"Oh, don't go!" Baron broke out, with a sudden expressiveness which made his voice, as it fell upon his ear, strike him as the voice of another. She gave a vague exclamation and, nodding slightly but not unsociably, passed back into the house. She had made an impression which remained till the other party to the conversation reached the railway-station, when it was superseded by the thought of his prospective discussion with Mr Locket. This was a proof of the intensity of that interest.

The aftertaste of the later conference was also intense for Peter Baron, who quitted his editor with his manuscript under his arm. He had had the question out with Mr Locket, and he was in a flutter which ought to have been a sense of triumph and which indeed at first he succeeded in regarding in this light. Mr Locket had had to admit that there was an idea in his story, and that was a tribute which Baron was in a position to make the most of. But there was also a scene which scandalised the editorial conscience and which the young man had promised to rewrite. The idea that Mr Locket had been so good as to disengage depended for clearness mainly on this scene; so it was easy to see his objection was perverse. This inference was probably a part of the joy in which Peter Baron walked as he carried home a contribution it pleased him to classify as accepted. He walked to work off his excitement and to think in what manner he should reconstruct. He went some distance without settling that point, and then, as it began to worry him, he looked vaguely into shop-windows for solutions and hints. Mr Locket lived in the depths of Chelsea, in a little panelled, amiable house, and Baron took his way homeward along the King's Road. There was a new amusement for him, a fresher bustle, in a London walk in the morning; these were hours that he habitually spent at his table, in the awkward attitude engendered by the poor piece of furniture, one of the rickety features of Mrs Bundy's second floor, which had to serve as his altar of literary sacrifice. If by exception he went out when the day was young he noticed that life seemed younger with it; there were livelier industries to profit by and shop-girls, often rosy, to look at; a different air was in the streets and a chaff of traffic for the observer of manners to catch. Above all, it was the time when poor Baron made his purchases, which were wholly of the wandering mind; his extravagances, for some mysterious reason, were all matutinal, and he had a foreknowledge that if ever he should ruin himself it would be well before noon. He felt lavish this morning, on the strength of what the Promiscuous would do for him; he had lost sight for the moment of what he should have to do for the Promiscuous. Before the old bookshops and printshops, the crowded panes of the curiosity-mongers and the desirable exhibitions of mahogany "done up," he used, by an innocent process, to commit luxurious follies. He refurnished Mrs Bundy with a freedom that cost her nothing, and lost himself in pictures of a transfigured second floor.

On this particular occasion the King's Road proved almost unprecedentedly expensive, and indeed this occasion differed from most others in containing the germ of real danger. For once in a way he had a bad conscience—he felt himself tempted to pick his own pocket. He never saw a commodious writing-table, with elbow-room and drawers and a fair expanse of leather stamped neatly at the edge with gilt, without being freshly reminded of Mrs Bundy's dilapidations. There were several such tables in the King's Road—they seemed indeed particularly numerous today. Peter Baron glanced at them all through the fronts of the shops, but there was one that detained him in supreme contemplation. There was a fine assurance about it which seemed a guarantee of masterpieces; but when at last he went in and, just to help himself on his way, asked the impossible price, the sum mentioned by the voluble vendor mocked at him even more than he had feared. It was far too expensive, as he hinted, and he was on the point of completing his comedy by a pensive retreat when the shopman bespoke his attention for another article of the same general character, which he described as remarkably cheap for what it was. It was an old piece, from a sale in the country, and it had been in stock some time; but it had got pushed out of sight in one of the upper rooms—they contained such a wilderness of treasures—and happened to have but just come to light. Peter suffered himself to be conducted into an interminable dusky rear, where he presently found himself bending over one of those square substantial desks of old mahogany, raised, with the aid of front legs, on a sort of retreating pedestal which is fitted with small drawers, contracted conveniences known immemorially to the knowing as davenports. This specimen had visibly seen service, but it had an old-time solidity and to Peter Baron it unexpectedly appealed.

He would have said in advance that such an article was

exactly what he didn't want, but as the shopman pushed up a chair for him and he sat down with his elbows on the gentle slope of the large, firm lid, he felt that such a basis for literature would be half the battle. He raised the lid and looked lovingly into the deep interior; he sat ominously silent while his companion dropped the striking words: "Now that's an article I personally covet!" Then when the man mentioned the ridiculous price (they were literally giving it away), he reflected on the economy of having a literary altar on which one could really kindle a fire. A davenport was a compromise, but what was all life but a compromise? He could beat down the dealer, and at Mrs Bundy's he had to write on an insincere cardtable. After he had sat for a minute with his nose in the friendly desk he had a queer impression that it might tell him a secret or two—one of the secrets of form, one of the sacrificial mysteries—though no doubt its career had been literary only in the sense of its helping some old lady to write invitations to dull dinners. There was a strange, faint odour in the receptacle, as if fragrant, hallowed things had once been put away there. When he took his head out of it he said to the shopman: "I don't mind meeting you halfway." He had been told by knowing people that that was the right thing. He felt rather vulgar, but the davenport arrived that evening at Jersey Villas.

II

"I DARESAY it will be all right; he seems quiet now," said the poor lady of the "parlours" a few days later, in reference to their litigious neighbour and the precarious piano. The two lodgers had grown regularly acquainted, and the piano had had much to do with it. Just as this instrument served, with the gentleman at No. 4, as a theme for discussion, so between Peter Baron and the lady of the parlours it had become a basis of peculiar agreement, a topic, at any rate, of conversation frequently renewed. Mrs Ryves was so prepossessing that Peter was sure that even if they had not had the piano he would have found something else to thresh out with her. Fortunately however they did have it, and he, at least, made the most of it, knowing more now about his new friend, who when, widowed and fatigued, she held her beautiful child in her arms, looked dimly like a modern Madonna. Mrs Bundy, as a letter of furnished lodgings, was characterised in general by a familiar domestic severity in respect to picturesque young women, but she had the highest confidence in Mrs Ryves. She was luminous about her being a lady, and a lady who could bring Mrs Bundy back to a gratified recognition of one of those manifestations of mind for which she had an independent esteem. She was professional, but Jersey Villas could be proud of a profession that didn't happen to be the wrong one—they had seen something of that. Mrs Ryves had a hundred a year (Baron wondered how Mrs Bundy knew this; he thought it unlikely Mrs Ryves had told her), and for the rest she depended on her lovely music. Baron judged that her music, even though lovely, was a frail dependence; it would hardly help to fill a concert-room, and he asked himself at first whether she played country-dances at children's parties or gave lessons to young ladies who studied above their station.

Very soon, indeed, he was sufficiently enlightened; it all went fast, for the little boy had been almost as great a help as the piano. Sidney haunted the doorstep of No. 3; he was eminently sociable, and had established independent relations with Peter, a frequent feature of which was an adventurous visit, upstairs, to picture books criticised for not being *all* geegees and walking sticks happily more conformable. The young man's window, too, looked out on their acquaintance; through a starched muslin curtain it kept his neighbour before him, made him almost more aware of her comings and goings than he felt he had a right to be. He was capable of a shyness of curiosity about her and of dumb little delicacies of consideration. She did give a few lessons; they were essentially local, and he ended by knowing more or less what she went out for and what she came in from. She had almost no visitors, only a decent old lady or two, and, every day, poor dingy Miss Teagle, who was also ancient and who came humbly enough to governess the infant of the parlours. Peter Baron's window had always, to his sense, looked out on a good deal of life, and one of the things it had most shown him was that there is nobody so bereft of joy as not to be able to command for twopence the services of somebody less joyous. Mrs Ryves was a struggler (Baron scarcely liked to think of it), but she occupied a pinnacle for Miss Teagle, who had lived on—and from a noble nursery—into a period of diplomas and humiliation.

Mrs Ryves sometimes went out, like Baron himself, with manuscripts under her arm, and, still more like Baron, she almost always came back with them. Her vain approaches were to the music-sellers; she tried to compose—to produce songs that would make a hit. A successful song was an income, she confided to Peter one of the first times he took Sidney, blasé and drowsy, back to his mother. It was not on one of these occasions, but once when he had come in on no better pretext than that of simply wanting to (she had after all virtually invited him), that she mentioned how only one song in a thousand was successful and that the terrible difficulty was in getting the right words. This rightness was just a vulgar "fluke"—there were lots of words really clever that were of no use at all. Peter said, laughing, that he supposed any words he should try to produce would be sure to be too clever; yet only three weeks after his first encounter with Mrs Ryves he sat at his delightful davenport (well aware that he had duties more pressing), trying to string together rhymes idiotic enough to make his neighbour's fortune. He was satisfied of the fineness of her musical gift—it had the touching note. The touching note was in her person as well.

The davenport was delightful, after six months of its tottering predecessor, and such a reënforcement to the young man's style was not impaired by his sense of something lawless in the way it had been gained. He had made the purchase in anticipation of the money he expected from Mr Locket, but Mr Locket's liberality was to depend on the ingenuity of his contributor, who now found himself confronted with the consequence of a frivolous optimism. The fruit of his labour presented, as he stared at it with his elbows on his desk, an aspect uncompromising and incorruptible. It seemed to look up at him reproachfully and to say, with its essential finish: "How could you promise anything so base; how could you pass your word to mutilate and dishonour me?" The alterations demanded by Mr Locket were impossible, the concessions to the platitude of his conception of the public mind were degrading. The public mind!—as if the public *had* a mind, or any principle of perception more discoverable than the stare of huddled sheep! Peter Baron felt that it concerned him to determine if he were only not clever enough or if he were simply not abject enough to rewrite his story. He might in truth have had less pride if he had had more skill, and more discretion if he had had more practice. Humility, in the profession of letters, was half of practice, and resignation was half of success. Poor Peter actually flushed with pain as he recognised that this was not success, the production of gelid prose which his editor could do nothing with on the one side and he himself could do nothing with on the other. The truth about his luckless tale was now the more bitter from his having managed, for some days, to taste it as sweet.

As he sat there, baffled and sombre, biting his pen and wondering what was meant by the "rewards" of literature, he generally ended by tossing away the composition deflowered by Mr Locket and trying his hand at the sort of twaddle that Mrs Ryves might be able to set to music. Success in these experiments wouldn't be a reward of literature, but it might very well become a labour of love. The experiments would be pleasant enough for him if they were pleasant for his inscrutable neighbour. That was the way he thought of her now, for he had learned enough about her, little by little, to guess how much there was still to learn. To spend his mornings over cheap rhymes for her was certainly to shirk the immediate question; but there were hours when he judged this question to be altogether too arduous, reflecting that he might quite as well perish by the sword as by famine. Besides, he did meet it obliquely when he considered that he shouldn't be an utter failure if he were to produce some songs to which Mrs Ryves's accompaniments would give a circulation. He had not ventured to show her anything yet, but one morning, at a moment when her little boy was in his room, it seemed to him that, by an inspiration, he had arrived at the happy middle course (it was an art by itself), between sound and sense. If the sense was not confused it was because the sound was so familiar.

He had said to the child, to whom he had sacrificed barley-sugar (it had no attraction for his own lips, yet in these days there was always some of it about), he had confided to the small Sidney that if he would wait a little he should be intrusted with something nice to take down to his parent. Sidney had absorbing occupation and, while Peter copied off the song in a pretty hand, roamed, gurgling and sticky, about the room. In this manner he lurched like a little toper into the rear of the davenport, which stood a few steps out from the recess of the window, and, as he was fond of beating time to his intensest joys, began to bang on the surface of it with a paper-knife which at that spot had chanced to fall upon the floor. At the moment Sidney committed this violence his kind friend had happened to raise the lid of the desk and, with his head beneath it, was rummaging among a mass of papers for a proper envelope. "I say, I say, my boy!" he exclaimed, solicitous for the ancient glaze of his most cherished possession. Sidney paused an instant; then, while Peter still hunted for the envelope, he administered another, and this time a distinctly disobedient, rap. Peter heard it from within and was struck with its oddity of sound—so much so that, leaving the child for a moment under a demoralising impression of impunity, he waited with quick curiosity for a repetition of the stroke. It came of course immediately, and then the young man, who had at the same instant found his envelope and ejaculated "Hallo, this thing has a false back!" jumped up and secured his visitor, whom with his left arm he held in durance on his knee while with his free hand he addressed the missive to Mrs Ryves.

As Sidney was fond of errands he was easily got rid of, and after he had gone Baron stood a moment at the window chinking pennies and keys in pockets and wondering if the charming composer would think his song as good, or in other words as bad, as he thought it. His eyes as he turned away fell on the wooden back of the davenport, where, to his regret, the traces of Sidney's assault were visible in three or four ugly scratches. "Confound the little brute!" he exclaimed, feeling as if an altar had been desecrated. He was reminded, however, of the observation this outrage had led him to make, and, for further assurance, he knocked on the wood with his knuckle. It sounded from that position commonplace enough, but his suspicion was strongly confirmed when, again standing beside the desk, he put his head beneath the lifted lid and gave ear while with an extended arm he tapped sharply in the same place. The back was distinctly hollow; there was a space between the inner and the outer pieces (he could measure it), so wide that he was a fool not to have noticed it before. The depth of the receptacle from front to rear was so great that it could sacrifice a certain quantity of room without detection.

The sacrifice could of course only be for a purpose, and the purpose could only be the creation of a secret compartment. Peter Baron was still boy enough to be thrilled by the idea of such a feature, the more so as every indication of it had been cleverly concealed. The people at the shop had never noticed it, else they would have called his attention to it as an enhancement of value. His legendary lore instructed him that where there was a hiding-place there was always a hidden spring, and he pried and pressed and fumbled in an eager search for the sensitive spot. The article was really a wonder of neat construction; everything fitted with a closeness that completely saved appearances.

It took Baron some minutes to pursue his inquiry, during which he reflected that the people of the shop were not such fools after all. They had admitted moreover that they had accidentally neglected this relic of gentility—it had been overlooked in the multiplicity of their treasures. He now recalled that the man had wanted to polish it up before sending it home, and that, satisfied for his own part with its honourable appearance and averse in general to shiny furniture, he had in his impatience declined to wait for such an operation, so that the object had left the place for Jersey Villas, carrying presumably its secret with it, two or three hours after his visit. This secret it seemed indeed capable of keeping; there was an absurdity in being baffled, but Peter couldn't find the spring. He thumped and sounded, he listened and measured again; he inspected every joint and crevice, with the effect of becoming surer still of the existence of a chamber and of making up his mind that his davenport was a rarity. Not only was there a compartment between the two backs, but there was distinctly something *in* the compartment! Perhaps it was a lost manuscript—a nice, safe, old-fashioned story that Mr Locket wouldn't object to. Peter returned to the charge, for it had occurred to him that he had perhaps not sufficiently visited the small drawers, of which, in two vertical rows, there were six in number, of different sizes, inserted sideways into that portion of the structure which formed part of the support of the desk. He took them out again and examined more minutely the condition of their sockets, with the happy result of discovering at last, in the place into which the third on the left-hand row was fitted, a small sliding panel. Behind the panel was a spring, like a flat button, which yielded with a click when he pressed it and which instantly produced a loosening of one of the pieces of the shelf forming the highest part of the davenport—pieces adjusted to each other with the most deceptive closeness.

This particular piece proved to be, in its turn, a sliding panel, which, when pushed, revealed the existence of a smaller receptacle, a narrow, oblong box, in the false back. Its capacity was limited, but if it couldn't hold many things it might hold precious ones. Baron, in presence of the ingenuity with which it had been dissimulated, immediately felt that, but for the odd chance of little Sidney Ryves's having hammered on the outside at the moment he himself happened to have his head in the desk, he might have remained for years without suspicion of it. This apparently would have been a loss, for he had been right in guessing that the chamber was not empty. It contained objects which, whether precious or not, had at any rate been worth somebody's hiding. These objects were a collection of small flat parcels, of the shape of packets of letters, wrapped in white paper and neatly sealed. The seals, mechanically figured, bore the impress neither of arms nor of initials; the paper looked old—it had turned faintly sallow; the packets might have been there for ages. Baron counted them—there were nine in all, of different sizes; he turned them over and over, felt them curiously and snuffed in their vague, musty smell, which affected him with the melancholy of some smothered human accent. The little bundles were neither named nor numbered—there was not a word of writing on any of the covers; but they plainly contained old

letters, sorted and matched according to dates or to author-
ship. They told some old, dead story—they were the ashes of
fires burned out.

As Peter Baron held his discoveries successively in his
hands he became conscious of a queer emotion which was not
altogether elation and yet was still less pure pain. He had
made a find, but it somehow added to his responsibility; he
was in the presence of something interesting, but (in a manner
he couldn't have defined) this circumstance suddenly constituted a danger. It was the perception of the danger, for
instance, which caused to remain in abeyance any impulse he
might have felt to break one of the seals. He looked at them all
narrowly, but he was careful not to loosen them, and he wondered uncomfortably whether the contents of the secret compartment would be held in equity to be the property of the
people in the King's Road. He had given money for the
davenport, but had he given money for these buried papers?
He paid by a growing consciousness that a nameless chill had
stolen into the air the penalty, which he had many a time paid
before, of being made of sensitive stuff. It was as if an occasion had insidiously arisen for a sacrifice—a sacrifice for the
sake of a fine superstition, something like honour or kindness
or justice, something indeed perhaps even finer still—a difficult deciphering of duty, an impossible tantalising wisdom.
Standing there before his ambiguous treasure and losing himself for the moment in the sense of a dawning complication,
he was startled by a light, quick tap at the door of his sitting-
room. Instinctively, before answering, he listened an instant
—he was in the attitude of a miser surprised while counting
his hoard. Then he answered "One moment, please!" and
slipped the little heap of packets into the biggest of the
drawers of the davenport, which happened to be open. The
aperture of the false back was still gaping, and he had not
time to work back the spring. He hastily laid a big book over
the place and then went and opened his door.

It offered him a sight none the less agreeable for being un-expected—the graceful and agitated figure of Mrs Ryves. Her agitation was so visible that he thought at first that something dreadful had happened to her child—that she had rushed up to ask for help, to beg him to go for the doctor. Then he perceived that it was probably connected with the desperate verses he had transmitted to her a quarter of an hour before; for she had his open manuscript in one hand and was ner-vously pulling it about with the other. She looked frightened and pretty, and if, in invading the privacy of a fellow-lodger, she had been guilty of a departure from rigid custom, she was at least conscious of the enormity of the step and incapable of treating it with levity. The levity was for Peter Baron, who endeavoured, however, to clothe his familiarity with respect, pushing forward the seat of honour and repeating that he rejoiced in such a visit. The visitor came in, leaving the door ajar, and after a minute during which, to help her, he charged her with the purpose of telling him that he ought to be ashamed to send her down such rubbish, she recovered herself sufficiently to stammer out that his song was exactly what she had been looking for and that after reading it she had been seized with an extraordinary, irresistible impulse—that of thanking him for it in person and without delay.

"It was the impulse of a kind nature," he said, "and I can't tell you what pleasure you give me."

She declined to sit down, and evidently wished to appear to have come but for a few seconds. She looked confusedly at the place in which she found herself, and when her eyes met his own they struck him as anxious and appealing. She was evidently not thinking of his song, though she said three or four times over that it was beautiful. "Well, I only wanted you to know, and now I must go," she added; but on his hearthrug she lingered with such an odd helplessness that he felt almost sorry for her.

"Perhaps I can improve it if you find it doesn't go,"

said Baron. "I'm so delighted to do anything for you I can."

"There may be a word or two that might be changed," she answered, rather absently. "I shall have to think it over, to live with it a little. But I like it, and that's all I wanted to say."

"Charming of you. I'm not a bit busy," said Baron.

Again she looked at him with a troubled intensity, then suddenly she demanded: "Is there anything the matter with you?"

"The matter with me?"

"I mean like being ill or worried. I wondered if there might be; I had a sudden fancy; and that, I think, is really why I came up."

"There isn't, indeed; I'm all right. But your sudden fancies are inspirations."

"It's absurd. You must excuse me. Good-by!" said Mrs Ryves.

"What are the words you want changed?" Baron asked.

"I don't want any—if you're all right. Good-by," his visitor repeated, fixing her eyes an instant on an object on his desk that had caught them. His own glanced in the same direction and he saw that in his hurry to shuffle away the packets found in the davenport he had overlooked one of them, which lay with its seals exposed. For an instant he felt found out, as if he had been concerned in something to be ashamed of, and it was only his quick second thought that told him how little the incident of which the packet was a sequel was an affair of Mrs Ryves's. Her conscious eyes came back to his as if they were sounding them, and suddenly this instinct of keeping his discovery to himself was succeeded by a really startled inference that, with the rarest alertness, she had guessed something and that her guess (it seemed almost supernatural), had been her real motive. Some secret sympathy had made her vibrate—had touched her with the knowledge that he had brought something to light. After an

instant he saw that she also divined the very reflection he was
then making, and this gave him a lively desire, a grateful,
happy desire, to appear to have nothing to conceal. For herself, it determined her still more to put an end to her momentary visit. But before she had passed to the door he exclaimed:

"All right? How can a fellow be anything else who has just
had such a find?"

She paused at this, still looking earnest and asking: "What
have you found?"

"Some ancient family papers, in a secret compartment of
my writing-table." And he took up the packet he had left
out, holding it before her eyes. "A lot of other things like
that."

"What are they?" murmured Mrs Ryves.

"I haven't the least idea. They're sealed."

"You haven't broken the seals?" She had come further
back.

"I haven't had time; it only happened ten minutes ago."

"I knew it," said Mrs Ryves, more gaily now.

"What did you know?"

"That you were in some predicament."

"You're extraordinary. I never heard of anything so miraculous; down two flights of stairs."

"*Are* you in a quandary?" the visitor asked.

"Yes, about giving them back." Peter Baron stood smiling
at her and rapping his packet on the palm of his hand. "What
do you advise?"

She herself smiled now, with her eyes on the sealed parcel.
"Back to whom?"

"The man of whom I bought the table."

"Ah then, they're not from *your* family?"

"No indeed, the piece of furniture in which they were
hidden is not an ancestral possession. I bought it at second
hand—you see it's old—the other day in the King's Road.
Obviously the man who sold it to me sold me more than he

meant; he had no idea (from his own point of view it was stupid of him), that there was a hidden chamber or that mysterious documents were buried there. Ought I to go and tell him? It's rather a nice question."

"Are the papers of value?" Mrs Ryves inquired.

"I haven't the least idea. But I can ascertain by breaking a seal."

"Don't!" said Mrs Ryves, with much expression. She looked grave again.

"It's rather tantalising—it's a bit of a problem," Baron went on, turning his packet over.

Mrs Ryves hesitated. "Will you show me what you have in your hand?"

He gave her the packet, and she looked at it and held it for an instant to her nose. "It has a queer, charming old fragrance," he said.

"Charming? It's horrid." She handed him back the packet, saying again more emphatically "Don't!"

"Don't break a seal?"

"Don't give back the papers."

"Is it honest to keep them?"

"Certainly. They're yours as much as the people's of the shop. They were in the hidden chamber when the table came to the shop, and the people had every opportunity to find them out. They didn't—therefore let them take the consequences."

Peter Baron reflected, diverted by her intensity. She was pale, with eyes almost ardent. "The table had been in the place for years."

"That proves the things haven't been missed."

"Let me show you how they were concealed," he rejoined; and he exhibited the ingenious recess and the working of the curious spring. She was greatly interested, she grew excited and became familiar; she appealed to him again not to do anything so foolish as to give up the papers, the rest of which, in their little blank, impenetrable covers, he placed in a row before her. "They might be traced—their history, their ownership," he argued; to which she replied that this was exactly why he ought to be quiet. He declared that women had not the smallest sense of honour, and she retorted that at any rate they have other perceptions more delicate than those of men. He admitted that the papers might be rubbish, and she conceded that nothing was more probable; yet when he offered to settle the point off-hand she caught him by the wrist, acknowledging that, absurd as it was, she was nervous. Finally she put the whole thing on the ground of his just doing her a favour. She asked him to retain the papers, to be silent about them, simply because it would please her. That would be reason enough. Baron's acquaintance, his agreeable relations with her, advanced many steps in the treatment of this question; an element of friendly candour made its way into their discussion of it.

"I can't make out why it matters to you, one way or the other, nor why you should think it worth talking about," the young man reasoned.

"Neither can I. It's just a whim."

"Certainly, if it will give you any pleasure, I'll say nothing at the shop."

"That's charming of you, and I'm very grateful. I see now that this was why the spirit moved me to come up—to save them," Mrs Ryves went on. She added, moving away, that now she had saved them she must really go.

"To save them for what, if I mayn't break the seals?" Baron asked.

"I don't know—for a generous sacrifice."

"Why should it be generous? What's at stake?" Peter demanded, leaning against the doorpost as she stood on the landing.

"I don't know what, but I feel as if something or other were in peril. Burn them up!" she exclaimed with shining eyes.

"Ah, you ask too much—I'm so curious about them!"

"Well, I won't ask more than I ought, and I'm much obliged to you for your promise to be quiet. I trust to your discretion. Good-by."

"You ought to *reward* my discretion," said Baron, coming out to the landing.

She had partly descended the staircase and she stopped, leaning against the baluster and smiling up at him. "Surely you've had your reward in the honour of my visit."

"That's delightful as far as it goes. But what will you do for me if I burn the papers?"

Mrs Ryves considered a moment. "Burn them first and you'll see!"

On this she went rapidly downstairs, and Baron, to whom the answer appeared inadequate and the proposition indeed in that form grossly unfair, returned to his room. The vivacity of her interest in a question in which she had discoverably nothing at stake mystified, amused and, in addition, irresistibly charmed him. She was delicate, imaginative, inflammable, quick to feel, quick to act. He didn't complain of it, it was the way he liked women to be; but he was not impelled for the hour to commit the sealed packets to the flames. He dropped them again into their secret well, and after that he went out. He felt restless and excited; another day was lost for work— the dreadful job to be performed for Mr Locket was still further off.

III

TEN days after Mrs Ryves's visit he paid by appointment another call on the editor of the Promiscuous. He found him in the little wainscoted Chelsea house, which had to Peter's sense the smoky brownness of an old pipebowl, surrounded with all the emblems of his office—a litter of papers, a hedge

of encyclopædias, a photographic gallery of popular con-
tributors—and he promised at first to consume very few of
the moments for which so many claims competed. It was Mr
Locket himself however who presently made the interview
spacious, gave it air after discovering that poor Baron had
come to tell him something more interesting than that he
couldn't after all patch up his tale. Peter had begun with this,
had intimated respectfully that it was a case in which both
practice and principle rebelled, and then, perceiving how little
Mr Locket was affected by his audacity, had felt weak and
slightly silly, left with his heroism on his hands. He had
armed himself for a struggle, but the Promiscuous didn't even
protest, and there would have been nothing for him but to go
away with the prospect of never coming again had he not
chanced to say abruptly, irrelevantly, as he got up from his
chair:

"Do you happen to be at all interested in Sir Dominick
Ferrand?"

Mr Locket, who had also got up, looked over his glasses.
"The late Sir Dominick?"

"The only one; you know the family's extinct."

Mr Locket shot his young friend another sharp glance, a
silent retort to the glibness of this information. "Very extinct indeed. I'm afraid the subject today would scarcely be
regarded as attractive."

"Are you very sure?" Baron asked.

Mr Locket leaned forward a little, with his finger-tips on his
table, in the attitude of giving permission to retire. "I might
consider the question in a special connection." He was silent a
minute, in a way that relegated poor Peter to the general; but
meeting the young man's eyes again he asked: "Are you—a—
thinking of proposing an article upon him?"

"Not exactly proposing it—because I don't yet quite see
my way; but the idea rather appeals to me."

Mr Locket emitted the safe assertion that this eminent

statesman had been a striking figure in his day; then he added: "Have you been studying him?"

"I've been dipping into him."

"I'm afraid he's scarcely a question of the hour," said Mr Locket, shuffling papers together.

"I think I could make him one," Peter Baron declared.

Mr Locket stared again; he was unable to repress an unattenuated "You?"

"I have some new material," said the young man, colouring a little. "That often freshens up an old story."

"It buries it sometimes. It's often only another tombstone."

"That depends upon what it is. However," Peter added, "the documents I speak of would be a crushing monument."

Mr Locket, hesitating, shot another glance under his glasses. "Do you allude to—a—revelations?"

"Very curious ones."

Mr Locket, still on his feet, had kept his body at the bowing angle; it was therefore easy for him after an instant to bend a little further and to sink into his chair with a movement of his hand toward the seat Baron had occupied. Baron resumed possession of this convenience, and the conversation took a fresh start on a basis which such an extension of privilege could render but little less humiliating to our young man. He had matured no plan of confiding his secret to Mr Locket, and he had really come out to make him conscientiously that other announcement as to which it appeared that so much artistic agitation had been wasted. He had indeed during the past days—days of painful indecision—appealed in imagination to the editor of the Promiscuous, as he had appealed to other sources of comfort; but his scruples turned their face upon him from quarters high as well as low, and if on the one hand he had by no means made up his mind not to mention his strange knowledge, he had still more left to the determination of the moment the question of how he should introduce the subject. He was in fact too nervous to decide; he only felt that he needed for his peace of mind to communicate his discovery. He wanted an opinion, the impression of somebody else, and even in this intensely professional presence, five minutes after he had begun to tell his queer story, he felt relieved of half his burden. His story was very queer; he could take the measure of that himself as he spoke; but wouldn't this very circumstance qualify it for the Promiscuous?

"Of course the letters may be forgeries," said Mr Locket at last.

"I've no doubt that's what many people will say."

"Have they been seen by any expert?"

"No indeed; they've been seen by nobody."

"Have you got any of them with you?"

"No; I felt nervous about bringing them out."

"That's a pity. I should have liked the testimony of my eyes."

"You may have it if you'll come to my rooms. If you don't care to do that without a further guarantee I'll copy you out some passages."

"Select a few of the worst!" Mr Locket laughed. Over Baron's distressing information he had become quite human and genial. But he added in a moment more dryly: "You know they ought to be seen by an expert."

"That's exactly what I dread," said Peter.

"They'll be worth nothing to me if they're not."

Peter communed with his innermost spirit. "How much will they be worth to *me* if they *are*?"

Mr Locket turned in his study-chair. "I should require to look at them before answering that question."

"I've been to the British museum—there are many of his letters there. I've obtained permission to see them, and I've compared everything carefully. I repudiate the possibility of forgery. No sign of genuineness is wanting; there are details, down to the very postmarks, that no forger could have invented. Besides, whose interest could it conceivably have been? A labor of unspeakable difficulty, and all for what advantage? There are so many letters, too—twenty-seven in all."

"Lord, what an ass!" Mr Locket exclaimed.

"It will be one of the strangest post-mortem revelations of which history preserves the record."

Mr Locket, grave now, worried with a paper-knife the crevice of a drawer. "It's very odd. But to be worth anything such documents should be subjected to a searching criticism—I mean of the historical kind."

"Certainly; that would be the task of the writer introducing them to the public."

Again Mr Locket considered; then with a smile he looked up. "You had better give up original composition and take to buying old furniture."

"Do you mean because it will pay better?"

"For you, I should think, original composition couldn't pay worse. The creative faculty's so rare."

"I do feel tempted to turn my attention to real heroes," Peter replied.

"I'm bound to declare that Sir Dominick Ferrand was never one of mine. Flashy, crafty, second-rate—that's how I've always read him. It was never a secret, moreover, that his private life had its weak spots. He was a mere flash in the pan."

"He speaks to the people of this country," said Baron.

"He did; but his voice—the voice, I mean, of his prestige—is scarcely audible now."

"They're still proud of some of the things he did at the Foreign Office—the famous 'exchange' with Spain, in the Mediterranean, which took Europe so by surprise and by which she felt injured, especially when it became apparent how much we had the best of the bargain. Then the sudden, unexpected show of force by which he imposed on the United States our interpretation of that tiresome treaty—I

could never make out what it was about. These were both
matters that no one really cared a straw about, but he made
every one feel as if they cared; the nation rose to the way he
played his trumps—it was uncommon. He was one of the few
men we've had, in our period, who took Europe, or took
America, by surprise, made them jump a bit; and the country
liked his doing it—it was a pleasant change. The rest of the
world considered that they knew in any case exactly what we
would do, which was usually nothing at all. Say what you
like, he's still a high name; partly also, no doubt, on account
of other things—his early success and early death, his political 'cheek' and wit; his very appearance—he certainly was
handsome—and the possibilities (of future personal supre-
macy) which it was the fashion at the time, which it's the
fashion still, to say had passed away with him. He had been
twice at the Foreign Office; that alone was remarkable for a
man dying at forty-four. What therefore will the country
think when it learns he was venal?"

Peter Baron himself was not angry with Sir Dominick
Ferrand, who had simply become to him (he had been
"reading up" feverishly for a week) a very curious subject of
psychological study; but he could easily put himself in the
place of that portion of the public whose memory was long
enough for their patriotism to receive a shock. It was some
time fortunately since the conduct of public affairs had wanted
for men of disinterested ability, but the extraordinary documents concealed (of all places in the world—it was as
fantastic as a nightmare) in a "bargain" picked up at second-
hand by an obscure scribbler, would be a calculable blow to
the retrospective mind. Baron saw vividly that if these relics
should be made public the scandal, the horror, the chatter
would be immense. Immense would be also the contribution
to truth, the rectification of history. He had felt for several
days (and it was exactly what had made him so nervous) as
if he held in his hand the key to public attention.

"There are too many things to explain," Mr Locket went on, "and the singular *provenance* of your papers would count almost overwhelmingly against them even if the other objections were met. There would be a perfect and probably a very complicated pedigree to trace. How did they get into your davenport, as you call it, and how long had they been there? What hands secreted them? what hands had, so incredibly, clung to them and preserved them? Who are the persons mentioned in them? who are the correspondents, the parties to the nefarious transactions? You say the transactions appear to be of two distinct kinds—some of them connected with public business and others involving obscure personal relations."

"They all have this in common," said Peter Baron, "that they constitute evidence of uneasiness, in some instances of painful alarm, on the writer's part, in relation to exposure— the exposure in the one case, as I gather, of the fact that he had availed himself of official opportunities to promote enterprises (public works and that sort of thing) in which he had a pecuniary stake. The dread of the light in the other connection is evidently different, and these letters are the earliest in date. They are addressed to a woman, from whom he had evidently received money."

Mr Locket wiped his glasses. "What woman?"

"I haven't the least idea. There are lots of questions I can't answer, of course; lots of identities I can't establish; lots of gaps I can't fill. But as to two points I'm clear, and they are the essential ones. In the first place the papers in my possession are genuine; in the second place they're compromising."

With this Peter Baron rose again, rather vexed with himself for having been led on to advertise his treasure (it was his interlocutor's perfectly natural scepticism that produced this effect), for he felt that he was putting himself in a false position. He detected in Mr Locket's studied detachment the fermentation of impulses from which, unsuccessful as he was, he himself prayed to be delivered.

Mr Locket remained seated; he watched Baron go across the room for his hat and umbrella. "Of course, the question would come up of whose property today such documents would legally be. There are heirs, descendants, executors to consider."

"In some degree perhaps; but I've gone into that a little. Sir Dominick Ferrand had no children, and he left no brothers and no sisters. His wife survived him, but she died ten years ago. He can have had no heirs and no executors to speak of, for he left no property."

"That's to his honour and against your theory," said Mr Locket.

"I *have* no theory. He left a largeish mass of debt," Peter Baron added. At this Mr Locket got up, while his visitor pursued: "So far as I can ascertain, though of course my inquiries have had to be very rapid and superficial, there is no one now living, directly or indirectly related to the personage in question, who would be likely to suffer from any steps in the direction of publicity. It happens to be a rare instance of a life that had, as it were, no loose ends. At least there are none perceptible at present."

"I see, I see," said Mr Locket. "But I don't think I should care much for your article."

"What article?"

"The one you seem to wish to write, embodying this new matter."

"Oh, I don't wish to write it!" Peter exclaimed. And then he bade his host good-by.

"Good-by," said Mr Locket. "Mind you, I don't say that I think there's nothing in it."

"You would think there was something in it if you were to see my documents."

"I should like to see the secret compartment," the caustic editor rejoined. "Copy me out some extracts."

"To what end, if there's no question of their being of use to you?"

"I don't say that—I might like the letters themselves."

"Themselves?"

"Not as the basis of a paper, but just to publish—for a sensation."

"They'd sell your number!" Baron laughed.

"I daresay I should like to look at them," Mr Locket conceded after a moment. "When should I find you at home?"

"Don't come," said the young man. "I make you no offer."

"I might make *you* one," the editor hinted.

"Don't trouble yourself; I shall probably destroy them." With this Peter Baron took his departure, waiting however just afterwards, in the street near the house, as if he had been looking out for a stray hansom, to which he would not have signalled had it appeared. He thought Mr Locket might hurry after him, but Mr Locket seemed to have other things to do, and Peter Baron returned on foot to Jersey Villas.

IV

ON the evening that succeeded this apparently pointless encounter he had an interview more conclusive with Mrs Bundy, for whose shrewd and philosophic view of life he had several times expressed, even to the good woman herself, a considerable relish. The situation at Jersey Villas (Mrs Ryves had suddenly flown off to Dover) was such as to create in him a desire for moral support, and there was a kind of domestic determination in Mrs Bundy which seemed, in general, to advertise it. He had asked for her on coming in, but had been told she was absent for the hour; upon which he had addressed himself mechanically to the task of doing up his dishonoured manuscript—the ingenious fiction about which Mr Locket had been so stupid—for further adventures and not improbable defeats. He passed a restless, ineffective afternoon, asking himself if his genius were a horrid delusion, looking out of his window for something that didn't happen, something that seemed now to be the advent of a persuasive Mr Locket and now the return, from an absence more disappointing even than Mrs Bundy's, of his interesting neighbour of the parlours. He was so nervous and so depressed that he was unable even to fix his mind on the composition of the note with which, on its next peregrination, it was necessary that his manuscript should be accompanied. He was too nervous to eat, and he forgot even to dine; he forgot to light his candles, he let his fire go out, and it was in the melancholy chill of the late dusk that Mrs Bundy, arriving at last with his lamp, found him extended moodily upon his sofa. She had been informed that he wished to speak to her, and as she placed on the malodorous luminary an oily shade of green pasteboard she expressed the friendly hope that there was nothing wrong with his 'ealth.

The young man rose from his couch, pulling himself together sufficiently to reply that his health was well enough but that his spirits were down in his boots. He had a strong disposition to "draw" his landlady on the subject of Mrs Ryves, as well as a vivid conviction that she constituted a theme as to which Mrs Bundy would require little pressure to tell him even more than she knew. At the same time he hated to appear to pry into the secrets of his absent friend; to discuss her with their bustling hostess resembled too much for his taste a gossip with a tattling servant about an unconscious employer. He left out of account however Mrs Bundy's knowledge of the human heart, for it was this fine principle that broke down the barriers after he had reflected reassuringly that it was not meddling with Mrs Ryves's affairs to try and find out if she struck such an observer as happy. Crudely, abruptly, even a little blushingly, he put the direct question to Mrs Bundy, and this led tolerably straight to another question, which, on his spirit, sat equally heavy (they were indeed but different phases of the same), and which the good woman answered with expression when she ejaculated: "Think it a liberty for you to run down for a few hours? If she do, my dear sir, just send her to me to talk to!" As regards happiness indeed she warned Baron against imposing too high a standard on a young thing who had been through so much, and before he knew it he found himself, without the responsibility of choice, in submissive receipt of Mrs Bundy's version of this experience. It was an interesting picture, though it had its infirmities, one of them congenital and consisting of the fact that it had sprung essentially from the virginal brain of Miss Teagle. Amplified, edited, embellished by the richer genius of Mrs Bundy, who had incorporated with it and now liberally introduced copious interleavings of Miss Teagle's own romance, it gave Peter Baron much food for meditation, at the same time that it only half relieved his curiosity about the causes of the charming woman's underlying strangeness. He sounded this note experimentally in Mrs Bundy's ear, but it was easy to see that it didn't reverberate in her fancy. She had no idea of the picture it would have been natural for him to desire that Mrs Ryves should present to him, and she was therefore unable to estimate the points in respect to which his actual impression was irritating. She had indeed no adequate conception of the intellectual requirements of a young man in love. She couldn't tell him why their faultless friend was so isolated, so unrelated, so nervously, shrinkingly proud. On the other hand she could tell him (he knew it already) that she had passed many years of her life in the acquisition of accomplishments at a seat of learning no less remote than Boulogne, and that Miss Teagle had been intimately acquainted with the late Mr Everard Ryves, who was a "most rising" young man in the city, not making any year less than his clear twelve hundred. "Now that he isn't there to make them, his mourning widow can't live as she had then, can she?" Mrs Bundy asked.

Baron was not prepared to say that she could, but he thought of another way she might live as he sat, the next day, in the train which rattled him down to Dover. The place, as he approached it, seemed bright and breezy to him; his roamings had been neither far enough nor frequent enough to make the cockneyfied coast insipid. Mrs Bundy had of course given him the address he needed, and on emerging from the station he was on the point of asking what direction he should take. His attention however at this moment was drawn away by the bustle of the departing boat. He had been long enough shut up in London to be conscious of refreshment in the mere act of turning his face to Paris. He wandered off to the pier in company with happier tourists and, leaning on a rail, watched enviously the preparation, the agitation of foreign travel. It was for some minutes a foretaste of adventure; but, ah, when was he to have the very draught? He turned away as he dropped this interrogative sigh, and in doing so perceived that in another part of the pier two ladies and a little boy were gathered with something of the same wistfulness. The little boy indeed happened to look round for a moment, upon which, with the keenness of the predatory age, he recognised in our young man a source of pleasures from which he lately had been weaned. He bounded forward with irrepressible cries of "Geegee!" and Peter lifted him aloft for an embrace. On putting him down the pilgrim from Jersey Villas stood confronted with a sensibly severe Miss Teagle, who had followed her little charge. "What's the matter with the old woman?" he asked himself as he offered her a hand which she treated as the merest detail. Whatever it was, it was (and very properly, on the part of a loyal *suivante*) the same complaint as that of her employer, to whom, from a distance, for Mrs

Ryves had not advanced an inch, he flourished his hat as she stood looking at him with a face that he imagined rather white. Mrs Ryves's response to this salutation was to shift her position in such a manner as to appear again absorbed in the Calais boat. Peter Baron, however, kept hold of the child, whom Miss Teagle artfully endeavoured to wrest from him— a policy in which he was aided by Sidney's own rough but instinctive loyalty; and he was thankful for the happy effect of being dragged by his jubilant friend in the very direction in which he had tended for so many hours. Mrs Ryves turned once more as he came near, and then, from the sweet, strained smile with which she asked him if he were on his way to France, he saw that if she had been angry at his having followed her she had quickly got over it.

"No, I'm not crossing; but it came over me that you might be, and that's why I hurried down—to catch you before you were off."

"Oh, we can't go—more's the pity; but why, if we could," Mrs Ryves inquired, "should you wish to prevent it?"

"Because I've something to ask you first, something that may take some time." He saw now that her embarrassment had really not been resentful; it had been nervous, tremulous, as the emotion of an unexpected pleasure might have been. "That's really why I determined last night, without asking your leave first to pay you this little visit—that and the intense desire for another bout of horse-play with Sidney. Oh, I've come to see you," Peter Baron went on, "and I won't make any secret of the fact that I expect you to resign yourself gracefully to the trial and give me all your time. The day's lovely, and I'm ready to declare that the place is as good as the day. Let me drink deep of these things, drain the cup like a man who hasn't been out of London for months and months. Let me walk with you and talk with you and lunch with you— I go back this afternoon. Give me all your hours in short, so that they may live in my memory as one of the sweetest occasions of life."

The emission of steam from the French packet made such an uproar that Baron could breathe his passion into the young woman's ear without scandalising the spectators; and the charm which little by little it scattered over his fleeting visit proved indeed to be the collective influence of the conditions he had put into words. "What is it you wish to ask me?" Mrs Ryves demanded, as they stood there together; to which he replied that he would tell her all about it if she would send Miss Teagle off with Sidney. Miss Teagle, who was always anticipating her cue, had already begun ostentatiously to gaze at the distant shores of France and was easily enough induced to take an earlier start home and rise to the responsibility of stopping on her way to contend with the butcher. She had however to retire without Sidney, who clung to his recovered prey, so that the rest of the episode was seasoned, to Baron's sense, by the importunate twitch of the child's little, plump, cool hand. The friends wandered together with a conjugal air and Sidney not between them, hanging wistfully, first, over the lengthened picture of the Calais boat, till they could look after it, as it moved rumbling away, in a spell of silence which seemed to confess—especially when, a moment later, their eyes met—that it produced the same fond fancy in each. The presence of the boy moreover was no hindrance to their talking in a manner that they made believe was very frank. Peter Baron presently told his companion what it was he had taken a journey to ask, and he had time afterwards to get over his discomfiture at her appearance of having fancied it might be something greater. She seemed disappointed (but she was forgiving) on learning from him that he had only wished to know if she judged ferociously his not having complied with her request to respect certain seals.

"How ferociously do you suspect me of having judged it?" she inquired.

"Why, to the extent of leaving the house the next moment."

They were still lingering on the great granite pier when he touched on this matter, and she sat down at the end while the breeze, warmed by the sunshine, ruffled the purple sea. She coloured a little and looked troubled, and after an instant she repeated interrogatively: "The next moment?"

"As soon as I told you what I had done. I was scrupulous about this, you will remember; I went straight downstairs to confess to you. You turned away from me, saying nothing; I couldn't imagine—as I vow I can't imagine now—why such a matter should appear so closely to touch you. I went out on some business and when I returned you had quitted the house. It had all the look of my having offended you, of your wishing to get away from me. You didn't even give me time to tell you how it was that, in spite of your advice, I determined to see for myself what my discovery represented. You must do me justice and hear what determined me."

Mrs Ryves got up from her seat and asked him, as a particular favour, not to allude again to his discovery. It was no concern of hers at all, and she had no warrant for prying into his secrets. She was very sorry to have been for a moment so absurd as to appear to do so, and she humbly begged his pardon for her meddling. Saying this she walked on with a charming colour in her cheek, while he laughed out, though he was really bewildered, at the endless capriciousness of women. Fortunately the incident didn't spoil the hour, in which there were other sources of satisfaction, and they took their course to her lodgings with such pleasant little pauses and excursions by the way as permitted her to show him the objects of interest at Dover. She let him stop at a wine-merchant's and buy a bottle for luncheon, of which, in its order, they partook, together with a pudding invented by Miss Teagle, which, as they hypocritically swallowed it, made them look at each other in an intimacy of indulgence. They came out again and, while Sidney grubbed in the gravel of the shore, sat selfishly on the Parade, to the disappointment of Miss Teagle, who had fixed her hopes on a fly and a ladylike visit to the castle. Baron had his eye on his watch—he had to think of his train and the dismal return and many other melancholy things; but the sea in the afternoon light was a more appealing picture; the wind had gone down, the Channel was crowded, the sails of the ships were white in the purple distance. The young man had asked his companion (he had asked her before) when she was to come back to Jersey Villas, and she had said that she should probably stay at Dover another week. It was dreadfully expensive, but it was doing the child all the good in the world, and if Miss Teagle could go up for some things she should probably be able to manage an extension. Earlier in the day she had said that she perhaps wouldn't return to Jersey Villas at all, or only return to wind up her connection with Mrs Bundy. At another moment she had spoken of an early date, an immediate reoccupation of the wonderful parlours. Baron saw that she had no plan, no real reasons, that she was vague and, in secret, worried and nervous, waiting for something that didn't depend on herself. A silence of several minutes had fallen upon them while they watched the shining sails; to which Mrs Ryves put an end by exclaiming abruptly, but without completing her sentence: "Oh, if you had come to tell me you had destroyed them—"

"Those terrible papers? I like the way you talk about 'destroying!' You don't even know what they are."

"I don't want to know; they put me into a state."

"What sort of a state?"

"I don't know; they haunt me."

"They haunted me; that was why, early one morning, suddenly, I couldn't keep my hands off them. I had told you I wouldn't touch them. I had deferred to your whim, your superstition (what is it?) but at last they got the better of me.

I had lain awake all night threshing about, itching with curiosity. It made me ill; my own nerves (as I may say) were irritated, my capacity to work was gone. It had come over me in the small hours in the shape of an obsession, a fixed idea, that there was nothing in the ridiculous relics and that my exaggerated scruples were making a fool of me. It was ten to one they were rubbish, they were vain, they were empty; that they had been even a practical joke on the part of some weakminded gentleman of leisure, the former possessor of the confounded davenport. The longer I hovered about them with such precautions the longer I was taken in, and the sooner I exposed their insignificance the sooner I should get back to my usual occupations. This conviction made my hand so uncontrollable that that morning before breakfast I broke one of the seals. It took me but a few minutes to perceive that the contents were not rubbish; the little bundle contained old letters—very curious old letters."

"I know—I know; 'private and confidential.' So you broke the other seals?" Mrs Ryves looked at him with the strange apprehension he had seen in her eyes when she appeared at his door the moment after his discovery.

"You know, of course, because I told you an hour later, though you would let me tell you very little."

Baron, as he met this queer gaze, smiled hard at her to prevent her guessing that he smarted with the fine reproach conveyed in the tone of her last words; but she appeared able to guess everything, for she reminded him that she had not had to wait that morning till he came downstairs to know what had happened above, but had shown him at the moment how she had been conscious of it an hour before, had passed on her side the same tormented night as he, and had had to exert extraordinary self-command not to rush up to his rooms while the study of the open packets was going on. "You're so sensitively organised and you've such mysterious powers that you're uncanny," Baron declared.

"I feel what takes place at a distance; that's all."

"One would think somebody you liked was in danger."

"I told you that that was what was present to me the day I came up to see you."

"Oh, but you don't like me so much as that," Baron argued, laughing.

She hesitated. "No, I don't know that I do."

"It must be for someone else—the other person concerned. The other day, however, you wouldn't let me tell you that person's name."

Mrs Ryves, at this, rose quickly. "I don't want to know it; it's none of my business."

"No, fortunately, I don't think it is," Baron rejoined, walking with her along the Parade. She had Sidney by the hand now, and the young man was on the other side of her. They moved toward the station—she had offered to go part of the way. "But with your miraculous gift it's a wonder you haven't divined."

"I only divine what I want," said Mrs Ryves.

"That's very convenient!" exclaimed Peter, to whom Sidney had presently come round again. "Only, being thus in the dark, it's difficult to see your motive for wishing the papers destroyed."

Mrs Ryves meditated, looking fixedly at the ground. "I thought you might do it to oblige me."

"Does it strike you that such an expectation, formed in such conditions, is reasonable?"

Mrs Ryves stopped short, and this time she turned on him the clouded clearness of her eyes. "What do you mean to do with them?"

It was Peter Baron's turn to meditate, which he did, on the empty asphalt of the Parade (the "season," at Dover, was not yet), where their shadows were long in the afternoon light. He was under such a charm as he had never known, and he wanted immensely to be able to reply: "I'll do anything you

like if you'll love me." These words, however, would have
represented a responsibility and have constituted what was
vulgarly termed an offer. An offer of what? he quickly asked
himself here, as he had already asked himself after making in
spirit other awkward dashes in the same direction—of what
but his poverty, his obscurity, his attempts that had come to
nothing, his abilities for which there was nothing to show?
Mrs Ryves was not exactly a success, but she was a greater
success than Peter Baron. Poor as he was he hated the sordid
(he knew she didn't love it), and he felt small for talking of
marriage. Therefore he didn't put the question in the words it
would have pleased him most to hear himself utter, but he
compromised, with an angry young pang, and said to her:
"What will you do for me if I put an end to them?"

She shook her head sadly—it was always her prettiest
movement. "I can promise nothing—oh, no, I can't promise!
We must part now," she added. "You'll miss your train."

He looked at his watch, taking the hand she held out to him.
She drew it away quickly, and nothing then was left him,
before hurrying to the station, but to catch up Sidney and
squeeze him till he uttered a little shriek. On the way back to
town the situation struck him as grotesque.

V

IT tormented him so the next morning that after threshing it
out a little further he felt he had something of a grievance.
Mrs Ryves's intervention had made him acutely uncomfortable, for she had taken the attitude of exerting pressure without, it appeared, recognising on his part an equal right. She
had imposed herself as an influence, yet she held herself aloof
as a participant; there were things she looked to him to do for
her, yet she could tell him of no good that would come to

him from the doing. She should either have had less to say or have been willing to say more, and he asked himself why he should be the sport of her moods and her mysteries. He perceived her knack of punctual interference to be striking, but it was just this apparent infallibility that he resented. Why didn't she set up at once as a professional clairvoyant and eke out her little income more successfully? In purely private life such a gift was disconcerting; her divinations, her evasions disturbed at any rate his own tranquillity.

What disturbed it still further was that he received early in the day a visit from Mr Locket, who, leaving him under no illusion as to the grounds of such an honour, remarked as soon as he had got into the room or rather while he still panted on the second flight and the smudged little slavey held open Baron's door, that he had taken up his young friend's invitation to look at Sir Dominick Ferrand's letters for himself. Peter drew them forth with a promptitude intended to show that he recognised the commercial character of the call and without attenuating the inconsequence of this departure from the last determination he had expressed to Mr Locket. He showed his visitor the davenport and the hidden recess, and he smoked a cigarette, humming softly, with a sense of unwonted advantage and triumph, while the cautious editor sat silent and handled the papers. For all his caution Mr Locket was unable to keep a warmer light out of his judicial eye as he said to Baron at last with sociable brevity—a tone that took many things for granted: "I'll take them home with me—they require much attention."

The young man looked at him a moment. "Do you think they're genuine?" He didn't mean to be mocking, he meant not to be; but the words sounded so to his own ear, and he could see that they produced that effect on Mr Locket.

"I can't in the least determine. I shall have to go into them at my leisure, and that's why I ask you to lend them to me."

He had shuffled the papers together with a movement

charged, while he spoke, with the air of being preliminary to that of thrusting them into a little black bag which he had brought with him and which, resting on the shelf of the davenport, struck Peter, who viewed it askance, as an object darkly editorial. It made our young man, somehow, suddenly apprehensive; the advantage of which he had just been conscious was about to be transferred by a quiet process of legerdemain to a person who already had advantages enough. Baron, in short, felt a deep pang of anxiety; he couldn't have said why. Mr Locket took decidedly too many things for granted, and the explorer of Sir Dominick Ferrand's irregularities remembered afresh how clear he had been after all about his indisposition to traffic in them. He asked his visitor to what end he wished to remove the letters, since on the one hand there was no question now of the article in the Promiscuous which was to reveal their existence, and on the other he himself, as their owner, had a thousand insurmountable scruples about putting them into circulation.

Mr Locket looked over his spectacles as over the battlements of a fortress. "I'm not thinking of the end—I'm thinking of the beginning. A few glances have assured me that such documents ought to be submitted to some competent eye."

"Oh, you mustn't show them to anyone!" Baron exclaimed.

"You may think me presumptuous, but the eye that I venture to allude to in those terms—"

"Is the eye now fixed so terribly on *me?*" Peter laughingly interrupted. "Oh, it would be interesting, I confess, to know how they strike a man of your acuteness!" It had occurred to him that by such a concession he might endear himself to a literary umpire hitherto implacable. There would be no question of his publishing Sir Dominick Ferrand, but he might, in due acknowledgment of services rendered, form the habit of publishing Peter Baron. "How long would it be your idea to retain them?" he inquired, in a manner which, he imme-

diately became aware, was what incited Mr Locket to begin
stuffing the papers into his bag. With this perception he came
quickly closer and, laying his hand on the gaping receptacle,
lightly drew its two lips together. In this way the two men
stood for a few seconds, touching, almost in the attitude of
combat, looking hard into each other's eyes.

The tension was quickly relieved however by the surprised
flush which mantled on Mr Locket's brow. He fell back a few
steps with an injured dignity that might have been a protest
against physical violence. "Really, my dear young sir, your
attitude is tantamount to an accusation of intended bad faith.
Do you think I want to steal the confounded things?" In reply
to such a challenge Peter could only hastily declare that he was
guilty of no discourteous suspicion—he only wanted a limit
named, a pledge of every precaution against accident. Mr
Locket admitted the justice of the demand, assured him he
would restore the property within three days, and completed,
with Peter's assistance, his little arrangements for removing
it discreetly. When he was ready, his treacherous reticule
distended with its treasures, he gave a lingering look at the
inscrutable davenport. "It's how they ever got into that thing
that puzzles one's brain!"

"There was some concatenation of circumstances that
would doubtless seem natural enough if it were explained, but
that one would have to remount the stream of time to ascertain. To one course I have definitely made up my mind: not
to make any statement or any inquiry at the shop. I simply
accept the mystery," said Peter, rather grandly.

"That would be thought a cheap escape if you were to put
it into a story," Mr Locket smiled.

"Yes, I shouldn't offer the story to *you*. I shall be impatient
till I see my papers again," the young man called out, as his
visitor hurried downstairs.

That evening, by the last delivery, he received, under the
Dover postmark, a letter that was not from Miss Teagle. It

was a slightly confused but altogether friendly note, written that morning after breakfast, the ostensible purpose of which was to thank him for the amiability of his visit, to express regret at any appearance the writer might have had of meddling with what didn't concern her, and to let him know that the evening before, after he had left her, she had in a moment of inspiration got hold of the tail of a really musical idea—a perfect accompaniment for the song he had so kindly given her. She had scrawled, as a specimen, a few bars at the end of her note, mystic, mocking musical signs which had no sense for her correspondent. The whole letter testified to a restless but rather pointless desire to remain in communication with him. In answering her, however, which he did that night before going to bed, it was on this bright possibility of their collaboration, its advantages for the future of each of them, that Baron principally expatiated. He spoke of this future with an eloquence of which he would have defended the sincerity, and drew of it a picture extravagantly rich. The next morning, as he was about to settle himself to tasks for some time terribly neglected, with a sense that after all it was rather a relief not to be sitting so close to Sir Dominick Ferrand, who had become dreadfully distracting; at the very moment at which he habitually addressed his preliminary invocation to the muse, he was agitated by the arrival of a telegram which proved to be an urgent request from Mr Locket that he would immediately come down and see him. This represented, for poor Baron, whose funds were very low, another morning sacrificed, but somehow it didn't even occur to him that he might impose his own time upon the editor of the Promiscuous, the keeper of the keys of renown. He had some of the plasticity of the raw contributor. He gave the muse another holiday, feeling she was really ashamed to take it, and in course of time found himself in Mr Locket's own chair at Mr Locket's own table—so much nobler an expanse than the slippery slope of the davenport—considering with quick intensity, in the white flash of certain words just brought out by his host, the quantity of happiness, of emancipation that might reside in a hundred pounds.

Yes, that was what it meant: Mr Locket, in the twenty-four hours, had discovered so much in Sir Dominick's literary remains that his visitor found him primed with an offer. A hundred pounds would be paid him that day, that minute, and no questions would be either asked or answered. "I take all the risks, I take all the risks," the editor of the Promiscuous repeated. The letters were out on the table, Mr Locket was on the hearthrug, like an orator on a platform, and Peter, under the influence of his sudden ultimatum, had dropped, rather weakly, into the seat which happened to be nearest and which, as he became conscious it moved on a pivot, he whirled round so as to enable himself to look at his tempter with an eye intended to be cold. What surprised him most was to find Mr Locket taking exactly the line about the expediency of publication which he would have expected Mr Locket not to take. "Hush it all up; a barren scandal, an offence that can't be remedied, is the thing in the world that least justifies an airing—" some such line as that was the line he would have thought natural to a man whose life was spent in weighing questions of propriety and who had only the other day objected, in the light of this virtue, to a work of the most disinterested art. But the author of that incorruptible masterpiece had put his finger on the place in saying to his interlocutor on the occasion of his last visit that, if given to the world in the pages of the Promiscuous, Sir Dominick's aberrations would sell the edition. It was not necessary for Mr Locket to reiterate to his young friend his phrase about their making a sensation. If he wished to purchase the "rights," as theatrical people said, it was not to protect a celebrated name or to lock them up in a cupboard. That formula of Baron's covered all the ground, and one edition was a low estimate of the probable performance of the magazine.

Peter left the letters behind him and, on withdrawing from the editorial presence, took a long walk on the Embankment. His impressions were at war with each other—he was flurried by possibilities of which he yet denied the existence. He had consented to trust Mr Locket with the papers a day or two longer, till he should have thought out the terms on which he might—in the event of certain occurrences—be induced to dispose of them. A hundred pounds were not this gentleman's last word, nor perhaps was mere unreasoning intractability Peter's own. He sighed as he took no note of the pictures made by barges—sighed because it all might mean money. He needed money bitterly; he owed it in disquieting quarters. Mr Locket had put it before him that he had a high responsibility —that he might vindicate the disfigured truth, contribute a chapter to the history of England. "You haven't a right to suppress such momentous facts," the hungry little editor had declared, thinking how the series (he would spread it into three numbers) would be the talk of the town. If Peter had money he might treat himself to ardour, to bliss. Mr Locket had said, no doubt justly enough, that there were ever so many questions one would have to meet should one venture to play so daring a game. These questions, embarrassments, dangers—the danger, for instance, of the cropping-up of some lurking litigious relative—he would take over unreservedly and bear the brunt of dealing with. It was to be remembered that the papers were discredited, vitiated by their childish pedigree; such a preposterous origin, suggesting, as he had hinted before, the feeble ingenuity of a third-rate novelist, was a thing he should have to place himself at the positive disadvantage of being silent about. He would rather give no account of the matter at all than expose himself to the ridicule that such a story would infallibly excite. Couldn't one see them in advance, the clever, taunting things the daily and weekly papers would say? Peter Baron had his guileless side, but he felt, as he worried with a stick that betrayed him the granite parapets of the Thames, that he was not such a fool as not to know how Mr Locket would "work" the mystery of his marvellous find. Nothing could help it on better with the public than the impenetrability of the secret attached to it. If Mr Locket should only be able to kick up dust enough over the circumstances that had guided his hand his fortune would literally be made. Peter thought a hundred pounds a low bid, yet he wondered how the Promiscuous could bring itself to offer such a sum—so large it loomed in the light of literary remuneration as hitherto revealed to our young man. The explanation of this anomaly was of course that the editor shrewdly saw a dozen ways of getting his money back. There would be in the "sensation," at a later stage, the making of a book in large type—the book of the hour; and the profits of this scandalous volume or, if one preferred the name, this reconstruction, before an impartial posterity, of a great historical humbug, the sum "down," in other words, that any lively publisher would give for it, figured vividly in Mr Locket's calculations. It was therefore altogether an opportunity of dealing at first hand with the lively publisher that Peter was invited to forego. Peter gave a masterful laugh, rejoicing in his heart that, on the spot, in the *repaire* he had lately quitted, he had not been tempted by a figure that would have approximately represented the value of his property. It was a good job, he mentally added as he turned his face homeward, that there was so little likelihood of his having to struggle with that particular pressure.

VI

WHEN, half an hour later, he approached Jersey Villas, he noticed that the house-door was open; then, as he reached the gate, saw it make a frame for an unexpected presence. Mrs Ryves, in her bonnet and jacket, looked out from it as if she were expecting something—as if she had been passing to and fro to watch. Yet when he had expressed to her that it was a delightful welcome she replied that she had only thought there might possibly be a cab in sight. He offered to go and look for one, upon which it appeared that after all she was not, as yet at least, in need. He went back with her into her sitting-room, where she let him know that within a couple of days she had seen clearer what was best; she had determined to quit Jersey Villas and had come up to take away her things, which she had just been packing and getting together.

"I wrote you last night a charming letter in answer to yours," Baron said. "You didn't mention in yours that you were coming up."

"It wasn't your answer that brought me. It hadn't arrived when I came away."

"You'll see when you get back that my letter is charming."

"I daresay." Baron had observed that the room was not, as she had intimated, in confusion—Mrs Ryves's preparations for departure were not striking. She saw him look round and, standing in front of the fireless grate with her hands behind her, she suddenly asked: "Where have you come from now?"

"From an interview with a literary friend."

"What are you concocting between you?"

"Nothing at all. We've fallen out—we don't agree."

"Is he a publisher?"

"He's an editor."

"Well, I'm glad you don't agree. I don't know what he wants, but, whatever it is, don't do it."

"He must do what *I* want!" said Baron.

"And what's that?"

"Oh, I'll tell you when he has done it!" Baron begged her to let him hear the "musical idea" she had mentioned in her letter; on which she took off her hat and jacket and, seating herself at her piano, gave him, with a sentiment of which the very first notes thrilled him, the accompaniment of his song. She phrased the words with her sketchy sweetness, and he sat there as if he had been held in a velvet vise, throbbing with the emotion, irrecoverable ever after in its freshness, of the young artist in the presence for the first time of "production"—the proofs of his book, the hanging of his picture, the rehearsal of his play. When she had finished he asked again for the same delight, and then for more music and for more; it did him such a world of good, kept him quiet and safe, smoothed out the creases of his spirit. She dropped her own experiments and gave him immortal things, and he lounged there, pacified and charmed, feeling the mean little room grow large and vague and happy possibilities come back. Abruptly, at the piano, she called out to him: "Those papers of yours—the letters you found—are not in the house?"

"No, they're not in the house."

"I was sure of it! No matter—it's all right!" she added. She herself was pacified—trouble was a false note. Later he was on the point of asking her how she knew the objects she had mentioned were not in the house; but he let it pass. The subject was a profitless riddle—a puzzle that grew grotesquely bigger, like some monstrosity seen in the darkness, as one opened one's eyes to it. He closed his eyes—he wanted another vision. Besides, she had shown him that she had extraordinary senses—her explanation would have been stranger than the fact. Moreover they had other things to talk about, in particular the question of her putting off her return to Dover till the

morrow and dispensing meanwhile with the valuable protection of Sidney. This was indeed but another face of the question of her dining with him somewhere that evening (where
else should she dine?)—accompanying him, for instance, just
for an hour of Bohemia, in their deadly respectable lives, to a
jolly little place in Soho. Mrs Ryves declined to have her life
abused, but in fact, at the proper moment, at the jolly little
place, to which she did accompany him—it dealt in macaroni
and Chianti—the pair put their elbows on the crumpled cloth
and, face to face, with their little emptied coffee-cups pushed
away and the young man's cigarette lighted by her command,
became increasingly confidential. They went afterwards to the
theatre, in cheap places, and came home in "busses" and under
umbrellas.

On the way back Peter Baron turned something over in his
mind as he had never turned anything before; it was the question of whether, at the end, she would let him come into her
sitting-room for five minutes. He felt on this point a passion
of suspense and impatience, and yet for what would it be but
to tell her how poor he was? This was literally the moment to
say it, so supremely depleted had the hour of Bohemia left
him. Even Bohemia was too expensive, and yet in the course
of the day his whole temper on the subject of certain fitnesses
had changed. At Jersey Villas (it was near midnight, and Mrs
Ryves, scratching a light for her glimmering taper, had said:
"Oh, yes, come in for a minute if you like!"), in her precarious parlour, which was indeed, after the brilliances of the
evening, a return to ugliness and truth, she let him stand while
he explained that he had certainly everything in the way of
fame and fortune still to gain, but that youth and love and
faith and energy—to say nothing of her supreme dearness—
were all on his side. Why, if one's beginnings were rough,
should one add to the hardness of the conditions by giving up
the dream which, if she would only hear him out, would make
just the blessed difference? Whether Mrs Ryves heard him out

or not is a circumstance as to which this chronicle happens to be silent; but after he had got possession of both her hands and breathed into her face for a moment all the intensity of his tenderness—in the relief and joy of utterance he felt it carry him like a rising flood—she checked him with better reasons, with a cold, sweet afterthought in which he felt there was something deep. Her procrastinating head-shake was prettier than ever, yet it had never meant so many fears and pains—impossibilities and memories, independences and pieties, and a sort of uncomplaining ache for the ruin of a friendship that had been happy. She had liked him—if she hadn't she wouldn't have let him think so!—but she protested that she had not, in the odious vulgar sense, "encouraged" him. Moreover she couldn't talk of such things in that place, at that hour, and she begged him not to make her regret her good-nature in staying over. There were peculiarities in her position, considerations insurmountable. She got rid of him with kind and confused words, and afterwards, in the dull, humiliated night, he felt that he had been put in his place. Women in her situation, women who after having really loved and lost, usually lived on into the new dawns in which old ghosts steal away. But there was something in his whimsical neighbour that struck him as terribly invulnerable.

VII

"I've had time to look a little further into what we're prepared to do, and I find the case is one in which I should consider the advisability of going to an extreme length," said Mr Locket. Jersey Villas the next morning had had the privilege of again receiving the editor of the Promiscuous, and he sat once more at the davenport, where the bone of contention, in the shape of a large, loose heap of papers that showed how much they had been handled, was placed well in view. "We shall see our way to offering you three hundred, but we shouldn't, I must positively assure you, see it a single step further."

Peter Baron, in his dressing-gown and slippers, with his hands in his pockets, crept softly about the room, repeating, below his breath and with inflections that for his own sake he endeavoured to make humorous: "Three hundred—three hundred." His state of mind was far from hilarious, for he felt poor and sore and disappointed; but he wanted to prove to himself that he was gallant—was made, in general and in particular, of undiscourageable stuff. The first thing he had been aware of on stepping into his front room was that a four-wheeled cab, with Mrs Ryves's luggage upon it, stood at the door of No. 3. Permitting himself, behind his curtain, a pardonable peep, he saw the mistress of his thoughts come out of the house, attended by Mrs Bundy, and take her place in the modest vehicle. After this his eyes rested for a long time on the sprigged cotton back of the landlady, who kept bobbing at the window of the cab an endlessly moralising old head. Mrs Ryves had really taken flight—he had made Jersey Villas impossible for her—but Mrs Bundy, with a magnanimity unprecedented in the profession, seemed to express a belief in the purity of her motives. Baron felt that his own separation had been, for the present at least, effected; every instinct of delicacy prompted him to stand back.

Mr Locket talked a long time, and Peter Baron listened and waited. He reflected that his willingness to listen would probably excite hopes in his visitor—hopes which he himself was ready to contemplate without a scruple. He felt no pity for Mr Locket and had no consideration for his suspense or for his possible illusions; he only felt sick and forsaken and in want of comfort and of money. Yet it was a kind of outrage to his dignity to have the knife held to his throat, and he was irritated above all by the ground on which Mr Locket put the question—the ground of a service rendered to historical truth. It might be—he wasn't clear; it might be—the question was deep, too deep, probably, for his wisdom; at any rate he had to control himself not to interrupt angrily such dry, interested palaver, the false voice of commerce and of cant. He stared tragically out of the window and saw the stupid rain begin to fall; the day was duller even than his own soul, and Jersey Villas looked so sordidly hideous that it was no wonder Mrs Ryves couldn't endure them. Hideous as they were he should have to tell Mrs Bundy in the course of the day that he was obliged to seek humbler quarters. Suddenly he interrupted Mr Locket; he observed to him: "I take it that if I should make you this concession the hospitality of the Promiscuous would be by that very fact unrestrictedly secured to me."

Mr Locket stared. "Hospitality—secured?" He thumbed the proposition as if it were a hard peach.

"I mean that of course you wouldn't—in courtesy, in gratitude—keep on declining my things."

"I should give them my best attention—as I've always done in the past."

Peter Baron hesitated. It was a case in which there would have seemed to be some chance for the ideally shrewd aspirant in such an advantage as he possessed; but after a moment the blood rushed into his face with the shame of the idea of pleading for his productions in the name of anything but their merit. It was as if he had stupidly uttered evil of them. Nevertheless he added the interrogation: "Would you for instance publish my little story?"

"The one I read (and objected to some features of) the other day? Do you mean—a—with the alteration?" Mr Locket continued.

"Oh, no, I mean utterly without it. The pages you want altered contain, as I explained to you very lucidly, I think, the very *raison d'être* of the work, and it would therefore, it seems to me, be an imbecility of the first magnitude to cancel them." Peter had really renounced all hope that his critic would understand what he meant, but, under favour of circumstances, he couldn't forbear to taste the luxury, which probably never again would come within his reach, of being really plain, for one wild moment, with an editor.

Mr Locket gave a constrained smile. "Think of the scandal, Mr Baron."

"But isn't this other scandal just what you're going in for?"

"It will be a great public service."

"You mean it will be a big scandal, whereas my poor story would be a very small one, and that it's only out of a big one that money's to be made."

Mr Locket got up—he too had his dignity to vindicate. "Such a sum as I offer you ought really to be an offset against all claims."

"Very good—I don't mean to make any, since you don't really care for what I write. I take note of your offer," Peter pursued, "and I engage to give you to-night (in a few words left by my own hand at your house) my absolutely definite and final reply."

Mr Locket's movements, as he hovered near the relics of the eminent statesman, were those of some feathered parent fluttering over a threatened nest. If he had brought his huddled brood back with him this morning it was because he had felt sure enough of closing the bargain to be able to be graceful. He kept a glittering eye on the papers and remarked that he was afraid that before leaving them he must elicit some assurance that in the meanwhile Peter would not place them in any other hands. Peter, at this, gave a laugh of harsher cadence than he intended, asking, justly enough, on what privilege his visitor rested such a demand and why he himself was disqualified from offering his wares to the highest bidder.

"Surely you wouldn't hawk such things about?" cried Mr Locket; but before Baron had time to retort cynically he added: "I'll publish your little story."

"Oh, thank you!"

"I'll publish anything you'll send me," Mr Locket continued, as he went out. Peter had before this virtually given his word that for the letters he would treat only with the Promiscuous.

The young man passed, during a portion of the rest of the day, the strangest hours of his life. Yet he thought of them afterwards not as a phase of temptation, though they had been full of the emotion that accompanies an intense vision of alternatives. The struggle was already over; it seemed to him that, poor as he was, he was not poor enough to take Mr Locket's money. He looked at the opposed courses with the self-possession of a man who has chosen, but this self-possession was in itself the most exquisite of excitements. It was really a high revulsion and a sort of noble pity. He seemed indeed to have his finger upon the pulse of history and to be in the secret of the gods. He had them all in his hand, the tablets and the scales and the torch. He couldn't keep a character together, but he might easily pull one to pieces. That would be "creative work" of a kind—he could reconstruct the character less pleasingly, could show an unknown side of it. Mr Locket had had a good deal to say about responsibility; and responsibility in truth sat there with him all the morning, while he revolved in his narrow cage and, watching the crude spring rain on the windows, thought of the dismalness to which, at Dover, Mrs Ryves was going back. This influence took in fact the form, put on the physiognomy of poor Sir Dominick Ferrand; he was at present as perceptible in it, as coldly and strangely personal, as if he had been a haunting ghost and had risen beside his own old hearthstone. Our friend was accustomed to his company and indeed had spent so many hours in it of late, following him up at the museum and comparing his different portraits, engravings and lithographs, in which there seemed to be conscious, pleading eyes for the betrayer, that their queer intimacy had grown as close as an embrace. Sir Dominick was very dumb, but he was terrible in his dependence, and Peter would not have encouraged him by so much curiosity nor reassured him by so much deference had it not been for the young man's complete acceptance of the impossibility of getting out of a tight place by exposing an individual. It didn't matter that the individual was dead; it didn't matter that he was dishonest. Peter felt him sufficiently alive to suffer; he perceived the rectification of history so conscientiously desired by Mr Locket to be somehow for himself not an imperative task. It had come over him too definitely that in a case where one's success was to hinge upon an act of extradition it would minister most to an easy conscience to let the success go. No, no—even should he be starving he couldn't make money out of Sir Dominick's disgrace. He was almost surprised at the violence of the horror with which, as he shuffled mournfully about, the idea of any such profit inspired him. What was Sir Dominick to him after all? He wished he had never come across him.

In one of his brooding pauses at the window—the window out of which never again apparently should he see Mrs Ryves glide across the little garden with the step for which he had liked her from the first—he became aware that the rain was about to intermit and the sun to make some grudging amends. This was a sign that he might go out; he had a vague perception that there were things to be done. He had work to look for, and a cheaper lodging, and a new idea (every idea he had ever cherished had left him), in addition to which the promised little word was to be dropped at Mr Locket's door. He looked at his watch and was surprised at the hour, for he had nothing but a heartache to show for so much time. He would have to dress quickly, but as he passed to his bedroom his eye was caught by the little pyramid of letters which Mr Locket had constructed on his davenport. They startled him and, staring at them, he stopped for an instant, half-amused, half-annoyed at their being still in existence. He had so completely destroyed them in spirit that he had taken the act for granted, and he was now reminded of the orderly stages of which an intention must consist to be sincere. Baron went at the papers with all his sincerity, and at his empty grate (where there lately had been no fire and he had only to remove a horrible ornament of tissue-paper dear to Mrs Bundy) he burned the collection with infinite method. It made him feel happier to watch the worst pages turn to illegible ashes—if happiness be the right word to apply to his sense, in the process, of something so crisp and crackling that it suggested the death-rustle of banknotes.

When ten minutes later he came back into his sitting-room, he seemed to himself oddly, unexpectedly in the presence of a bigger view. It was as if some interfering mass had been so displaced that he could see more sky and more country. Yet the opposite houses were naturally still there, and if the grimy little place looked lighter it was doubtless only because the rain had indeed stopped and the sun was pouring in. Peter went to the window to open it to the altered air, and in doing so beheld at the garden gate the humble "growler" in which a few hours before he had seen Mrs Ryves take her departure. It was unmistakable—he remembered the knock-kneed white horse; but this made the fact that his friend's luggage no longer surmounted it only the more mystifying. Perhaps the cabman had already removed the luggage—he was now on his box smoking the short pipe that derived relish from inaction paid for. As Peter turned into the room again his ears caught a knock at his own door, a knock explained, as soon as he had responded, by the hard breathing of Mrs Bundy.

"Please, sir, it's to say she've come back."

"What has she come back for?" Baron's question sounded ungracious, but his heartache had given another throb, and he felt a dread of another wound. It was like a practical joke.

"I think it's for you, sir," said Mrs Bundy. "She'll see you for a moment, if you'll be so good, in the old place."

Peter followed his hostess downstairs, and Mrs Bundy ushered him, with her company flourish, into the apartment she had fondly designated.

"I went away this morning, and I've only returned for an instant," said Mrs Ryves, as soon as Mrs Bundy had closed the door. He saw that she was different now; something had happened that had made her indulgent.

"Have you been all the way to Dover and back?"

"No, but I've been to Victoria. I've left my luggage there —I've been driving about."

"I hope you've enjoyed it."

"Very much. I've been to see Mr Morrish."

"Mr Morrish?"

"The musical publisher. I showed him our song. I played it for him, and he's delighted with it. He declares it's just the thing. He has given me fifty pounds. I think he believes in us," Mrs Ryves went on, while Baron stared at the wonder—too sweet to be safe, it seemed to him as yet—of her standing there again before him and speaking of what they had in common. "Fifty pounds! fifty pounds!" she exclaimed, fluttering at him her happy cheque. She had come back, the first thing, to tell him, and of course his share of the money would be the half. She was rosy, jubilant, natural, she chattered like a happy woman. She said they must do more, ever so much more. Mr Morrish had practically promised he would take anything that was as good as that. She had kept her cab because she was going to Dover; she couldn't leave the others alone. It was a vehicle infirm and inert, but Baron, after a little, appreciated its pace, for she had consented to his getting in with her and driving, this time in earnest, to Victoria. She had only come to tell him the good news—she repeated this assurance more than once. They talked of it so profoundly that it drove everything else for the time out of his head—his duty to Mr Locket, the remarkable sacrifice he had just achieved, and even the odd coincidence, matching with the oddity of all the others, of her having reverted to the house again, as if with one of her famous divinations, at the very moment the trumpery papers, the origin really of their intimacy, had ceased to exist. But she, on her side, also had evidently forgotten the trumpery papers: she never mentioned them again, and Peter Baron never boasted of what he had done with them. He was silent for a while, from curiosity to see if her fine nerves had really given her a hint; and then later, when it came to be a question of his permanent attitude, he was silent, prodigiously, religiously, tremulously silent, in consequence of an extraordinary conversation that he had with her.

This conversation took place at Dover, when he went down to give her the money for which, at Mr Morrish's bank, he had exchanged the cheque she had left with him. That cheque, or rather certain things it represented, had made somehow all the difference in their relations. The difference was huge, and Baron could think of nothing but this confirmed vision of their being able to work fruitfully together that would account for so rapid a change. She didn't talk of impossibilities now—she didn't seem to want to stop him off; only when, the day following his arrival at Dover with the fifty pounds (he had after all to agree to share them with her —he couldn't expect her to take a present of money from him), he returned to the question over which they had had their little scene the night they dined together—on this occasion (he had brought a portmanteau and he was staying) she mentioned that there was something very particular she had it on her conscience to tell him before letting him commit himself. There dawned in her face as she approached the subject a light of warning that frightened him; it was charged with something so strange that for an instant he held his breath. This flash of ugly possibilities passed however, and it was with the gesture of taking still tenderer possession of her, checked indeed by the grave, important way she held up a finger, that he answered: "Tell me everything—tell me!"

"You must know what I am—who I am; you must know especially what I'm not! There's a name for it, a hideous, cruel name. It's not my fault! Others have known, I've had to speak of it—it has made a great difference in my life. Surely you must have guessed!" she went on, with the thinnest quaver of irony, letting him now take her hand, which felt as cold as her hard duty. "Don't you see I've no belongings, no relations, no friends, nothing at all, in all the world, of my own? I was only a poor girl."

"A poor girl?" Baron was mystified, touched, distressed, piecing dimly together what she meant, but feeling, in a great surge of pity, that it was only something more to love her for.

"My mother—my poor mother," said Mrs Ryves. She paused with this, and through gathering tears her eyes met his as if to plead with him to understand. He understood, and drew her closer, but she kept herself free still, to continue: "She was a poor girl—she was only a governess; she was alone, she thought he loved her. He did—I think it was the only happiness she ever knew. But she died of it."

"Oh, I'm so glad you tell me—it's so grand of you!" Baron murmured. "Then—your father?" He hesitated, as if with his hands on old wounds.

"He had his own troubles, but he was kind to her. It was all misery and folly—he was married. He wasn't happy—there were good reasons, I believe, for that. I know it from letters, I know it from a person who's dead. Everyone is dead now—it's too far off. That's the only good thing. He was very kind to me; I remember him, though I didn't know then, as a little girl, who he was. He put me with some very good people—he did what he could for me. I think, later, his wife knew—a lady who came to see me once after his death. I was a very little girl, but I remember many things. What he could he did —something that helped me afterwards, something that helps me now. I think of him with a strange pity—I *see* him!" said Mrs Ryves, with the faint past in her eyes. "You mustn't say anything against him," she added, gently and gravely.

"Never—never; for he has only made it more of a rapture to care for you."

"You must wait, you must think; we must wait together," she went on. "You can't tell, and you must give me time. Now that you know, it's all right; but you had to know. Doesn't it make us better friends?" asked Mrs Ryves, with a tired smile which had the effect of putting the whole story further and further away. The next moment, however, she added quickly, as if with the sense that it couldn't be far enough: "You don't know, you can't judge, you must let it settle. Think of it, think of it; oh you will, and leave it so. I must have time myself, oh I must! Yes, you must believe me."

She turned away from him, and he remained looking at her a moment. "Ah, how I shall work for you!" he exclaimed.

"You must work for yourself; I'll help you." Her eyes had met his eyes again, and she added, hesitating, thinking: "You had better know, perhaps, who he was."

Baron shook his head, smiling confidently. "I don't care a straw."

"I do—a little. He was a great man."

"There must indeed have been some good in him."

"He was a high celebrity. You've often heard of him."

Baron wondered an instant. "I've no doubt you're a princess!" he said with a laugh. She made him nervous.

"I'm not ashamed of him. He was Sir Dominick Ferrand."

Baron saw in her face, in a few seconds, that she had seen something in his. He knew that he stared, then turned pale; it had the effect of a powerful shock. He was cold for an instant, as he had just found her, with the sense of danger, the confused horror of having dealt a blow. But the blood rushed back to its courses with his still quicker consciousness of safety, and he could make out, as he recovered his balance, that his emotion struck her simply as a violent surprise. He gave a muffled murmur: "Ah, it's you, my beloved!" which lost itself as he drew her close and held her long, in the intensity of his embrace and the wonder of his escape. It took more than a minute for him to say over to himself often enough, with his hidden face: "Ah, she must never, never know!"

She never knew; she only learned, when she asked him casually, that he had in fact destroyed the old documents she had had such a comic caprice about. The sensibility, the curiosity they had had the queer privilege of exciting in her had lapsed with the event as irresponsibly as they had arisen, and she appeared to have forgotten, or rather to attribute now to other causes, the agitation and several of the odd incidents that accompanied them. They naturally gave Peter Baron rather more to think about, much food, indeed, for clandestine meditation, some of which, in spite of the pains he took not to be caught, was noted by his friend and interpreted, to his knowledge, as depression produced by the long probation she succeeded in imposing on him. He was more patient than she could guess, with all her guessing, for if he was put to the proof she herself was not left undissected. It came back to him again and again that if the documents he had burned proved anything they proved that Sir Dominick Ferrand's human errors were not all of one order. The woman he loved was the daughter of her father, he couldn't get over that. What was more to the point was that as he came to know her better and better—for they did work together under Mr Morrish's pro-tection—his affection was a quantity still less to be neglected. He sometimes wondered, in the light of her general straight-ness (their marriage had brought out even more than he believed there was of it) whether the relics in the davenport were genuine. That piece of furniture is still almost as useful to him as Mr Morrish's patronage. There is a tremendous run, as this gentleman calls it, on several of their songs. Baron nevertheless still tries his hand also at prose, and his offerings are now not always declined by the magazines. But he has never approached the Promiscuous again. This periodical published in due course a highly eulogistic study of the remarkable career of Sir Dominick Ferrand.

COLLABORATION

I DON'T know how much people care for my work, but they like my studio (of which indeed I am exceedingly fond myself), as they show by their inclination to congregate there at dusky hours on winter afternoons, or on long dim evenings when the place looks well with its rich combinations and low-burning lamps and the bad pictures (my own) are not particularly visible. I won't go into the question of how many of these are purchased, but I rejoice in the distinction that my invitations are never declined. Some of my visitors have been good enough to say that on Sunday evenings in particular there is no pleasanter place in Paris—where so many places are pleasant—none friendlier to easy talk and repeated cigarettes, to the exchange of points of view and the comparison of accents. The air is as international as only Parisian air can be; women, I surmise, think they look well in it; they come also because they fancy they are doing something Bohemian, just as many of the men come because they suppose they are doing something correct. The old heraldic cushions on the divans, embossed with rusty gold, are favourable both to expansion and to contraction—that of course of contracting parties—and the Italian brocade on the walls appeals to one's highest feelings. Music makes its home there—though I confess I am not quite the master of *that* house, and when it is going on in a truly receptive hush I enjoy the way my company leans back and gazes through the thin smoke of cigarettes up at the distant Tiepolo in the almost palatial ceiling. I make sure the piano, the tobacco and the tea are all of the best.

For the conversation, I leave that mostly to take care of

itself. There are discussions of course and differences—sometimes even a violent circulation of sense and sound; but I have a consciousness that beauty flourishes and that harmonies prevail in the end. I have occasionally known a visitor to be rude to me because he disliked another visitor's opinions—I had seen an old habitué slip away without bidding me good night on the arrival of some confident specimen of *les jeunes;* but as a general thing we have it out together on the spot—the place is really a chamber of justice, a temple of reconciliation: we understand each other if we only sit up late enough. Art protects her children in the long run—she only asks them to trust her. She is like the Catholic Church—she guarantees paradise to the faithful. Music moreover is a universal solvent; though I've not an infallible ear I've a sufficient sense of the matter for that. Ah, the wounds I've known it to heal—the bridges I've known it to build—the ghosts I've known it to lay! Though I've seen people stalk out I've never observed them not to steal back. My studio in short is the theatre of a cosmopolite drama, a comedy essentially "of character."

One of the liveliest scenes of the performance was the evening, last winter, on which I became aware that one of my compatriots—an American, my good friend Alfred Bonus—was engaged in a controversy somewhat acrimonious, on a literary subject, with Herman Heidenmauer, the young composer who had been playing to us divinely a short time before and whom I thought of neither as a disputant nor as an Englishman. I perceived in a moment that something had happened to present him in this combined character to poor Bonus, who was so ardent a patriot that he lived in Paris rather than in London, who had met his interlocutor for the first time on this occasion, and who apparently had been misled by the perfection with which Heidenmauer spoke English—he spoke it really better than Alfred Bonus. The young musician, a born Bavarian, had spent a few years in England, where he had a commercial step-brother planted and more or less prosperous

—a helpful man who had watched over his difficult first steps, given him a temporary home, found him publishers and pupils, smoothed the way to a stupefied hearing for his first productions. He knew his London and might at a first glance have been taken for one of its products; but he had, in addition to a genius of the sort that London fosters but doesn't beget, a very German soul. He brought me a note from an old friend on the other side of the Channel, and I liked him as soon as I looked at him; so much indeed that I could forgive him for making me feel thin and empirical, conscious that *he* was one of the higher kind whom the future has looked in the face. He had met through his gold spectacles her deep eyes, and some mutual communication had occurred. This had given him a confidence which passed for conceit only with those who didn't know the reason.

I guessed the reason early, and, as may be imagined, he didn't grudge me the knowledge. He was happy and various— as little as possible the mere long-haired musicmonger. His hair was short—it was only his legs and his laughter that were long. He was fair and rosy, and his gold spectacles glittered as if in response to the example set them by his beautiful young golden beard. You would have been sure he was an artist without going so far as to decide upon his particular passion; for you would have been conscious that whatever this passion might be it was acquainted with many of the others and mixed with them to its profit. Yet these discoveries had not been fully made by Alfred Bonus, whose occupation was to write letters to the American journals about the way the "boys" were coming on in Paris; for in such a case he probably would not have expected such nebulous greatness to condense at a moment's notice. Bonus is clever and critical, and a sort of self-appointed emissary or agent of the great republic. He has it at heart to prove that the Americans in Europe *do* get on— taking for granted on the part of the Americans at home an interest in this subject greater, as I often assure him, than any really felt. "Come, now, do *I* get on?" I often ask him; and I sometimes push the inquiry so far as to stammer: "And you, my dear Bonus, do *you* get on?" He is apt to look a little injured on such occasions, as if he would like to say in reply: "Don't you call it success to have Sunday evenings at which I'm a regular attendant? And can you question for a moment the figure I make at them?" It has even occurred to me that he suspects me of painting badly on purpose to spite him—that is to interfere with his favourite dogma. Therefore to spite me in return he's in the heroic predicament of refusing to admit that I'm a failure. He takes a great interest in the plastic arts, but his intensest sympathy is for literature. This sentiment is somewhat starved, as in that school the boys languish as yet on a back seat. To show what they are doing Bonus has to retreat upon the studios, but there is nothing he enjoys so much as having, when the rare chance offers, a good literary talk. He follows the French movement closely and explains it profusely to our compatriots, whom he mystifies, but who guess he's rather loose.

I forget how his conversation with Heidenmauer began—it was, I think, some difference of opinion about one of the English poets that set them afloat. Heidenmauer knows the English poets, and the French, and the Italian, and the Spanish, and the Russian—he is a wonderful representative of that Germanism which consists in the negation of intellectual frontiers. It is the English poets that, if I'm not mistaken, he loves best, and probably the harm was done by his having happened to say so. At any rate Alfred Bonus let him have it, without due notice perhaps, which is rather Alfred's way, on the question (a favourite one with my compatriot) of the backward state of literature in England, for which after all Heidenmauer was not responsible. Bonus believes in responsibility—the responsibility of others, an attitude which tends to make some of his friends extremely secretive, though perhaps it would have been justified—as to this I'm not sure—

had Heidenmauer been, under the circumstances, technically British. Before he had had time to explain that he was not, the other persons present had become aware that a kind of challenge had passed—that nation, in a sudden startled flurry, somehow found itself pitted against nation. There was much vagueness at first as to which of the nations were engaged and as to what their quarrel was about, the question coming presently to appear less simple than the spectacle (so easily conceivable) of a German's finding it hot for him in a French house, a house French enough at any rate to give countenance to the idea of his quick defeat.

How could the right cause fail of protection in any house of which Madame de Brindes and her charming daughter were so good as to be assiduous frequenters? I recollect perfectly the pale gleam of joy in the mother's handsome face when she gathered that what had happened was that a detested German was on his defence. She wears her eternal mourning (I admit it's immensely becoming) for a triple woe, for multiplied griefs and wrongs, all springing from the crash of the Empire, from the battlefields of 1870. Her husband fell at Sedan, her father and her brother on still darker days; both her own family and that of M. de Brindes, their general situation in life, were, as may be said, creations of the Empire, so that from one hour to the other she found herself sinking with the wreck. You won't recognise her under the name I give her, but you may none the less have admired, between their pretty lemon-coloured covers, the touching tales of Claude Lorrain. She plies an ingenious, pathetic pen and has reconciled herself to effort and privation for the sake of her daughter. I say privation, because these distinguished women are poor, receive with great modesty and have broken with a hundred of those social sanctities that are dearer to French souls than to any others. They have gone down into the market-place, and Paule de Brindes, who is three-and-twenty to-day and has a happy turn for keeping a water-colour liquid, earns a hundred francs here and there. She is not so handsome as her mother, but she has magnificent hair and what the French call a look of race, and is, or at least was till the other day, a frank and charming young woman. There is something exquisite in the way these ladies are earnestly, conscientiously modern. From the moment they accept necessities they accept them all, and poor Madame de Brindes flatters herself that she has made her dowerless daughter one of us others. The girl goes out alone, talks with young men and, although she only paints landscape, takes a free view of the *convenances*. Nothing can please either of them more than to tell them they have thrown over their superstitions. They haven't, thank heaven; and when I want to be reminded of some of the prettiest in the world—of a thousand fine scruples and pleasant forms, and of what grace can do for the sake of grace—I know where to go for it.

It was a part of this pious heresy—much more august in the way they presented it than some of the aspects of the old faith—that Paule should have become "engaged," quite like a *jeune mees*, to my brilliant friend Félix Vendemer. He is such a votary of the modern that he was inevitably interested in the girl of the future and had matched one reform with another, being ready to marry without a penny, as the clearest way of expressing his appreciation, this favourable specimen of the type. He simply fell in love with Mademoiselle de Brindes and behaved, on his side, equally like one of us others, except that he begged me to ask her mother for her hand. I was inspired to do so with eloquence, and my friends were not insensible of such an opportunity to show that they now lived in the world of realities. Vendemer's sole fortune is his genius, and he and Paule, who confessed to an answering flame, plighted their troth like a pair of young rustics or (what comes for French people to the same thing) young Anglo-Saxons. Madame de Brindes thinks such doings at bottom very vulgar; but vulgar is what she tries hard to be, she is so convinced it is the only way to make a living. Vendemer had had at that time only the first of his successes, which was not, as you will remember—and unfortunately for Madame de Brindes—of this remunerative kind. Only a few people recognised the perfection of his little volume of verse: my acquaintance with him originated in my having been one of the few. A volume of verse was a scanty provision to marry on, so that, still like a pair of us others, the luckless lovers had to bide their time. Presently however came the success (again a success only with those who care for quality, not with the rough and ready public) of his comedy in verse at the Français. This charming work had just been taken off (it had been found not to make money), when the various parties to my little drama met Heidenmauer at my studio.

Vendemer, who has, as indeed the others have, a passion for music, was tremendously affected by hearing him play two or three of his compositions, and I immediately saw that the immitigable German quality was a morsel much less bitter for him than for the two uncompromising ladies. He went so far as to speak to Heidenmauer frankly, to thank him with effusion, an effort of which neither of the quivering women would have been capable. Vendemer was in the room the night Alfred Bonus raised his little breeze; I saw him lean on the piano and listen with a queer face looking however rather wonderingly at Heidenmauer. Before this I had noticed the instant paleness (her face was admirably expressive) with which Madame de Brindes saw her prospective son-in-law make up, as it were, to the original Teuton, whose national character was intensified to her aching mind, as it would have been to that of most Frenchwomen in her place, by his wash of English colour. A German was bad enough—but a German with English aggravations! Her senses were too fine to give her the excuse of not feeling that his compositions were interesting, and she was capable, magnanimously, of listening to them with dropped eyes; but (much as it ever cost her not to be perfectly courteous), she couldn't have made even the most superficial speech to him about them. Marie de Brindes could never have spoken to Herman Heidenmauer. It was a narrowness if you will, but a narrowness that to my vision was enveloped in a dense atmosphere—a kind of sunset bloom—of enriching and fortifying things. Herman Heidenmauer himself, like the man of imagination and the lover of life that he was, would have entered into it delightedly, been charmed with it as a fine case of bigotry. This was conspicuous in Marie de Brindes: her loyalty to the national idea was that of a *dévote* to a form of worship. She never spoke of France, but she always made me think of it, and with an authority which the women of her race seem to me to have in the question much more than the men. I dare say I'm rather in love with her, though, being considerably younger, I've never told her so—as if she would in the least mind that! I have indeed been a little checked by a spirit of allegiance to Vendemer; suspecting always (excuse my sophistication) that in the last analysis it is the mother's charm that he feels—or originally felt—in the daughter's. He spoke of the elder lady to me in those days with the insistence with which only a Frenchman can speak of the objects of his affection. At any rate there was always something symbolic and slightly ceremonial to me in her delicate cameo-face and her general black-robed presence; she made me think of a priestess or a mourner, of revolutions and sieges, detested treaties and ugly public things. I pitied her, too, for the strife of the elements in her—for the way she must have felt a noble enjoyment mutilated. She was too good for that, and yet she was too rigid for anything else; and the sight of such dismal perversions made me hate more than ever the stupid terms on which nations have organised their intercourse.

When she gathered that one of my guests was simply cramming it down the throat of another that the English literary mind was not even literary, she turned away with a vague shrug and a pitiful look at her daughter for the taste of people who took their pleasure so poorly: the truth in question would be so obvious that it was not worth making a scene about. Madame de Brindes evidently looked at any scene between the English and the Americans as a quarrel proceeding vaguely from below stairs—a squabble sordidly domestic. Her almost immediate departure with her daughter operated as a lucky interruption, and I caught for the first time in the straight, spare girl, as she followed her mother, a little of the air that Vendemer had told me he found in her, the still exaltation, the brown uplifted head that we attribute, or that at any rate he made it visible to me that he attributed, to the dedicated Maid. He considered that his intended bore a striking resemblance to Jeanne d'Arc, and he marched after her on this occasion like a square-shouldered armour-bearer. He reappeared, however, after he had put the ladies into a cab, and half an hour later the rest of my friends, with the sole exception of Bonus, having dispersed, he was sitting up with me in the empty studio for another *bout de causerie*. At first perhaps I was too occupied with reprimanding my compatriot to give much attention to what Vendemer might have to say; I remember at any rate that I had asked Bonus what had induced him to make so grave a blunder. He was not even yet, it appeared, aware of his blunder, so that I had to inquire by what odd chance he had taken Heidenmauer for a bigoted Briton.

"If I spoke to him as one he answered as one; that's bigoted enough," said Alfred Bonus.

"He was confused and amused at your onslaught: he wondered what fly had stung you."

"The fly of patriotism," Vendemer suggested.

"Do *you* like him—a beast of a German?" Bonus demanded.

"If he's an Englishman he isn't a German—*il faut opter*. We can hang him for the one or for the other, we can't hang him for both. I was immensely struck with those things he played."

"They had no charm for me, or doubtless I too should have been demoralised," Alfred said. "He seemed to know nothing about Miss Brownrigg. Now Miss Brownrigg's great."

"I like the things and even the people you quarrel about, you big babies of the same breast. *C'est à se tordre!*" Vendemer declared.

"I may be very abject, but I *do* take an interest in the American novel," Alfred rejoined.

"I hate such expressions: there's no such thing as the American novel."

"Is there by chance any such thing as the French?"

"*Pas davantage*—for the artist himself: how can you ask? I don't know what is meant by French art and English art and American art: those seem to me mere cataloguers' and reviewers' and tradesmen's names, representing preoccupations utterly foreign to the artist. Art is art in every country, and the novel (since Bonus mentions that) is the novel in every tongue, and hard enough work they have to live up to that privilege, without our adding another muddle to the problem. The reader, the consumer may call things as he likes, but we leave him to his little amusements." I suggested that we were all readers and consumers; which only made Vendemer continue: "Yes, and only a small handful of us have the ghost of a palate. But you and I and Bonus are of the handful."

"What do you mean by the handful?" Bonus inquired.

Vendemer hesitated a moment. "I mean the few intelligent people, and even the few people who are not——" He paused again an instant, long enough for me to request him not to say what they were "not," and then went on: "People in a word who have the honour to live in the only country worth living in."

"And pray what country is that?"

"The land of dreams—the country of art."

"Oh, the land of dreams! I live in the land of realities!"
Bonus exclaimed. "What do you all mean then by chattering
so about *le roman russe?*"

"It's a convenience—to identify the work of three or four,
là-bas, because we're so far from it. But do you see them
writing 'le roman russe?'"

"I happen to know that that's exactly what they want to
do, some of them," said Bonus.

"Some of the idiots, then! There are plenty of those everywhere. Anything born under that silly star is sure not to
count."

"Thank God I'm not an artist!" said Bonus.

"Dear Alfred's a critic," I explained.

"And I'm not ashamed of my country," he subjoined.

"Even a critic perhaps may be an artist," Vendemer mused.

"Then as the great American critic Bonus may be the great
American artist," I went on.

"Is that what you're supposed to give us—'American'
criticism?" Vendemer asked, with dismay in his expressive,
ironic face. "Take care, take care, or it will be more American
than critical, and then where will *you* be? However," he continued, laughing and with a change of tone, "I may see the
matter in too lurid a light, for I've just been favoured with a
judgment conceived in the purest spirit of our own national
genius." He looked at me a moment and then he remarked:
"That dear Madame de Brindes doesn't approve of my
attitude."

"Your attitude?"

"Toward your German friend. She let me know it when I
went down stairs with her—told me I was much too cordial,
that I must observe myself."

"And what did you reply to that?"

"I answered that the things he had played were extraordinarily beautiful."

"And how did she meet that?"

"By saying that he's an enemy of our country."

"She had you there," I rejoined.

"Yes, I could only reply '*Chère madame, voyons!*'"

"That was meagre."

"Evidently, for it did no more for me than to give her a chance to declare that he can't possibly be here for any good and that he belongs to a race it's my sacred duty to loathe."

"I see what she means."

"I don't then—where artists are concerned. I said to her: '*Ah, madame, vous savez que pour moi il n'y a que l'art!*'"

"It's very exciting!" I laughed. "How could she parry that?"

"'I know it, my dear child—but for *him?*' That's the way she parried it. 'Very well, for him?' I asked. 'For him there's the insolence of the victor and a secret scorn for our incurable illusions!'"

"Heidenmauer has no insolence and no secret scorn."

Vendemer was silent a moment. "Are you very sure of that?"

"Oh, I like him! He's out of all that, and far above it. But what did Mademoiselle Paule say?" I inquired.

"She said nothing—she only looked at me."

"Happy man!"

"Not a bit. She looked at me with strange eyes, in which I could read 'Go straight, my friend—go straight!' Oh, *les femmes, les femmes!*"

"What's the matter with them now?"

"They've a mortal hatred of art!"

"It's a true, deep instinct," said Alfred Bonus.

"But what passed further with Madame de Brindes?" I went on.

"She only got into her cab, pushing her daughter first; on which I slammed the door rather hard and came up here. *Cela m'a porté sur les nerfs.*"

"I'm afraid I haven't soothed them," Bonus said, looking for his hat. When he had found it he added: "When the English have beaten us and pocketed our *milliards* I'll forgive them; but not till then!" And with this he went off, made a little uncomfortable, I think, by Vendemer's sharper alternatives, while the young Frenchman called after him: "My dear fellow, at night all cats are grey!"

Vendemer, when we were left alone together, mooned about the empty studio awhile and asked me three or four questions about Heidenmauer. I satisfied his curiosity as well as I could, but I demanded the reason of it. The reason he gave was that one of the young German's compositions had already begun to haunt his memory; but that was a reason which, to my sense, still left something unexplained. I didn't however challenge him, before he quitted me, further than to warn him against being deliberately perverse.

"What do you mean by being deliberately perverse?" He fixed me so with his intensely living French eye that I became almost blushingly conscious of a certain insincerity and, instead of telling him what I meant, tried to get off with the deplorable remark that the prejudices of Mesdames de Brindes were after all respectable. "That's exactly what makes them so odious!" cried Vendemer.

A few days after this, late in the afternoon, Herman Heidenmauer came in to see me and found the young Frenchman seated at my piano—trying to win back from the keys some echo of a passage in the *Abendlied* we had listened to on the Sunday evening. They met, naturally, as good friends, and Heidenmauer sat down with instant readiness and gave him again the page he was trying to recover. He asked him for his address, that he might send him the composition, and at Vendemer's request, as we sat in the firelight, played half-a-dozen other things. Vendemer listened in silence but to my surprise took leave of me before the lamp was brought in. I asked him to stay to dinner (I had already appealed to

Heidenmauer to stay), but he explained that he was engaged
to dine with Madame de Brindes—*à la maison* as he always
called it. When he had gone Heidenmauer, with whom on
departing he had shaken hands without a word, put to me the
same questions about him that Vendemer had asked on the
Sunday evening about the young German, and I replied that
my visitor would find in a small volume of remarkable verse
published by Lemerre, which I placed in his hands, much of the
information he desired. This volume, which had just appeared,
contained, beside a reprint of Vendemer's earlier productions,
many of them admirable lyrics, the drama that had lately been
played at the Français, and Heidenmauer took it with him
when he left me. But he left me late, and before this occurred,
all the evening, we had much talk about the French nation. In
the foreign colony of Paris the exchange of opinions on this
subject is one of the most inevitable and by no means the
least interesting of distractions; it furnishes occupation to
people rather conscious of the burden of leisure. Heidenmauer
had been little in Paris, but he was all the more open to impressions; they evidently poured in upon him and he gave
them a generous hospitality. In the diffused white light of his
fine German intelligence old colours took on new tints to me,
and while we spun fancies about the wonderful race around us
I added to my little stock of notions about his own. I saw that
his admiration for our neighbours was a very high tide, and I
was struck with something bland and unconscious (noble and
serene in its absence of precautions) in the way he let his doors
stand open to it. It would have been exasperating to many
Frenchmen; he looked at them through his clear spectacles
with such an absence of suspicion that they might have anything to forgive him, such a thin metaphysical view of
instincts and passions. He had the air of not allowing for
recollections and nerves, and would doubtless give them
occasion to make afresh some of their reflections on the tact
of *ces gens-là*.

COLLABORATION

A couple of days after I had given him Vendemer's book he came back to tell me that he found great beauty in it. "It speaks to me—it speaks to me," he said with his air of happy proof. "I liked the songs—I liked the songs. Besides," he added, "I like the little romantic play—it has given me wonderful ideas; more ideas than anything has done for a long time. Yes—yes."

"What kind of ideas?"

"Well, this kind." And he sat down to the piano and struck the keys. I listened without more questions, and after a while I began to understand. Suddenly he said: "Do you know the words of *that?*" and before I could answer he was rolling out one of the lyrics of the little volume. The poem was strange and obscure, yet irresistibly beautiful, and he had translated it into music still more tantalizing than itself. He sounded the words with his German accent, barely perceptible in English but strongly marked in French. He dropped them and took them up again; he was playing with them, feeling his way. "*This* is my idea!" he broke out; he had caught it, in one of its mystic mazes, and he rendered it with a kind of solemn freshness. There was a phrase he repeated, trying it again and again, and while he did so he chanted the words of the song as if they were an illuminating flame, an inspiration. I was rather glad on the whole that Vendemer didn't hear what his pronunciation made of them, but as I was in the very act of rejoicing I became aware that the author of the verses had opened the door. He had pushed it gently, hearing the music; then hearing also his own poetry he had paused and stood looking at Heidenmauer. The young German nodded and laughed and, irreflectively, spontaneously, greeted him with a friendly "*Was sagen Sie dazu?*" I saw Vendemer change colour; he blushed red and, for an instant, as he stood wavering, I thought he was going to retreat. But I beckoned him in and, on the divan beside me, patted a place for him to sit.

He came in but didn't take this place; he went and stood before the fire to warm his feet, turning his back to us. Heidenmauer played and played, and after a little Vendemer turned round; he looked about him for a seat, dropped into it and sat with his elbows on his knees and his head in his hands. Presently Heidenmauer called out, in French, above the music: "I like your songs—I like them immensely!" but the young Frenchman neither spoke nor moved. When however five minutes later Heidenmauer stopped he sprang up with an entreaty to him to go on, to go on for the love of God. "*Foilà—foilà!*" cried the musician, and with hands for an instant suspended he wandered off into mysterious worlds. He played Wagner and then Wagner again—a great deal of Wagner; in the midst of which, abruptly, he addressed himself again to Vendemer, who had gone still further from the piano, launching to me, however from his corner a "*Dieu, que c'est beau!*" which I saw that Heidenmauer caught. "I've a conception for an opera, you know—I'd give anything if you'd do the libretto!" Our German friend laughed out, after this, with clear good nature, and the rich appeal brought Vendemer slowly to his feet again, staring at the musician across the room and turning this time perceptibly pale.

I felt there was a drama in the air, and it made me a little nervous; to conceal which I said to Heidenmauer: "What's your conception? What's your subject?"

"My conception would be realized in the subject of M. Vendemer's play—if he'll do that for me in a great lyric manner!" And with this the young German, who had stopped playing to answer me, quitted the piano and Vendemer got up to meet him. "The subject is splendid—it has taken possession of me. Will you do it with me? Will you work with me? We shall make something great!"

"Ah, you don't know what you ask!" Vendemer answered, with his pale smile.

"I do—I do: I've thought of it. It will be bad for me in my

country; I shall suffer for it. They won't like it—they'll abuse me for it—they'll say of me *pis que pendre.*" Heidenmauer pronounced it *bis que bendre.*

"They'll hate my libretto so?" Vendemer asked.

"Yes, your libretto—they'll say it's immoral and horrible. And they'll say *I'm* immoral and horrible for having worked with you," the young composer went on, with his pleasant healthy lucidity. "You'll injure my career. Oh yes, I shall suffer!" he joyously, exultingly cried.

"*Et moi donc!*" Vendemer exclaimed.

"Public opinion, yes. I shall also make *you* suffer—I shall nip your prosperity in the bud. All that's *des bêtises—tes pêtisses,*" said poor Heidenmauer. "In art there are no countries."

"Yes, art is terrible, art is monstrous," Vendemer replied, looking at the fire.

"I love your songs—they have extraordinary beauty."

"And Vendemer has an equal taste for *your* compositions," I said to Heidenmauer.

"Tempter!" Vendemer murmured to me, with a strange look.

"*C'est juste!* I mustn't meddle—which will be all the easier as I'm dining out and must go and dress. You two make yourselves at home and fight it out here."

"Do you *leave* me?" asked Vendemer, still with his strange look.

"My dear fellow, I've only just time."

"We will dine together—he and I—at one of those characteristic places, and we will look at the matter in its different relations," said Heidenmauer. "Then we will come back here to finish—your studio is so good for music."

"There are some things it *isn't* good for," Vendemer remarked, looking at our companion.

"It's good for poetry—it's good for truth," smiled the composer.

"You'll stay *here* and dine together," I said; "my servant can manage that."

"No, no—we'll go out and we'll walk together. We'll talk a great deal," Heidenmauer went on. "The subject is so comprehensive," he said to Vendemer, as he lighted another cigar.

"The subject?"

"Of your drama. It's so universal."

"Ah, the universe—*il n'y a que ça!*" I laughed, to Vendemer, partly with a really amused sense of the exaggerated woe that looked out of his poetic eyes and that seemed an appeal to me not to forsake him, to throw myself into the scale of the associations he would have to stifle, and partly to encourage him, to express my conviction that two such fine minds couldn't in the long run be the worse for coming to an agreement. I might have been a more mocking Mephistopheles handing over his pure spirit to my literally German Faust.

When I came home at eleven o'clock I found him alone in my studio, where, evidently, for some time, he had been moving up and down in agitated thought. The air was thick with Bavarian fumes, with the reverberation of mighty music and great ideas, with the echoes of that "universe" to which I had so mercilessly consigned him. But I judged in a moment that Vendemer was in a very different phase of his evolution from the one in which I had left him. I had never seen his handsome, sensitive face so intensely illumined.

"*Ça y est—ça y est!*" he exclaimed, standing there with his hands in his pockets and looking at me.

"You've really agreed to do something together?"

"We've sworn a tremendous oath—we've taken a sacred engagement."

"My dear fellow, you're a hero."

"Wait and see! *C'est un très-grand esprit.*"

"So much the better!"

"*C'est un bien beau génie.* Ah, we've risen—we soar; *nous sommes dans les grandes espaces!*" my friend continued with his dilated eyes.

"It's very interesting—because it will cost you something."

"It will cost me everything!" said Félix Vendemer in a tone I seem to hear at this hour. "That's just the beauty of it. It's the chance of chances to testify for art—to affirm an indispensable truth."

"An indispensable truth?" I repeated, feeling myself soar too, but into the splendid vague.

"Do you know the greatest crime that can be perpetrated against it?"

"Against it?" I asked, still soaring.

"Against the religion of art—against the love for beauty—against the search for the Holy Grail?" The transfigured look with which he named these things, the way his warm voice filled the rich room, was a revelation of the wonderful talk that had taken place.

"Do you know—for one of *us*—the really damnable, the only unpardonable, sin?"

"Tell me, so that I may keep clear of it!"

"To profane *our* golden air with the hideous invention of patriotism."

"It was a clever invention in its time!" I laughed.

"I'm not talking about its time—I'm talking about its place. It was never anything but a fifth-rate impertinence here. In art there are no countries—no idiotic nationalities, no frontiers, nor *douanes*, nor still more idiotic fortresses and bayonets. It has the unspeakable beauty of being the region in which those abominations cease, the medium in which such vulgarities simply can't live. What therefore are we to say of the brutes who wish to drag them all in—to crush to death with them all the flowers of such a garden, to shut out all the light of such a sky?" I was far from desiring to defend the "brutes" in question, though there rose before me even at that moment a sufficiently vivid picture of the way, later on, poor Vendemer would have to face them. I quickly perceived indeed that the picture was, to his own eyes, a still more crowded canvas. Félix Vendemer, in the centre of it, was an admirable, a really sublime figure. If there had been wonderful talk after I quitted the two poets the wonder was not over yet—it went on far into the night for my benefit. We looked at the prospect in many lights, turned the subject about almost every way it would go; but I am bound to say there was one relation in which we tacitly agreed to forbear to consider it. We neither of us uttered the name of Paule de Brindes—the outlook in that direction would be too serious. And yet if Félix Vendemer, exquisite and incorruptible artist that he was, had fallen in love with the idea of "testifying," it was from that direction that the finest part of his opportunity to do so would proceed.

I was only too conscious of this when, within the week, I received a hurried note from Madame de Brindes, begging me as a particular favour to come and see her without delay. I had not seen Vendemer again, but I had had a characteristic call from Heidenmauer, who, though I could imagine him perfectly in a Prussian helmet, with a needle-gun, perfectly, on definite occasion, a sturdy, formidable soldier, gave me a renewed impression of inhabiting, in the expansion of his genius and the exercise of his intelligence, no land of red tape, no province smaller nor more pedantically administered than the totality of things. I was reminded afresh too that *he* foresaw no striking salon-picture, no *chic* of execution nor romance of martyrdom, or at any rate devoted very little time to the consideration of such objects. He doubtless did scant justice to poor Vendemer's attitude, though he said to me of him by the way, with his rosy deliberation: "He has good ideas—he has good ideas. The French mind has—for me—the taste of a very delightful *bonbon!*" He only measured the angle of convergence, as he called it, of their two projections. He was in short not preoccupied with the personal gallantry of their experiment; he was preoccupied with its "æsthetic and harmonic basis."

It was without her daughter that Madame de Brindes received me, when I obeyed her summons, in her scrap of a *quatrième* in the Rue de Miromesnil.

"Ah, *cher monsieur,* how could you have permitted such a horror—how could you have given it the countenance of your roof, of your influence?" There were tears in her eyes, and I don't think that for the moment I have ever been more touched by a reproach. But I pulled myself together sufficiently to affirm my faith as well as to disengage my responsibility. I explained that there was no horror to me in the matter, that if I was not a German neither was I a Frenchman, and that all I had before me was two young men inflamed by a great idea and nobly determined to work together to give it a great form.

"A great idea—to go over to *ces gens-là?*"

"To go over to them?"

"To put yourself on their side—to throw yourself into the arms of those who hate us—to fall into their abominable trap!"

"What do you call their abominable trap?"

"Their false *bonhomie,* the very impudence of their intrigues, their profound, scientific deceit and their determination to get the advantage of us by exploiting our generosity."

"You attribute to such a man as Heidenmauer too many motives and too many calculations. He's quite ideally superior!"

"Oh, German idealism—we know what that means! We've no use for their superiority; let them carry it elsewhere—let them leave us alone. Why do they thrust themselves in upon us and set old wounds throbbing by their detested presence? We don't go near *them*, or ever wish to hear their ugly names or behold their *visages de bois;* therefore the most rudimentary good taste, the tact one would expect even from naked

savages, might suggest to them to seek their amusements elsewhere. But *their* taste, *their* tact—I can scarcely trust myself
to speak!"

Madame de Brindes did speak however at considerable
further length and with a sincerity of passion which left one
quite without arguments. There was no argument to meet the
fact that Vendemer's attitude wounded her, wounded her
daughter, *jusqu'au fond de l'âme,* that it represented for them
abysses of shame and suffering and that for himself it meant a
whole future compromised, a whole public alienated. It was
vain doubtless to talk of such things; if people didn't *feel* them,
if they hadn't the fibre of loyalty, the high imagination of
honour, all explanations, all supplications were but a waste of
noble emotion. M. Vendemer's perversity was monstrous—
she had had a sickening discussion with him. What she
desired of me was to make one last appeal to him, to put the
solemn truth before him, to try to bring him back to sanity.
It was as if he had temporarily lost his reason. It was to be
made clear to him, *par exemple,* that unless he should recover
it Mademoiselle de Brindes would unhesitatingly withdraw
from her engagement.

"Does she *really* feel as you do?" I asked.

"Do you think I put words into her mouth? She feels as a
fille de France is obliged to feel!"

"Doesn't she love him then?"

"She adores him. But she won't take him without his
honour."

"I don't understand such refinements!" I said.

"Oh, *vous autres!*" cried Madame de Brindes. Then with
eyes glowing through her tears she demanded: "Don't you
know she knows how her father died?" I was on the point of
saying "What has that to do with it?" but I withheld the
question, for after all I could conceive that it might have something. There was no disputing about tastes, and I could only
express my sincere conviction that Vendemer was pro-

COLLABORATION

it by making her a sacrifice!" my strenuous hostess replied; to
which I rejoined that I would repeat our conversation to him
and put the matter before him as strongly as I could. I delayed a little to take leave, wondering if the girl would not
come in—I should have been so much more content to receive
her strange recantation from her own lips. I couldn't say this
to Madame de Brindes; but she guessed I meant it, and before
we separated we exchanged a look in which our mutual mis-
trust was written—the suspicion on her side that I should not
be a very passionate intercessor and the conjecture on mine
that she might be misrepresenting her daughter. This slight
tension, I must add, was only momentary, for I have had a
chance of observing Paule de Brindes since then, and the two
ladies were soon satisfied that I pitied them enough to have
been eloquent.

My eloquence has been of no avail, and I have learned (it
has been one of the most interesting lessons of my life) of
what transcendent stuff the artist may sometimes be made.
Herman Heidenmauer and Félix Vendemer are, at the hour I
write, immersed in their monstrous collaboration. There were
postponements and difficulties at first, and there will be more
serious ones in the future, when it is a question of giving the
finished work to the world. The world of Paris will stop its
ears in horror, the German Empire will turn its mighty back,
and the authors of what I foresee (oh, I've been treated to
specimens!) as a perhaps really epoch-making musical revelation (is Heidenmauer's style rubbing off on me?) will perhaps
have to beg for a hearing in communities fatally unintelligent.
It may very well be that they will not obtain any hearing at all
for years. I like at any rate to think that time works for them.
At present they work for themselves and for each other, amid
drawbacks of several kinds. Separating after the episode in
Paris, they have met again on alien soil, at a little place on the
Genoese Riviera where sunshine is cheap and tobacco bad,

and they live (the two together) for five francs a day, which is all they can muster between them. It appears that when Heidenmauer's London step-brother was informed of the young composer's unnatural alliance he instantly withdrew his subsidy. The return of it is contingent on the rupture of the unholy union and the destruction by flame of all the manuscript. The pair are very poor and the whole thing depends on their staying power. They are so preoccupied with their opera that they have no time for potboilers. Vendemer is in a feverish hurry, lest perhaps he should find himself chilled. There are still other details which contribute to the interest of the episode and which, for me, help to render it a most refreshing, a really great little case. It rests me, it delights me, there is something in it that makes for civilization. In their way they are working for human happiness. The strange course taken by Vendemer (I mean his renunciation of his engagement) must moreover be judged in the light of the fact that he was really in love. Something had to be sacrificed, and what he clung to most (he's extraordinary, I admit) was the truth he had the opportunity of proclaiming. Men give up their love for advantages every day, but they rarely give it up for such discomforts.

Paule de Brindes was the less in love of the two; I see her often enough to have made up my mind about that. But she's mysterious, she's odd; there was at any rate a sufficient wrench in her life to make her often absent-minded. Does her imagination hover about Félix Vendemer? A month ago, going into their rooms one day when her mother was not at home (the *bonne* had admitted me under a wrong impression) I found her at the piano, playing one of Heidenmauer's compositions—playing it without notes and with infinite expression. How had she got hold of it? How had she learned it? This was her secret—she blushed so that I didn't pry into it. But what is she doing, under the singular circumstances, with a composition of Herman Heidenmauer's? She never met him, she never heard him play but that once. It will be a pretty complication if it shall appear that the young German genius made on that occasion more than one intense impression. This needn't appear, however, inasmuch as, being naturally in terror of the discovery by her mother of such an anomaly, she may count on me absolutely not to betray her. I hadn't fully perceived how deeply susceptible she is to music. She must have a strange confusion of feelings—a dim, haunting trouble, with a kind of ache of impatience for the wonderful opera somewhere in the depths of it. Don't we live fast after all, and doesn't the old order change? Don't say art isn't mighty! I shall give you some more illustrations of it yet.

GREVILLE FANE

COMING in to dress for dinner, I found a telegram: "Mrs Stormer dying; can you give us half a column for to-morrow evening? Let her off easy, but not too easy." I was late; I was in a hurry; I had very little time to think, but at a venture I dispatched a reply: "Will do what I can." It was not till I had dressed and was rolling away to dinner that, in the hansom, I bethought myself of the difficulty of the condition attached. The difficulty was not of course in letting her off easy but in qualifying that indulgence. "I simply won't qualify it," I said to myself. I didn't admire her, but I liked her, and I had known her so long that I almost felt heartless in sitting down at such an hour to a feast of indifference. I must have seemed abstracted, for the early years of my acquaintance with her came back to me. I spoke of her to the lady I had taken down, but the lady I had taken down had never heard of Greville Fane. I tried my other neighbour, who pronounced her books "too vile." I had never thought them very good, but I should let her off easier than that.

I came away early, for the express purpose of driving to ask about her. The journey took time, for she lived in the northwest district, in the neighbourhood of Primrose Hill. My apprehension that I should be too late was justified in a fuller sense than I had attached to it—I had only feared the house would be shut up. There were lights in the windows, and the temperate tinkle of my bell brought a servant immediately to the door, but poor Mrs Stormer had passed into a state in which the resonance of no earthly knocker was to be feared. A lady, in the hall, hovering behind the servant, came forward when she heard my voice. I recognised Lady Luard, but she had mistaken me for the doctor.

"Excuse my appearing at such an hour," I said; "it was the first possible moment after I heard."

"It's all over," Lady Luard replied. "Dearest mamma!"

She stood there under the lamp with her eyes on me; she was very tall, very stiff, very cold, and always looked as if these things, and some others beside, in her dress, her manner and even her name, were an implication that she was very admirable. I had never been able to follow the argument, but that is a detail. I expressed briefly and frankly what I felt, while the little mottled maidservant flattened herself against the wall of the narrow passage and tried to look detached without looking indifferent. It was not a moment to make a visit, and I was on the point of retreating when Lady Luard arrested me with a queer, casual, drawling "Would you—a— would you, perhaps, be *writing* something?" I felt for the instant like an interviewer, which I was not. But I pleaded guilty to this intention, on which she rejoined: "I'm so very glad—but I think my brother would like to see you." I detested her brother, but it wasn't an occasion to act this out; so I suffered myself to be inducted, to my surprise, into a small back room which I immediately recognised as the scene, during the later years, of Mrs Stormer's imperturbable industry. Her table was there, the battered and blotted accessory to innumerable literary lapses, with its contracted space for the arms (she wrote only from the elbow down) and the confusion of scrappy, scribbled sheets which had already become literary remains. Leolin was also there, smoking a cigarette ~~before~~ the fire and looking impudent even in his grief, sincere as it well might have been.

To meet him, to greet him, I had to make a sharp effort; for the air that he wore to me as he stood before me was quite that of his mother's murderer. She lay silent for ever upstairs —as dead as an unsuccessful book, and his swaggering erect-ness was a kind of symbol of his having killed her. I wondered if he had already, with his sister, been calculating what they could get for the poor papers on the table; but I had not long to wait to learn, for in reply to the scanty words of sympathy I addressed him he puffed out: "It's miserable, miserable, yes; but she has left three books complete." His words had the oddest effect; they converted the cramped little room into a seat of trade and made the "book" wonderfully feasible. He would certainly get all that could be got for the three. Lady Luard explained to me that her husband had been with them but had had to go down to the House. To her brother she explained that I was going to write something, and to me again she made it clear that she hoped I would "do mamma justice." She added that she didn't think this had ever been done. She said to her brother: "Don't you think there are some things he ought thoroughly to understand?" and on his instantly exclaiming "Oh, thoroughly—thoroughly!" she went on, rather austerely: "I mean about mamma's birth."

"Yes, and her connections," Leolin added.

I professed every willingness, and for five minutes I listened, but it would be too much to say that I understood. I don't even now, but it is not important. My vision was of other matters than those they put before me, and while they desired there should be no mistake about their ancestors I became more and more lucid about themselves. I got away as soon as possible, and walked home through the great dusky, empty London—the best of all conditions for thought. By the time I reached my door my little article was practically composed—ready to be transferred on the morrow from the polished plate of fancy. I believe it attracted some notice, was thought "graceful" and was said to be by some one else. I had to be pointed without being lively, and it took some tact. But what I said was much less interesting than what I thought —especially during the half-hour I spent in my armchair by

the fire, smoking the cigar I always light before going to bed.
I went to sleep there, I believe; but I continued to moralise
about Greville Fane. I am reluctant to lose that retrospect
altogether, and this is a dim little memory of it, a document
not to "serve." The dear woman had written a hundred
stories, but none so curious as her own.

When first I knew her she had published half-a-dozen
fictions, and I believe I had also perpetrated a novel. She was
more than a dozen years older than I, but she was a person
who always acknowledged her relativity. It was not so very
long ago, but in London, amid the big waves of the present,
even a near horizon gets hidden. I met her at some dinner and
took her down, rather flattered at offering my arm to a
celebrity. She didn't look like one, with her matronly, mild,
inanimate face, but I supposed her greatness would come out
in her conversation. I gave it all the opportunities I could, but
I was not disappointed when I found her only a dull, kind
woman. This was why I liked her—she rested me so from
literature. To myself literature was an irritation, a torment;
but Greville Fane slumbered in the intellectual part of it like
a Creole in a hammock. She was not a woman of genius, but
her faculty was so special, so much a gift out of hand, that I
have often wondered why she fell below that distinction. This
was doubtless because the transaction, in her case, had remained incomplete; genius always pays for the gift, feels the
debt, and she was placidly unconscious of obligation. She
could invent stories by the yard, but she couldn't write a page
of English. She went down to her grave without suspecting
that though she had contributed volumes to the diversion of
her contemporaries she had not contributed a sentence to the
language. This had not prevented bushels of criticism from
being heaped upon her head; she was worth a couple of
columns any day to the weekly papers, in which it was
shown that her pictures of life were dreadful but her
style really charming. She asked me to come and see her, and

I went. She lived then in Montpellier Square; which helped me to see how dissociated her imagination was from her character.

An industrious widow, devoted to her daily stint, to meeting the butcher and baker and making a home for her son and daughter, from the moment she took her pen in her hand she became a creature of passion. She thought the English novel deplorably wanting in that element, and the task she had cut out for herself was to supply the deficiency. Passion in high life was the general formula of this work, for her imagination was at home only in the most exalted circles. She adored, in truth, the aristocracy, and they constituted for her the romance of the world or, what is more to the point, the prime material of fiction. Their beauty and luxury, their loves and revenges, their temptations and surrenders, their immoralities and diamonds were as familiar to her as the blots on her writing-table. She was not a belated producer of the old fashionable novel, she had a cleverness and a modernness of her own, she had freshened up the fly-blown tinsel. She turned off plots by the hundred and—so far as her flying quill could convey her—was perpetually going abroad. Her types, her illustrations, her tone were nothing if not cosmopolitan. She recognised nothing less provincial than European society, and her fine folk knew each other and made love to each other from Doncaster to Bucharest. She had an idea that she resembled Balzac, and her favourite historical characters were Lucien de Rubempré and the Vidame de Pamiers. I must add that when I once asked her who the latter personage was she was unable to tell me. She was very brave and healthy and cheerful, very abundant and innocent and wicked. She was clever and vulgar and snobbish, and never so intensely British as when she was particularly foreign.

This combination of qualities had brought her early success, and I remember having heard with wonder and envy of what she "got," in those days, for a novel. The revelation gave

GREVILLE FANE

me a pang: it was such a proof that, practising a totally different style, I should never make my fortune. And yet when, as I knew her better, she told me her real tariff and I saw how rumour had quadrupled it, I liked her enough to be sorry. After a while I discovered too that if she got less it was not that *I* was to get any more. My failure never had what Mrs Stormer would have called the banality of being relative—it was always admirably absolute. She lived at ease however in those days—ease is exactly the word, though she produced three novels a year. She scorned me when I spoke of difficulty —it was the only thing that made her angry. If I hinted that a work of art required a tremendous licking into shape she thought it a pretension and a *pose*. She never recognised the "torment of form"; the furthest she went was to introduce into one of her books (in satire her hand was heavy) a young poet who was always talking about it. I couldn't quite understand her irritation on this score, for she had nothing at stake in the matter. She had a shrewd perception that form, in prose at least, never recommended any one to the public we were condemned to address, and therefore she lost nothing (putting her private humiliation aside) by not having any. She made no pretence of producing works of art, but had comfortable tea-drinking hours in which she freely confessed herself a common pastrycook, dealing in such tarts and puddings as would bring customers to the shop. She put in plenty of sugar and of cochineal, or whatever it is that gives these articles a rich and attractive colour. She had a serene superiority to observation and opportunity which constituted an inexpugnable strength and would enable her to go on indefinitely. It is only real success that wanes, it is only solid things that melt. Greville Fane's ignorance of life was a resource still more unfailing than the most approved receipt. On her saying once that the day would come when she should have written herself out I answered: "Ah, you look into fairyland, and the fairies love you, and *they* never change. Fairyland is always there; it

438

always was from the beginning of time, and it always will be
to the end. They've given you the key and you can always
open the door. With me it's different; I try, in my clumsy way,
to be in some direct relation to life." "Oh, bother your direct
relation to life!" she used to reply, for she was always annoyed by the phrase—which would not in the least prevent
her from using it when she wished to try for style. With no
more prejudices than an old sausage-mill, she would give forth
again with patient punctuality any poor verbal scrap that had
been dropped into her. I cheered her with saying that the dark
day, at the end, would be for the like of *me;* inasmuch as,
going in our small way by experience and observation, we
depended not on a revelation, but on a little tiresome process.
Observation depended on opportunity, and where should we
be when opportunity failed?

One day she told me that as the novelist's life was so
delightful and during the good years at least such a comfortable support (she had these staggering optimisms) she meant
to train up her boy to follow it. She took the ingenious view
that it was a profession like another and that therefore everything was to be gained by beginning young and serving an
apprenticeship. Moreover the education would be less expensive than any other special course, inasmuch as she could
administer it herself. She didn't profess to keep a school, but
she could at least teach her own child. It was not that she was
so very clever, but (she confessed to me as if she were afraid I
would laugh at her) that *he* was. I didn't laugh at her for that,
for I thought the boy sharp—I had seen him at sundry times.
He was well grown and good-looking and unabashed, and
both he and his sister made me wonder about their defunct
papa, concerning whom the little I knew was that he had been
a clergyman. I explained them to myself by suppositions and
imputations possibly unjust to the departed; so little were they
—superficially at least—the children of their mother. There
used to be, on an easel in her drawing-room, an enlarged

photograph of her husband, done by some horrible post-
humous "process" and draped, as to its florid frame, with a
silken scarf, which testified to the candour of Greville Fane's
bad taste. It made him look like an unsuccessful tragedian; but
it was not a thing to trust. He may have been a successful
comedian. Of the two children the girl was the elder, and
struck me in all her younger years as singularly colourless.
She was only very long, like an undecipherable letter. It was
not till Mrs Stormer came back from a protracted residence
abroad that Ethel (which was this young lady's name) began
to produce the effect, which was afterwards remarkable in her,
of a certain kind of high resolution. She made one apprehend
that she meant to do something for herself. She was long-
necked and near-sighted and striking, and I thought I had
never seen sweet seventeen in a form so hard and high and dry.
She was cold and affected and ambitious, and she carried an
eyeglass with a long handle, which she put up whenever she
wanted not to see. She had come out, as the phrase is, immensely; and yet I felt as if she were surrounded with a spiked
iron railing. What she meant to do for herself was to marry,
and it was the only thing, I think, that she meant to do for any
one else; yet who would be inspired to clamber over that
bristling barrier? What flower of tenderness or of intimacy
would such an adventurer conceive as his reward?

This was for Sir Baldwin Luard to say; but he naturally
never confided to me the secret. He was a joyless, jokeless
young man, with the air of having other secrets as well, and a
determination to get on politically that was indicated by his
never having been known to commit himself—as regards any
proposition whatever—beyond an exclamatory "Oh!" His
wife and he must have conversed mainly in prim ejaculations,
but they understood sufficiently that they were kindred
spirits. I remember being angry with Greville Fane when she
announced these nuptials to me as magnificent; I remember
asking her what splendour there was in the union of the

daughter of a woman of genius with an irredeemable mediocrity. "Oh! he's awfully clever," she said; but she blushed
for the maternal fib. What she meant was that though Sir
Baldwin's estates were not vast (he had a dreary house in
South Kensington and a still drearier "Hall" somewhere in
Essex, which was let), the connection was a "smarter" one
than a child of hers could have aspired to form. In spite of the
social bravery of her novels she took a very humble and dingy
view of herself, so that of all her productions "my daughter
Lady Luard" was quite the one she was proudest of. That personage thought her mother very vulgar and was distressed
and perplexed by the occasional license of her pen, but had a
complicated attitude in regard to this indirect connection with
literature. So far as it was lucrative her ladyship approved of
it, and could compound with the inferiority of the pursuit by
doing practical justice to some of its advantages. I had reason
to know (my reason was simply that poor Mrs Stormer told
me) that she suffered the inky fingers to press an occasional
banknote into her palm. On the other hand she deplored the
"peculiar style" to which Greville Fane had devoted herself,
and wondered where an author who had the convenience of so
lady-like a daughter could have picked up such views about
the best society. "She might know better, with Leolin and
me," Lady Luard had been known to remark; but it appeared
that some of Greville Fane's superstitions were incurable. She
didn't live in Lady Luard's society, and the best was not good
enough for her—she must make it still better.

I could see that this necessity grew upon her during the
years she spent abroad, when I had glimpses of her in the shifting sojourns that lay in the path of my annual ramble. She
betook herself from Germany to Switzerland and from Switzerland to Italy; she favoured cheap places and set up her desk in
the smaller capitals. I took a look at her whenever I could, and
I always asked how Leolin was getting on. She gave me
beautiful accounts of him, and whenever it was possible the

boy was produced for my edification. I had entered from the first into the joke of his career—I pretended to regard him as a consecrated child. It had been a joke for Mrs Stormer at first, but the boy himself had been shrewd enough to make the matter serious. If his mother accepted the principle that the intending novelist cannot begin too early to see life, Leolin was not interested in hanging back from the application of it. He was eager to qualify himself, and took to cigarettes at ten, on the highest literary grounds. His poor mother gazed at him with extravagant envy and, like Desdemona, wished heaven had made *her* such a man. She explained to me more than once that in her profession she had found her sex a dreadful drawback. She loved the story of Madame George Sand's early rebellion against this hindrance, and believed that if she had worn trousers she could have written as well as that lady. Leolin had for the career at least the qualification of trousers, and as he grew older he recognised its importance by laying in an immense assortment. He grew up in gorgeous apparel, which was his way of interpreting his mother's system. Whenever I met her I found her still under the impression that she was carrying this system out and that Leolin's training was bearing fruit. She was giving him experience, she was giving him impressions, she was putting a *gagne-pain* into his hand. It was another name for spoiling him with the best conscience in the world. The queerest pictures come back to me of this period of the good lady's life and of the extraordinarily virtuous, muddled, bewildering tenor of it. She had an idea that she was seeing foreign manners as well as her petticoats would allow; but, in reality she was not seeing anything, least of all fortunately how much she was laughed at. She drove her whimsical pen at Dresden and at Florence, and produced in all places and at all times the same romantic and ridiculous fictions. She carried about her box of properties and fished out promptly the familiar, tarnished old puppets. She believed in them when others couldn't, and as they were like nothing that was to be seen under the sun it was impossible to prove by comparison that they were wrong. You can't compare birds and fishes; you could only feel that, as Greville Fane's characters had the fine plumage of the former species, human beings must be of the latter.

It would have been droll if it had not been so exemplary to see her tracing the loves of the duchesses beside the innocent cribs of her children. The immoral and the maternal lived together in her diligent days on the most comfortable terms, and she stopped curling the mustaches of her Guardsmen to pat the heads of her babes. She was haunted by solemn spinsters who came to tea from continental *pensions*, and by unsophisticated Americans who told her she was just loved in *their* country. "I had rather be just paid there," she usually replied; for this tribute of transatlantic opinion was the only thing that galled her. The Americans went away thinking her coarse; though as the author of so many beautiful love-stories she was disappointing to most of these pilgrims, who had not expected to find a shy, stout, ruddy lady in a cap like a crumbled pyramid. She wrote about the affections and the impossibility of controlling them, but she talked of the price of *pension* and the convenience of an English chemist. She devoted much thought and many thousands of francs to the education of her daughter, who spent three years at a very superior school at Dresden, receiving wonderful instruction in sciences, arts and tongues, and who, taking a different line from Leolin, was to be brought up wholly as a *femme du monde*. The girl was musical and philological; she made a specialty of languages and learned enough about them to be inspired with a great contempt for her mother's artless accents. Greville Fane's French and Italian were droll; the imitative faculty had been denied her, and she had an unequalled gift, especially pen in hand, of squeezing big mistakes into small opportunities. She knew it, but she didn't care; correctness was the virtue in the world that, like her

heroes and heroines, she valued least. Ethel, who had perceived in her pages some remarkable lapses, undertook at one
time to revise her proofs; but I remember her telling me a year
after the girl had left school that this function had been very
briefly exercised. "She can't read me," said Mrs Stormer; "I
offend her taste. She tells me that at Dresden—at school—I
was never allowed." The good lady seemed surprised at this,
having the best conscience in the world about her lucubra-
tions. She had never meant to fly in the face of anything, and
considered that she grovelled before the Rhadamanthus of the
English literary tribunal, the celebrated and awful Young
Person. I assured her, as a joke, that she was frightfully in-
decent (she hadn't in fact that reality any more than any other)
my purpose being solely to prevent her from guessing that her
daughter had dropped her not because she was immoral but
because she was vulgar. I used to figure her children closeted
together and asking each other while they exchanged a gaze
of dismay: "Why should she *be* so—and so *fearfully* so—
when she has the advantage of our society? Shouldn't *we* have
taught her better?" Then I imagined their recognising with a
blush and a shrug that she was unteachable, irreformable. Indeed she was, poor lady; but it is never fair to read by the light
of taste things that were not written by it. Greville Fane had,
in the topsy-turvy, a serene good faith that ought to have
been safe from allusion, like a stutter or a *faux pas*.

    She didn't make her son ashamed of the profession to which
he was destined, however; she only made him ashamed of the
way she herself exercised it. But he bore his humiliation much
better than his sister, for he was ready to take for granted that
he should one day restore the balance. He was a canny and far-
seeing youth, with appetites and aspirations, and he had not a
scruple in his composition. His mother's theory of the happy
knack he could pick up deprived him of the wholesome discipline required to prevent young idlers from becoming cads.
He had, abroad, a casual tutor and a snatch or two of a Swiss

school, but no consecutive study, no prospect of a university or a degree. It may be imagined with what zeal, as the years went on, he entered into the pleasantry of there being no manual so important to him as the massive book of life. It was an expensive volume to peruse, but Mrs Stormer was willing to lay out a sum in what she would have called her *premiers frais*. Ethel disapproved—she thought this education far too unconventional for an English gentleman. Her voice was for Eton and Oxford, or for any public school (she would have resigned herself) with the army to follow. But Leolin never was afraid of his sister, and they visibly disliked, though they sometimes agreed to assist, each other. They could combine to work the oracle—to keep their mother at her desk.

When she came back to England, telling me she had got all the continent could give her, Leolin was a broad-shouldered, red-faced young man, with an immense wardrobe and an extraordinary assurance of manner. She was fondly obstinate about her having taken the right course with him, and proud of all that he knew and had seen. He was now quite ready to begin, and a little while later she told me he *had* begun. He had written something tremendously clever, and it was coming out in the *Cheapside*. I believe it came out; I had no time to look for it; I never heard anything about it. I took for granted that if this contribution had passed through his mother's hands it had practically become a specimen of her own genius, and it was interesting to consider Mrs Stormer's future in the light of her having to write her son's novels as well as her own. This was not the way she looked at it herself; she took the charming ground that he would help her to write hers. She used to tell me that he supplied passages of the greatest value to her own work—all sorts of technical things, about hunting and yachting and wine—that she couldn't be expected to get very straight. It was all so much practice for him and so much alleviation for her. I was unable to identify these pages, for I had long since ceased to "keep up" with Greville Fane;

but I was quite able to believe that the wine-question had been put, by Leolin's good offices, on a better footing, for the dear lady used to mix her drinks (she was perpetually serving the most splendid suppers) in the queerest fashion. I could see that he was willing enough to accept a commission to look after that department. It occurred to me indeed, when Mrs Stormer settled in England again, that by making a shrewd use of both her children she might be able to rejuvenate her style. Ethel had come back to gratify her young ambition, and if she couldn't take her mother into society, she would at least go into it herself. Silently, stiffly, almost grimly, this young lady held up her head, clenched her long teeth, squared her lean elbows and made her way up the staircases she had elected. The only communication she ever made to me, the only effusion of confidence with which she ever honoured me, was when she said: "I don't want to know the people mamma knows; I mean to know others." I took due note of the remark, for I was not one of the "others." I couldn't trace therefore the steps of her process; I could only admire it at a distance and congratulate her mother on the results. The results were that Ethel went to "big" parties and got people to take her. Some of them were people she had met abroad, and others were people whom the people she had met abroad had met. They ministered alike to Miss Ethel's convenience, and I wondered how she extracted so many favours without the expenditure of a smile. Her smile was the dimmest thing in the world, diluted lemonade, without sugar, and she had arrived precociously at social wisdom, recognising that if she was neither pretty enough nor rich enough nor clever enough, she could at least in her muscular youth be rude enough. Therefore if she was able to tell her mother what really took place in the mansions of the great, give her notes to work from, the quill could be driven at home to better purpose and precisely at a moment when it would have to be more active than ever. But if she did tell, it would appear that poor Mrs

Stormer didn't believe. As regards many points this was not a wonder; at any rate I heard nothing of Greville Fane's having developed a new manner. She had only one manner from start to finish, as Leolin would have said.

She was tired at last, but she mentioned to me that she couldn't afford to pause. She continued to speak of Leolin's work as the great hope of their future (she had saved no money) though the young man wore to my sense an aspect more and more professional if you like, but less and less literary. At the end of a couple of years there was something monstrous in the impudence with which he played his part in the comedy. When I wondered how she could play *her* part I had to perceive that her good faith was complete and that what kept it so was simply her extravagant fondness. She loved the young impostor with a simple, blind, benighted love, and of all the heroes of romance who had passed before her eyes he was by far the most brilliant. He was at any rate the most real —she could touch him, pay for him, suffer for him, worship him. He made her think of her princes and dukes, and when she wished to fix these figures in her mind's eye she thought of her boy. She had often told me she was carried away by her own creations, and she was certainly carried away by Leolin. He vivified, by potentialities at least, the whole question of youth and passion. She held, not unjustly, that the sincere novelist should feel the whole flood of life; she acknowledged with regret that she had not had time to feel it herself, and it was a joy to her that the deficiency might be supplied by the sight of the way it was rushing through this magnificent young man. She exhorted him, I suppose, to let it rush; she wrung her own flaccid little sponge into the torrent. I knew not what passed between them in her hours of tuition, but I gathered that she mainly impressed on him that the great thing was to live, because that gave you material. He asked nothing better; he collected material, and the formula served as a universal pretext. You had only to look at him to see that, with his rings and breastpins, his cross-barred jackets, his early *embonpoint*, his eyes that looked like imitation jewels, his various indications of a dense, full-blown temperament, his idea of life was singularly vulgar; but he was not so far wrong as that his response to his mother's expectations was not in a high degree practical. If she had imposed a profession on him from his tenderest years it was exactly a profession that he followed. The two were not quite the same, inasmuch as *his* was simply to live at her expense; but at least she couldn't say that he hadn't taken a line. If she insisted on believing in him he offered himself to the sacrifice. My impression is that her secret dream was that he should have a *liaison* with a countess, and he persuaded her without difficulty that he had one. I don't know what countesses are capable of, but I have a clear notion of what Leolin was.

He didn't persuade his sister, who despised him—she wished to work her mother in her own way, and I asked myself why the girl's judgment of him didn't make me like her better. It was because it didn't save her after all from a mute agreement with him to go halves. There were moments when I couldn't help looking hard into his atrocious young eyes, challenging him to confess his fantastic fraud and give it up. Not a little tacit conversation passed between us in this way, but he had always the best of it. If I said: "Oh, come now, with *me* you needn't keep it up; plead guilty, and I'll let you off," he wore the most ingenuous, the most candid expression, in the depths of which I could read: "Oh, yes, I know it exasperates you—that's just why I do it." He took the line of earnest inquiry, talked about Balzac and Flaubert, asked me if I thought Dickens *did* exaggerate and Thackeray *ought* to be called a pessimist. Once he came to see me, at his mother's suggestion he declared, on purpose to ask me how far, in my opinion, in the English novel, one really might venture to "go." He was not resigned to the usual pruderies—he suffered under them already. He struck out the brilliant idea that nobody knew how far we might go, for nobody had ever tried. Did I think *he* might safely try—would it injure his mother if he did? He would rather disgrace himself by his timidities than injure his mother, but certainly some one ought to try. Wouldn't *I* try—couldn't I be prevailed upon to look at it as a duty? Surely the ultimate point ought to be fixed—he was worried, haunted by the question. He patronised me unblushingly, made me feel like a foolish amateur, a helpless novice, inquired into my habits of work and conveyed to me that I was utterly *vieux jeu* and had not had the advantage of an early training. I had not been brought up from the germ, I knew nothing of life—didn't go at it on *his* system. He had dipped into French feuilletons and picked up plenty of phrases, and he made a much better show in talk than his poor mother, who never had time to read anything and could only be vivid with her pen. If I didn't kick him down-stairs it was because he would have alighted on her at the bottom.

When she went to live at Primrose Hill I called upon her and found her weary and wasted. It had waned a good deal, the elation caused the year before by Ethel's marriage; the foam on the cup had subsided and there was a bitterness in the draught. She had had to take a cheaper house and she had to work still harder to pay even for that. Sir Baldwin was obliged to be close; his charges were fearful, and the dream of her living with her daughter (a vision she had never mentioned to me) must be renounced. "I would have helped with things, and I could have lived perfectly in one room," she said; "I would have paid for everything, and—after all—I'm some one, ain't I? But I don't fit in, and Ethel tells me there are tiresome people she *must* receive. I can help them from here, no doubt, better than from there. She told me once, you know, what she thinks of my picture of life. 'Mamma, your picture of life is preposterous!' No doubt it is, but she's vexed with me for letting my prices go down; and I had to write three novels to pay for all her marriage cost me. I did it very well—I mean the outfit and the wedding; but that's why I'm here. At any rate she doesn't want a dingy old woman in her house. I should give it an atmosphere of literary glory, but literary glory is only the eminence of nobodies. Besides, she doubts my glory —she knows I'm glorious only at Peckham and Hackney. She doesn't want her friends to ask if I've never known nice people. She can't tell them I've never been in society. She tried to teach me better once, but I couldn't learn. It would seem too as if Peckham and Hackney had had enough of me; for (don't tell any one!) I've had to take less for my last than I ever took for anything." I asked her how little this had been, not from curiosity, but in order to upbraid her, more disinterestedly than Lady Luard had done, for such concessions. She answered "I'm ashamed to tell you," and then she began to cry.

I had never seen her break down, and I was proportionately moved; she sobbed, like a frightened child, over the extinction of her vogue and the exhaustion of her vein. Her little workroom seemed indeed a barren place to grow flowers, and I wondered, in the after years (for she continued to produce and publish) by what desperate and heroic process she dragged them out of the soil. I remember asking her on that occasion what had become of Leolin, and how much longer she intended to allow him to amuse himself at her cost. She rejoined with spirit, wiping her eyes, that he was down at Brighton hard at work—he was in the midst of a novel—and that he *felt* life so, in all its misery and mystery, that it was cruel to speak of such experiences as a pleasure. "He goes beneath the surface," she said, "and he *forces* himself to look at things from which he would rather turn away. Do you call that amusing yourself? You should see his face sometimes! And he does it for me as much as for himself. He tells me everything—he comes home to me with his *trouvailles*. We are artists together, and to the artist all things are pure. I've often heard you say so yourself." The novel that Leolin was engaged in at Brighton was never published, but a friend of mine and of Mrs Stormer's who was staying there happened to mention to me later that he had seen the young apprentice to fiction driving, in a dogcart, a young lady with a very pink face. When I suggested that she was perhaps a woman of title with whom he was conscientiously flirting my informant replied: " She is indeed, but do you know what her title is? " He pronounced it—it was familiar and descriptive—but I won't reproduce it here. I don't know whether Leolin mentioned it to his mother: she would have needed all the purity of the artist to forgive him. I hated so to come across him that in the very last years I went rarely to see her, though I knew that she had come pretty well to the end of her rope. I didn't want her to tell me that she had fairly to give her books away—I didn't want to see her cry. She kept it up amazingly, and every few months, at my club, I saw three new volumes, in green, in crimson, in blue, on the book-table that groaned with light literature. Once I met her at the Academy soirée, where you meet people you thought were dead, and she vouchsafed the information, as if she owed it to me in candour, that Leolin had been obliged to recognise insuperable difficulties in the question of *form*, he was so fastidious; so that she had now arrived at a definite understanding with him (it was such a comfort) that *she* would do the form if he would bring home the substance. That was now his position—he foraged for her in the great world at a salary. "He's my 'devil,' don't you see? as if I were a great lawyer: he gets up the case and I argue it." She mentioned further that in addition to his salary he was paid by the piece: he got so much for a striking character, so much for a pretty name, so much for a plot, so much for an incident, and had so much promised him if he would invent a new crime.

"He *has* invented one," I said, "and he's paid every day of his life."

"What is it?" she asked, looking hard at the picture of the year, "Baby's Tub," near which we happened to be standing.

I hesitated a moment. "I myself will write a little story about it, and then you'll see."

But she never saw; she had never seen anything, and she passed away with her fine blindness unimpaired. Her son published every scrap of scribbled paper that could be extracted from her table-drawers, and his sister quarrelled with him mortally about the proceeds, which showed that she only wanted a pretext, for they cannot have been great. I don't know what Leolin lives upon, unless it be on a queer lady many years older than himself, whom he lately married. The last time I met him he said to me with his infuriating smile: "Don't you think we can go a little further still—just a little?" *He* really goes too far.

THE WHEEL OF TIME

I

"AND your daughter?" said Lady Greyswood; "tell me about her. She must be nice."

"Oh, yes, she's nice enough. She's a great comfort." Mrs Knocker hesitated a moment, then she went on: "Unfortunately she's not good-looking—not a bit."

"That doesn't matter, when they're not ill-natured," rejoined, insincerely, Lady Greyswood, who had the remains of great beauty.

"Oh, but poor Fanny is quite extraordinarily plain. I assure you it does matter. She knows it herself; she suffers from it. It's the sort of thing that makes a great difference in a girl's life."

"But if she's charming, if she's clever!" said Lady Greyswood, with more benevolence than logic. "I've known plain women who were liked."

"Do you mean *me*, my dear?" her old friend straightforwardly inquired. "But I'm not so awfully liked!"

"You?" Lady Greyswood exclaimed. "Why, you're grand!"

"I'm not so repulsive as I was when I was young perhaps, but that's not saying much."

"As when you were young!" laughed Lady Greyswood. "You sweet thing, you *are* young. I thought India dried people up."

"Oh, when you're a mummy to begin with!" Mrs Knocker returned, with her trick of self-abasement. "Of course I've not been such a fool as to keep my children there. My girl *is* clever," she continued, "but she's afraid to show it.

453

Therefore you may judge whether, with her unfortunate appearance, she's charming."

"She shall show it to *me!* You must let me do everything for her."

"Does that include finding her a husband? I should like her to show it to someone who'll marry her."

"*I*'ll marry her!" said Lady Greyswood, who was handsomer than ever when she laughed and looked capable.

"What a blessing to meet you this way on the threshold of home! I give you notice that I shall cling to you. But that's what I meant; that's the thing the want of beauty makes so difficult—as if it were not difficult enough at the best."

"My dear child, one meets plenty of ugly women with husbands," Lady Greyswood argued, "and often with very nice ones."

"Yes, mine is very nice. There are men who don't mind one's face, for whom beauty isn't indispensable, but they are rare. I don't understand them. If I'd been a man about to marry I should have gone in for looks. However, the poor child will *have* something," Mrs Knocker continued.

Lady Greyswood rested thoughtful eyes on her. "Do you mean she'll be well off?"

"We shall do everything we can for her. We're not in such misery as we used to be. We've managed to save in India, strange to say, and six months ago my husband came into money (more than we had ever dreamed of), by the death of his poor brother. We feel quite opulent (it's rather nice!) and we should expect to do something decent for our daughter. I don't mind it's being known."

"It *shall* be known!" said Lady Greyswood, getting up. "Leave the dear child to me!" The old friends embraced, for the porter of the hotel had come in to say that the carriage ordered for her ladyship was at the door. They had met in Paris by the merest chance, in the court of an inn, after a separation of years, just as Lady Greyswood was going home.

She had been to Aix-les-Bains early in the season and was resting on her way back to England. Mrs Knocker and the General, bringing their eastern exile to a close, had arrived only the night before from Marseilles and were to wait in Paris for their children, a tall girl and two younger boys, who, inevitably dissociated from their parents, had been for the past two years with a devoted aunt, their father's maiden sister, at Heidelberg. The reunion of the family was to take place with jollity in Paris, whither this good lady was now hurrying with her drilled and demoralized charges. Mrs Knocker had come to England to see them two years before, and the period at Heidelberg had been planned during this visit. With the termination of her husband's service a new life opened before them all, and they had plans of comprehensive re-joicing for the summer—plans involving however a con-tinuance, for a few months, of useful foreign opportunities, during which various questions connected with the organiza-tion of a final home in England were practically to be dealt with. There was to be a salubrious house on the continent, taken in some neighbourhood that would both yield a stimulus to plain Fanny's French (her German was much commended), and permit of frequent "running over" for the General. With these preoccupations Mrs Knocker, after her delightful encounter with Lady Greyswood, was less keenly conscious of the variations of destiny than she had been when, at the age of twenty, that intimate friend of her youth, beautiful, loveable and about to be united to a nobleman of ancient name, was brightly, almost insolently alienated. The less attractive of the two girls had married only several years later, and her marriage had perhaps emphasised the diver-gence of their ways. To-day however the inequality, as Mrs Knocker would have phrased it, rather dropped out of the impression produced by the somewhat wasted and faded dowager, exquisite still, but unexpectedly appealing, who made no secret (an attempt that in an age of such publicity would have been useless), of what she had had, in vulgar parlance, to put up with, or of her having been left badly off. She had spoken of her children—she had had no less than six—but she had evidently thought it better not to speak of her husband. That somehow made up, on Mrs Knocker's part, for some ancient aches.

It was not till a year after this incident that, one day in London, in her little house in Queen Street, Lady Greyswood said to her third son, Maurice—the one she was fondest of, the one who on his own side had given her most signs of affection:

"I don't see what there is for you but to marry a girl of a certain fortune."

"Oh, that's not my line! I may be an idiot, but I'm not mercenary," the young man declared. He was not an idiot, but there was an examination, rather stiff indeed, to which, without success, he had gone up twice. The diplomatic service was closed to him by this catastrophe; nothing else appeared particularly open; he was terribly at leisure. There had been a theory none the less that he was the ablest of the family. Two of his brothers had been squeezed into the army and had declared rather crudely that they would do their best to keep Maurice out. They were not put to any trouble in this respect however, as he professed a complete indifference to the trade of arms. His mother, who was vague about everything except the idea that people ought to like him, if only for his extraordinary good looks, thought it strange there shouldn't be some opening for him in political life, or something to be picked up even in the City. But no bustling borough solicited the advantage of his protection, no eminent statesman in want of a secretary took him by the hand, no great commercial house had been keeping a stool for him. Maurice, in a word, was not "approached" from any quarter, and meanwhile he was as irritating as the intending traveller who allows you the pleasure of looking out his railway-connections. Poor Lady

Greyswood fumbled the social Bradshaw in vain. The young man had only one marked taste, with which his mother saw no way to deal—an invincible passion for photography. He was perpetually taking shots at his friends, but she couldn't open premises for him in Baker Street. He smoked endless cigarettes—she was sure they made him languid. She would have been more displeased with him if she had not felt so vividly that someone ought to do something for him; nevertheless she almost lost patience at his remark about not being mercenary. She was on the point of asking him what he called it to live on his relations, but she checked the words as she remembered that she herself was the only one who did much for him. Nevertheless, as she hated open professions of disinterestedness, she replied that that was a nonsensical tone. Whatever one should get in such a way one would give quite as much, even if it didn't happen to be money; and when he inquired in return what it was (beyond the disgrace of his failures) that she judged a fellow like him would bring to his bride, she replied that he would bring himself, his personal qualities (she didn't like to be more definite about his appearance), his name, his descent, his connections—good honest commodities all, for which any girl of proper feeling would be glad to pay. Such a name as that of the Glanvils was surely worth something, and she appealed to him to try what he could do with it.

"Surely I can do something better with it than sell it," said Maurice.

"I should like then very much to hear what," she replied very calmly, waiting reasonably for his answer. She waited to no purpose; the question baffled him, like those of his examinations. She explained that she meant of course that he should care for the girl, who might easily have a worse fault than the command of bread and butter. To humour her, for he was always good-natured, he said after a moment, smiling:

"Dear mother, is she pretty?"

"Is who pretty?"

"The young lady you have in your eye. Of course I see you've picked her out."

She coloured slightly at this—she had planned a more gradual revelation. For an instant she thought of saying that she had only had a general idea, for the form of his question embarrassed her; but on reflection she determined to be frank and practical. "Well, I confess I *am* thinking of a girl —a very nice one. But she hasn't great beauty."

"Oh, then it's of no use."

"But she's delightful, and she'll have thirty thousand pounds down, to say nothing of expectations."

Maurice Glanvil looked at his mother. "She must be hideous—for you to admit it. Therefore if she's rich she becomes quite impossible; for how can a fellow have the air of having been bribed with gold to marry a monster?"

"Fanny Knocker isn't the least a monster, and I can see that she'll improve. She's tall, and she's quite strong, and there's nothing at all disagreeable about her. Remember that you can't have everything."

"I thought you contended that I could!" said Maurice, amused at his mother's description of her young friend's charms. He had never heard anyone damned, as regards that sort of thing, with fainter praise. He declared that he would be perfectly capable of marrying a poor girl, but that the prime necessity in any young person he should think of would be the possession of a face—to put it at the least—that it would give him positive pleasure to look at. "I don't ask for much, but I do ask for beauty," he went on. "My eye must be gratified—I must have a wife I can photograph."

Lady Greyswood was tempted to answer that he himself had good looks enough to make a handsome couple, but she withheld the remark as injudicious, though effective, for it was a part of her son's amiability that he appeared to have no conception of his plastic side. He would have been disgusted if she had put it forward; if he had the ideal he had just described it was not because his own profile was his standard. What she herself saw in it was a force for coercing heiresses. She had however to be patient, and she promised herself to be adroit; which was all the easier as she really liked Fanny Knocker.

The girl's parents had at last taken a house in Ennismore Gardens, and the friend of her mother's youth had been confronted with the question of redeeming the pledges uttered in Paris. This unsophisticated and united family, with relations to visit and schoolboys' holidays to outlive, had spent the winter in the country and had but lately begun to talk of itself, extravagantly of course, through Mrs Knocker's droll lips, as open to social attentions. Lady Greyswood had not been false to her vows; she had on the contrary recognised from the first that, if he could only be made to see it, Fanny Knocker would be just the person to fill out poor Maurice's blanks. She had kept this confidence to herself, but it had made her very kind to the young lady. One of the forms of this kindness had been an ingenuity in keeping her from coming to Queen Street until Maurice should have been prepared. Was he to be regarded as prepared now that he asserted he would have nothing to do with Miss Knocker? This was a question that worried Lady Greyswood, who at any rate said to herself that she had told him the worst. Her idea had been to sound her old friend only after the young people should have met and Fanny should have fallen in love. Such a catastrophe for Fanny belonged for Lady Greyswood to that order of convenience that she could always take for granted.

She had found the girl, as she expected, ugly and awkward, but had also discovered a charm of character in her intelligent timidity. No one knew better than this observant woman how thankless a task in general it was in London to "take out" a plain girl; she had seen the nicest creatures, in the brutality of balls, participate only through wistful, almost tearful eyes; her little drawing-room, at intimate hours, had been shaken by the confidences of desperate mothers. None the less she felt sure that Fanny's path would not be rugged; thirty thousand pounds were a fine set of features, and her anxiety was rather on the score of the expectations of the young lady's parents. Mrs Knocker had dropped remarks suggestive of a high imagination, of the conviction that there might be a real efficacy in what they were doing for their daughter. The danger, in other words, might well be that no younger son need apply—a possibility that made Lady Greyswood take all her precautions. The acceptability of her favourite child was consistent with the rejection of those of other people—on which indeed it even directly depended. She remembered on the other hand the proverb about taking your horse to the water; the crystalline spring of her young friend's homage might overflow, but she couldn't compel her boy to drink. The clever way was to break down his prejudice—to get him to consent to give poor Fanny a chance. Therefore if she was careful not to worry him she let him see her project as something patient and deeply wise; she had the air of waiting resignedly for the day on which, in the absence of other solutions, he would say to her: "Well, let me have a look at my fate!" Meanwhile moreover she was nothing if not conscientious, and as she had made up her mind about the girl's susceptibility she had a scruple against exposing her. This exposure would not be justified so long as Maurice's theoretic rigour should remain unabated.

She felt virtuous in carrying her scruple to the point of rudeness; she knew that Jane Knocker wondered why, though so attentive in a hundred ways, she had never definitely included the poor child in any invitation to Queen Street. There came a moment when it gave her pleasure to suspect that her old friend had begun to explain this omission by the idea of a positive exaggeration of good faith—an honest recognition of the detrimental character of the young man in ambush there. As Maurice, though much addicted to kissing his mother at home, never dangled about her in public, he had remained a mythical figure to Mrs Knocker: he had been absent (culpably—there was a touch of the inevitable incivility in it), on each of the occasions on which, after their arrival in London, she and her husband dined with Lady Greyswood. This astute woman knew that her delightful Jane was whimsical enough to be excited good-humouredly by a mystery: she might very well want to make Maurice's acquaintance in just the degree in which she guessed that his mother's high sense of honour kept him out of the way. Moreover, she desired intensely that her daughter should have the sort of experience that would help her to take confidence. Lady Greyswood knew that no one had as yet asked the girl to dinner and that this particular attention was the one for which her mother would be most grateful. No sooner had she arrived at these illuminations than, with deep diplomacy, she requested the pleasure of the company of her dear Jane and the General. Mrs Knocker accepted with delight—she always accepted with delight—so that nothing remained for Lady Greyswood but to make sure of Maurice in advance. After this was done she had only to wait. When the dinner, on a day very near at hand, took place (she had jumped at the first evening on which the Knockers were free), she had the gratification of seeing her prevision exactly fulfilled. Her whimsical Jane had thrown the game into her hands, had been taken at the very last moment with one of her Indian headaches and, infinitely apologetic and explanatory, had hustled poor Fanny off with the General. The girl, flurried and frightened by her responsibility, sat at dinner next to Maurice, who behaved beautifully—not in the least as the victim of a trick; and when a fortnight later Lady Greyswood was able to divine that her mind from that evening had been filled with a virginal ecstasy, she was also fortunately able to feel serenely, delightfully guiltless.

II

SHE knew this fact about Fanny's mind, she believed, some
time before Jane Knocker knew it; but she also had reason to
think that Jane Knocker had known it for some time before
she spoke of it. It was not till the middle of June, after a succession of encounters between the young people, that her old
friend came one morning to discuss the circumstance. Mrs
Knocker asked her if she suspected it, and she promptly
replied that it had never occurred to her. She added that she
was extremely sorry and that it had probably in the first
instance been the fault of that injudicious dinner.

"Ah, the day of my headache—my miserable headache?"
said her visitor. "Yes, very likely that did it. He's so dreadfully good-looking."

"Poor child, he can't help that. Neither can I!" Lady
Greyswood ventured to add.

"He comes by it honestly. He seems very nice."

"He's nice enough, but he hasn't a farthing, you know, and
his expectations are *nil*." They considered, they turned the
matter about, they wondered what they had better do. In the
first place there was no room for doubt; of course Mrs
Knocker hadn't sounded the girl, but a mother, a true mother
was never reduced to that. If Fanny was in every relation of
life so painfully, so constitutionally awkward, the still depths
of her shyness, of her dissimulation even, in such a predicament as this, might easily be imagined. She would give no
sign that she could possibly smother, she would say nothing
and do nothing, watching herself, poor child, with trepidation; but she would suffer, and some day when the question
of her future should really come up—it might after all in the
form of some good proposal—they would find themselves

beating against a closed door. That was what they had to think of; that was why Mrs Knocker had come over. Her old friend cross-examined her with a troubled face, but she was very impressive with her reasons, her intuitions.

"I'll send him away in a moment, if you'd like that," Lady Greyswood said at last. "I'll try and get him to go abroad."

Her visitor made no direct reply to this, and no reply at all for some moments. "What does he expect to do—what does he want to do?" she asked.

"Oh, poor boy, he's looking—he's trying to decide. He asks nothing of anyone. If he would only knock at a few doors! But he's too proud."

"Do you call him *very* clever?" Fanny's mother demanded.

"Yes, decidedly—and good and kind and true. But he has been unlucky."

"Of course he can't bear her!" said Mrs Knocker with a little dry laugh.

Lady Greyswood stared; then she broke out: "Do you mean you'd be willing?——"

"He's very charming."

"Ah, but you must have great ideas."

"He's very well connected," said Mrs Knocker, snapping the tight elastic on her umbrella.

"Oh, my dear Jane—'connected'!" Lady Greyswood gave a sigh of the sweetest irony.

"He's connected with you, to begin with."

Lady Greyswood put out her hand and held her visitor's for a moment. "Of course it isn't as if he were a different sort of person. Of course I should like it!" she added.

"Does he dislike her *very* much?"

Lady Greyswood looked at her friend with a smile. "He resembles Fanny—he doesn't tell. But what would her father say?" she went on.

"He doesn't know it."

"You've not talked with him?"

Mrs Knocker hesitated a moment. "He thinks she's all right." Both the ladies laughed a little at the density of men; then the visitor said: "I wanted to see you first."

This circumstance gave Lady Greyswood food for thought; it suggested comprehensively that in spite of a probable deficiency of zeal on the General's part the worthy man would not be the great obstacle. She had begun so quickly to turn over in her mind the various ways in which this new phase of the business might make it possible the real obstacle should be surmounted that she scarcely heard her companion say next: "The General will only want his daughter to be happy. He has no definite ambitions for her. I dare say Maurice could make him like him." It was something more said by her companion about Maurice that sounded sharply through her reverie. "But unless the idea appeals to *him* a bit there's no use talking about it."

At this Lady Greyswood spoke with decision. "It *shall* appeal to him. Leave it to me! Kiss your dear child for me," she added as the ladies embraced and separated.

In the course of the day she made up her mind, and when she again broached the question to her son (it befell that very evening) she felt that she stood on firmer ground. She began by mentioning to him that her dear old friend had the same charming dream—for the girl—that *she* had; she sketched with a light hand a picture of their preconcerted happiness in the union of their children. When he replied that he couldn't for the life of him imagine what the Knockers could see in a poor beggar of a younger son who had publicly come a cropper, she took pains to prove that he was as good as anyone else and much better than many of the young men to whom persons of sense were often willing to confide their daughters. She had been in much tribulation over the circumstance announced to her in the morning, not knowing whether, in her present enterprise, to keep it back or put it forward. If Maurice should happen not to take it in the right way it was the sort of thing that might dish the whole experiment. He might be bored, he might be annoyed, he might be horrified—there was no limit, in such cases, to the perversity, to the possible brutality of even the most amiable man. On the other hand he might be pleased, touched, flattered—if he didn't dislike the girl too much. Lady Greyswood could indeed imagine that it might be unpleasant to know that a person who was disagreeable to you was in love with you; so that there was just that risk to run. She determined to run it only if there should be absolutely no other card to play. Meanwhile she said: "Don't you see, now, how intelligent she is, in her quiet way, and how perfect she is at home—without any nonsense or affectation or ill-nature? She's not a bit stupid, she's remarkably clever. She can do a lot of things; she has no end of talents. Many girls with a quarter of her abilities would make five times the show."

"My dear mother, she's a great swell, I freely admit it. She's far too good for me. What in the world puts it into your two heads that she would look at me?"

At this Lady Greyswood was tempted to speak; but after an instant she said instead: "She *has* looked at you, and you've seen how. You've seen her several times now, and she has been remarkably nice to you."

"Nice? Ah, poor girl, she's frightened to death!"

"Believe me—I read her," Lady Greyswood replied.

"She knows she has money and she thinks I'm after it. She thinks I'm a ravening wolf and she's scared."

"I happen to know as a fact that she's in love with you!" Before she could check herself Lady Greyswood had played her card, and though she held her breath a little after doing so she felt that it had been a good moment. "If I hadn't known it," she hastened further to declare, "I should never have said another word." Maurice burst out laughing—how in the world *did* she know it? When she put the evidence before him she had the pleasure of seeing that he listened without irritation; and this emboldened her to say: "Don't you think you could *try* to like her?"

Maurice was lounging on a sofa opposite to her; jocose but embarrassed, he had thrown back his head, and while he stretched himself his eyes wandered over the upper expanse of the room. "It's very kind of her and of her mother, and I'm much obliged and all that, though a fellow feels rather an ass in talking about such a thing. Of course also I don't pretend—before such a proof of wisdom—that I think her in the least a fool. But, oh, dear——!" And the young man broke off with laughing impatience, as if he had too much to say. His mother waited an instant, then she uttered a persuasive, interrogative sound, and he went on: "It's only a pity she's so awful!"

"So awful?" murmured Lady Greyswood.

"Dear mother, she's about as ugly a woman as ever turned round on you. If there were only just a touch or two less of it!"

Lady Greyswood got up: she stood looking in silence at the tinted shade of the lamp. She remained in this position so long that he glanced at her—he was struck with the sadness in her face. He would have been in error however if he had suspected that this sadness was assumed for the purpose of showing him that she was wounded by his resistance, for the reflection that his last words caused her to make was as dis-interested as it was melancholy. Here was an excellent, a charming girl—a girl, she was sure, with a rare capacity for devotion—whose future was reduced to nothing by the mere accident, in her face, of a certain want of drawing. A man could settle her fate with a laugh, could give her away with a snap of his fingers. She seemed to see Maurice administer to poor Fanny's image the little displeased shove with which he would have disposed of an ill-seasoned dish. Moreover he greatly exaggerated. Her heart grew heavy with a sense of the hardness of the lot of women, and when she looked again at her son there were tears in her eyes that startled him. "Poor girl—poor girl!" she simply sighed, in a tone that was to reverberate in his mind and to constitute in doing so a real appeal to his imagination. After a moment she added: "We'll talk no more about her—no, no!"

All the same she went three days later to see Mrs Knocker and say to her: "My dear creature, I think it's all right."

"Do you mean he'll take us up?"

"He'll come and see you, and you must give him plenty of chances." What Lady Greyswood would have liked to be able to say, crudely and comfortably, was: "He'll try to manage it—he promises to do what he can." What she did say, however, was: "He's greatly prepossessed in the dear child's favour."

"Then I dare say he'll be very nice."

"If I didn't think he'd behave like a gentleman I wouldn't raise a finger. The more he sees of her the more he'll be sure to like her."

"Of course with poor Fanny that's the only thing one can build on," said Mrs Knocker. "There's so much to get over."

Lady Greyswood hesitated a moment. "Maurice *has* got over it. But I should tell you that at first he doesn't want it known."

"Doesn't want what known?"

"Why, the footing on which he comes. You see it's just the least bit experimental."

"For what do you take me?" asked Mrs Knocker. "The child shall never dream that anything has passed between us. No more of course shall her father."

"It's too delightful of you to leave it that way," Lady Greyswood replied. "We must surround her happiness with every safeguard."

Mrs Knocker sat pensive for some moments. "So that if nothing comes of it there's no harm done? That idea—that nothing may come of it—makes one a little nervous," she added.

"Of course I can't absolutely answer for my poor boy!" said Lady Greyswood, with just the faintest ring of impatience. "But he's much affected by what he knows—I told him. That's what moves him."

"He must of course be perfectly free."

"The great thing is for her not to know."

Mrs Knocker considered. "Are you very sure?" She had apparently had a profounder second thought.

"Why, my dear—with the risk!"

"Isn't the risk, after all, greater the other way? Mayn't it help the matter on, mayn't it do the poor child a certain degree of good, the idea that, as you say, he's prepossessed in her favour? It would perhaps cheer her up, as it were, and encourage her, so that by the very fact of being happier about herself she may make a better impression. That's what she wants, poor thing—to be helped to hold up her head, to take herself more seriously, to believe that people can like her. And fancy, when it's a case of such a beautiful young man who's all ready to!"

"Yes, he's all ready to," Lady Greyswood conceded. "Of course it's a question for your own discretion. I can't advise you, for you know your child. But it seems to me a case for tremendous caution."

"Oh, trust me for that!" said Mrs Knocker. "We shall be very kind to him," she smiled, as her visitor got up.

"He'll appreciate that. But it's too nice of you to leave it so."

Mrs Knocker gave a hopeful shrug. "He has only to be civil to Blake!"

"Ah, he isn't a brute!" Lady Greyswood exclaimed, caressing her.

After this she passed a month of no little anxiety. She asked her son no question, and for two or three weeks he offered her

no other information than to say two or three times that Miss
Knocker really could ride; but she learned from her old friend
everything she wanted to know. Immediately after the conference of the two ladies Maurice, in the Row, had taken an
opportunity of making up to the girl. She rode every day with
her father, and Maurice rode, though possessed of nothing in
life to put a leg across; and he had been so well received that
this proved the beginning of a custom. He had a canter with
the young lady most days in the week, and when they parted
it was usually to meet again in the evening. His relations with
the household in Ennismore Gardens were indeed not left
greatly to his initiative; he became on the spot the subject of
perpetual invitations and arrangements, the centre of the
friendliest manœuvres; so that Lady Greyswood was struck
with Jane Knocker's feverish energy in the good cause—the
ingenuity, the bribery, the cunning that an exemplary mother
might be inspired to practise. She herself did nothing, she left
it all to poor Jane, and this perhaps gave her for the moment
a sense of contemplative superiority. She wondered if *she*
would in any circumstances have plotted so almost fiercely for
one of her children. She was glad her old friend's design had
her full approbation; she held her breath a little when she
said to herself: "Suppose I hadn't liked it—suppose it had
been for Chumleigh!" Chumleigh was the present Lord
Greyswood, whom his mother still called by his earlier desig-
nation. Fanny Knocker's thirty thousand would have been by
no means enough for Chumleigh. Lady Greyswood, in spite
of her suspense, was detached enough to be amused when her
accomplice told her that "Blake" had said that Maurice really
could ride. The two mothers thanked God for the riding—
the riding would see them through. Lady Greyswood had
watched Fanny narrowly in the Park, where, in the saddle,
she looked no worse than lots of girls. She had no idea how
Maurice got his mounts—she knew Chumleigh had none to
give him; but there were directions in which she would have

encouraged him to incur almost any liability. He was evidently amused and beguiled; he fell into comfortable attitudes on the soft cushions that were laid for him and partook with relish of the dainties that were served; he had his fill of the theatres, of the opera—entertainments of which he was fond. She could see he didn't care for the sort of people he met in Ennismore Gardens, but this didn't matter: so much as that she didn't ask of him. She knew that when he should have something to tell her he would speak; and meanwhile she pretended to be a thousand miles away. The only thing that worried her was that he had dropped photography. She said to Mrs Knocker more than once: "Does he make love?—that's what I want to know!" to which this lady replied with her incongruous drollery: "My dear, how can I make out? He's so little like Blake!" But she added that she believed Fanny was intensely happy. Lady Greyswood had been struck with the girl's looking so, and she rejoiced to be able to declare in perfectly good faith that she thought her greatly improved. "Didn't I tell you?" returned Mrs Knocker to this with a certain accent of triumph. It made Lady Greyswood nervous, for she took it to mean that Fanny had had a hint from her mother of Maurice's possible intentions. She was afraid to ask her old friend directly if this were definitely true: poor Fanny's improvement was after all not a gain sufficient to make up for the cruelty that would reside in the sense of being rejected.

One day, in Queen Street, Maurice said in an abrupt, conscientious way: "You were right about Fanny Knocker—she's a remarkably clever and a thoroughly nice girl; a fellow can really talk with her. But oh mother!"

"Well, my dear?"

The young man's face wore a strange smile. "Oh mother!" he expressively, quite tragically repeated. "But it's all right!" he presently added in a different tone, and Lady Greyswood was reassured. This confidence, however, received a shock a little later, on the evening of a day that had been intensely hot. A torrid wave had passed over London, and in the suffocating air the pleasures of the season had put on a purple face. Lady Greyswood, whose own fine lowness of tone no temperature could affect, knew, in her bedimmed drawing-room, exactly the detail of her son's engagements. She pitied him—*she* had managed to keep clear; she had in particular a vision of a distribution of prizes, by one of the princesses, at a big horticultural show; she saw the sweltering starers (and at what, after all?) under a huge glass roof, while there passed before her, in a blur of crimson, the glimpse of uncomfortable cheeks under an erratic white bonnet, together also with the sense that some of Jane Knocker's ideas of pleasure were of the oddest (she had such *lacunes*), and some of the ordeals to which she exposed poor Fanny singularly ill-chosen. Maurice came in, perspiring but pale (nothing could make *him* ugly!) to dress for dinner, and though he was in a great hurry he found time to pant: "Oh mother, what I'm going through for you!"

"Do you mean rushing about so—in this weather? We shall have a change to-night."

"I hope so! There are people for whom it doesn't do at all; ah, not a bit!" said Maurice with a laugh that she didn't fancy. But he went upstairs before she could think of anything to reply, and after he had dressed he passed out without speaking to her again. The next morning, on entering her room, her maid mentioned as a delicate duty that Mr Glanvil, whose door stood wide open and whose bed was untouched, had apparently not yet come in. While, however, her ladyship was in the first freshness of meditation on this singular fact the morning's letters were brought up, and as it happened that the second envelope she glanced at was addressed in Maurice's hand she was quickly in possession of an explanation still more startling than his absence. He wrote from a club, at nine o'clock the previous evening, to announce that he was taking the night train for the continent. He hadn't dressed for dinner,

THE WHEEL OF TIME

he had dressed otherwise, and having stuffed a few things with surreptitious haste into a Gladstone bag, had slipped unperceived out of the house and into a hansom. He had sent to Ennismore Gardens, from his club, an apology—a request he should not be waited for; and now he should just have time to get to Charing Cross. He was off he didn't know where, but he was off he did know why. "You'll know why, dear mother too, I think," this wonderful communication continued; "you'll know why, because I haven't deceived you. I've done what I could, but I've broken down. I felt to-day that it was no use; there was a moment, at that beastly exhibition, when I saw it, when the question was settled. The truth rolled over me in a stifling wave. After that I made up my mind there was nothing to do but to bolt. I meant to put it off till to-morrow, and to tell you first, but while I was dressing to-day it struck me irresistibly that my true course is to break now—never to enter the house or go near her again. I was afraid of a scene with you about this. I haven't uttered a word of 'love' to her (heaven save us!) but my position this afternoon became definitely false, and that fact prescribes the course I am taking. You shall hear from me again in a day or two. I have the greatest regard for her, but I can't bear to look at her. I don't care a bit for money, but, hang it, I *must* have beauty! Please send me twenty pounds, *poste restante*, Boulogne."

"What I want, Jane, is to get at *this*," Lady Greyswood said, later in the day, with an austerity that was sensible even through her tears. "Does the child know, or doesn't she, what was at stake?"

"She hasn't an inkling of it—how should she? I recognised that it was best not to tell her—and I didn't."

On this, as Mrs Knocker's tears had also flowed, Lady Greyswood kissed her. But she didn't believe her. Fanny herself, however, for the rest of the season, proved inscrutable. "She's a character!" Lady Greyswood reflected with admiration. In September, in Yorkshire, the girl was taken seriously ill.

III

AFTER luncheon at the Crisfords'—the big Sunday banquets of twenty people and a dozen courses—the men, lingering a little in the dining-room, dawdling among displaced chairs and dropped napkins while the ladies rustled away, ended by shuffling in casual pairs up to the studio, where coffee was served and where, presently, before the cigarettes were smoked out, Mrs Crisford always reappeared to usher in her contingent. The studio was high and handsome, and luncheon at the Crisfords' was, in the common esteem, more amusing than almost anything else in London except dinner. It was Bohemia with excellent service—Bohemia not debtor but creditor. Upstairs the pictures, finished or nearly finished, and arranged in a shining row, gave an obviousness of topic, so that conversation could easily touch bottom. Maurice Glanvil, who had never been in the house before, looked about and wondered; he was struck with the march of civilization— the rise of the social tide. There were new notes in English life, which he caught quickly with his fresh sense; during his long absence— twenty years of France and Italy—all sorts of things had happened. In his youth, in England, artists and authors and actors—people of that general kind—were not nearly so "smart." Maurice Glanvil was forty-nine to-day, and he thought a great deal of his youth. He regretted it, he missed it, he tried to beckon it back; but the differences in London made him feel that it had gone forever. There might perhaps be some sudden compensation in being fifty, some turn of the dim telescope, some view from the brow of the hill; it was a round, gross, stupid number, which probably would make one pompous, make one think one's self venerable. Meanwhile at any rate it was odious to be forty-nine. Maurice observed the young now more than he had ever done; observed them, that is, as the young. He wished he could have had a son, to be twenty with again; his daughter was only eighteen, but fond as he was of her he couldn't live instinctively into her girlishness. It was not that there was not plenty of it, for she was simple, sweet, indefinite, without the gifts that the boy would have had, the gifts—what had become of them now?—that he himself used to have.

The youngest person present, before the ladies came in, was the young man who had sat next to Vera and whom, being on the same side of the long table, he had not had under his eye. Maurice noticed him now, noticed that he was very good-looking, fair and fresh and clean, impeccable in his straight smoothness; also that apparently knowing none of the other guests and moving by himself about the studio with visible interest in the charming things, he had the modesty of his age and of his position. He had however something more besides, which had begun to prompt this observer to speak to him in order to hear the sound of his voice—a strange, elusive resemblance, lost in the profile but flickering straight out of the full face, to someone Maurice had known. For a minute Glanvil was worried by it—he had a sense that a name would suddenly come to him if he should see the lips in motion; but as he was on the point of laying the ghost by an experiment Mrs Crisford led in her companions. His daughter was among them, and in company, as he was constantly anxious about her appearance and her attitude, she had at moments the faculty of drawing his attention from everything else. The poor child, the only fruit of his odd, romantic union, the *coup de foudre* of his youth, with her strangely beautiful mother, whose own mother had been a Russian and who had died in giving birth to her—his short, colourless, insignificant Vera was excessively, incorrigibly plain. She had been the disappointment of his life, but he greatly pitied her. Her want of beauty, with her antecedents, had been one of the strangest tricks of fate; she was acutely conscious of it and, being good and docile, would have liked to please. She did sometimes, to her father's delight, in spite of everything; she had been educated abroad, on foreign lines, near her mother's people. He had brought her to England to take her out, to do what he could for her; but he was not unaware that in England her manners, which had been thought very pretty on the continent, would strike some persons as artificial. They were exactly what her mother's had been; they made up to a certain extent for the want of other resemblance. An extreme solicitude at any rate as to the impression they might make was the source of his habit, in London, of watching her covertly. He tried to see at a given moment how she looked, if she were happy; it was always with an intention of encouragement, and there was a frequent exchange between them of little invisible affectionate signs. She wore charming clothes, but she was terribly short; in England the girls were gigantic and it was only the tallest who were noticed. Their manners, alas, had nothing to do with it—many of them indeed hadn't any manners. As soon as he had got near Vera he said to her, scanning her through his single glass from head to foot:

"Who is the young man who sat next you? the one at the other end of the room."

"I don't know his name, papa—I didn't catch it."

"Was he civil—did he talk to you?"

"Oh, a great deal, papa—about all sorts of things."

Something in the tone of her voice made him look with greater intensity and even with greater tenderness than usual into her little dim green eyes. "Then you're all right—you're getting on?"

She gave her effusive smile—the one that perhaps wouldn't do in England. "Oh beautifully, papa—everyone's so kind."

She never complained, was a brave little optimist, full of sweet resources; but he had detected to-day as soon as he looked at her the particular shade of her content. It made him continue, after an hesitation: "He didn't say anything about his relations—anything that could give you a clue?"

Vera thought a moment. "Not that I can remember—unless that Mr Crisford is painting the portrait of his mother. Ah, there it is!" the girl exclaimed, looking across the room at a large picture on an easel, which the young man had just approached and from which their host had removed the drapery that covered it. Maurice Glanvil had observed this drapery, and as the artist unveiled the canvas with a flourish he saw that he had been waiting for the ladies to show it, to produce a surprise, a grand effect. Everyone moved toward it, and Maurice, with his daughter beside him, recognised that the production, a portrait, was striking, a great success for Crisford—the figure, down to the knees, with an extraordinary look of life, of a tall, handsome woman of middle age, in full dress, in black. Yet he saw it for the moment vaguely, through a preoccupation, that of a discovery which he had just made and which had recalled to him an incident of his youth —his juxtaposition, in London, at a dinner, to a girl, insurmountably charmless to him, who had fallen in love with him (so that she was nearly to die of it), within the first five minutes, before he had even spoken; as he had subsequently learned from a communication made him by his poor mother —a reminder uttered with a pointless bitterness that he had failed to understand and accompanied with unsuspected details, much later—too late, long after his marriage and shortly before her death. He said to himself that he must look out, and he wondered if poor Vera would also be insurmountably charmless to the good-looking young man. "But what a likeness, papa—what a likeness!" he heard her murmur at his elbow with suppressed excitement.

"How can you tell, my dear, if you haven't seen her?"

"I mean to the gentleman—the son."

Everyone was exclaiming "How wonderfully clever—how beautiful!" and under cover of the agitation and applause

Maurice Glanvil had drawn nearer the picture. The movement had brought him close to the young man of whom he
had been talking with Vera and who, with his happy eyes on
the painted figure, seemed to smile in acknowledgment of the
artist's talent and of the sitter's charm.

"Do you know who the lady is?" Maurice said to him.

He turned his bright face to his interlocutor. "She's my
mother—Mrs Tregent. Isn't it wonderful?"

His eyes, his lips, his voice flashed a light into Glanvil's
uncertainty—the tormenting resemblance was simply a prolonged echo of Fanny Knocker, in whose later name, precisely, he recognised the name pronounced by the young man.
Maurice Glanvil stared in some bewilderment; this stately,
splendid lady, with a face so vivid that it was handsome, was
what that unfortunate girl had become? The eyes, as if they
picked him out, looked at him strangely from the canvas; the
face, with all its difference, asserted itself, and he felt himself
turning as red as if he had been in the presence of the original.
Young Tregent, pleased and proud, had given way to the
pressing spectators, placing himself at Vera's other side; and
Maurice heard the girl exclaim to him in one of her pretty
effusions: "How beautiful she must be, and how amiable!"

"She is indeed—it's not a bit flattered." And while Maurice
still stared, more and more mystified—for "flattered, flattered!" was the unspoken solution in which he had instantly
taken refuge—his neighbour continued: "I wish you could
know her—you must; she's delightful. She couldn't come here
to-day—they asked her: she has people lunching at home."

"I should be so glad; perhaps we may meet her somewhere," said Vera.

"If I ask her and if you'll let her I'm sure she'll come to see
you," the young man responded. Maurice had glanced at him
while the face of the portrait watched them with the oddest,
the grimmest effect. He was filled with a confusion of feelings,
asking himself half-a-dozen questions at once. Was young

Tregent, with his attentive manner, "making up" to Vera? was he going out of his way in answering for his mother's civility? Little did he know what he was taking on himself! Above all was Fanny Knocker to-day this extraordinary figure—extraordinary in the light of the early plainness that had made him bolt? He became conscious of an extreme curiosity, an irresistible desire to see her.

"Oh, papa," said Vera, "Mr Tregent's so kind; he's so good as to promise us a visit from his mother."

The young man's friendly eyes were still on the child's face. "I'll tell her all about you. Oh, if I ask her she'll come!" he repeated.

"Does she do everything you ask her?" the girl inquired.

"She likes to know my friends!"

Maurice hesitated, wondering if he were in the presence of a smooth young humbug to whom compliments cost nothing, or in that of an impression really made—made by his little fluttered, unpopular Vera. He had a horror of exposing his child to risks, but his curiosity was greater than his caution. "Your mother mustn't come to us—it's our duty to go to her," he said to Mr Tregent; "I had the honour of knowing her—a long time ago. Her mother and mine were intimate friends. Be so good as to mention my name to her, that of Maurice Glanvil, and to tell her how glad I have been to make your acquaintance. And now, my dear child," he added to Vera, "we must take leave."

During the rest of that day it never occurred to him that there might be an awkwardness in his presenting himself, even after many years, before a person with whom he had broken as he had broken with Fanny Knocker. This was partly because he held, justly enough, that he had never committed himself, and partly because the intensity of his desire to measure with his own eyes the change represented—misrepresented perhaps—by the picture was a force greater than any embarrassment. His mother had told him that the poor girl had cruelly suffered, but there was no present intensity in that idea. With her expensive portrait, her grand air, her handsome son, she somehow embodied success, whereas he himself, standing for mere bereavement and disappointment, was a failure not to be surpassed. With Vera that evening he was very silent; she saw him smoke endless cigarettes and wondered what he was thinking of. She guessed indeed, but she was too subtle a little person to attempt to fall in with his thoughts or to be willing to betray her own by asking him random questions about Mrs Tregent. She had expressed as they came away from their luncheon-party a natural surprise at the coincidence of his having known the mother of her amusing neighbour, but the only other words that dropped from her on the subject were contained in a question that, before she went to bed, she put to him with abrupt gaiety, while she carefully placed a marker in a book she had not been reading.

"When is it then that we're to call upon this wonderful old friend?"

He looked at her through the smoke of his cigarette. "I don't know. We must wait a little, to allow her time to give some sign."

"Oh, I see!" And Vera took leave of him with one of her sincere little kisses.

IV

HE had not long to wait for the sign from Mrs Tregent; it arrived the very next morning in the shape of an invitation to dinner. This invitation was immediately accepted, but a fortnight was still to intervene—a trial to Maurice Glanvil's patience. The promptitude of the demonstration gave him pleasure—it showed him no bitterness had survived. What place was there indeed for resentment, since she had married and given birth to children and thought so well of the face God had conferred on her as to wish to hand it on to her posterity? Her husband was in Parliament, or had been—that came back to him from his mother's story. He caught himself reverting to her with a frequency that surprised him; he was haunted by the image of that bright, strong woman on Crisford's canvas, in whom there was just enough of Fanny Knocker to put a sort of defiance into the difference. He wanted to see it again, and his opportunity was at hand in the form of a visit to Mrs Crisford. He called on this lady, without his daughter, four days after he had lunched with her, and, finding her at home, he presently led the conversation to the portrait and to his ardent desire for another glimpse of it. Mrs Crisford gratified this eagerness—perhaps he struck her as a possible sitter; it was late in the afternoon and her husband was out: she led him into the studio. Mrs Tregent, splendid and serene, stood there as if she had been watching for him. There was no doubt the picture was a masterpiece. Maurice had mentioned that he had known the original years before and then had lost sight of her. He questioned his hostess with artful detachment.

"What sort of a person has she become—agreeable, popular?"

"Everyone adores her—she's so clever."

"Really—remarkably?"

"Extraordinarily—one of the cleverest women I've ever known, and quite one of the most charming."

Maurice looked at the portrait—at the super-subtle smile which seemed to tell him Mrs Tregent knew they were talking about her; a kind of smile he had never expected to live to see in Fanny Knocker's eyes. Then he asked: "Has she literally become as handsome as that?"

Mrs Crisford hesitated. "She's beautiful."

"Beautiful?" Maurice echoed.

"What shall I say? It's a peculiar charm! It's her spirit. One sees that her life has been beautiful in spite of her sorrows!" Mrs Crisford added.

"What sorrows has she had?" Maurice coloured a little as soon as he had spoken.

"Oh, lots of deaths. She has lost her husband; she has lost several children."

"Ah, that's new to me. Was her marriage happy?"

"It must have been for Mr Tregent. If it wasn't for her, no one ever knew."

"But she has a son," said Maurice.

"Yes, the only one—such a dear. She thinks all the world of him."

At this moment a message was brought to Mrs Crisford, and she asked to be excused while she went to say a word to someone who was waiting. Maurice Glanvil in this way was left alone for five minutes with the intensity of the presence evoked by the artist. He found himself agitated, excited by it: the face of the portrait was so intelligent and conscious that as he stood there he felt as if some strange communication had taken place between his being and Mrs Tregent's. The idea made him nervous: he moved about the room and ended by turning his back. Mrs Crisford reappeared, but he soon took leave of her; and when he had got home (he had settled himself in South Kensington, in a little undiscriminated house which he had hated from the first), he learned from his daughter that she had had a visit from young Tregent. He had asked first for Mr Glanvil and then, in the second instance, for herself, telling her when admitted, as if to attenuate his possible indiscretion, that his mother had charged him to try to see her even if he should not find her father. Vera had never before received a gentleman alone, and the incident had left traces of emotion. "Poor little thing!" Maurice said to himself: he always took a melancholy view of any happiness of his daughter's, tending to believe, in his pessimism, that it could

only lead to some refinement of humiliation. He encouraged
her however to talk about young Tregent, who, according to
her account, had been extravagantly amusing. He had said
moreover that his mother was tremendously impatient to
renew such an old acquaintance. "Why in the world doesn't
she, then?" Maurice asked himself; "why doesn't she come
and see Vera?" He reflected afterwards that such an expectation was unreasonable, but it represented at the moment a
kind of rebellion of his conscience. Then, as he had begun
to be a little ashamed of his curiosity, he liked to think that
Mrs Tregent would have quite as much. On the morrow he
knocked at her door—she lived in a "commodious" house in
Manchester Square—and had the satisfaction, as he had
chosen his time carefully, of learning that she had just come in.

Upstairs, in a high, quiet, old-fashioned drawing-room,
she was before him. What he saw was a tall woman in black, in
her bonnet, with a white face, smiling intensely—smiling and
smiling before she spoke. He quickly perceived that she was
agitated and was making an heroic effort, which would
presently be successful, not to show it. But it was above all
clear to him that she wasn't Fanny Knocker—was simply
another person altogether. She had nothing in common with
Fanny Knocker—it was impossible to meet her on the ground
of any former acquaintance. What acquaintance had he ever
had with this graceful, harmonious, expressive English
matron, whose smile had a singular radiance? That rascal of a
Crisford had done her such perfect justice that he felt as if
he had before him the portrait of which the image in the studio
had been the original. There were nevertheless things to be
said, and they said them on either side, sinking together, with
friendly exclamations and exaggerated laughs, on the sofa,
where her nearness seemed the span of all the distance that
separated her from the past. The phrase that hummed through
everything, to his sense, was his own inarticulate "How could
I have known? how could I have known?" How could he

have foreseen that time and life and happiness (it was probably more than anything happiness), would transpose her into such a different key? Her whole personality revealed itself from moment to moment as something so agreeable that even after all these years he felt himself blushing for the crass stupidity of his mistake. Yes, he was turning red, and she could see it and would know why: a perception that could only constitute for her a magnificent triumph, a revenge. All his natural and acquired coolness, his experience of life, his habit of society, everything that contributed to make him a man of the world, were of no avail to cover his confusion. He took refuge from it almost angrily in trying to prove to himself that she had on a second look a likeness to the ugly girl he had not thought good enough—in trying to trace Fanny Knocker in her fair, ripe bloom, the fine irregularity of her features. To put his finger on the identity would make him feel better. Some of the facts of the girl's crooked face were still there—conventional beauty was absent; but the proportions and relations had changed, and the expression and the spirit: she had accepted herself or ceased to care—had found oblivion and activity and appreciation. What Maurice mainly discovered however in this intenser observation was an attitude of hospitality toward himself which immediately effaced the presumption of "triumph." Vulgar vanity was far from her, and the grossness of watching her effect upon him: she was watching only the lost vision that had come back, the joy that, if for a single hour, she had found again. She herself had no measure of the alteration that struck him, and there was no substitution for her in the face that her deep eyes seemed to brush with their hovering. Presently they were talking like old friends, and before long each was in possession of the principal facts concerning the other. Many things had come and gone and the common fate had pressed them hard. Her parents were dead, and her husband and her first-born children. He, on his side, had lost his mother and his wife. They matched bereavements and compared bruises, and in the way she expressed herself there was a charm which forced him, as he wondered, to remember that Fanny Knocker had at least been intelligent.

"I wish I could have seen your wife—you must tell me all about her," she said. "Haven't you some portraits?"

"Some poor little photographs. I'll show them to you. She was very pretty and very gentle; she was also very un-English. But she only lived a year. She wasn't clever and accomplished—like you."

"Ah, me; you don't know *me!*"

"No, but I want to—oh particularly. I'm prepared to give a good deal of time to the study."

"We must be friends," said Mrs Tregent. "I shall take an extraordinary interest in your daughter."

"She'll be grateful for it. She's a good little reasonable thing, without a scrap of beauty."

"You care greatly for that," said Mrs Tregent.

He hesitated a moment. "Don't you?"

She smiled at him with her basking candour. "I used to. That's my husband," she added, with an odd, though evidently accidental, inconsequence. She had reached out to a table for a photograph in a silver frame. "He was very good to me."

Maurice saw that Mr Tregent had been many years older than his wife—a prosperous, prosaic, parliamentary person whom she couldn't impose on a man of the world. He sat an hour, and they talked of the mutilated season of their youth: he wondered at the things she remembered. In this little hour he felt his situation change—something strange and important take place: he seemed to see why he had come back to England. But there was an implication that worried him—it was in the very air, a reverberation of that old assurance of his mother's. He wished to clear the question up—it would matter for the beginning of a new friendship. Had she had any sense of injury when he took to his heels, any glimpse of the understanding on which he had begun to come to Ennismore Gardens? He couldn't find out to-day except by asking her, which, at their time of life, after so many years and consolations, would be legitimate and even amusing. When he took leave of her he held her hand a moment, hesitating; then he brought out:

"Did they ever tell you—a hundred years ago—that between your mother and mine there was a great question of our marrying?"

She stared—she broke into a laugh. "*Was* there?"

"Did you ever know it? Did you ever suspect it?"

She hesitated and, for the first time since he had been in the room, ceased for an instant to look straight at him. She only answered, still laughing however: "Poor dears—they were altogether too deep!"

She evidently wished to convey that she had never known. Maurice was a little disappointed: at present he would have preferred her knowledge. But as he walked home across the park, through Kensington Gardens, he felt it impossible to believe in her ignorance.

V

At the end of a month he broke out to her. "I can't get over it, it's so extraordinary—the difference between your youth and your maturity!"

"Did you expect me to be an eternal child?" Mrs Tregent asked composedly.

"No, it isn't that." He stopped—it would be difficult to explain.

"What is it then?" she inquired, with her systematic refusal to acknowledge a complication. There was always, to

Maurice Glanvil's ear, in her impenetrability to allusion, the faintest, softest glee, and it gave her on this occasion the appearance of recognising his difficulty and being amused at it. She would be excusable to be a little cold-blooded. He really knew however that the penalty was all in his own reflections, for it had not taken him even a month to perceive that she was supremely, almost strangely indulgent. There was nothing he was ready to say that she might not hear, and her absence of coquetry was a remarkable rest to him.

"It isn't what I expected—it's what I didn't expect. To say exactly what I mean, it's the way you've improved."

"I've improved? I'm so glad!"

"Surely you've been aware of it—you've been conscious of the transformation."

"As an improvement? I don't know. I've been conscious of changes enough—of all the stages and strains and lessons of life. I've been aware of growing old, and I hold, in dissent from the usual belief, that there's no fool like a young fool. One is never, I suppose, such a fool as one *has* been, and that may count perhaps as amelioration. But I can't flatter myself that I've had two different identities. I've had to make one, such as it is, do for everything. I think I've been happier than I originally supposed I should be—and yet I had my happiness too as a girl. At all events if you were to scratch me, as they say, you'd still find——" She paused a moment, and he really hung upon her lips: there was such a charm of tone in whatever she said. "You'd still find, underneath, the blowsy girl——" With this she again checked herself and, slightly to his surprise, gave a nervous laugh.

"The blowsy girl?" he repeated, with an artlessness of interrogation that made her laugh again.

"Whom you went with that hot day to see the princess give the prizes."

"Oh yes—that dreadful day!" he answered gravely, musingly, with the whole scene pictured by her words and without contesting the manner in which she qualified herself. It was the nearest allusion that had passed between them to that crudest conception of his boyhood, his flight from Ennismore Gardens. Almost every day for a month he had come to see her, and they had talked of a thousand things; never yet however had they made any explicit mention of this remote instance of premature wisdom. Moreover if he now felt the need of going back it was not to be apologetic, to do penance; he had nothing to explain, for his behaviour, as he considered it, still struck him, given the circumstances, as natural. It was to himself indeed that explanations were owing, for he had been the one who had been most deceived. He liked Mrs Tregent better than he had ever liked a woman—that is he liked her for more reasons. He had liked his poor little wife only for one, which was after all no reason at all: he had been in love with her. In spite of the charm that the renewal of acquaintance with his old friend had so unexpectedly added to his life there was a vague torment in his relation with her, the sense of a revenge (oh a very kind one!) to take, a haunting idea that he couldn't pacify. He could still feel sore at the trick that had been played him. Even after a month the curiosity with which he had approached her was not assuaged; in a manner indeed it had only borrowed force from all she had insisted on doing for him. She was literally doing everything now; gently, gaily, with a touch so familiar that protestations on his part would have been pedantic, she had taken his life in hand. Rich as she was she had known how to give him lessons in economy; she had taught him how to manage in London on his means. A month ago his servants had been horrid—to-day they were the best he had ever known. For Vera she was plainly a providence—her behaviour to Vera was transcendent.

He had privately made up his mind that Vera had in truth had her *coup de foudre*—that if she had had a chance she would have laid down her little life for Arthur Tregent; yet two circumstances, he could perceive, had helped to postpone, to attenuate even somewhat, her full consciousness of what had befallen her. One of these influences had been the prompt departure of the young man from London; the other was simply the diversion produced by Mrs Tregent's encompassing art. It had had immediate consequences for the child: it was like a drama in perpetual climaxes. This surprising benefactress rejoiced in her society, took her "out," treated her as if there were mysterious injustices to repair. Vera was agitated not a little by such a change in her life; she had English kindred enough, uncles and aunts and cousins; but she had felt herself lost in her father's family and was principally aware, among them, of their strangeness and their indifference. They affected her mainly as mere number and stature. Mrs Tregent's was a performance unpromised and uninterrupted, and the girl desired to know if all English people took so generous a view of friendship. Maurice laughed at this question and, without meeting his daughter's eyes, answered in the negative. Vera guessed so many things that he didn't know what she would be guessing next. He saw her caught up to the blue like Ganymede, and surrendered her contentedly. She had been the occupation of his life, yet to Mrs Tregent he was willing to part with her; this lady was the only person of whom he would not have been jealous. Even in the young man's absence moreover Vera lived with the son of the house and breathed his air; Manchester Square was full of him, his photograph was on every table. How often she spoke of him to his mother Maurice had no means of knowing, nor whether Mrs Tregent encouraged such a topic; he had reason to believe indeed that there were reserves on either side, and he felt that he could trust his old friend's prudence as much as her liberality. The attitude of forbearance from rash allusions, which was Maurice's own, could not at any rate keep Arthur from being a presence in the little drama which had begun for them all, as the older man was more and more to recognise

with nervous prefigurements, on that occasion at the Crisfords'.

Arthur Tregent had gone to Ireland to spend a few weeks
with an old university friend—the gentleman indeed, at Cam-
bridge, had been his tutor—who had lately, in a district classi-
fied as "disturbed," come into a bewildering heritage. He had
chosen in short for a study of the agrarian question on the spot
the moment of the year when London was most absorbing.
Maurice Glanvil made no remark to his mother on this
anomaly, and she offered him no explanation of it; they talked
in fact of almost everything except Arthur. Mrs Tregent had
to her constant visitor the air of feeling that she owed him in
relation to her son an apology which she had not the materials
for making. It was certainly a high standard of courtesy that
would suggest to her that he ought to have put himself out
for these social specimens; but it was obvious that her standard was high. Maurice Glanvil smiled when he thought to
what bare civility the young man would have deemed himself
held had he known of a certain passage of private history. But
he knew nothing—Maurice was sure of that; his reason for
going away had been quite another matter. That Vera's
brooding parent should have had such an insight into the
young man's motives is a proof of the amount of reflection
that he devoted to him. He had not seen much of him and in
truth he found him provoking, but he was haunted by the odd
analogy of which he had had a glimpse on their first encounter. The late Mr Tregent had had "interests in the north," and
the care of them had naturally devolved upon his son, who
by the mother's account had shown an admirable capacity for
business. The late Mr Tregent had also been actively political,
and it was fondly hoped, in Manchester Square at least, that
the day was not distant when his heir would, in turn and as
a representative of the same respectabilities, speak reported
words in debate. Maurice himself, vague about the House of
Commons, had nothing to say against his making a figure

there. Accordingly if these natural gifts continued to remind him of his own fastidiously clever youth, it was with the difference that Arthur Tregent's cleverness struck him as much the greater of the two. If the changes in England were marked this indeed was in general one of them, that the sharp young men were still sharper than of yore. When they had ability at anyrate they showed it all; Maurice would never have pretended that he had shown all his. He had not cared whether anyone knew it. It was not however this superior intensity which provoked him, and poor young Tregent could not be held responsible for his irritation. If the circumstance in which they most resembled each other was the disposition to escape from plain girls who aspired to them, such a characteristic, as embodied in the object of Vera's admiration, was purely interesting, was even amusing, to Vera's father; but it would have gratified him to be able to ascertain from Mrs Tregent whether, to her knowledge, her son thought his child really repulsive, and what annoyed him was the fact that such an inquiry was practically impossible. Arthur was provoking in short because he had an advantage—an advantage residing in the fact that his mother's friend couldn't ask questions about him without appearing to indulge in hints and overtures. The idea of this officiousness was odious to Maurice Glanvil; so that he confined himself to meditating in silence on the happiness it would be for poor Vera to marry a beautiful young man with a fortune and a future.

Though the opportunity for this recreation—it engaged much of his time—should be counted as one of the pleasant results of his intimacy with Mrs Tregent, yet the sense, perverse enough, that he had a ground of complaint against her subsisted even to the point of finally steadying him while he expressed his grievance. This happened in the course of one of those afternoon hours that had now become indispensable to him—hours of belated tea and egotistical talk in the long summer light and the chastened roar of London.

"No, it wasn't fair," he said, "and I wasn't well used—a hundred years ago. I'm sore about it now; you ought to have notified me, to have instructed me. Why didn't you, in common honesty? Why didn't my poor mother, who was so eager and shrewd? Why didn't yours? She used to talk to me. Heaven forgive me for saying it, but our mothers weren't up to the mark! You may tell me they didn't know; to which I reply that mine was universally supposed, and by me in particular, to know everything that could be known. No, it wasn't well managed, and the consequence has been this odious discovery, an awful shock to a man of my time of life and under the effect of which I now speak to you, that for a quarter of a century I've been a fool."

"What would you have wished us to do?" Mrs Tregent asked as she gave him another cup of tea.

"Why, to have said 'Wait, wait—at any price; have patience and hold on!' They ought to have told me, *you* ought to have told me, that your conditions at that time were a temporary phase and that you would infallibly break your shell. You ought to have warned me, they ought to have warned me, that there would be wizardry in the case, that you were to be the subject, at a given moment, of a transformation absolutely miraculous. I couldn't know it by inspiration; I measured you by the common law—how could I do anything else? But it wasn't kind to leave me in error."

Maurice Glanvil treated himself without scruple to this fine ironic flight, this sophistry which eased his nerves, because though it brought him nearer than he had yet come to putting his finger, visibly to Mrs Tregent, on the fact that he had once tried to believe he could marry her and had found her too ugly, their present relation was so extraordinary and his present appreciation so liberal as to make almost any freedom excusable, especially as his companion had the advantage of being to all intents and purposes a different person from the one he talked of, while he suffered the ignominy of being the same.

"There has been no miracle," said Mrs Tregent after a moment. "I've never known anything but the common, ah the very common, law, and anything that I may have become only the common things have made me."

He shook his head. "You wore a disfiguring mask, a veil, a disguise. One fine day you dropped them all and showed the world the real creature."

"It wasn't one fine day—it was little by little."

"Well, one fine day I saw the result; the process doesn't matter. To arrive at a goal invisible from the starting-point is no doubt an incident in the life of a certain number of women. But what is absolutely unprecedented is to have traversed such a distance."

"Hadn't I a single redeeming point?" Mrs Tregent demanded.

He hesitated a little, and while he hesitated she looked at him. Her look was but of an instant, but it told him everything, told him, in one misty moonbeam, all she had known of old. She had known perfectly—she had been as conscious of the conditions of his experiment as of the invincibility of his repugnance. Whether her mother had betrayed him didn't matter; she had read everything clear and had had to accept the cruel truth. He was touched as he had never been by that moment's communication; he was, unexpectedly, almost awe-struck, for there was something still more in it than he had guessed. "I was letting my fancy play just now," he answered, apologetically. "It was I who was wanting—it was I who was the idiot!"

"Don't say that. You were so kind." And hereupon Mrs Tregent startled her visitor by bursting into tears.

She recovered herself indeed, and they forbore on that occasion, in the interest of the decorum expected of persons of their age and in their circumstances, to rake over these smouldering ashes; but such a conversation had made a difference, and from that day onward Maurice Glanvil was

awake to the fact that he had been the passion of this extraordinary woman's life. He felt humiliated for an hour, but
after that his pleasure was almost as great as his wonder. For
wonder there was plenty of room, but little by little he saw
how things had come to pass. She was not subjected to the
ordeal of telling him or to the abasement of any confession,
but day by day he sounded, with a purity of gratitude that
renewed, in his spirit, the sources of youth, the depths of
everything that her behaviour implied. Of such a studied
tenderness as she showed him the roots could only be in some
unspeakably sacred past. She had not to explain, she had not
to clear up inconsistencies, she had only to let him be with her.
She had striven, she had accepted, she had conformed, but she
had thought of him every day of her life. She had taken up
duties and performed them, she had banished every weakness
and practised every virtue, but the still, hidden flame had
never been quenched. His image had interposed, his reality
had remained, and she had never denied herself the sweetness
of hoping that she should see him again and that she should
know him. She had never raised a little finger for it, but fortune had answered her prayer. Women were capable of these
mysteries of sentiment, these intensities of fidelity, and there
were moments in which Maurice Glanvil's heart beat strangely
before a vision really so sublime. He seemed to understand
now by what miracle Fanny Knocker had been beautified—
the miracle of heroic docilities and accepted pangs and vanquished egotisms. It had never come in a night, but it had
come by living for others. She was living for others still; it
was impossible for him to see anything else at last than that
she was living for him. The time of passion was over, but the
time of service was long. When all this became vivid to him
he felt that he couldn't recognise it enough and yet that recognition might only be tacit and, as it were, circuitous. He
couldn't say to her even humorously "It's very kind of you to
be in love with such a donkey," for these words would have

implied somehow that he had rights—an attitude from which his renovated delicacy shrank. He bowed his head before such charity and seemed to see moreover that Mrs Tregent's desire to befriend him was a feeling independent of any prospect of gain and indifferent to any chance of reward. It would be described vulgarly, after so much had come and gone, as the state of being "in love"—the state of the instinctive and the simple, which they both had left far behind; so that there was a certain sort of reciprocity which would almost constitute an insult to it.

VI

HE soared on these high thoughts till, toward the end of July (Mrs Tregent stayed late in town—she was awaiting her son's return) he made the discovery that to some persons, perhaps indeed to many, he had all the air of being in love. This image was flashed back to him from the irreverent lips of a lady who knew and admired Mrs Tregent and who professed amusement at his surprise, at his artless declaration that he had no idea he had made himself conspicuous. She assured him that everyone was talking about him—though people after all had a tenderness for elderly romance; and she left him divided between the acute sense that he was comical (he had a horror of that) and the pale perception of something that he could "help" still less. At the end of a few hours of reflection he had sacrificed the penalty to the privilege; he was about to be fifty, and he knew Fanny Knocker's age—no one better; but he cared no straw for vulgar judgments and moreover could think of plenty of examples of unions admired even after longer delays. For three days he enjoyed the luxury of admitting to himself without reserve how indispensable she had become to him; as the third drew to a close he was more

nervous than really he had ever been in his life, for this was
the evening on which, after many hindrances, Mrs Tregent
had agreed to dine with him. He had planned the occasion for
a month—he wanted to show her how well he had learned
from her how to live on his income. Her occupations had
always interposed—she was teaching him new lessons; but
at last she gave him the joy of sitting at his table. At the
evening's end he begged her to remain after the others, and he
asked one of the ladies who had been present, and who was
going to a pair of parties, to be so good as to take Vera away.
This indeed had been arranged in advance, and when, in the
discomposed drawing-room, of which the windows stood
open to the summer night, he was alone with his old friend, he
saw in her face that she knew it had been arranged. He saw
more than this—that she knew what he was waiting to say
and that if, after a visible reluctance, she had consented to
come, it was in order to meet him, with whatever effort, on
the ground he had chosen—meet him once and then leave it
forever. This was why, without interrupting him, but before
he had finished, putting out her hand to his own, with a
strange clasp of refusal, she was ready to show him, in a woeful but beautiful headshake to which nothing could add, that
it was impossible at this time of day for them to marry. She
stayed only a moment, but in that moment he had to accept
the knowledge that by as much as it might have been of old,
by so much might it never be again. After she had gone he
walked up and down the drawing-room half the night. He sent
the servants to bed, he blew out the candles; the forsaken place
was lighted only by the lamps in the street. He gave himself
the motive of waiting for Vera to come back, but in reality he
threshed about in the darkness because his cheeks had begun
to burn. There was a sting for him in Mrs Tregent's refusal,
and this sting was sharper even than the disappointment of his
desire. It was a reproach to his delicacy; it made him feel as if
he had been an ass for the second time. When she was young

and free his faith had been too poor and his perceptions too dense; he had waited to show her that he only bargained for certainties and only recognised success. He dropped into a chair at last and sat there a long time, his elbows on his knees, his face in his hands, trying to cover up his humiliation, waiting for it to ebb. As the sounds of the night died away it began to come back to him that she had given him a promise to which a rich meaning could be attached. What was it that before going away she had said about Vera, in words he had been at the moment too disconcerted to take in? Little by little he reconstructed these words with comfort; finally, when after hearing a carriage stop at the door he hastily pulled himself together and went down to admit his daughter, the sight of the child on his threshold, as the brougham that had restored her drove away, brought them all back in their generosity.

"Have you danced?" he asked.

She hesitated. "A little, papa."

He knew what that meant—she had danced once. He followed her upstairs in silence; she had not wasted her time—she had had her humiliation. Ah, clearly she was too short! Yet on the landing above, where her bedroom candle stood, she tried to be gay with him, asking him about his own party and whether the people had stayed late.

"Mrs Tregent stayed after the others. She spoke very kindly of you."

The girl looked at her father with an anxiety that showed through her smile. "What did she say?"

He hesitated, as Vera had done a moment before. "That you must be our compensation."

His daughter's eyes, still wondering, turned away. "What did she mean?"

"That it's all right, darling!" And he supplied the deficiencies of this explanation with a long kiss for good-night.

The next day he went to see Mrs Tregent, who wore the

air of being glad to have something at once positive and pleasant to say. She announced immediately that Arthur was coming back.

"I congratulate you." Then, as they exchanged one of their looks of unreserved recognition, Maurice added: "Now it's for Vera and me to go."

"To go?"

"Without more delay. It's high time we should take ourselves off."

Mrs Tregent was silent a moment. "Where shall you go?"

"To our old haunts, abroad. We must see some of our old friends. We shall spend six months away."

"Then what becomes of *my* months?"

"Your months?"

"Those it's all arranged she's to spend at Blankley." Blankley was Mrs Tregent's house in Derbyshire, and she laughed as she went on: "Those that I spoke of last evening. Don't look as if we had never discussed it and settled it!"

"What shall I do without her?" Maurice Glanvil presently demanded.

"What will you do *with* her?" his hostess replied, with a world of triumphant meaning. He was not prepared to say, in the sense of her question, and he took refuge in remarking that he noted her avoidance of any suggestion that he too would be welcome in Derbyshire; which led her to continue, with unshrinking frankness: "Certainly, I don't want you a bit. Leave us alone."

"Is it safe?"

"Of course I can't absolutely answer for anything, but at least it will be safer than with *you*," said Mrs Tregent.

Maurice Glanvil turned this over. "Does he dislike me?"

"What an idea!"

But the question had brought the colour to her face, and the sight of this, with her evasive answer, kindled in Maurice's heart a sudden relief, a delight almost, that was strange

enough. Arthur was in opposition, plainly, and that was why
he had so promptly quitted London, that was why Mrs
Tregent had refused Mr Glanvil. The idea was an instant
balm. "He'd be quite right, poor fellow!" Maurice declared.
"I'll go abroad alone."

"Let me keep her six months," said Mrs Tregent. "I'll
try it—I'll try it!"

"I wouldn't interfere for the world."

"It's an immense responsibility; but I should like so to
succeed."

"She's an angel!" Maurice said.

"That's what gives me courage."

"But she mustn't dream of any plot," he added.

"For what do you take me?" Mrs Tregent exclaimed with
a smile which lightened up for him intensely that far-away
troubled past as to which she had originally baffled his
inquiry.

The joy of perceiving in an aversion to himself a possible
motive for Arthur's absence was so great in him that before
he took leave of her he ventured to say to his old friend:
"Does he like her at all?"

"He likes her very much."

Maurice remembered how much he had liked Fanny
Knocker and been willing to admit it to his mother; but he
presently observed: "Of course he can't think her in the least
pretty."

"As you say, she's an angel," Mrs Tregent rejoined.

"She would pass for one better if she were a few inches
taller."

"It doesn't matter," said Mrs Tregent.

"One must remember that in that respect, at her age, she
won't change," Maurice pursued, wondering after he had
spoken whether he had pressed upon the second pronoun.

"No, she won't change. But she's a darling!" Mrs Tregent
exclaimed; and it was in these meagre words, which were only

half however of what passed between them, that an extraordinary offer was made and accepted. They were so ready
to understand each other that no insistence and no professions
now were necessary, and that Maurice Glanvil had not even
broken into a murmur of gratitude at this quick revelation of
his old friend's beautiful conception of a nobler remedy—the
endeavour to place their union outside themselves, to make
their children know the happiness they had missed. They had
not needed to teach each other what they saw, what they
guessed, what moved them with pity and hope, and there
were transitions enough safely skipped in the simple conversation I have preserved. But what Mrs Tregent was ready to
do for him filled Maurice Glanvil, for days after this, with an
even greater wonder, and it seemed to him that not till then
had she fully shown him that she had forgiven him.

Six months, however, proved much more than sufficient for
her attempt to test the plasticity of her son. Maurice Glanvil
went abroad, but was nervous and restless, wandering from
place to place, revisiting old scenes and old friends, reverting,
with a conscious, an even amused incongruity, and yet with an
effect that was momentarily soothing, to places at which he
had stayed with his wife, but feeling all the while that he was
really staking his child's happiness. It only half reassured him
to feel that Vera would never know what poor Fanny
Knocker had been condemned to know, for the daily contact
was cruel from the moment the issue was uncertain; and it
only half helped him to reflect that she was not so plain as
Fanny, for had not Arthur Tregent given him the impression
that the young man of the present was intrinsically even more
difficult to please than the young man of the past? The letters
he received from Blankley conveyed no information about
Arthur beyond the fact that he was at home; only once Vera
mentioned that he was "remarkably good" to her. Toward
the end of November he found himself in Paris, submitting
reluctantly to social accidents which put off from day to day

his return to London, when, one morning in the Rue de Rivoli, he had to stop short to permit the passage of a vehicle which had emerged from the court of an hotel. It was an open cab—the day was mild and bright—with a small quantity of neat, leathery luggage, which Maurice vaguely recognised as English, stowed in the place beside the driver—luggage from which his eyes shifted straight to the occupant of the carriage, a young man with his face turned to the allurements of travel and the urbanity of farewell to bowing waiters still visible in it. The young man was so bright and so on his way, as it were, that Maurice, standing there to make room for him, felt for the instant that he too had taken a tip. The feeling became acute as he recognised that this humiliating obligation was to no less a person than Arthur Tregent. It was Arthur who was so much on his way—it was Arthur who was catching a train. He noticed his mother's friend as the cab passed into the street, and, with a quick demonstration, caused the driver to pull up. He jumped out, and under the arcade the two men met with every appearance of cordiality, but with conscious confusion. Each of them coloured perceptibly, and Maurice was angry with himself for blushing before a boy. Long afterwards he remembered how cold, and even how hard, was the handsome clearness of the young eyes that met his own in an artificial smile.

"You here? I thought you were at Blankley."

"I left Blankley yesterday; I'm on my way to Spain."

"To Spain? How charming!"

"To join a friend there—just for a month or two."

"Interesting country—well worth seeing. Your mother's all right?"

"Oh, yes, all right. And Miss Glanvil——" Arthur Tregent went on, cheerfully.

"Vera's all right?" interrupted Maurice, with a still gayer tone.

"Everyone, everything's all right!" Arthur laughed.

"Well, I mustn't keep you. Bon voyage!"

Maurice Glanvil, after the young man had driven on, flattered himself that in this brief interview he had suppressed every indication of surprise; but that evening he crossed the Channel, and on the morrow he went down to Blankley. "To Spain—to Spain!" the words kept repeating themselves in his ears. He, when he had taken flight in a similar conjunction, had only got, for the time, as far as Boulogne; and he was reminded afresh of the progress of the species. When he was introduced into the drawing-room at Blankley—a chintzy, flowery, friendly expanse—Mrs Tregent rose before him alone and offered him a face that she had never shown before. She was white and she looked scared; she faltered in her movement to meet him.

"I met Arthur in Paris, so I thought I might come."

Oh, yes; there was pain in her face, and a kind of fear of him that frightened him, but their hands found each other's hands while she replied: "He went off—I didn't know it."

"But you had a letter the next morning," Maurice said.

She stared. "How did you know that?"

"Who should know better than I? He wrote from London, explaining."

"I did what I could —I believed in it!" said Mrs Tregent. "He was charming, for a while."

"But he broke down. She's too short, eh?" Maurice asked.

"Don't laugh; she's ill."

"What's the matter with her?"

Mrs Tregent gave the visitor a look in which there was almost a reproach for the question. "She has had a chill; she's in bed. You must see her."

She took him upstairs and he saw his child. He remembered what his mother had told him of the grievous illness of Fanny Knocker. Poor little Vera lay there in the flush of a feverish cold which had come on the evening before. She grew worse from the effect of a complication, and for three days he was anxious about her; but even more than with his alarm he held his breath before the distress, the disappointment, the humility of his old friend. Up to this hour he had not fully measured the strength of her desire to do something for him, or the intensity of passion with which she had wished to do it in the particular way that had now broken down. She had counted on her influence with her son, on his affection and on the maternal art, and there was anguish in her compunction for her failure, for her false estimate of the possible. Maurice Glanvil reminded her in vain of the consoling fact that Vera had known nothing of any plan, and he guessed indeed the reason why this theory had no comfort. No one could be better aware than Fanny Tregent of how much girls knew who knew nothing. It was doubtless this same sad wisdom that kept her sombre when he expressed a confidence that his child would promptly recover. She herself had had a terrible fight—and yet with the physical victory, had she recovered? Her apprehension for Vera was justified, for the poor girl was destined finally to forfeit even the physical victory. She got better, she got up, she quitted Blankley, she quitted England with her father, but her health had failed and a year later it gave way. Overtaken in Rome by a second illness, she succumbed; unlike Fanny Knocker she was never to have her revenge.

A NOTE ON THE TEXT

In preparing these tales for publication, the editor had to choose between James's original magazine texts, those published in book form soon afterwards and those revised and rewritten for the New York Edition. The obvious choice, it seemed to him, was the original book form of the story where there was one. In that form it had the benefit of revision from magazine to volume; and in that form it was best known to James's generation. It seemed to the editor that in a chronological edition of James's shorter fictions, the New York Edition texts had no relevance. They belong exclusively to the edition for which they were designed; particularly since the revisions were often made several decades after the original publication.

The original magazine publications of the tales in this volume were as follows:

"Brooksmith," *Harper's Weekly* and *Black and White*, 2 May 1891.

"The Marriages," *Atlantic Monthly*, August 1891.

"The Chaperon," *Atlantic Monthly*, November–December 1891.

"Sir Edmund Orme," *Black and White*, 25 November 1891.

"Nona Vincent," *English Illustrated Magazine*, February–March 1892.

"The Private Life," *Atlantic Monthly*, April 1892.

"The Real Thing," *Black and White*, 16 April 1892.

"Lord Beaupré," *Macmillan's Magazine*, April–June 1892 (entitled "Lord Beauprey").

"The Visits," *Black and White*, 28 May 1892 (entitled "The Visit").

"Sir Dominick Ferrand," *Cosmopolitan Magazine*, July–August 1892 (entitled "Jersey Villas").

"Collaboration," *English Illustrated Magazine*, September 1892.

"Greville Fane," *Illustrated London News*, 17 and 24 September 1892.

"The Wheel of Time," *Cosmopolitan Magazine*, December 1892–January 1893.

"Brooksmith," "The Marriages" and "Sir Edmund Orme" were first reprinted in *The Lesson of the Master* (London and New York, 1892), "The Chaperon," "Nona Vincent," "The Real Thing," "Sir Dominick Ferrand" and "Greville Fane" in *The Real Thing* (London and New York, 1893) and "The Private Life," "Lord Beaupré," "The Visits," "Collaboration" and "The Wheel of Time" in *The Private Life* (London 1893). The text of these first book publications has been used here.

For the complete bibliography of the tales the reader is referred to *A Bibliography of the Writings of Henry James* by Leon Edel and Dan H. Laurence (second edition, revised, London, 1961) in the Soho Bibliographies published by Rupert Hart-Davis.